OCTAVIA

M.M. Holt

Copyright © 2024
All rights reserved by the author.
No part of this book may be reproduced in any form without permission in writing from the author. Reviewers may quote brief passages in reviews.

ISBN: 9798328623094

Contents

Part 1 : Sinistra 5
Part 2 : Grenda 119
Part 3 : Flavia 247
Part 4 : Octavia 361
Epilogue..461
This is not the end 488
Sample Chapter: 'Fifty Degrees South'........492
Acknowledgements 500
Author's notes 501
Who is M.M. Holt? 502

Dedicated to the continuing struggle
against the Accord of Nations.

Part One: Sinistra

"Character is destiny."

                A philosopher from the Hyacinth planet.

1

Historian's Remarks

In the sixth month of the mission, before the trouble began, the great warship Herculaneum cruised into a remote region of the galaxy known as Ilium.

In Ilium, the Herculaneum altered its course and proceeded toward a location identified by the ship's astronomer as the Point of Acceleration.

At the Point of Acceleration, the Herculaneum's captain would order the chief engineer to engage the large Acceleration engines. The ship would then increase its speed to a velocity greater than that of light.

Propelled forward as this astonishing rate, the Herculaneum would cross the galaxy, traveling between the billons of stars and planets, all the way to a region on the galaxy's far side.

The mission destination was a nine-planet solar system and a minor planet named Hyacinth. Hyacinth was the word for blue in the language of the creatures who dominated that planet at the time.

The mission, as stated in the Admiralty's orders was as follows.

TO CAPTAIN TIBERIUS, SENATE NAVY.
YOUR MISSION

'Greet the inhabitants of the Hyacinth planet. Prepare the leaders for our imminent arrival in the transport ships. Employ the arts of diplomacy to reassure the Hyacinth leaders of our intentions.

'Do not reveal your mission's true purpose. Instead, stress that you wish to form a friendship between our worlds.

'Above all, do not alarm the Hyacinth creatures. Do not reveal your great ship to them, nor your weaponry, nor the number of your ship's crew. Nor must you reveal your natural body forms. The sight of these will cause mistrust, panic, and terror.

'Instead, you must adopt the form of the Hyacinth creatures themselves, in all their frailty, limitations, and irrationality. Remain in the Hyacinth-creature form, in both sexes, at all times during the voyage and on the Hyacinth planet.

'Finally, you must also call yourselves by Hyacinth-creature names, and you must speak the Hyacinth language at all times during the mission, as well as using the Hyacinth units of measurement, as difficult as that might be. Effective, natural communication will be essential when meeting the Hyacinth leaders.

'That is all.'

Centuries later, many historians, including myself, concluded that these last instructions caused the problems aboard the Herculaneum, and especially the disastrous actions of Second Lieutenant Sinistra.

They also led to the catastrophe that followed.

2

On the morning of the Acceleration, alone in her cabin, Second Lieutenant Sinistra woke from the sixtieth act of sleep in her life.

As usual, Lieutenant Sinistra awoke exhausted and afraid. She had experienced a terrifying nightmare. The nightmare was always the same: her childhood self, a dark silent forest, and someone stalking her through the trees—someone who intended violence.

Sinistra sat up on her berth, rubbed her Hyacinth-creature eyes, and shook the nightmare away. This morning she had to concentrate on the Acceleration above all else. But first, and to her great displeasure, she had to cope with her Hyacinth-creature body.

She had to dress this awkward arrangement of abdomen, arms, and legs. She had to touch it. She had to clean it. She had to look at it. Then, she had to endure its weaknesses, its confusing senses, its unscaled, vulnerable skin, and the torrents of strange thoughts, urges, and emotions.

Keeping her eyes closed, she breathed slowly in and out. It was better to delay her first glance at the body's floppy limbs, its writhing fingers, useless claws, vulnerable feet, creaking joints, Hyacinth female sex organs, and its face.

Yes, the face: she especially loathed that.

'I must endure it,' she said to the empty cabin. 'Hoc ferrendum est,' she said in the singsong Hyacinth language. This must be borne. I must make the best of it. She breathed in, filling her lungs with the metallic air from the Herculaneum's atmosphere pumps.

When she had breathed in and out three times, she began the process of preparing the body for duty. She swung her Hyacinth-creature legs over the edge of the berth and onto the deck. Then she stood up, swaying on her unreliable feet.

The body complained.

Her bizarre toes recoiled from the cold metal, squirming like worms. The armpits itched and required scratching with the pathetic claws. The knee joints cracked and wouldn't unlock. The back spiked with pain above the ludicrous buttocks. And the digestive organs flopped in the abdomen —useless and heavy.

Next, she peeled off her sleeping uniform and stood naked. This was the worst moment of all, when the body's watery reflection appeared in the metal bulkhead. There it was, with its yellow cranial hair; its round, shell-shaped ears; the strange curves at its waist; the pointy useless nose; the tiny mouth; the too-small teeth; the sickly, glittering blue eyes with their staring, round pupils.

Ugh! Sinistra thought. Too many colors. Too many cartilage protrusions. So many elbows, knees, ankles, and not enough girth in the neck! The skin was too vulnerable to scratches and the cold. There was not enough height and no strength worth mentioning. To move in this body was to be crippled.

Worse!

For Sinistra's own particular Hyacinth creature body, there was so very little of what the crew regarded as pulchritudo. Beauty. Others aboard the Herculaneum strolled the passageways in perfectly symmetrical forms.

Their bodies resembled statues of Hyacinth gods and Hyacinth emperors.

But not Sinistra's Hyacinth-creature body.

I look like a sick flower, she thought, a sick yellow flower. No, not even a flower. I look like a pale shrub from the Northern Forests on the home planet. I'm a noxious shrub growing in space.

She opened her locker. Her uniform waited on its hanger. The uniform was her great consolation. It made her form almost bearable. She pulled its rich blue cloth over the awkward arms, legs, and abdomen. Then she looked at the reflection once more. This was better. She looked like a leader, calm and controlled—at least, on the outside.

She brushed some lint from her name patch. The patch read 'Secundus Tenens Sinistra.' Second Lieutenant Sinistra. Then she checked the reflection once more. There she was, the third in command of the Senate Navy vessel Herculaneum, a ship the size of a city. She stood as upright as her body would let her, as if she could make the name patch more prominent than herself.

The ship's bell tolled three times in her mind. Time to go.

But before she left for the ship's bridge, she looked at the few luxuries the Admiralty allowed her: photographs from home, each fixed flat to the bulkhead. She saw the photograph of her graduation from the naval academy; a photograph of her last command, the navy ship Drast; and a picture of her only friend in the world, Lieutenant Nim.

Nim, she thought. Can you hear me? Today is the day. Nim, are you there? But Nim never replied. Or if she did, her thoughts never made it across the depths of space from the home planet.

Have it your way, Sinistra thought. Keep me waiting.

She took a last look at her reflection, at the officer's uniform, and the name patch. Would these be good enough for her commanding officer, First Lieutenant Flavia?

Probably not. Flavia made it her special duty to find fault with Sinistra, to humiliate her, and upbraid her in front of the crew.

But I have my skills, Sinistra thought. I have my dedication. I have my service record. I have my experience. Flavia can't deny me those. She needs me. She knows I'm indispensable.

Someone knocked at the door.

Sinistra drew a breath and called, 'Veni!'

The cabin door opened. Private Volso of the Navy's Marines stood saluting. His other hand was on his sidearm. Like most of the marines, Volso had been issued a Hyacinth-creature form that was tall and broad at the shoulders. He stood a full Hyacinth-creature head above Sinistra.

As Volso saluted, The Herculaneum's sounds and smells surged through the open cabin door: the growling Acceleration engines idling astern; the odors of metal, sweat, and laundered uniforms; the faint reek of animal hide, and what Sinistra described as the scent of order that ruled the ten thousand members of the crew.

Private Volso said, 'Third Lieutenant Cadmus's duty, Second Lieutenant Sinistra.'

'Only you today, Volso? Where is Sergeant Opiter Is something wrong?'

'I don't know, Lieutenant.'

'Why don't you know, Private?'

She looked at Volso's face. The skin beneath his dark eyes was puffy. Like most of the crew, Volso had family caught in the catastrophic eruptions on the home planet. He came from the Ishank province. A long dormant volcano known as Arakan (Big Claw) had recently dumped ash and lava over the province capital.

She softened her tone. 'Has something happened?'

'Beg pardon, Lieutenant Sinistra,' Volso said. 'Marine Captain Ranant didn't say.'

'Well, let's get going,' she said, and limped from the cabin. Volso stepped aside and said, 'Begging your pardon, Lieutenant Sinistra.'

'What is it?'

'Third Lieutenant Cadmus has ordered a car for your use, if you please.'

Sinistra pictured the long walk forward to the bridge through the crowded passageways, and then inside the packed shuttle train. A car would save her at least a half hora. Today, of all the days, she should use the car.

'No,' she said. 'I prefer to walk. I want to inspect the hold on the way.'

This display of extra dedication would no doubt impress First Lieutenant Flavia and Captain Tiberius.

'Let's go,' she said.

'Aye, Lieutenant,' said Volso, keeping his eyes up and away from Sinistra's lame right foot.

There was one and a half Hyacinth horae to go until the Acceleration.

3

Sinistra and Volso entered the great passageway, the major artery from the ship's stern to its stem, running almost ten Hyacinth milia forward. The passageway was heavy with pre-Acceleration traffic.

As the mission orders demanded, every crew member was in Hyacinth-creature form, and the sight of so many small figures made the passageway appear like a giant basilica not a ship's thoroughfare. It was only to be expected. The passageway, like the Herculaneum itself, had been constructed for a much taller, much wider crew.

Either side of Sinistra and Volso, the engineer's mates streamed aft to the engine deck, along with the dropship mechanics heading to the stern for one last test of the dropship fleet mountings. Technical specialists passed forward and aft, descending below decks to inspect the hull. Beside them, the stewards scoured the passageway for loose objects.

The rest of the crew hurried to their Acceleration stations. The armorer's mates, the gunner's mates, the surgeon's mates, the planetographers, astronomers, marines, and the seaman from the last watch, headed fore, aft, aloft, and below, to strap themselves into harnesses for the great jolt, which the ship's surgeon had warned could damage their Hyacinth-creature organs and crack their Hyacinth-creature spines and necks.

The crew saluted Sinistra as she limped along, touching a knuckle to their foreheads. Sinistra replied with a small smile, her one dependable expression. Some crewmen even called out encouragements to her, such as, 'Good luck, Lieutenant,' and 'Won't be long now, Lieutenant,' as if Sinistra were commanding the ship herself, not First Lieutenant Flavia.

But despite the crew's cheerfulness, each member was afraid. No one had experienced an Acceleration before, not even Gabinus, the chief engineer. And everyone knew that on the last mission to Hyacinth, the navy ship Parthia had exploded in this very same region of Ilium. All the Parthia crew had died in the explosion or perished in open space. And that was in their natural forms. What would happen to a crew ordered to remain in the weak, vulnerable bodies of Hyacinth creatures?

Sinistra and Volso pressed on through the crowd towards the shuttle station. After boarding the shuttle, they would reach the bridge and Lieutenant Flavia in just twenty minuta. All was going well until they passed the elevator leading to the hold. Here, Sinistra said, 'Wait a moment, Private. I'm going to take a look.'

With Volso following her, Sinistra limped across the traffic to the passageway's starboard side. Then she looked over the rail into the dark hold below. Under the lamplights, the master's mates were moving the giant terraforming machinery from port to starboard.

This was bad. Sinistra had supervised the stowing of the hold herself. After several weeks with the master's mates, she had achieved a good balance for the Acceleration. Now, not two horae before the great engines would fire, someone had ordered a change.

But who would do such a thing? And why wouldn't they consult Sinistra first? Which senior officer could possibly be so reckless?

But Sinistra knew all too well which officer had ordered the change.

Her organs squirmed in her abdomen. The usual contest began: the contest between her duty to serve the mission and her desire to win First Lieutenant Flavia's approval, or at the very least, to avoid Flavia's temper.

Sinistra's small hands squeezed the rail. Her forehead creased. Her breath came in short, shallow puffs, then stopped altogether. Her left sleeve swelled, straining the four button threads. Red flesh appeared in the cuff vents.

Volso stood beside her, his eyes on Sinistra's sleeve.

'Beg pardon, Lieutenant, but are you all right?'

The sleeve relaxed and the angry red flesh cooled.

In a flat, expressionless voice, Sinistra said, 'Mutatio consilli, Privatus Volso. Descendere debemus.' A change of plan, Private Volso. I must descend to the hold.

The ship's bell tolled six times in Sinistra's mind. There was only one hora to go—one hora until the great engines would fire and the Herculaneum would hurtle across the galaxy.

But first, Sinistra would have to restore the terraforming machines.

Worse!

She would be late.

4

Twenty Hyacinth minuta before the Acceleration, Sinistra limped into the area known as the forward stateroom, just aft the ship's bridge.

She was flustered. Her hands quivered, her face flushed pink, and the fold of skin beneath her left eye twitched. This was not a good beginning to the most important watch of the mission.

The marine sentries stood to attention while Sinistra pressed a finger to the skin beneath her eye and stifled the twitch. Then she closed her eyes and breathed slowly. Finally, she opened her eyes and said, 'Aperi ianuam, Corporalis Stolo.' Open the door, Corporal Stolo.

The lever swung back; the wheel turned. The heavy door unsealed and swung open. Warm air and the scent of electrical circuity rushed out. Sinistra drew one more breath, two breaths, and stepped over the threshold.

Inside, there was near darkness. The only illumination came from the bright rectangles of light from the display screens on the forward-bulkhead. Before each screen sat a technical specialist, each monitoring the status of the ship's engines, exterior sensors, ballast, atmosphere, hull integrity, weapons, and heading.

Sinistra waited for her weak Hyacinth-creature eyes to adjust to the dark. Then she hobbled towards her station: the station to monitor the starboard side for rogue objects. But before she could walk more than a few passus, an imperious female voice spoke to her from the gloom.

'Stop, Second Lieutenant Sinistra. Stop right there.'

Sinistra's lame foot paused, dangling in the air. She settled it onto the deck and waited. This was what she had feared. She lifted her eyes to the formidable figure of First Lieutenant Flavia.

'You are late for the watch,' Flavia said. She spoke the singsong Hyacinth language in big round vowels, like the voice of a queen addressing her subjects.

'Yes, Lieutenant Flavia,' Sinistra said.

'And this is not just any watch, is it?'

'No, Lieutenant Flavia.'

'In fact,' said Flavia, looking about the bridge, inviting the crew to listen, 'You are late to the most critical watch of the mission—the mission to Hyacinth, the mission to save our people. You are aware of that, aren't you, Second Lieutenant Sinistra?'

'Of course.'

'Then how is it, Second Lieutenant, that all the rest of the bridge crew is at their stations, and yet, the Herculaneum's third in command is late—and late after two months of drills for this very moment?'

'Begging your pardon, First Lieutenant Flavia,' said Sinistra. 'Someone had commandeered the forward-aft shuttle for use re-stowing the hold.'

'That someone was me,' said Flavia. 'I ordered the hold to be re-stowed. I also ordered the shuttle to be available for the purser's sole use.'

'Beg pardon, First Lieutenant. I was not informed.'

'What did you say, Lieutenant?' said Flavia. 'I can't understand your accent. Try again. This time, enunciate.'

First Lieutenant Flavia's chair rested on a plinth in the centre of the bridge. Beside her sat the ship's captain, Tiberius. Both Flavia and Tiberius had been issued Hyacinth forms modeled on Hyacinth statues observed on previous missions. The statues were those depicting Hyacinth emperors, empresses, gods, and goddesses. Lieutenant Flavia had also been issued with dark red hair, a swaying gait, a pale complexion, and vivid green eyes.

Captain Tiberius was the male equivalent. He was tall and upright, with golden curls and a prominent chin. If Sinistra resembled a withered shrub from the bogs of the North, First Lieutenant Flavia and Captain Tiberius were exotic flowers in bloom on the home planet's equator.

'Beg pardon, First Lieutenant,' Sinistra said. 'There was no mention of the change of plan in the final briefing. I had already approved the hold.'

'Even so, you could have walked here instead of taking the shuttle. It is not the captain's problem nor mine that you have not yet mastered Hyacinth-creature locomotion, is it, Second Lieutenant?'

'No, First Lieutenant. Of course not.'

'If you could walk or run as fast as the rest of us, you would have been here at the beginning of the watch, wouldn't you?'

'Yes, First Lieutenant.'

'Fortunately for you, and for us, we are not yet at the Point of Acceleration.' Flavia swung her noble head away, flourishing thick, red hair. 'How long now, Astronomer Manius?'

Beneath the large screen on the bridge's port side, the chief astronomer looked up. Like Captain Tiberius and Flavia, Astronomer Manius had been assigned the body shape of a young Hyacinth emperor. His face was unlined, his skin was clear, his shoulders broad, his posture immaculate.

Astronomer Manius said, 'You can start the sequence in the next few minuta, First Lieutenant.'

'Thank you, Manius,' said Flavia. She turned to Sinistra. 'You may go to your station, Second Lieutenant.'

'Thank you, Lieutenant Flavia.'

On her plinth, Flavia said to the air, 'Light the navigation screen.'

At the forward extreme of the bridge, a great screen lit up. There was an intake of breath from the crew. On the screen, the spiral shape of the galaxy appeared, glistening with its billions of stars, all represented by tiny points of light.

On the spiral's port side, a small dark shape displayed the Herculaneum's position in the region known as Ilium. Across the spiral, on the galaxy's far side, the blue planet of Hyacinth blinked, as if calling to the Herculaneum for help.

Connecting these two points, a single straight line showed the Herculaneum's Acceleration course between the planets, stars, comets, and space debris.

The sight of the galaxy spiral and the Herculaneum's course was a thrilling moment. Six months before, the Herculaneum had launched from the home planet, carrying the entire population's hopes for survival. Now, the ship had reached the mission's most critical stage. Every crew member on the bridge watched, waited and hoped all would go well.

Astronomer Manius broke the silence. 'Quinque minuta, Lieutenant Flavia.' Five minutes.

'Good,' Flavia replied. 'Let's start the sequence.' She held out a hand, palm up. Fourth Lieutenant Priscus rushed forward from the rear bulkhead and handed her a sheet of paper listing the final pre-Acceleration steps. Flavia tossed back her lustrous hair and prepared to speak.

Down at her station, Sinistra focused on her screen. Her task for the Acceleration was to monitor the space immediately surrounding the ship for rogue detritus that might strike the Herculaneum just as it made its astonishing leap in velocity.

For now, Sinistra's screen was blank. Nothing out there—nothing forward, aft, to starboard, to port, aloft, or below. So far, the Ilium region was as calm as a lake in a lonely forest.

'Thank Owanthan,' whispered Sinistra, using the old phrase of gratitude to the gods. At least something was going right.

But just as Flavia called out the pre-Acceleration sequence, Sinistra noticed something unusual, something that caused her Hyacinth-creature heart to skip. She leaned in towards the screen. She raised a hand to her Hyacinth-creature mouth and for a moment stopped breathing entirely.

Impossible as it seemed, a small object had appeared in the screen's top right corner.

Something was out there in space, hurtling towards the ship.

5

First Lieutenant Flavia began the sequence.

'Navigation,' she called to Astronomer Manius.

'The way is clear, First Lieutenant.'

'Helm?'

'Steady and responding,' replied Helmsman Corvinus.

Then, Flavia spoke to the comms device.

'Quartermaster?'

'Ready,' said Quartermaster Antias.

'Engineering?' said Flavia.

'Chief Engineer Gabinus reports three minuta,' said Technical Officer Paulus.

'Holds?'

'Re-stowed and secure, First Lieutenant. All vehicles, provisions, weapons, herbicide tanks, and materials are tied down, all a "tanto."'

'Domum Deck?'

'All clear of personnel, First Lieutenant,' said Chief Purser Seta. 'The lakes are drained. The forest is secure.'

'What about Telepathy?' said Flavia.

'Telepathy is in contact with the Senate,' said Chief Communications Officer Domitian. 'He's ready to transmit the captain's speech—when the captain is ready, of course.'

'Of course. Marines?'

'Armed and standing by,' said Marine Captain Ranant from the rear bulkhead of the bridge. Flavia turned and smiled at Ranant, who smiled in return.

'Stern ramp?' said Flavia.

'Stern port sealed, First Lieutenant,' came the voice over the comms. 'All dropships are secure above their pads.'

'Armory?'

'Inventoried, First Lieutenant. All weapons accounted for and stowed in their clips. Hatches dogged shut. Armed Marine sentries are stationed outside.'

'Medical deck?'

'All surgery has ceased, First Lieutenant,' said Surgeon's Mate Cordinaus. 'Patients are strapped to their beds. All personnel are at their stations.'

'Good. Bridge crew harnesses?'

'Fastened and tight, First Lieutenant,' said Antias.

'All right,' said Flavia. 'Now to the last checks. Hull integrity?'

'No breaches, First Lieutenant. Atmosphere is steady at Hyacinth pressure.'

'Good. Topside watch?'

'All clear of approaching objects, First Lieutenant.'

'Keel?'

'Also clear of objects approaching from below, First Lieutenant.'

'Starboard watch?'

'Clear of objects, First Lieutenant. Nothing's out there. Not a thing.'

'Bow?'

'As you see, First Lieutenant. All clear ahead to the Point of Acceleration.'

'Praeclarus,' said First Lieutenant Flavia. Excellent. 'Gun deck?'

'Secured, Lieutenant. Gun ports are closed. Cannons are

inactive and secured.'

'All right,' Flavia said. Then she looked through the gloom at Sinistra. By now, Sinistra's nose was almost touching her screen, and the twitch had returned to the skin beneath her left eye.

'Port side watch?' Flavia repeated.

No reply came.

'Lieutenant Sinistra, did you hear me?'

Lieutenant Sinistra's blue, Hyacinth-creature eyes did not move. She was thinking quickly, as fast as her Hyacinth-creature mind could work.

Was there really an object out there, she wondered. Why wasn't it detected days ago? And if there is an object, she thought, what is it? Frozen gas? Icicles from waste jettisoned from the scuttles? Or something worse?

'We're waiting, Lieutenant Sinistra,' called Flavia. 'Is the port-side clear of objects or isn't it?'

Sinistra looked up. She saw Flavia's luminous green eyes, lustrous hair, and one eyebrow riding high, a rare Hyacinth-creature facial expression, which Sinistra had learned meant a question combined with impatience.

Sinistra said, 'All clear of objects, as Astronomer Manius predicted, First Lieutenant.'

'Faster, next time,' said Flavia.

'Yes, Lieutenant.'

Then, Flavia turned and addressed a tall male wearing long snowy-white robes with a purple sash across his chest, the robes of the future governor of Hyacinth.

'Advisor Cicero,' Flavia said. 'The captain will now address the Senate.'

Advisor Cicero replied from his special chair by the rear bulkhead. 'The members of the Senate are ready and waiting, First Lieutenant.'

'Good,' said Flavia. She turned to the noble profile of the captain. 'Tiberius, the crew and the Senate are standing by.'

Captain Tiberius raised his noble chin and smiled. Despite his youthful face, he was old—over three times the average age of the crew, and twice as old as Sinistra. His appointment to the mission had been a curious one. There had been younger, more able candidates, yet he was the Senate's only choice.

'Thank you, Lieutenant Flavia,' Captain Tiberius said. 'I will now address the crew and the Senate listening at home. Given the volume of engine noise astern, I will break with protocol and speak to you in your minds.'

The captain lowered his head and closed his eyes. A moment later, Sinistra heard his voice in her head, pronouncing the singsong Hyacinth words in the same round tones used by Flavia.

Shipmates, said Captain Tiberius's voice, fellow officers and members of the Senate, we are embarked on the most important mission of our lives: a mission to create a new world in order to save our people from the volcanic forces destroying our old world.

The distance we must travel is great, and the voyage is hazardous. We will be far from home in the company of a strange species. However, we should not be afraid. In the past, no less than two of our missions have reached Hyacinth, and in ships less magnificent than the Herculaneum. So there is no reason we will not do the same. Remember that in the deep past, our ancestors made equally perilous voyages across the galaxy to a new planet, a new home. We are about to emulate their great voyage, and do the same.

The captain's face turned grave. Deep creases appeared on his smooth forehead.

Of course, we must never forget the crew of the ill-fated ship, Parthia, which perished here in Ilium on its return voyage a century ago. There were five thousand crew members aboard. I know that many of them were family members or relatives of those hearing my voice today.

The technicians lowered the heads. Flavia reached a slender hand to her face and pressed it over her eyes.

The captain's voice paused, then began again.

So, let us go forth knowing that if each of us does our duty, we will succeed. For those of you who are religiously minded, let me quote some words from the Old Book, "Where we go, the gods of our fathers go with us."

He looked up.

His voice said, 'Ad Hyacinth!'

'To Hyacinth!' said the technicians on the bridge. 'To Hyacinth!' came the shouts of ten thousand voices around the ship.

'To Hyacinth,' whispered Sinistra, her eyes on her screen, and without realizing, she added, 'May the gods go with us.'

When all was quiet, the captain smiled at Flavia, who smiled back.

'Thank you, Captain,' Flavia said. 'We are ready.' She switched on the comms device beside her.

'Chief Engineer?'

'What?' came the grumpy voice of Chief Engineer Gabinus.

'Begin.'

'Aye, aye,' said the voice. 'Better hold on to your round Hyacinth creature behind, Flavia. It's going to be loud and hard.'

As soon as he had spoken, a deep, low moan surged from behind the rear bulkhead. Throughout the ship, thousands of harnesses tightened, and prayers were uttered to the old god, Owanthan, by people who had never prayed in their lives.

The Acceleration was about to take place.

The moan of the great engines intensified. It changed in pitch, rising from melancholy and woeful, to a plaintive whine. Finally, the noise became three yowls, more like animals than engines—furious animals warning everyone to keep away lest they be scratched.

The deck quivered, the screens flickered, the bulkheads rattled. Pens and notepads dropped to the deck. The ship's mascot, Gothi, fled to the rear bulkhead and hid behind the armored legs of Captain Ranant and the two marine sentries. At the helm, Corvinus adjusted his stance for astonishing jolt.

And above them, the great navigation screen shone forth. The galaxy's white spiral glittered. The Herculaneum's course flashed, disappeared, then re-emerged in a series of bright segments, dotting their way across the spiral to the blue light of the planet Hyacinth, waiting, waiting, waiting, an almost immeasurable distance away.

Everyone thrilled to this prospect, from the crew rattling in their chairs on the orlop, to the mechanics on the stern ramp watching the fleet of dropships quiver on their docking pads. The months of hardship had ended. Hyacinth was in reach. The business of saving the people on the home planet was finally about to begin. Everyone looked ahead.

But not quite everyone.

Not Second Lieutenant Sinistra.

Down at her station, Sinistra re-covered her mouth with her hand and concentrated on her screen. 'Please don't let it happen,' she whispered. 'Please don't let it happen.'

But *it* really was happening. The speck in the screen's top right corner had returned. Now it blinked, over and over, announcing its presence, demanding attention.

'Please don't let this happen,' Sinistra said. She almost added, 'Go away,' because now, she couldn't deny the truth. Out there in the black void of Ilium, at a distance of one hundred thousand milia off the port bow, an object hurtled through the gloom.

The sensor could not yet measure the object's size. However, it could predict its path. If nothing changed, the object would streak across a point two thousand Hyacinth milia directly ahead of the Herculaneum's present position.

But the object would not cross the Herculaneum's bow and roll away into oblivion. Instead, it would strike the Herculaneum just as it accelerated. And when the collision occurred, the ship's hull would be smashed, the ten thousand crew members would be killed by the impact, and any survivors would die in agony.

Worst of all, the mission would fail, and the families and friends on the home planet would suffer and die. Sinistra's old comrade, Nim, would be among them.

And Sinistra's career would be over.

She calmed her nerves, slowed her breath, and dabbled at the nagging twitch beneath her eye. Then, she tried to think. Was she really so certain that a collision was imminent?

Then, a brief battle took place in her mind—a battle between her duty to the mission and Sinistra's need to avoid Flavia's disapproval.

Duty seemed to win, but fear of Flavia was a formidable enemy. Of course, she couldn't risk another humiliation in front of the crew. But if she said nothing, what then?

Finally, Sinistra made her choice.

She switched on her comms device, drew a breath of the metallic air, and spoke the words she dreaded most.

'Lieutenant Flavia,' she called, detesting the sound of her voice, and hating yet another turn of bad luck in a morning of bad luck. 'Lieutenant, there's something approaching the ship.'

6

'Lieutenant Flavia!'

But Flavia did not reply. She and Captain Tiberius gazed at the forward screen, smiling at the galaxy and the Herculaneum's path across it. In their eyes, a glorious destiny waited in which they would be leaders, heroes, aristocrats, just as their ancestors had been on the home planet.

Sinistra tried again.

'Lieutenant Flavia!' she called. 'Captain Tiberius!'

No response. They couldn't hear or didn't care. Destiny had called them on.

Sinistra re-scanned her screen to check if anything had changed. Yes, the horrible object was still there, blinking in the screen's top right corner, proclaiming its course—its horrible, mission-destroying, career-wrecking course.

Sinistra raised her hand and dabbed a finger at the object, as if she could push it deep into space, but the object kept blinking, still advancing. Sinistra snatched her hand back. It was trembling.

Soon, fearful, defensive thoughts returned to her mind. What if I really do say nothing? What if I just keep quiet? The object might miss. The ship might accelerate past it.

What if I wait?

Yes, she thought, but what if the object doesn't miss? What then?

But she knew 'what then.' The impact would cause more than a catastrophe for the mission. It would cause a catastrophe for the home planet, too, and the billions of people.

'Captain Tiberius,' she shouted again. 'Lieutenant Flavia.'

This time, she was heard. Antias, the quartermaster, looked over his shoulder from where he stood strapped to his station beside the helm, and then Lieutenant Flavia's green eyes swung away from the screens and onto Sinistra. Her lips compressed into a red smear of displeasure.

'There's an object approaching from port!' Sinistra said. 'It will hit the ship before we accelerate.' Then she added. 'It came from nowhere. It wasn't on the screen before. It just appeared.'

But Lieutenant Flavia's response was to raise her shoulders. Sinistra didn't know what this expression meant. So she tried again, shouting this time.

'There's an object, Lieutenant Flavia! There's an object that will strike the ship. We must change course or abort the Acceleration.'

Now, Flavia made another curious expression. She held out her arms, revealing her two slender palms. So, Sinistra broke with mission protocol and sent out a telepathic thought.

Lieutenant Flavia, we must abort the Acceleration! Object approaching from port: nature unknown, size unknown, velocity immense. The strike point will be just before we accelerate. We must change course or abort the mission or, at the very least, order the gun deck to fire on it.

This time, Flavia's face showed a new expression. Both her eyebrows rose. Then her deep, round, assertive voice spoke in Sinistra's mind.

Lieutenant Sinistra, we will abort nothing. Not until we assess the danger. There is enough time. Send your image to the main screen. Astronomer Manius will estimate the object's velocity and heading.

Sinistra sent a thought back. It's already calculated, Lieutenant. (Why didn't Flavia know this?) I've just done it. The implication is clear. The object will strike us.

Astronomer Manius himself interrupted her. It's impossible, his voice said. There should be no object anywhere. The port-side space has been clear for weeks. You are mistaken.

It's there, Sinatra replied. The sensors missed it. We must abort, or we must order the gun deck to fire.

Send me the image, Lieutenant, said Astronomer Manius's voice. And watch your tone when you speak to me.

Now the rest of the bridge crew turned to look. Heads swiveled in the dark as everyone looked at each other for an explanation. Everyone was confused.

Then, the great screen changed its image from the spiral galaxy to a view of space from the ship's port side. All eyes turned towards it.

There was no sunlight in the Ilium region and so there was no light to view objects as they really appeared. Instead, the screen displayed a graphical representation.

Out there in space, an object tumbled in the gloom, lumbering and mindless, rolling on towards the ship, unaware of the destruction it would cause to the crew and an entire planet's population.

Flavia turned to Captain Tiberius and shouted in his right ear. The captain's Hyacinth-emperor brow creased. Advisor Cicero leaned forward, holding his robes to his chest. He too shouted in the captain's ear. The captain nodded as Cicero spoke. Then, he raised his chin and said, We will proceed. Our destiny cannot be delayed. The home planet expects it. The people depend on us.

But on Sinistra's screen, the blinking object continued on its course. Someone else's voice now spoke. It might have been Technical Officer Paulus.

We have a magnified image, Lieutenant Flavia.

Now, on the large, forward screen, a gray, box-shaped object loomed in the darkness.

What is it, Astronomer? An asteroid?

No, said Manius. Look at its sides. They're flat.

Then what? Ice vapor?

Possibly, but not with that shape.

Then what? What else is can it be?

It might be some kind of machine.

A machine, Astronomer? A machine coming from where? From whom?

Astronomer Manius scratched his neck. I don't know. It doesn't make sense.

Could it be from the Parthia? Flavia said. Wreckage from centuries ago?

Astronomer Manius held up both hands and raised each of his shoulders in the curious Hyacinth-creature way of conveying incomprehension.

Flavia's voice said, How long until impact?

Uno minuta, said Sinistra.

Captain Tiberius, your orders? said Flavia.

The captain raised his chin a second time. We will proceed, Lieutenant.

But it might strike us, Tiberius.

We will proceed, Lieutenant. We will proceed.

Yes, Captain.

The Herculaneum closed in on the Point of Acceleration; the engines shrieked; the entire bridge shook as if it were shivering with fear.

Then, Sinistra made a second decision. She unstrapped her harness and climbed from behind her station.

'Put your harness back on and sit down, Lieutenant!'

shouted Flavia.

'Beg pardon,' shouted Sinistra over the engine noise. 'If we follow the captain's orders, we risk the ship. We must abort the Acceleration or fire on the object—one or the other.'

'Captain Tiberius has made his decision, Lieutenant.'

Sinistra ignored her. She had never spoken this way to any officer in her career. 'We must order the gun deck to fire,' she shouted. 'While there's time.'

Lieutenant Flavia blinked at Sinistra, then came to a decision of her own. She spoke into her comms device. 'Captain Ranant?'

'Yes, Lieutenant,' said the captain of the Marines from the rear bulkhead.

'Arrest Lieutenant Sinistra and escort her from the bridge.'

'Aye, Lieutenant. But we are about to accelerate.'

'Now, Captain!'

At the rear bulkhead, Marine Captain Ranant turned and shouted to his men. Two tall armored marines stepped forward.

'Don't Captain,' said Sinistra, and then added. 'Please.'

'Sorry, Sin,' said Ranant. 'Orders.'

The marines grabbed Sinistra's arms and lifted her from the deck.

'Brace for impact,' called the quartermaster

Everyone gripped the armrests on their chairs. Around the ship, ten thousand crew members did the same. And on the forward screen, the box-like object raced to the collision point.

But all of a sudden, like the snapping of a tight rope, like the release of a ferocious grip, the entire ship went slack. The shuddering bulkheads relaxed. The engine shriek faded, as if it were a howling animal struck down with a weapon.

For a moment, all was quiet on the bridge—so quiet that Sinistra could hear the squelch of the marines' boots on the metallic deck.

Then, everything changed.

The great ship Herculaneum seemed to hit a wall in space. Everything came to a stop. Around the bridge, each technical specialist flew forward in his or her harness. Their arms flung out as if they were shoving someone away. Inside their abdomens, the flopping Hyacinth-creature organs crashed into their ribs. Then, each body came to a violent stop, and their heads snapped down, their chins stabbing the notch above each sternum.

Meanwhile, Sinistra was yanked from her feet towards and flung towards the forward bulkhead. The heavy marines came beside her. The three of them hit the display screens, splintering them into shards of glass.

Then, as they dropped to the deck, alarms rang fore and aft, and a series of bangs and crashes sounded deep in the ship, one after the after, as if a giant were stomping his way forward, one cabin at a time, all while someone on the bridge screamed 'My leg! My hind leg!'

At the navigation screens, the ship's astronomer, Manius, clutched his face where a shiny medal from Flavia's uniform detached from her chest and struck his cheekbone, and everywhere, crew members clutched at their chins, throats, and chests.

'Calm!' called Captain Tiberius. 'Stay calm, everyone.'

Sinistra pulled herself up on one elbow and opened her mouth to speak, while from her chair and straining harness, Flavia glared down at her with an expression Sinistra did not dare to understand.

And around the bridge, the crew began to realise what had just happened. The ship had not been hit, as every feared. Instead, the object had missed and rolled away into space.

But this was not the reason for the sudden halt. It was something else. The Acceleration engines had failed just before the leap to faster-than-light speed.

Now, the Herculaneum was still in Ilium, and Hyacinth's blue oceans, white mountains, and shining cities remained out of reach, across the galaxy, far, far away.

Sinistra risked another glance at Flavia. Then, she had seen Flavia's expression for the second time, she wished she'd never raised her head.

Nim, she thought. Something dreadful has happened. I have done a terrible thing, a most terrible, terrible thing. I'll never win their approval now.

But what Sinistra did not yet realize was that out in space, the object had not rolled away. When the screens came back on, they revealed a shocking sight.

The object had returned.

Somehow it had crouched like a gray, malevolent predator, locked directly ahead of the Herculaneum's bow at a distance of one leuga.

And it stayed there no matter how fast or slow the Herculaneum moved.

7

As the next bell tolled, Captain Tiberius issued the order to stand down.

Flavia dismissed the Acceleration crew from the bridge. Third Lieutenant Cadmus assumed command. He ordered the ship to heave to and stand by for new orders.

The object remained a leagua from the bow.

At the ship's stern, several milia aft the bridge, projecting out into cold dark space, the Herculaneum's enormous exhaust funnels cooled. Deep in the engineering hall, the Acceleration engines themselves, known as Jupiter, Mars, and Apollo, sat blackened and smoking in their pits. The engineer's mates watched them from the bulkheads. The mates had learned a new Hyacinth-creature expression: a bewildered scratch of the head.

Meanwhile, the ship's other ten thousand crew members returned to their routines. The morning watch went to their bunks for Hyacinth-creature sleep. The rest of the crew went to their stations, or to the newsroom for the latest about the volcanic eruptions on the home planet.

Everyone discussed the aborted Acceleration. Superstitious crew members said it was because of the presence of a strange hand-shaped constellation that appeared in Ilium a week ago. Others said it was only to be expected, given the rush to launch the mission when neither the crew nor the ship was ready. More still had heard a rumor that the object was still around, blocking the ship's progress.

Then, the crew returned to the usual subject of conversation: How would the actual Hyacinth creatures on Hyacinth react when they met the visitors from the stars? Would the Hyacinth creatures welcome them? Or would they sense something wrong? What about the Hyacinth females—what would they think of the visitor men?

'I'll just say to them, you're a woman, I'm a man, and take it from there,' said Seaman Vitus.

'And what will any Hyacinth woman say if she sees your real self?' This was Petty Officer Gracchus from the stern.

'They'll think we're monsters, of course,' said Vitus. 'That's what they'll think. Scary monsters. Monstra terribilia—most very horrible monstra terribilia.'

'Speak for yourself,' said Gracchus. 'I'm no monster.'

'What about that rash on your neck, Gracchus?' said Vitus. 'The Hyacinth creatures will think you're a freak.'

'They'll think we're all freaks,' said Able Seaman Testa, also from the stern. 'All of us—even beautiful First Lieutenant Flavia.'

'They will think we're freaks if they ever hear beautiful First Lieutenant Flavia speak to her second lieutenant.'

'Why does she put up with it?'

'Who? Flavia?'

'No. Sinistra.'

'She has to put up with it. What can she do?'

'But imagine. She's third in command and the officers speak to her like dirt.'

Everyone was silent for a moment.

'To think we might be there by now,' said Gracchus. 'Just imagine. We'd be on that planet, looking at the blue oceans and the white mountains.'

Meanwhile, Captain Tiberius had ordered the most senior naval officers, senior warrant officers, and senior petty officers, to present themselves to the great cabin at the very next bell. Second Lieutenant Sinistra would be among them.

8

In Captain Tiberius's great cabin, a large painting dominated the port bulkhead.

Titled, 'The Fate of The People' and created by mission artist Petty Officer Bucco, the painting depicted the most significant event in the people's folklore: the moment, eons ago, when the people fled the old planet and trekked across the galaxy to conquer a new planet, the planet they now called the home planet, or home.

The scene in the painting was epic in style. On a grim, black mountaintop blasted by volcanic ash, the ancient god Owanthan pointed to the evening sky. His meaning was unmistakable. 'That is the way. Up there in the stars! There lies salvation from the terrors you face. There waits your new home.'

Standing beside Owanthan, the ancient ruler, King Angwor stared at the stars, his face rippled with concern. Beside the king stood Queen Angwere, his wife, twisting Angwor's left sleeve with her hands. The king's advisors stood nearby. Some looked to the stars, others gazed at the planet they would soon leave behind.

Behind the advisors, trailing down the mountain's storm-blasted slopes, the masses huddled in fear, waiting for the gods, the king, and his advisors, to lead them to the new world.

For the mission, Captain Tiberius ordered Petty Officer Bucco to make two bold changes to the traditional representation of this event. First, the ancient gods and the ancient people should be depicted as Hyacinth creatures. Yes, Hyacinth creatures. Second, the advisors standing closest to the king should resemble the Herculaneum's captain and his senior officers in their Hyacinth-creature forms.

There were good reasons for these requests. Many of the old patrician families claimed their ancestors had been present at the famous moment. The Admiralty and the Senate chose the Herculaneum's officers for this very reason. They wanted the ship's crew to know that the old families would once again lead them from catastrophe to a safe new world.

Now, in the captain's great cabin, the descendants of the figures represented in the painting gathered beneath it, waiting for Captain Tiberius to arrive, and for the debriefing to begin. There was Chief Engineer Gabinus, Chief Astronomer Manius, Master Gunner Decimus, Chief Communications Officer Domitian, Chief Purser Seta, and First Lieutenant Flavia.

All these officers had been issued Hyacinth-creature forms that were young, handsome, and strong, according to Hyacinth-creature ideas of beauty. It didn't matter that, in reality, the officers were aged, bent, doddering, forgetful, and at the end of undistinguished careers. As Hyacinth-creatures, they were in the bloom of health. They looked like leaders.

The only officer not represented in Petty Officer Bucco's work was Second Lieutenant Sinistra. If the epic moment on the mountain had actually occurred, her ancestors wouldn't have stood beside the god and the king. They would have been shivering with the masses, filled with fear and resentment, waiting to be led.

Lieutenant Sinistra stood alone in the centre of the stateroom, her hands penitently clasped. In the presence of so much Hyacinth creature beauty, she felt more like a withered yellow shrub than ever, all of which made her need to win approval more intense, especially after the debacle during the Acceleration.

When should I speak? she wondered. How can I talk without treading on any toes? She stole a glance at Flavia, who was adjusting her chin so that she matched the woman in scarlet robes in the painting. Sinistra watched her until Flavia's green eyes swung away from the painting and caught Sinistra staring at her. Flavia was about to speak when the stateroom door opened.

Captain Tiberius strode inside. Everyone stood and saluted. 'At ease,' the captain said. 'At ease. I just left Telepathy. Advisor Cicero and I have spoken with the Senate. The Senators want answers. They want to know why the Herculaneum is not already in the Hyacinth solar system. They want to know how we intend to get there and what we intend to do about this object off our bow. The people on the home planet need good news, not failed Accelerations.'

Here, the captain paused and turned to Chief Purser Seta. 'The Admiralty also sends its condolences, Seta. The eruption at Grankat was a terrible blow to your family and to many members of the service.'

'Thank you, Captain,' Seta said.

'Sir,' said Flavia. 'Don't the Senators want to know more about the object itself? Surely they realize we must send a survey crew over to it.'

'Survey crew?' said chief Gunner Decimus. 'We're going to blast it to pieces, aren't we? Boosh!' He raised his hands and slowly drew them apart.

'The only thing I want to know about the object,' said Astronomer Manius, 'is that it's behind us.'

'That is what we're going to discuss,' said Captain Tiberius.

'I hope, Captain,' said Flavia, 'that we are also going to discuss the wider implication of what happened on the bridge this morning.'

'Flavia, if you're referring to Second Lieutenant Sinistra,' said Tiberius, 'we will address her actions separately.'

'Yes, Captain,' Flavia said. 'Thank you, but I'm talking about something else: that the object looks to be part of a machine, possibly another vessel, probably the Parthia. It might be wreckage. There might be survivors.'

'We don't know that, Lieutenant, not unless we see the object up close, which we can't. The magnifying instruments show only a blur, and the lantern beams can't reach it.'

'But Manius said it's a machine.'

'I did not,' replied Manius. 'I said it resembled a machine, nothing more. It's likely just a fragment of an asteroid—a box-shaped asteroid.'

'Or it could be wreckage from the Parthia,' said Flavia, 'which means Parthia survivors might be inside it. That's why it's blocking our path. Captain Strahklan is trying to get our attention.'

'Or it could just be debris,' said Manius. 'That's the most logical explanation, in which case Decimus is right. We must blast it away. The mission must come first, just as in the past.'

At the words, 'The mission must come first,' each of the senior officers looked at 'The fate of the people,' and at their historical counterparts. Without realizing it, some officers adjusted their poses. Gabinus placed a hand on his chest. Seta pushed her raven dark hair behind her ears.

Chief Petty Officer Domitian broke the silence.

'And what if the object is something else entirely? What if

it's a machine, as Flavia says, but not from the Parthia?'

'What are you saying?' scoffed Astronomer Manius. 'That it's from another civilization? Don't be ridiculous, Domitian. Who is here in the galaxy but ourselves and the Hyacinth creatures?'

'What I'm saying,' said Domitian, 'is that the object might be a message from the gods themselves. They're trying to help us in this time of crisis.'

Everyone turned to look at him. No one spoke. No one wanted to mention the gods, or Owanthan, or the other gods in the pantheon, or religion, or even the Old Book. The gods were fine for paintings and old stories, but not much more. And so, without speaking, the senior officers turned away from Domitian and back to the captain.

'It's an asteroid,' said Astronomer Manius. 'A rogue asteroid that crossed our path and, for some reason, was attracted by the ship. My crew is working to discover why, Captain.'

'No,' said Flavia. 'The most logical explanation, Chief Astronomer, is that it is either wreckage from the Parthia or that it's a form of lifeboat. You had a relative on the Parthia, didn't you, Manius? What was his name? Was it Lieutenant Grista? We all had relatives aboard. Captain Strahklan is a cousin of mine.'

Manius ignored her and spoke to the captain. 'Tiberius, we have priorities—mission priorities. We must put the mission objective first, and that is to reach Hyacinth, not waste time investigating asteroids, no matter how diverting the distractions might be.'

'And I say,' said Flavia, 'that if there are Parthia survivors inside that object, their rescue will give hope to the people at home. Imagine the boost to morale. Imagine greeting our relatives again. Wasn't your wife's nephew the Parthia's engineer?'

'There isn't time, cousin Flavia,' said Manius. 'We've got

to find a new Acceleration point.'

'There's time if we say there is, cousin Manius. And in case you forgot, it's the naval officers who decide the mission's course, not the warrant officers.'

'Are you pulling rank, cousin Flavia?'

'Are you being insubordinate, cousin Manius?'

They glared at each other, each beautiful face scowling.

Tiberius said, 'These questions can be answered if we could only see the object clearly. Chief Astronomer, why can't we bring the Herculaneum closer to it? What keeps it locked on our path? And if there are Parthia survivors, why don't they answer Telepathy's messages?'

'As I said, we're working on it, Captain,' said Manius. 'But we are running out of time before we have to move on.'

'And I say,' said Flavia, 'that if we don't investigate this object, we'll be abandoning our relatives, our fellow Navy service members.'

Both Flavia and Manius glared at each other, then both turned to the captain, awaiting his judgement. Now, it was Captain Tiberius who looked at the painting of the 'The Fate Of The People, ' as if the old god Owanthan would speak from the canvas and offer him advice, just as he'd advised King Angwor, all those centuries ago.

Chief Communications Officer Domitian saw him and was about to mention something more about the gods and the Old Book, when a small, thin voice spoke from the center of the room.

'Captain Tiberius?' the voice said.

As soon as she had spoken, Sinistra regretted opening her mouth. A range of Hyacinth-creature faces swung on her like weapons, armed and ready to fire. The barrage was so fierce that she took a step backwards onto her lame right foot and almost tripped. She couldn't interpret most Hyacinth-creature expressions, but there was no mistaking the meanings of those faces, and those body gestures.

She saw Manius's open mouth, Seta's tightly compressed lips, Gabinus's hand on one hip, Decimus's abrupt sniff, and Flavia's incandescent green glare.

If she didn't know better, Sinistra might have concluded all these beautiful people were in pain. But she knew just enough from her two months aboard to see the truth: all these gestures meant disdain, impatience, annoyance, and in Flavia's case something worse.

Only Chief Domitian smiled, and only Captain Tiberius looked interested in what Sinistra had to say.

'Yes, Lieutenant Sinistra,' Tiberius said. 'What is it?'

Sinistra thought about excusing herself and saying she hadn't meant to interrupt, but guessing that this would only bring more disdain, she said, 'May I make a suggestion?'

9

The bell tolled. Secunda passed. No one spoke. Only the hiss of the atmosphere pumps disturbed the silence.

Eventually, Captain Tiberius said, 'Yes, Lieutenant Sinistra. Of course. What is your suggestion?'

Sinistra opened her mouth, but Chief Engineer Gabinus interrupted her. 'Captain, I thought that only the most important officers would attend this debriefing.'

'Now, Chief Engineer,' said Tiberius. 'We've discussed this.'

'That's not what I mean. It's not about her rank.'

'Yes, I know, Gabinus, but on this mission, Lieutenant Sinistra's presence is important. I would argue it's essential. Also, the Senate wants her to be here.'

Decimus, the gunner, raised his chin and spoke. 'I'm the same as Gabinus, Captain. I don't like it either, this social experiment. We should have replaced Lieutenant Commodus with someone more appropriate—someone like Lieutenant Sylla, my brother-in-law, not this … this …'

The captain stood to his full height. 'No, Chief Gunner, I disagree. Fresh blood—that's what we need, as the Hyacinth-creature expression goes. We need people of competence regardless of where they are from. The mission requires it.'

'Competence?' said Gunner Decimus. 'What competence? It was this lieutenant who caused the trouble. And you heard the way she spoke to Flavia! It's intolerable.'

'Lieutenant Flavia will address that matter later,' said Tiberius. 'In the meantime, I shouldn't need to remind you that Lieutenant Sinistra outranks all of you, except for Flavia and myself.'

'But just look at her,' added Chief Peta Officer Seta. Her grief over her family's deaths during the recent eruptions had apparently subsided. 'The state of her!'

'The lieutenant's looks are not important,' said Tiberius. 'It's her competence that matters. I value her experience, her record, her counsel. So does Lieutenant Flavia, so does Advisor Cicero, as do the Admiralty and the Senate. You underestimate her. Lieutenant Sinistra has served in many naval actions. Who here can claim the same?'

'We don't underestimate her,' said Gabinus. 'It's just that she … she's not …'

'Enough!' said Tiberius. 'Really, Gabinus! That's enough.'

Tiberius turned to Sinistra.

'Now, Second Lieutenant, what is your suggestion?'

Sinistra stood with her hands clasped. These aristocratic officers were wrong about her. She didn't want to be one of them. Not at all. She wanted their approval. She wanted validation from those with the power to harm her. Without approval, the darkest fears came, the shame and self loathing turned up, and on this mission, in the strange Hyacinth-creature form, the nightmares showed up, too.

Now, she had drawn the worst of these aristocratic officers' opinions. Nim, she thought. Nim, if you're listening, give me some advice. But Nim did not reply. Nim never replied, and it was dangerous to even send her a message. You never knew who might read your mind.

'I think,' Sinistra began, 'that the chief astronomer and

the first lieutenant both have valid ideas.'

'Oh, well, thank you!' said Flavia to the deckhead above. Her red fingernails splayed over the blue uniform on her famous waist.

'I also think there might be a way to address both their concerns.'

'Tiberius, please,' said Flavia. 'There are more important things than—what did you call it, Decimus—social experiments?'

'Quiet, Flavia,' said Tiberius. 'Please go on, Lieutenant Sinistra.'

'If the Astronomer can tell us how long we have until the next Acceleration opportunity, there might be time to investigate the object.'

Flavia sighed. Manius closed his eyes in forbearance. Seta glowered. Gabinus had turned his back and studied his likeness in the painting, the tall, fair-haired figure with the defiant chin.

'Well, Chief Astronomer,' said Tiberius. 'How long do we have?'

'It's not that simple, Captain.'

'Well, what is it, then?'

'It depends on Chief Engineer Gabinus and how soon he can repair the Acceleration engines.'

'Well, Gabinus?' said Tiberius. 'Gabinus, are you listening?'

Gabinus turned from the painting and glared at Sinistra. 'Four Hyacinth days at the soonest,' he said. 'Apollo needs repair. The other two engines—Jupiter and Mars—they're all right, but my boys will check them just in case.'

'Your boys?'

'I mean my crew. I call them boys. We don't have any females in engineering.'

'Four Hyacinth days? Are you sure?'

'Four at least,' said Gabinus. 'Maybe more. Apollo can be

difficult.'

The captain turned to Manius. 'Well, Chief Astronomer, how much time can we spare before the next Acceleration?'

'That also depends, Captain.'

'Depends on what?'

'We have missed our chance here in Ilium. The way across the galaxy is blocked. Stars have drifted into the road along with their solar systems.

'Can't we go around them?'

'We can, Captain. However, at Acceleration speed, we can't change course. So, we will overshoot Hyacinth.'

'Can't we cruise back?'

'The cruise back could take several Hyacinth years.'

'Well, that's no good,' said the captain. 'The home planet will be ash by then, and the people … well, let's not think about that.'

'I have plotted a second course,' said Manius, 'from the Gordium region. A clear path will open there in seven Hyacinth days.'

'The Gordium region?'

'Gordium is our last opportunity, Captain. If we miss it, we must wait six Hyacinth months for a path in the Nostrum region.'

'How far to this Gordium?'

'Three Hyacinth days at cruising speed.'

'Chief Engineer Gabinus,' said Tiberius. 'Can our cruise engines take us there while you repair the large engines?'

'Maybe,' said Gabinus. 'With Owanthan's blessing.'

The captain tilted his head to one side. 'Did you say Owanthan's blessing, Chief Engineer? That's a strange expression to use. '

Chief Domitian interrupted. 'Faith in the old gods is returning, Captain,' he said. 'The crew have new interest in Owanthan, and in Sirhain, and the rest of the gods. They're even asking for copies of the Old Book.'

As before, the officers looked at Domitian as if he were mad. Then they turned back to Captain Tiberius and Engineer Gabinus.

Gabinus said, 'I used that old expression, Captain, because we'll need a miracle from the gods to be ready in time.'

'Well, then,' said the captain. 'With Owanthan's blessing, let us proceed.'

The captain stood up.

'But wait,' said Flavia. 'What about the object? We haven't discussed how to investigate it. I suggest we send a manned dropship across as soon as possible.'

Captain Tiberius sat down.

'A manned dropship?'

'Imagine, Captain. The Parthia officers are waiting for us. We must greet them with all naval courtesy. It will make a great subject for Bucco to paint. It will be a companion picture for "The Fate of The People."'

'But that sounds risky,' the captain said. 'Who will lead this manned dropship?'

'I will, Captain,' said Flavia.

'You? But you have so little experience of open space, Flavia, and none of dropships.'

Once again, the small voice spoke from the center of the room.

'Captain?' said Sinistra. Instantly, the hostile faces rotated towards her. Now it was Flavia's turn to close her eyes in forbearance and Manius's turn to look at the deckhead.

Sinistra continued. 'May I make another suggestion?'

'Not again,' said Flavia. 'Don't imagine you'll be the one commanding the dropship, Second Lieutenant, because you won't. This mission calls for the right people to lead it.'

'Not now, Flavia,' said Tiberius. 'Let's hear what the lieutenant has to say.'

'Thank you, Captain,' Sinistra said. 'Before we send a

manned mission, I suggest we send out the unmanned probes. They can see any markings, and can even take samples of the object's material, or if necessary, knock out a message on the object's side.'

'The probes!' said Tiberius. 'Of course! I knew we would find a use for them. Flavia, why didn't you suggest the probes?'

'I was just about to,' said Flavia, 'but you chose instead to listen to our overweening second lieutenant.'

Tiberius said, 'Who has the next watch?'

'I do, Captain,' said Sinistra.

'Good. Then you will command the ship while we send the probes forth. If the object turns out to be an asteroid, we will weigh anchor immediately and set sail for Gordium. And Decimus, you can use your guns to … what did you say.'

'I said "Boosh," Captain. That's what will happen when we blow it apart.'

'And if it's not an asteroid?' said Flavia. 'If it's the Parthia survivors?'

'Then we will discuss the possibility of a manned mission.'

The captain turned to leave once more, but after a few steps he turned back and looked at Sinistra.

'Lieutenant?'

'Yes, Captain.'

'Get some rest before your watch. You look tired. Are you having trouble resting? You aren't as used to the Hyacinth-creature form as the rest of us.'

'Yes, Captain. Thank you, Captain.'

When the officers had left, Sinistra limped after them. Flavia said, 'Lieutenant Sinistra, where do you think you are going?'

Sinistra stopped. Her frail body quivered beneath her uniform.

'To rest, First Lieutenant, as the captain recommended.'

'Stay where you are. There's something I want to say to you.'

10

'Yes, First Lieutenant?' Sinistra replied.

Flavia crossed her arms and said, 'As much as I'd like to, I can't dismiss you—not from this mission, nor from this ship. Not while the Senate exerts such pressure on the captain.'

Sinistra said nothing.

'I could almost bear your presence the first two months because you kept out of the way, but after this morning, I see it's going to get worse, and I simply refuse to suffer you for the rest of the mission.'

A series of wrinkles spread down Flavia's beautiful, smooth forehead. 'There's something wrong with you,' she said. 'And I don't just mean the way you look, speak, and move.'

Sinistra said, 'I am learning the language as fast as I can, Lieutenant, and my leg is much stronger now. I hope to be walking naturally by the time we greet the Hyacinth creatures.'

'That's not what I mean. I'm talking about something else.'

'I'm only trying to serve the navy and my superior officers, especially yourself, Lieutenant.'

'There!' said Flavia. 'That! You're doing it again.'

'Doing what, Lieutenant?'

'Speaking that way. Saying those words. Looking at me with that face. It makes my scales crawl.'

'I'm sorry, Lieutenant. I'm just trying to do my best.'

'Were you always like this? Have you always been this way?'

Sinistra did not reply, but the truth was she *had* always been this way—with Lieutenant Trant, Commander Akra, Captain Uralant, and the rest of the officers she'd served on her way to surpassing them. But they had been people like herself, the ordinary people who made up most of the home planet's population. None of them were like Flavia, a descendent from an old patrician family, and the granddaughter of the famous Admiral Guern.

Flavia said, 'What am I going to do with you?'

'In the future, Lieutenant, I will be more respectful of your rank?'

'That's not it. You don't see. It's that … I can't stand you. That's what I mean. I simply can't stand you.'

Sinistra made no reply. Flavia turned her back and looked at 'The Fate of The People' as if seeking answers from the red-haired woman in the scarlet robe.

Sinistra waited, her mind churning for a way to reverse the situation. If she could just show Flavia how competent she was, how deserving of praise. If she could only hear an encouraging word, then everything would be all right and the black feelings of shame and worthlessness would release their hold.

'Beg pardon, Lieutenant,' she said, 'but is there anything more?' She waited. 'Then, with your permission, I would like to do as the captain commanded. I'd like to rest before my watch.'

Flavia turned from the painting. She smiled. 'Maybe there is something I can do after all.'

'Yes, Lieutenant?' Sinistra replied.

'Go and open the door. I want the captain's steward.'

Sinistra hobbled to the door and opened it. Steward Frumentius looked up from his station, then shot to his feet.

'You!' said Flavia.

'Yes, First Lieutenant?'

'Pass the word for Doctor Galen.'

'Doctor Galen, Lieutenant? Is everything all right?'

'Tell him I want an evaluation of an officer's mental fitness.'

'Yes, Lieutenant. I'll message the medical deck.'

Frumentius disappeared.

'It's a great pity we lost Lieutenant Commodus,' said Flavia. 'She was a cousin of mine. Everyone liked her. If she were alive, you wouldn't be here. You'd be back on the home planet, causing trouble for someone else.'

'Do you mind me asking what happened to Lieutenant Commodus?'

'Yes,' said Flavia. 'I mind extremely.'

Frumentius returned. 'Doctor Galen is not on the medical deck, Lieutenant.'

'Then where is he?'

'I don't know. Only that he'll be back next watch.'

Flavia stamped her foot and spoke an obscenity in the growls of the native language. Sinistra and Frumentius flinched. Flavia clutched at her neck. The Hyacinth-creature throat could not pronounce the native language's growls and shrieks.

Sinistra said, 'Lieutenant Flavia, with your permission, I'd prefer to visit Doctor Galen after my watch, after we've sent out the probes.'

Flavia placed a hand over her forehead as if she were in pain.

'Then you will report to Doctor Galen the second your watch is complete.'

'Thank you.'

'You are dismissed, Second Lieutenant.'

Sinistra saluted, then backed away, keeping her face toward Flavia until she reached the door, as if Flavia were royalty and Sinistra a courtier.

'Wait,' said Flavia without turning around. Sinistra stopped. 'Look at the painting.'

Sinistra looked.

'Do you see the figure in green behind the Hyacinth creature who looks like Chief Petty Officer Decimus?'

'Yes, Lieutenant.'

'That is Doctor Galen's ancestor.'

'Yes, Lieutenant. I can see the likeness.'

Flavia smiled. 'Unfortunately, I can't remove you from command, but Doctor Galen can. Oh, yes. Doctor Galen can.'

11

In the afternoon watch, the Herculaneum lay heaved to at the edge of Ilium. The beacon flashed on the hull above the bridge. The lanterns beamed into the gloom, fore and aft. The cruise engines idled. Meanwhile, the crew rotated into and out of their watches, according to the strike of the bell.

On the bridge, investigations into the object were under way. The mission anthropologist was present, so too were the planetographer, and the chiefs of gunnery, engineering, navigation, and communications. Second Lieutenant Sinistra commanded the watch.

Down beneath the ship's keel, just forward of the hold, a hatch slid open, revealing a bright rectangle of light. A probe, measuring two Hyacinth creatures in height, descended from the hatch. It dropped beneath the clutter of pipes, antennae, hooks, and sensors, and, for a moment, floated motionless, as if stunned by the sight of the limitless void.

Then, a puff of mist burst from the small stern, and the probe pushed forward beneath the keel until it emerged from under the Herculaneum's bow. The forward lanterns flared on the probe's gray hull as it pushed away from the ship and into the gloom, like a child drifting away from its giant parent.

On the bridge, First Lieutenant Flavia stood watching the probe through the forward viewport. Her hands were on her hips. Her legs were planted apart. Her red lips curled up at one corner of her mouth.

'This will clear up the question once and for all, Captain,' she said.

Captain Tiberius and his senior officers stood watching the screen. Sinistra, the officer of the watch, stood to the side of the captain's vacant chair. The bridge crew attended to their own screens, awed by so many officers in one place.

For the moment, everyone watched the forward viewport as the small probe, a sliver of white in the forward lantern beam, drifted towards the object, a leuga away, out of sight in the gloom.

'Whatever it is, Flavia,' said Captain Tiberius. 'We must prioritize the mission, no matter how much we might wish otherwise.'

'But that's what I'm saying, Tiberius. This *is* for the mission—and for our relatives.'

'There was a crew of five thousand aboard the Parthia, Lieutenant, not just our family members.'

'Yes, of course. There was the crew. Naturally! But you know what I mean. Think of your cousin Kantra, and of Captain Strahklan. They might be alive and watching.'

Tiberius kept his eyes on the screen. By now, nothing showed up at all, except the darkness of space.

Tiberius looked over his shoulder. 'Lieutenant Sinistra!'

'Yes, Captain.'

'Why can't we see anything?'

'The object is beyond the range of the lantern beams, Captain, but the close view is coming up from the probe lights.'

Scapula, the anthropologist, said, 'What if it's not from the Parthia, and not an asteroid, either?'

Flavia said, 'We've already discussed this, Scapula—the idea of other civilizations, I mean. There are only ourselves and the Hyacinth creatures. There's no one else, unless you know something the rest of us don't.'

'We could argue that there is also the Goths,' said Scapula.

'They're hardly civilized,' said Flavia. 'They eat, hunt, kill, and fornicate. That's not a civilization. It's barely a culture. And what would they be doing out here?'

Everyone was silent while they recalled the huge, fur covered creatures who dominated the home planet until the ancestors from the old planet arrived. Even today, the terrifying Goths still posed a threat to anyone who entered their forests in the planet's north, where Sinistra grew up.

Chief Petty Officer Domitian interrupted everyone's thoughts. He said, 'That's not quite true, though, is it? There's another civilization.'

'What's not quite true?' said Flavia.

'There are also the gods. The gods were here once upon a time, too. They might still be a civilization.'

'Yes,' said Flavia. 'You're right, Domitian. The gods and their culture were here, but only in our ancestors' fantasies. I thought you were a scientist, Dom.'

'No one, not even a scientist, can dismiss with certainty that the gods never existed, Flavia. They are still with us, even if only in our culture.'

Among the bridge crew, looks were exchanged, and Technical officer Paulus mouthed a silent prayer. Other ordinary crew members bowed their heads.

'Why doesn't the object come closer?' said Engineer Gabinus. 'Why does it keep its distance from us? And are you sure it won't retreat from the probe?'

'There will be an explanation,' said Flavia. 'Perhaps the survivors are protecting us from something dangerous.'

'Like what?' said Manius.

'I don't know—an affliction of some kind, a contagious

disease they brought from Hyacinth.'

Chief Domitian said, 'Everything about this object is odd. If our own people are aboard it, why would they behave this way? Why come so close to crashing into us and then keep away?'

'That's easily explained,' said Flavia. 'The near collision was because of poor seamanship on our part. It was nothing to do with the object.'

She looked over her shoulder at Sinistra. 'Yes,' said Flavia, 'very poor seamanship, very poor behavior from one of our officers. Don't you agree, Captain?'

The captain's eyes remained on the small probe pushing into the dark. 'We've spoken about this, Flavia.'

'But you agree, don't you?'

'Not now, Lieutenant.'

'No, Tiberius, I insist. Do you agree or not?'

Tiberius sighed. 'To my thinking, Lieutenant Sinistra was only trying to help in difficult circumstances.'

Flavia removed her hands from her hips and raised her palms in the air.

Sinistra looked over at Gabinus. No one blamed him for the engine failure. Gabinus saw Sinistra's glance and warned her away by raising his noble chin.

Across the bridge, sitting at his console, the probe pilot, Lepidus, broke the tension. He opened his mouth to speak, but a coughing fit overcame him, and he barked and spluttered into his hands. When he recovered himself, he looked at Sinistra and pointed at his screen. Sinistra understood.

'Captain Tiberius. We can bring up the view from the probe now, if you please.'

Tiberius drew a weary breath. 'Yes, Lieutenant. Switch them on and then let's see what this thing is about.'

A screen flickered into life on the forward bulkhead. It showed nothing but distant stars. Finally, the object's gray, mournful face slowly emerged from the gloom.

'What in the galaxy is that?' said Gunner Decimus. 'Some kind of dropship?'

'It's not the Parthia,' said Gabinus, 'not any part I recognize. It's not any part of any ship.'

'Then, what is it?' said Tiberius. 'What can it be?'

Scapula, the anthropologist, said, 'I think I know what it is.'

'And what's that?' said the captain. 'What do you see?'

'Well, I've only read a description of these things from the first mission to Hyacinth, but to my mind it can only be one thing.'

'And what's that?'

'Believe it or not, I think it's a Hyacinth temple.'

12

Silence on the bridge. No sound at all, except for the hum of the electrical circuitry and the regular bip of the sensors.

Then Manius unfolded his arms and said, 'A Hyacinth temple? You sound very certain, Scapula. How do you know?'

'It's the columns,' said Scapula. 'If not for the columns, it might look just like a house or a windowless building.'

'It looks so strange,' said Seta. 'Not like a place anyone would want to enter. How do you think it got here?'

As Seta spoke, the probe pushed on. Its beams lit up the temple's columns. Dark shadows stretched and retreated on the gray cella wall and the plinth.

'Anyone see an entrance?' said Scapula.

When no one answered, Decimus the gunner, said, 'Captain, just say the word. I'll message the gun deck and this thing will be gone in under a minuta.'

No one replied.

'Obviously, it's an archaeological relic brought back by Captain Strahklan,' said Flavia. 'He must have had a reason.'

'What's at the base?' said Domitian.

'You mean the podium,' said Scapula.

Ignoring him, Domitian said, 'Sin, ask the pilot to enlarge

it.'

Flavia sniffed at Domitian's use of the name, 'Sin.'

Sinistra looked across the bridge at Lepidus, who was about to say, 'Aye, aye,' but instead he doubled over in another fit of coughs. Then he sent the instruction to the probe. Soon, the object's podium filled the screen. A series of symbols appeared in a row. They stood up from the surface, each symbol casting a shifting shadow of its own.

'Is that the Hyacinth language?' said Tiberius.

'Not one that I recognize,' said Scapula. 'But it might be a language non-Romans speak. Unfortunately, we know nothing about them—the other Hyacinth civilisations.'

'How will we find out what it means?' said Manius.

Chief Domitian said, 'No need. We can read it already.'

'Read it how?' said Scapula.

'Those characters are familiar to all of us—or they should be. They're familiar to our culture, to our ancestors, and to our gods.'

'Well, what are they?' said Flavia.

'They're from the Old Book?'

'The Old Book?' said Tiberius. 'Our Old Book? *The* Old Book?'

'That's the original language,' Domitian said. 'It's the language our ancestors spoke. The language the gods used to dictate the Old Book to the first scribes.'

'Well, what's it say?' said Scapula.

'I don't know,' replied Domitian.

'Can you make anything out?'

'No, but one character might be the word for destiny.'

'Destiny?'

'I'm guessing. It might mean something else.'

Tiberius said, 'Well, let's not guess. Does anyone aboard read the ancient language?' He looked about the bridge. 'Didn't anyone pay attention to their history lessons?'

'You forget, Captain,' said Scapula, 'that history classes

ended centuries ago—after you graduated.'

'Chief Domitian,' Tiberius said. 'Order Telepathy to send an image of these characters to the Senate. Ask them for a translation.'

Flavia spoke. 'Perhaps this sentence is a coded message—an instruction on how to enter.'

'Or a plea for help,' said Scapula.

'Or a warning,' said Domitian.

'A warning against what?' said Flavia.

'About the Parthia accident. A warning to avoid the same fate.'

'But why the old language?' said Tiberius.

Domitian said, 'Perhaps it's there to keep unwanted visitors out.'

'Not again,' said Manius. 'Who would be the unwanted visitors? Who else is there in the galaxy apart from ourselves?'

'All right,' said Tiberius. 'Let's move on. Lieutenant Sinistra?'

'Sir?'

'Send the probe on. Maybe the back or sides will tell us more.'

Sinistra nodded to Lepidus. The view on the screen changed. The sharp edge of the temple's podium slid by. For a moment, there was nothing but blackness and pinpricks of light as the probe's camera looked at the stars. Then, the stars swung away and the probe's bright circle of lamplight found the flat, gray surface of the object's port side.

'Anyone see what I see?' said the captain.

'I do,' said Domitian. 'But I can't quite believe it.'

Everyone was silent while they looked at the screen.

'Just say the word, Captain,' said Decimus once more. 'Say the word and I'll call my crew to fire. I'll tell them to let the cannons feast.'

'To feast, Chief Gunner?'

'I read it in a history of Hyacinth warfare, Tiberius. They used the expression, "Let the weapons feast." That's what's needed here.'

But no one paid Decimus any attention.

The probe's lights had illuminated a carving. The carving showed an image of the object itself, floating in space: a gray box with an angled roof and a columned front—a cella and an entablature. However, the carving also displayed something else: a vessel with the Herculaneum's unmistakable shape with lantern beams streaming forth from its bow and stern. This carved Herculaneum glowered at the object like an enormous sea creature hunting tiny prey.

'It can't be possible,' said Scapula. 'Who carved it? And when did they carve it—if carving is what it is?'

'There's no mistaking the shape,' said Gabinus. 'That's us. Look at the exhaust funnels. There's no mistaking them.'

'I think the question is now settled, Captain,' said Flavia, her hands back on her hips.

'I disagree. I think we need to know more,' said Tiberius.

'How much more?' said Flavia. 'We'll only be wasting time.'

Chief Domitian came back onto the bridge.

'From Telepathy, Captain. The Senate's translation of the symbols.'

'And what does it say?' said Flavia.

'It says, "May Owanthan save us. May Sirhain inspire us." It's a passage from the Old Book.'

'Which part of the Old Book?' said Astronomer Manius.

'It's from the section dealing with the migration from the old planet to the new. Both Owanthan and the demon god Sirhain were there, according to the Old Book. Owanthan led the people to the home planet. Sirhain argued with him and fought with him.'

No one spoke until Flavia said, 'Who else could have written it but survivors from the Parthia? Now we just have to decide who will go to greet them.' She looked at Sinistra. 'And who will definitely not go.'

'It's like a call to emulate our ancestors,' said Domitian. 'Just like in the painting.'

'All right,' said Tiberius. 'Let's not discuss this here. We'll meet later in my stateroom. But first, let's see what's on the other sides.'

The bell tolled. Third Lieutenant Cadmus came onto the bridge. Sinistra returned his salute and stepped down from the small podium. Flavia intercepted her before she could reach the captain. 'Second Lieutenant, don't you have an appointment with Doctor Galen?'

'Yes, Lieutenant, but shouldn't I stay while we explore the other sides? I might be able to help.'

'Doctor Galen is waiting for you.'

'Yes, Lieutenant. I'll send the doctor an apology. I believe it's more important for me to …'

Flavia interrupted.

'Permission denied, Lieutenant. No, don't think about asking Captain Tiberius. I'll let him know about the doctor. You are unwell and need attention.'

'But Lieutenant, I have piloted many dropship missions, several of them from here on the Herculaneum. It might be of use to …'

'Of course you have, Lieutenant. Don't we all know it? But I disagree with you. Doctor Galen is more important, and believe it or not, we can discuss the mission without you. You are dismissed, Lieutenant. You. Are. Dismissed.'

13

Sinistra limped down the Great Passageway. Her destination: the Domum Deck at the ship's stern where Doctor Galen waited. As usual, her lame foot dragged, but now her right knee ached too, and a new pain stabbed her lower back. But all these aches and pains were nothing compared to the turmoil in her mind.

Until now, her mission had gone reasonably well. Despite her troubles with her Hyacinth-creature form, the Hyacinth language, and sleep, she performed all her duties with competence and skill. She kept her watches on the bridge; she managed the crew, and regularly toured the holds, the gun decks, and the lower the decks with the experienced eye of an officer who had served on the Herculaneum three times before, and captained it during a long mission.

Each week, she mustered the crew for the captain to inspect, and she managed the third, fourth, and fifth lieutenants, while cautiously liaising with Manius about the ship's heading, and with Seta about the ship's maintenance, and with Gabinus about the engines.

Under Sinistra's command, the Herculaneum had glided toward Ilium for two months without incident. Captain Tiberius had praised her for good management. Flavia had said nothing, but Sinistra took this as praise by omission, while Flavia was in mourning over the tragic death of her friend Lieutenant Commodus. True, there had been no chance for Sinistra to distinguish herself in any other ways, but on such a mission as this, the opportunities would surly come.

But as the ship neared the Point of Acceleration, all that changed, as if the Herculaneum had sailed into a turbulent sea. Manius, Gabinus, and Decimus became terse and unfriendly. Flavia ordered Sinistra to perform technical duties way beneath her rank. The captain had grown remote.

Then the object had shown up and Sinistra's fortunes had plunged. Now, she was denied a chance to redeem herself. Worse! She must submit to Doctor Galen's examination, which she predicted would amount to one more humiliation.

The doctor also posed a new and dangerous threat. Like all medical crew, Doctor Galen would ask her about her mind. This was bad. Sinistra's mind was a like a black box. Inside it lay fears and urges Sinistra didn't want to see, let alone reveal to those with power over her career.

But she would have to provide answers to the doctor's questions. She didn't want to seem evasive. Seeming evasive could lead to the doctor asking even more questions. It was a frustrating dilemma. Her organs squirmed at the thought of it.

Nim, what will I say to him? Nim, are you listening? Nim. Are you there? Send me a thought—even if it's a short one.

But Nim didn't reply. She never did.

In the Great Passageway, traffic was heavy. The bell had rung. The watches were changing. Crew members surged forward and aft, overtaking Sinistra's limping progress, or rushing past, saluting as they went, dragging with them the reek of the hold, or the chemical smell of the laundry, or the oil and ash smells from engineering. Everyone seemed to sneak glances at the second lieutenant's uniquely ill-formed body: her lame right foot, her lopsided posture, her oily hair, and flaking skin.

Sinistra was used to it and tried not to care. She didn't want approval or admiration from the crew—not the way she needed it from Flavia and the captain. Flavia and the captain were different. They had power. Without their approval, the dread and the feelings of shame formed, and the images from her nightmares rose like creatures from the dark bog of her memory—things she could never reveal to anyone, not even Nim.

She limped into the second of the large staterooms. This was the stateroom in which the Hyacinth leaders would be welcomed, entertained, and eventually threatened. For now, it was noisy with linguists, astronomers, biologists, planetographers, construction engineers, and junior warrant officers, who all used this stateroom as an informal clubroom.

Someone called out 'Attendite!' and the noise faded. Everyone stiffened and saluted. Sinistra returned the salutes and said, 'Ad otium.' At ease. At least here, her rank commanded respect.

As soon as everyone relaxed, questions were called about the Acceleration, about the object, the rumored discovery of wreckage from the Parthia, of the possibility of survivors, and just how much longer would it take to reach Hyacinth.

'The captain will make an announcement,' Sinistra said. 'No, we're not in any danger. We will reach Hyacinth as planned. Our families and all the people at home depend on us. With luck, they'll soon be on their way, too.'

As she left the stateroom, she noticed the number of crew with necks oozing with angry rashes. Some rashes were bright red; others were stripes of festering sores. Then, just as she walked out of the stateroom, she noticed something else. Over at the port bulkhead, two petty officers, Venti and Sirena, male and female, turned to one another and engaged in a furtive Hyacinth-creature kiss, an act forbidden by the mission code.

It's the Hyacinth-creature form, thought Sinistra. That must be it. It makes experienced officers act like children. Its surging emotions make us act like fools, or cringe in fear. I can feel them now, in this Hyacinth-creature body, like an ache or a dread squirming in my viscera.

And for a moment she remembered the dream of the dark forest, her childhood self, fleeing in terror from someone or some thing. She closed her eyes and squinted, squeezing the images from her mind. But they only retreated to her mind's dark regions, waiting for their next chance.

Just before she reached the shuttle station, she passed the large version of the painting, 'The Fate of The People.' She saw the god Owanthan pointing the way to the home planet. She saw the faces of Captain Tiberius, Flavia, Gabinus, Decimus, Seta, Domitian, and Doctor Galen. Then she noticed something else.

Behind the advisors, one extra figure stood watching on. Bearded, stern-faced, wild-haired, and with his fists on his hips, a wild-looking male glared at Owanthan's head as if he were trying to stare through it, or burn it with his gaze, or perhaps to rush at him, fists flying. He was fascinating. He stole all the attention. So who was he? Why was he there?

Perhaps, thought Sinistra, the figure was the so-called demon god Sirhain, the one mentioned in the inscription on the object. But why was he not shown in the captain's version of the painting? She made a note to ask Chief Petty Officer Domitian.

By the time she reached the Domum Deck entrance, Sinistra had exhausted herself thinking of responses to imagined questions from Doctor Galen. Every answer sounded resentful to Flavia or too defensive about her state of mind. She walked towards the entrance with dread.

Two stewards greeted her, both female, and both with

graying hair and the lined faces of aged Hyacinth creatures. They leaped to their feet as she approached. Then, they saluted, and without meeting her eye, broke into a strange exchange of words.

'Hail, Lieutenant Sinistra!'
'Hail!'
'The time has come.'
'What must be done?'
'What must be won?'
'Great deeds.'
'Evil deeds.'
'All hail Lieutenant Sinistra.'

But Sinistra walked on without upbraiding them or threatening them with brig time. Her mind was elsewhere. She passed through the heavy doors and into the Domun Deck's surreal domain, still anxious about Doctor Galen's questions and her answers.

Say as little as possible, she thought. Don't lie. Say enough and no more.

Just before she stepped onto the lavender plain, she thought of a better idea. She should say, 'I was only doing my duty, Doctor. In these extreme times, it's only natural that there should be disagreements between senior officers.'

Yes, that was it. It was simple, obvious, and true. She was only doing her duty, not courting Flavia's approval, and not undermining it, either. Nothing like that. Doing her duty. That's it. Making tough decisions under pressure, just like an officer should. Even a doctor would understand that.

But that's when she heard the voice of Telepathy, the ship's telepath, speaking clearly in her mind.

Telepathy's voice said, I would be careful what you say to the doctor if I were you, Lieutenant Sinistra. Oh yes, very, very careful.

14

The Domum Deck was a pleasure deck, a re-creation of the home planet's deserts, forests, plains, and lakes, as they existed before the erupting volcanoes ruined the land with tides of lava, and thick, choking ash that blocked the sun.

The Domum Deck's dimensions were vast. Its height was that of several normal decks, and its length stretched from the stern ramp several milia forward.

Most officers visited the Domum Deck several times each Hyacinth week to sit quietly, to shed their uniforms, and to throw off the constrictive Hyacinth-creature form, and expand to the height, freedom and power of their natural bodies.

But unlike most officers, Sinistra never wandered through the deck's purple fields, or crossed the desert's tumbling dunes. Nor did she ever explore the cool dark forest or drag her lame foot along the lake's wet shore. And never in her two months aboard did she expand from her small, withered-shrub state to the height and strength of her home-planet self.

When Sinistra stepped onto the deck, it was dawn. She stood on the lavender plain. The day felt warm and summery. The artificial breeze gentled the field into rolling purple waves, and the lavender scent was rich and thick.

Beyond the plain lay the orange desert, like a frozen sea of dunes. Further away, a forest rose like a brown and green wall holding back the sand. The forest was thick, dark, and sinister, like the wintery forests of Sinistra's childhood in the north of the home planet. She almost expected to see a huge Goth push his snout from the shadows and sniff the air for prey.

Aft the lavender plain, the imposing figure of Telepathy squatted in his enclosure. Telepathy was the mission communicator between the ship and the home planet. Before the navy recruited him, Telepathy (original name Malawg) had been a violent criminal, but one with extraordinary telepathic powers.

Telepathy wasn't free aboard the ship. He lived behind reinforced bulkheads. He was permitted to remain expanded in his natural form to maximize his telepathic powers, but because of his dangerous past, Captain Tiberius ordered him to be tethered him to the deck by chains.

As Sinistra entered, she heard Telepathy's deep voice in her head speaking in the growls of the native language.

I would be careful what you say to Doctor Galen, he repeated.

'So, you hear my thoughts, Petty Officer?' said Sinistra in the Hyacinth language. 'You hear them without me opening my mind.'

I hear everyone's thoughts, said Telepathy's voice, when every thinker is in Hyacinth form. I hear so many thoughts at once that they tangle in my mind like wires. It's a talent I never knew I had. The gods have blessed me, Lieutenant Sinistra. The gods have also cursed me.

'Why have they cursed you?'

Do you think I want to hear everyone's thoughts, to hear their fears, their pain, and resentments?

'It must be tiring.'

Yes. Hyacinth-creature thoughts are more mischievous than our own thoughts, as you well know, Lieutenant.

'I keep my thoughts in harness, Petty Officer. I make them serve me, not hinder me.'

Serve you? Are you sure that's what you do? Could it be the reverse—that it's you who serve your thoughts instead—especially the unconscious ones?

'I think the thoughts, so I know who serves who, Petty Officer.'

It's whom, Lieutenant, not who.

'I should know who serves whom?'

Yes, Lieutenant, but I'm talking about your dreams. Over them, you have no control.

'My dreams? What dreams?'

You know which dreams I mean, Lieutenant.

'No. I don't know what you're talking about.'

You have a role to play in this story, said Telepathy's voice, suddenly sounding low and strange. You just don't know it yet.

'What role? What story?'

But Telepathy turned away. His chains rattled and his silhouette hunched. He raised a great claw to his head and pulled it down to his chest.

Do me a kindness, Lieutenant.

'What kindness?'

Hurry!

'Hurry what?'

The Acceleration. Get the ship out of this cursed Ilium region. Take us to the other side of the galaxy as fast as you can. Get us to Hyacinth, where thoughts from the home planet can't reach me. I hear too much about the devastation, the lost lives, the agonizing deaths. Hurry, so that I can swim in Hyacinth's cool blue oceans with an empty mind.

'We're trying, Petty Officer.'

Make it soon.

'What did you mean before about being careful about what I say to the doctor?'

Destiny calls you, Lieutenant. Yes, even with your broken Hyacinth-creature body. Make sure you can answer the call. Don't let the doctor stop you.

'You make no sense, Petty Officer Telepathy. What destiny? What call?'

But Telepathy's body spasmed, as if he were in pain, as if stomach cramps had struck. He clutched his chest and rocked from side to side. His chains rattled.

'What's wrong? Are you all right?'

There is a message from the home planet, Telepathy growled. Another eruption, a bad one, near Grantakranz. Millions killed. Many family members of the crew are dead. It will be another heavy day—another terrible, heavy day.

He turned away and hunched lower over his chains.

'Have you seen the doctor, Petty Officer? Where he is?'

In the forest, Telepathy moaned. He's waiting in a clearing by a log.

Sinistra watched Telepathy's silhouette swaying in pain. Then, she limped through the chest-high lavender to the desert, and trudged for a quarter bell across the yielding dunes, her lame foot dragging a trail, until she arrived hot and out of breath at the thick palisades of the forest edge.

She peered inside. The forest was much older than she imagined and much darker. It was so much like an old natural forest she could hear the trees creak and smell the reek of decay. Birdsong of at least three different species echoed unseen, and a cold, soft breeze, almost like a breath, chilled her sweating neck.

The forest was supposed to be a place to relax, but this forest created the opposite effect: a strong sense of unease, as if something malevolent waited inside. Sinistra immediately recalled the dark, winter forests of her childhood, and the dream in which she ran, pursued by someone with violence on their mind.

Not now, she thought. Not now, and especially not before Doctor Galen examines you. You're not in a real forest like the ones in the dream. You're on a giant navy warship, the size of the city, alone in a remote region of the galaxy. And you are the third in command.

And then, for the first time on this voyage— the first of many times over the next Hyacinth creature week— she limped over the twisting roots of the first rank of trees, and pushed on into the forest depths.

15

After a quarter bell of hobbling through the sighing trees, Sinistra heard a sneeze. She followed the sound to a clearing. There Doctor Galen stood at the clearing's far edge beside an uprooted tree that had fallen during the failed Acceleration. The doctor wiped his nose on a white cloth.

'Doctor Galen!' Sinistra called.

The doctor looked up, raised a languid hand, and Sinistra limped across the clearing towards him.

Like Captain Tiberius and the senior warrant-officers, the doctor resembled a statue of one of the Hyacinth emperors or gods. He looked about thirty Hyacinth-creature years in age, with a clear complexion and curly brown hair. He wore a snowy, white toga not a uniform, and his bare right arm was muscular and toned.

However, unlike the captain, Doctor Galen wore a beard. This was in order to emulate the famous Roman medical philosopher, Claudius Galenus, whose name the doctor assumed. The beard made the doctor appear both wise and young.

In reality, Doctor Galen was a century older than Captain Tiberius, and in his natural form was feeble, slow, and unable to expand more than twice his Hyacinth-creature size.

Sinistra approached him, smiling but wary.

'Secundus Tenens Sinistra!' the doctor said.

'Hello, Doctor Galen.'

'Salvete.'

'Salvete, Doctor.'

'Favere. Ut reveles!' To befriend. To discover. 'That is our mission motto, is it not?'

'Yes, Doctor. Favere. Ut reveles.'

'Come and join me. I am taking some time away from the patients. We have so many cases of what the crew call miseria or lurgia. It's a baffling affliction of the Hyacinth epidermis and lungs.'

'Is it serious, Doctor, this miseria? Should we be concerned?'

'Well, the case numbers increase every day, but so far, only a few have died from it. I hope that the pure Hyacinth air will heal us all. Have you read about the Hyacinth air, Lieutenant?'

As he spoke, the doctor's gazed flicked to Sinistra's legs, her waist, and neck. Then he smiled, blinking at her.

'Beg your pardon, Doctor. I am short of time. There is a briefing in Captain Tiberius's stateroom about the object blocking our path. I must attend it. To be honest, I am not sure why Lieutenant Flavia ordered me to see you. I feel perfectly fine. There's no need for concern. I won't trouble you for long.'

On hearing this, the doctor smiled even more. Then he carried on as if he hadn't heard her, as if she were a sick patient whom he must coddle, coax, and cosset.

Sinistra grew wary.

'You walk more freely, Lieutenant. Your limp is less pronounced. You no longer creep along with your head down.'

'Thank you, Doctor. I am trying. I walk several milia each

day in the Great Passageway.'

'And the rash on your neck is less angry. I was worried it might be miseria. And your general appearance, Lieutenant, is … well … it … have you any news?'

'No, Doctor, the Admiralty denied my request. I must stay in this form until further orders.'

'Oh, that's a pity. An officer must look the part, as well as act it. Yes, it's a pity. And what of your name? What was the one you requested?'

'Lavinia, Doctor Galen, a traditional Hyacinth name. But this request was also denied.'

'By who?'

'By Lieutenant Flavia?'

'Well,' the doctor said. 'Lavinia is quite a grand name in the Hyacinth history. Perhaps it was too grand—for you.'

'Perhaps, Doctor.'

'Well, never mind, Lieutenant. The Admiralty and Lieutenant Flavia know what they're doing. The good news is that you are progressing. Before long, you will stride the Hyacinth hills like a native, and chat with the Hyacinth creatures about the weather.'

'I hope so, Doctor—after the Acceleration, of course. That is the most important thing. But there's also this strange object in our way. That's why I can't spare much time today. I hope you will excuse me.'

Once again, the doctor seemed not to hear her, and Sinistra thought it better not to force to make a decision too soon.

'How I look forward to studying them,' the doctor said. 'I mean the Hyacinth creatures. There are many things we don't know about them—their digestive systems, for example. We've had no success with replicating them—unlike their sexual organs. We had great success with those.'

Sinistra smiled patiently and said nothing.

The doctor pulled his white robes over his prominent

chest. His family crest pin—a sun beaming over dark clouds—settled on his Hyacinth-creature heart.

'All right, Lieutenant,' he said. 'Let me ask you some questions.'

Sinistra drew a breath of the loamy forest air, and waited.

'Why do you think Lieutenant Flavia wants me to examine you?'

'I don't know, Doctor.'

'Lieutenant Flavia thinks you might be mentally strained. Why would she think that?'

'I cannot speak for Lieutenant Flavia.'

'Have you had any problems performing your duties?'

'None, Doctor.'

'Have you been under strain? My assistants say you are the busiest officer aboard. They say you are always about the ship. They see you from stern to stem, as we used to say on the seas.'

'A second lieutenant has many duties, Doctor, beyond that of commanding the bridge. The Herculaneum is a large ship with a full crew and many weapons of war, as well as a full hold of … machines.'

'Indeed, and do you have any trouble sleeping? Hyacinth-creature sleep is a fearful thing for many. Some consider it a kind of death.'

'No,' Sinistra lied.

'Do you experience dreams? It is quite natural to experience visions while asleep.'

'No,' lied Sinistra a second time, adding a vigorous shake of her head, a new Hyacinth-creature gesture she'd learned from Lieutenant Cadmus. 'No dreams. No. Nothing like that.'

'You seem very sure. It's possible to dream but not recall the dream when waking. Are you aware of that?'

'No, Doctor, but I am sure I am not troubled.'

'Do you have any family members caught up in the

eruptions?'

'No, Doctor. I have no family that I know of.'

'Of course! I beg your pardon, Lieutenant. After reading your file, I know of the orphanage you attended in the Northern Forests. Tell me, when was the last time you expanded to your natural form?'

'Not since I boarded the Krast.'

'The what?'

'Krast is the name of the cutter that brought me to the Herculaneum.'

'So no expansion for two months—is that right?'

'Yes, Doctor.'

'Why, my dear Lieutenant Sinistra, that must be it.'

'Must be what, Doctor?'

'Expansion. It's essential to good physical and mental health. To avoid expansion is to invite stress, tension, and possibly reduced function.'

'I know, Doctor. However, the Admiralty ordered me to remain in Hyacinth form.'

'But that time passed weeks ago. Have you tried to expand?'

'No, Doctor.'

'Why not?'

'I fear I that might not contract, Doctor. I might trap myself on this deck in an overextended form and so be unable to perform my duties.'

'But, as an officer,' said Doctor Galen, 'you have a duty to expand in order to be at your best—for yourself, and for the crew.'

Sinistra made no reply.

'What about this friction between you and Lieutenant Flavia?'

Sinistra considered the doctor. Did he know about the bridge incident? Of course he did. There are no secrets aboard a navy ship.

'I only ask you for the sake of the mission,' the doctor said. 'Is there some tension between you and the first lieutenant?'

Sinistra chose her words carefully. 'There was a small incident, Doctor. I questioned the first lieutenant's orders. At the time, I thought there was danger to the ship.' Sinistra paused before adding, 'I was only doing my duty, Doctor.'

She instantly regretted this remark. The doctor looked irritated. He reached his bare arm across his chest and straightened his family crest a second time.

'Now I understand. I think I know what's going on, here. If we are to succeed on this mission, Lieutenant, respect for rank, and especially for the natural social order, is essential. You see that, don't you?'

'Yes, Doctor. I remind myself of it daily.'

'Just imagine if such behavior spread. Imagine if we had a mutiny. I hesitate to even mention that word. It brings up memories of the terrible, tyrant dictators who troubled the people in the past. You see the danger, don't you, Lieutenant? You see what might happen if you question orders.'

'Of course, Doctor, but that is not that kind of tension between the first lieutenant and myself. I have no ambition for high command, only to help Captain Tiberius create the new world on Hyacinth. Nothing more.'

Doctor Galen regarded Sinistra while quietly nodding to himself.

'I think I had better see you expand, Lieutenant.'

'Now, Doctor?'

'Try to expand while there is no one else here.'

'But the briefing with the captain. We are planning a manned mission to the object.'

'Even so, please try.'

'I have tried before, Doctor, in my cabin. I failed.'

'Did you remove your clothing, Lieutenant? Clothes are

an impediment.'

'With your permission, I will expand another time, Doctor.'

'I'm not making a suggestion, Lieutenant. Expansion is a condition of you continuing with your duties. No, don't protest, Lieutenant. That's my decision.'

Sinistra looked at the doctor's face. A vertical crease had formed on his forehead. His smile was gone. His eyes stared straight into hers.

'All right, Doctor. If you insist, I will try.'

'Yes, I do insist.'

Sinistra clasped her hands together and closed her eyes.

'You forget, Lieutenant. I need to see a full expansion. Please remove your uniform.'

Sinistra looked at the doctor's handsome face. She didn't want to be naked in front of him, not with her blotched skin, spindly legs, and her other imperfections. They embarrassed her enough when she wore her uniform.

She drew another breath of the sickly forest air. 'If I must, Doctor.'

'Yes, Lieutenant. You must—for the mission.'

16

Sinistra knelt and unlaced her boots. Then she unbuttoned her shirt and let it drop. Then she unclipped her belt. The uniform slid down her thin legs, exposing the kink in her right ankle. Finally, she stood exposed to the weak sunlight. She covered her chest with her arms.

'All right,' said the doctor. 'Now try.'

Sinistra closed her eyes and concentrated on the sensations of her natural form. She recalled its towering height, its freedom of movement, its weight, its muscles, its scales, its claws, and jaws.

'You are shivering, Lieutenant,' said the doctor, but you are not expanding. 'You remember how to do it, don't you? Try again.'

Sinistra focused her mind solely on the sensation of strength. She saw herself rising above the treetops until she could see over the forest to the lake.

Then, something happened. She heard a bang and a shriek.

She opened her eyes. She was on her side with one elbow sunk into the damp soil. The doctor had fallen beside her.

'What did you do?' the doctor said.

'Nothing, Doctor.'

She tried to climb to her feet, but fell down. One of her legs was much longer, thicker, and scalier than the other. Her right arm was as thick as a cable. Her left arm dangled like a wilting branch of a yellow shrub.

'You kicked me,' said Doctor Galen.

'I'm sorry, Doctor. I couldn't help it.'

'And you've soiled my robes.'

'I beg your pardon, Doctor.'

The doctor stood up and brushed the leaves from his sleeve. Then he examined the long smear of brown mud stretching from his knee to the toga's hem.

'It's no good, Lieutenant. No, don't get up. You look quite obscene.'

Sinistra lay back down, breathing hard, afraid her body would lock itself in this disfigured state. She closed her eyes and imagined her limbs in her Hyacinth-creature form. Slowly, painfully, her long leg and bulging arm shrank. The scales faded away. Her pale skin returned.

She looked up at the doctor. 'I'm fine, Doctor,' she said. 'There's no need to worry. I think this small expansion helped. Now that I've made a start, I'll keep practicing. I feel relieved. I really do. I feel confident about resuming my duties.'

'No, Lieutenant. It's no good.'

'But you saw me expand.'

'Yes, but not nearly enough. I'm sorry. I think Flavia must reduce your duties for the time being.'

'But you haven't fully examined me.'

'No, it's not just your inability to expand.'

'Doctor, I'm fine.'

'I've been a navy doctor for centuries, Lieutenant. There's no use in pretending.'

'But Doctor, if I can't do my duty, the ship will be at the mercy of …'

The Doctor stopped brushing his robe and said, 'At the

mercy of what, Lieutenant? What do you mean, or rather, whom do you mean? What exactly are you implying?'

'Nothing, Doctor. Nothing and no one. I only meant that not all the officers have the same experience as I have. That's why the Admiralty ordered me to join the mission. My experience, Doctor.'

But the doctor looked up suddenly. There was noise in the forest.

'Pardon me, Lieutenant, but now it is I who must leave. Here is Cordinaus, my assistant.'

Sinistra saw a male figure at the far end of the clearing. He waited with his hands clasped in front of his white robe, like a monk in the old paintings of the days when the people worshipped Owanthan and the old gods.

'Won't you let me try again, Doctor?' Sinistra said, but Doctor Galen had walked away, his sandals sinking in the soil, his hands lifting the hem of his robe above the wet grass.

'Doctor?'

But now the doctor had entered the trees and disappeared.

Sinistra pulled on her uniform. She looked at the artificial sky. A rank of clouds advanced towards her over the treetops. She was so distracted by her misery that she didn't hear the clomp of a heavy footstep deep in the forest, coming her way.

17

Once she was out of the clearing and back in the forest's interior, Sinistra limped as fast as her lame foot could drag across the loamy soil, hurrying to the captain's meeting while there was still time.

If I can get there before the doctor speaks up, I can contribute, I can impress. The captain will insist I'm part of the mission.

She limped in the direction she thought was 'south,' back to the desert, the lavender plain, and the exit to the Great Passageway. But with each limp, the forest thickened, and the darkness grew.

Sinistra soon realized she had lost her way. So she stopped to take a bearing. She looked up and searched the gaps in the forest canopy for a glimpse of the sun, and listened for the growl of the engines astern.

But no sunlight filtered down. The canopy was too thick. The clouds had settled in. Forward looked the same as aft.

How embarrassing, Sinistra thought: a navy lieutenant unable to locate herself at sea. She considered retracing her steps to the clearing, but that would take time, and her pride wouldn't permit it.

I know what to do. I'll walk until I reach the edge. It can't be too far to a bulkhead. And so she limped on through the trees. Several minuta later, she entered a grassy glade. It was a gloomy, unfriendly place, but at least she had a view of the sky. But where was the sun? There it was! It was hiding behind a cumulonimbus cloud of white and gray. She had been traveling in the right direction all along.

With the sun on her starboard side, she limped aft, but only managed two steps before she heard the branches cracking high in the canopy, and heavy footsteps thumping into the soil.

Is it Telepathy, she thought. Surely he hadn't broken his chains. So who was it? From the height at which the branches snapped, someone as tall as Telepathy walked nearby. Perhaps it was Doctor Galen, or one of the other officers. Then, for a dark moment, a voice whispered in her mind, 'Or the someone from your dreams.'

A shadow passed over her, chilling the air.

'Petty Officer Telepathy!' Sinistra called. 'Is that you?'

But there was no reply.

The shadow thickened and spread on the forest floor. A foul breeze riffled Sinistra's oily hair, and a giant, scaly claw thumped into the glade behind her, tossing up twigs, leaves, and mud, and squelching as it sank into the soil.

Sinistra turned around to face it. Months had passed since she had seen anyone in their natural state, in expanded form. Now, here was someone of unusual height and girth. Sinistra's eyes traveled up along the big claws, the ranks of black, interlocking scales, the hill-scape of calve muscles, the pulsing veins beneath, and above them, the massive pelvis, the heaving abdomen, and the enormous head and snout, and the eyes slitted like those of a predator.

'Salve!' said Sinistra. Good day. 'Or should I say good afternoon? It's sometimes hard to tell the time of day in here.'

Her pleasantries had no effect. The colossal head did not

move. The clamped maw did not open. The maw's black hem did not stretch into a friendly curve.

'Beg your pardon,' said Sinistra. 'I have disturbed you.' Every officer knew you did not ask questions on the Domum Deck.

'Vale,' she said. Goodbye. Then she limped away, but the shadow darkened around her. Then, a second great claw planted itself in her way, churning the loam, and tossing chips of mud onto her uniform.

'What's the matter?' Sinistra said, looking up. 'I said I'm sorry.'

And then when no reply came, she said, 'Is that you, Chief Domitian? Chief, I don't have time right now. I'm heading to the captain's stateroom.'

The yellow, slitted eyes burnt down at her with a ferocity that didn't need interpretation. They radiated hostility—an enemy's hate.

Sinistra tried once more. 'Would you mind moving, please?'

The great claw remained half buried in the soil. Then, slowly, the claw pulled itself up and out, shedding wet sods, and squelching obscenely. 'Thank you,' Sinistra said, and began her unsteady limp around the crater's edge.

Once back in the dark forest, she heard a deep bass voice whispering in the growls and barks of the native language— so different to the singsong tones of Hyacinth.

'You really think he respects you, don't you?' said the growl. 'Don't you? Well, you'll find out exactly how he feels soon enough. Oh, yes. You'll find out.' Sinistra hurried on as fast as her lame foot would let her.

Outside, at the reception, the two stewards jumped to their feet and saluted.

'Who is on the deck?' Sinistra said.

'Yourself, Lieutenant.'

'Who came after me?'

'We cannot say, Lieutenant.'

'Can't say or won't say?'

'We must obey our orders, Lieutenant. Surely, the Lieutenant knows the Domum Deck's privacy protocol.'

'I know it wasn't Telepathy,' Sinistra snapped. 'Was it Lieutenant Flavia?'

'We cannot say.'

'Just answer the question or you'll both find yourselves beneath the ship's keel sizzling in open space.'

When neither steward replied, Sinistra felt her arms bubbling. Her left shirt sleeve filled, the buttons strained. She was achieving through anger what she could not achieve through practicing expansion. Her mind filled with rage.

When, the ship's bell tolled in her mind, she turned away from the stewards and limped up the Great Passageway towards the forward-aft shuttle. But when she arrived at Captain Tiberius's stateroom, the captain's steward, Frumentius told her the meeting was over.

'Where is the captain?' Sinistra said.

'He is resting, Lieutenant, and is not to be disturbed for two bells.'

'What did the meeting decide?'

'Beg pardon, Lieutenant. I don't know. I was only in there to set out the stationery. It was over quickly.'

'Tell me wha you heard when you were in there.'

'Only that orders are being prepared for the mission in the first watch.'

'Orders for whom?'

Frumentius showed her four envelopes, each with a name printed on the front: Lieutenant Flavia, Chief Domitian, Marine Captain Ranant, and Ensign Vopiscus.

'But there's no one to control the ship,' Sinistra said.

'There is also this envelope, Lieutenant.' Frumentius showed her. The name on the front was that of Lepidus, the technical officer who had controlled the probes from the bridge.

So there it was. The mission to the object would take place and Sinistra would not be aboard.

Flavia had gotten her way.

18

Later, Sinistra heard what happened at the meeting.

Captain Tiberius initially insisted that Sinistra lead the mission to the object. But Flavia had put her slender foot down in its Goth hide boot. Only an old family member could lead the mission and only an old family member should greet the Parthia captain and his officers. There was no room for anyone else, especially the second lieutenant, who would only embarrass the ship and cause disharmony.

Defeated, Sinistra left the captain's stateroom, wondering what to do. Should she petition the captain as soon as he was available or should she hide away and lick her wounds?

She slunk along the Great Passageway. The crew surged either side of her. Sinistra hardly noticed them. She looked straight ahead as if she were the only crew member there.

'Salve, Lieutenant,' someone said. Sinistra looked up. She saw Ensign Candida saluting her. He was a tall, dark-haired junior officer. 'Hello, Candida,' she said, no expression in her voice.

'Are you all right, Lieutenant?'

But Sinistra hobbled on without replying.

On her way to the shuttle station, Sinistra limped past the gallery of imagined scenes from the home planet and

Hyacinth. Here, Petty Officer Bucco had depicted the home planet Senate building; the capital city of Ranator; the great lavender plains, the Northern Forests, and the deserts—all in murals, three Hyacinth creatures high.

Finally, Bucco had depicted one of the Goths, the giant, dangerous animals who occupied the planet's forests. In Bucco's impression, the Goth was terrifying. It stood on its hind limbs with its teeth bared, its terrible yellow claws unsheathed, its dark fur shimmering.

Such a strange choice, thought Sinistra. She could understand Bucco paying tribute to the Goths, knowing they would die on the home planet when everyone else fled to Hyacinth, but the painting was terrifying, as anyone who had actually seen a Goth would know.

Next, Sinistra passed along the imagined lands of Hyacinth. These were more cheerful. She saw the aquamarine oceans with giant sea creatures leaping; the green and white mountains; the wheeling birds; the tall forests; the undulating deserts; and the shining cities, clean streets, and rows of statues of emperors and gods. The sight of them dulled the feeling of worthlessness sliding around Sinistra's organs.

Then she saw renditions of a Hyacinth male and female in actual size. The male was fair-haired. The woman's hair was light brown. Both were smiling in their white robes, standing on a grassy hillside in bright light. The female held a smiling baby. The three of them looked so innocent, so pure, and so unaware of the great black leviathan sliding across the galaxy like a monstrous reptile.

What will they think of us, those poor creatures? When they see our real selves, what will they think? After we have deceived them into welcoming us into their cities, what will they think? Monsters! That's what they'll think. Monsters—horrible, invading, terrifying monsters.

And by then, it will be too late.

She reached the forward-aft shuttle station. As always, the large version of 'The Fate of The People' dominated the passageway. Chief Domitian stood beneath it, gazing up at it as if he'd just discovered it. She liked Domitian. He was the only senior officer who was friendly to her. Usually, she would stop to chat with him, but for now, she wanted to be alone with her thoughts, so she limped behind him without saying hello.

But Domitian saw her and said, 'Wonderful, isn't it, Sin?'

Sinistra stopped and forced her face into a weak smile—her one dependable expression. 'What is, Chief? The painting?'

'Yes, the painting, of course, but also much more.'

'More, Chief?'

'There's a figure up there that represents my ancestor. See! There he is, in the green robes, holding an arm out to Owanthan. He's right there in front of that old devil Sirhain.'

'Yes,' said Sinistra. 'I saw it in the stateroom.'

'I'm drawing inspiration from him—my ancestor, I mean. I feel like I'm walking in his footsteps. There's a proverb in the Old Book, Sin. It says, "Character is destiny." Something like that. It's one to remember. When a crisis threatens the people, those with the qualities to lead step forward to save the day.' Domitian smiled. Then his smile dropped into a frown. 'Or is it "Crisis reveals character?"' He looked up. 'Or maybe it's "Cometh the hour, cometh the man."' He looked down again. 'Anyway, it's one of those.'

'Wonderful, Chief,' Sinistra said in a flat voice. 'They're all inspiring thoughts.' She took a step toward the shuttle station. 'My best wishes to you for the object mission.'

'Thank you, Sin. Thank you.'

Sinistra noticed Domitian's brown eyes flick over her face —her uneven features, tangled teeth, and hurt eyes. Obviously, in Domitian's mind, the crisis did not call for someone as unlikely as herself to save the day. And, as far as her character and destiny were concerned, her fate was obviously to play a secondary role to those born to lead.

But Domitian surprised her.

'If it's any consolation, Sin, I think you should be in the mission party. Open space is no jaunt. We don't know what's out there. None of us has been on a mission like this. And we don't really know what the object might be, despite Flavia's enthusiasm. You're the only one with any experience.'

'Thank you, Chief. But you will be safe. Lepidus is a good pilot. You'll be all right.'

'I hope so, Sin, but just between ourselves, I'm a little concerned about the mention of the demon god Sirhain. When I get back, I'll tell you about him and what he did all those centuries ago. He fought wars against Owanthan and tried to take the throne. He even tried to stop the migration to the home planet, and worse. Much, much worse!'

Sinistra looked up at this demon god in the painting. Before, he had looked wild and angry, but now simply looked disappointed. That was all. He'd been left out. So had she. She could empathize with him.

But what Sinistra didn't know was that Sirhain had eventually taken revenge.

'Thank you, Chief,' she said. 'I'd like to hear all about Sirhain, but not today.'

A quarter bell later, she reached her cabin. Before she opened the door, two marine sentries came up the small passageway and saluted.

'Ego dormian duabus horis,' Sinistra said. I will rest for the next two horae. 'So keep things quiet out here.'

'Yes, Lieutenant.'

Once inside, Sinistra looked at the bleak, minimal world of her cabin, its bulkheads and the narrow berth—the berth where the nightmares waited. She shivered, another new Hyacinth creature gesture.

Then, she tried to rest, but then got up from the berth and

stood looking at her watery reflection in the metal bulkhead. The withered yellow shrub stared unhappily back at her, wanting her to do something to relieve the pain of rejection, and to avoid the terrible fears that waited for their chance to torment her the moment she fell asleep.

Nim, Sinistra said in a thought message. Are you there? What would you do if you were me? She waited. Nim did not reply. Nim never replied. And even if she could, how would she ever know how Sinistra felt? How could Nim imagine what it was like to be in this emotion-filled Hyacinth-creature body with all its urges, resentments, and longings?

Sinistra stood halfway between the cabin door and her lonely bunk, listening for a whisper from across the galaxy. But all she heard was the low growl of the engines and the toll of the bell.

Then, she decided.

She opened the cabin door and stepped outside. The two sentries snapped to attention and saluted. She told them to wait. Then she limped to the far end of the passageway to a cabin door in the marine officers' section.

She was going to do the thing she'd promised herself she would never do again. She knocked on the door of the cabin occupied by handsome Captain Ranant.

19

A deep, male Hyacinth-creature from inside the cabin said, 'Veni.'

Sinistra opened the door. Captain Ranant of the Senate's Navy Marines sat at his desk. He held a small square object in both his hands. From the doorway, Sinistra could see Ranant's bunk reflected in the object's surface, but from Ranant's position, the object reflected his own handsome face.

'Does Captain Tiberius know you have that?' Sinistra said, trying to sound as casual as she could. 'They're banned, as you well know, Captain Ranant.'

'Sinistra!' Ranant said. 'I didn't expect to see you.'

'I'm only kidding about the mirror,' Sinistra said. 'Kidding —is that the right word, "iocari"'?

'Don't ask me,' said Ranant. 'I'm no good at the vocabulary, except for military commands.'

'Don't you pay attention in class?'

'I've stopped taking lessons. What's the point? I'm a marine, not a diplomat.'

Ranant's Hyacinth-creature form was tall. His head was a full Hyacinth hand higher than Sinistra. She had to look up to see his face. She liked that. She liked his face, too. Ranant's face resembled the faces on the statues of gods, even though Ranant was not from one of the old, patrician families.

She stepped closer to him.

'I haven't seen you since before the Acceleration,' she said, 'not really seen you. I wanted to. Don't think I didn't. But we had to stop, Ran. For the mission's sake, we had to stop.'

Ranant put the mirror down on the desk. Sinistra looked at his hands. When would they reach out to her?

'What's the matter?' Sinistra said. 'Don't tell me you're afraid of breaking a rule. I thought marines are rebellious by nature.'

'It's not that. There's only one hora until the mission. I have to muster the men.'

'You have time. There are two horae to go, not one, Captain.'

She wanted to move closer, but she waited for Ranant to move first, to touch her cheek, her neck.

'So you do have time,' she said. 'Don't you?'

'Even if I did, which I don't, it's not the right time, Sinistra. I've got to prepare. I've got to think about what might happen out there.'

'Sinistra? Who is Sinistra? You called me Sin last time.'

'Like I said. It's not the right time, Sin.'

'I know, but doesn't that make it more interesting?'

Ranant smiled, but at the bulkhead, not at Sinistra. 'We better not. I have to think about what I'll do if something goes wrong. Open space, Sin. Open space! Have you ever been out there—really out there?'

'Many times.'

'Then you know how dangerous it is.'

'You'll be safe. It's not really open space. You're sealed up in a dropship.'

'Yes, but I've never been in a dropship, either.'

'It's a short trip, only a leagua from the bow.'

'True, but there's Flavia's to consider. You know how she

can be.'

For once, Sinistra didn't react to the mention of Flavia's name. Instead, she said, 'Why don't you try to relax, Ran?'

'I can't relax. As I keep saying, now's not the time.'

'But I want to keep going, like we did last time. You want to as well, don't you? We don't have to follow the rules all the time.'

This time, she reached out and touched his shoulder. Touching him was fascinating. The uniform's rough cloth thrilled her Hyacinth-creature fingers. The strange bump on his shoulder was fascinating, too. So was the uniform's laundry smell, and beneath it the scent of Hyacinth-creature sweat. She slid her hand over his Ranant's chest.

'You enjoyed it last time, didn't you—what we did?'

Ranant stood up, pushing the chair back. Sinistra's hand slipped from his uniform.

'No.'

'No? Did you say no?'

Sinistra sensed the usual feelings arriving. Here they come: rejection, appraisal, dismissal, worthlessness, shame. They were the same feelings she felt all her life, but that didn't mean they hurt any less. In fact, they stung even more, intensified by the Hyacinth-creature form.

'Why?' she said. 'Is there another reason—apart from the object mission? What is it? What's happened? Tell me.'

'Let's talk about this when I get back. We should both be thinking about the survival of our people, of establishing the new world on Hyacinth. We should never forget that.'

'You're very serious all of a sudden. What happened to the irreverent Captain Ranant? What's going on?'

'Nothing's going on.'

But Sinistra's senses were raw and sharp from a day of harsh words and disappointments.

'I think there is,' she said.

She looked about the room at the tidy bunk with its taut

sheets, the hanging rack of uniforms with the shoulders all parallel. Then, she looked at the desk, saw the mirror, and then she realized. It was obvious. Why hadn't she made the connection already?

'You think you're too beautiful for me, don't you?'

'What?'

'You've just discovered it, haven't you? It's taken a while, but now you know.'

'Don't be silly.'

'You've discovered that females like you.'

'I don't know what you mean.'

'Don't you? I know something about you, Captain Ranant. Before the mission, you were no catch. But look at you now. They're running at you.'

'Running at me? What are you talking about?'

'Running at you, dreaming about you, throwing themeless at you. You know what I mean. You can't keep them away, can you? You have more options than a bull Goth in spring.'

'You're being oversensitive, Sin.'

'Oversensitive—is that it? Or is it that there's no need for poor Sinistra anymore? Poor, willing Sinistra, the one who looks like a yellow shrub.'

'A yellow what? What are you talking about?'

'You can have anyone you want now, is that it? There's no need for me any more?'

'You're being foolish, Sin. That's not very officer-like. You're emotional like a Hyacinth creature. That's dangerous.'

'What about Petty Officer Rufus? They say she's a perfect example of female Hyacinth beauty. How about Ensign Poplicola with her dark skin? Don't tell me you haven't thought about her? What about Warrant Officer Falto and the way she sways up the passageway? Or is it all of them, like a procession knocking on your door between watches?'

Ranant stood up. 'I don't have time for this, Sin. I've got to get to my men.'

But Sinistra wasn't finished.

'Or is it someone else—someone higher up the chain of command, someone really beautiful, someone who demands exclusivity?'

'We'll talk later, Sin,' Ranant warned.

'Will we? Will we all meet up later? You, me, and your …' she couldn't find the words, so she broke with protocol and growled in the native language. Then she doubled over, clutched her throat, and coughed so hard she had to put a hand on the bulkhead to steady herself.

Ranant tried to push past her. Sinistra grabbed his sleeve. Ranant stopped and looked down at her hand as it twisted his the sleeve tighter, like Queen Angwere clutching at King Angwor on the ash-blasted hill of the old planet.

'Will we really talk about it later,' Sinistra said, 'or will you be too busy in the first lieutenant's cabin? Yes, I saw her smile at you during the Acceleration. Don't think I didn't notice.'

'You're being stupid, Sin, and naïve. You can see that, can't you?'

Then, suddenly, Sinistra's shirt sleeve tightened. The stitching burst on the sleeve placket. The stitches securing the cuff buttons strained and unravelled. One button flew at the bulkhead and clattered to the deck.

Next, Sinistra's face swelled. The Hyacinth bones beneath it straightened and stretched. Her whole body filled with fury. Her legs bulged. Her knee joints thickened. Her pants cuffs climbed above her boots. A foul taste filled her mouth.

Then she saw Ranant's expression. She'd never seen one like it before. The squinting eyes, the screwed up nose, the recoiling neck—they were all new. But their meaning was clear.

Revulsion.

She let go of him.

Ranant pushed past her a second time. Sinistra let him. Then, Ranant opened the cabin door and stood between the jambs, slowly shaking his handsome, Hyacinth-creature head.

'I didn't know you would be like this, Sin.'

Sinistra felt a Hyacinth-creature tear form in her left eye. 'Neither did I,' she said, wiping the tear away. 'Neither did I.'

'You try too hard. Do you know that? You try too hard. That's your problem. Everyone says so.'

Sinistra's shamed eyes were on her torn sleeves.

'Yes,' she said. The self-loathing overwhelmed her. 'I try too hard. I have to do better. I need rest. Because if I don't rest I …'

The dream vision played in her mind: the forest, her childhood self, someone pursuing her through the trees, calling to her, someone with violence on their mind. The terrible blows of the weapon called a brak, came down on her arms and the backs of her legs.

'What did you say, Sin? Something about dread?'

'No,' she said. 'I … I don't know what I said. I have to try harder. That's what I mean. I just have to try harder.'

Ranant drew a long breath. 'Get some rest, Sin. Just get some rest. Lock the door when you leave. I've heard we now have thieves aboard.'

And then he left.

Sinistra stood alone in the cabin with the hissing atmosphere pumps, the rumble of the idling engines, the creak of the bulkheads, and a fear so great it was like an unwanted guest turning up and slinging insults in a deep sneering voice.

'Don't,' she whispered to the voice. 'I can try harder. Much harder. I must.'

'You're bad,' whispered the voice. 'You've always been

bad, and you always will.'

'I know,' Sinistra said. 'I know, but I can try harder.'

A half bell later, she felt able to leave the cabin.

She got up, wiped her face on her sleeve, and straightened her shirt. Then she opened the door, locked it, and limped into the passageway.

It's over now, she thought. Nothing to do but rest. Then I'll feel better. There's always tomorrow. Tomorrow, they'll want me. They'll have to. If they don't, well maybe I can find a way out into open space where none of this matters.

But there would be no rest—not today, not tomorrow, not for many days, and perhaps never.

In the distance, down the passageway, someone waited outside her cabin door.

20

The someone was an ensign, sent from the bridge. The ensign saluted and said, 'Fifth Lieutenant Basilus's duty, Second Lieutenant Sinistra.'

'Yes. What do you want?' She looked at the name patch. 'What is it, Ensign Frugi?'

'New orders from Captain Tiberius, Second Lieutenant.'

Sinistra knew about Ensign Frugi. His family was caught in the same eruption tragedy as Domitian's family weeks before. As a result, Ensign Frugi had suffered severe trauma, and spent a week on the medical deck.

Now he was back on duty. He looked thin. There was a red rash on one side of his neck, and something glistened at the roots of his short dark hair.

'What new orders?'

'I don't know, Second Lieutenant, but I have this.'

He held out an envelope. The captain's seal was stamped into a blob of red wax on the envelope's flap. The use of a seal was unusual. It was a formality reserved for special orders, such as the order to stand down from duties. Sinistra didn't want to touch it, let alone open it and read whatever was inside.

'Make your best guess, Ensign.'

Ensign Frugi cleared his throat. 'Well, Lieutenant, Petty Officer Triarius—he was on duty in the stateroom with the captain—he said it was something to do with Lepidus.'

'Lepidus, the probe pilot?'

'Yes, Lieutenant.'

'What about Lepidus?'

'He's with Doctor Galen.'

'Why? Is he ill?'

'I'm not sure, Lieutenant. Maybe he has the lurgy. Lots of the crew have it.'

'Lurgy? Do you mean the miseria?'

'The hands call it lurgy. Some of them call it the malady. Like this.' He pulled his collar aside to reveal more of the rash. It was red, angry, and slimy with ooze. 'It comes on fast. One minute you're fine. The next, you're tearing at your own throat.'

'You should see Doctor Galen yourself, Ensign Frugi.'

'I don't have the fever yet, Lieutenant. That's when you know the miseria has you—that and you can't breathe the Hyacinth air anymore.'

'How sick is Lepidus?'

'I don't know, Second Lieutenant. I think the doctor just wants to make sure he's all right for the rescue mission.'

'It's not a rescue mission, Ensign Frugi. It's a survey.'

'Yes, Lieutenant. Beg pardon. Rescue mission is what some of the hands call it. Some had family on the Parthia.'

Sinistra took the envelope from Frugi's outstretched hand.

'Thank you, Frugi. You are dismissed.'

Frugi saluted but did not walk away.

'Lieutenant?'

'Yes?'

'Some of the hands have questions, too.'

'What questions?'

'Is the mission all right? Are we going to make it to Hyacinth?'

'Why do the hands think we won't reach Hyacinth?'

'Someone saw a constellation that looks like a Hyacinth creature hand. It's a bad omen, that hand. That's what they say—the crew, I mean.'

Sinistra weighed her words. She chose an old phrase.

'With Owanthan's blessing and our trust in the captain, we'll make it. There's no question of failure.'

Ensign Frugi smiled. 'Yes, Lieutenant. Thank you, Lieutenant. The hands and the other midshipmen—they think what you did in the Acceleration was the right thing to do. Some remember you from the Grantakran.'

Frugi saluted, then spun around and walked back towards the Great Passageway.

Sinistra broke the envelope's red seal and pulled out the single sheet inside. The orders were short and definite. 'Report to the stern ramp at two bells in the first watch. Wait beside the dropship Albus.'

She felt a tingle in her armpits and on the backs of her knees. The orders gave her a sense of being summoned to something immense, something larger than just an investigation of the object or a chance to prove herself worthy of admiration.

It was like an opportunity had suddenly arrived—an opportunity that had waited for her all her life. She re-read the orders with a mixture of relief and fear. The relief was natural. She understood about the relief. It was the fear that made her wonder.

What was she afraid of? The danger? The unknown? The delay this short mission would cause when everyone knew they had to reach Gordium as soon as possible?

Then, she made a guess.

'Ensign Frugi!'

Frugi stopped and turned around.

'Yes, Second Lieutenant?'

'Does Lieutenant Flavia know about these orders?'

'I don't know, Lieutenant.'

She has to know, thought Sinistra. She has to know. If she is leading the mission, she has to know. But how will she react?

In three bells' time, Sinistra would find out.

21

As the bell tolled, Sinistra stepped onto the vast expanse of the Herculaneum's stern ramp.

It was called the stern ramp, but really it was where the dropships docked on their pads. The true ramp was at the stern port—the port leading to open space and through which the dropships launched and returned.

Sinistra saw no one and nothing but the high deckhead above and the fleet of white ships floating above their pads. The dropships were broad at the top, tapering down to a narrow keel. They looked like upended, Hyacinth-creature teardrops, and they smelled like metal, oil, rubber, and detergent.

They're like a forest, Sinistra thought, a forest of tears. I've just noticed it. They're a silent, forest of tears, frozen in place.

But whose tears?

She knew the answer before she posed the question. She imagined the poor Hyacinth creatures, their land devastated, their cities burned, their oceans fouled, and the invaders, her shipmates, descending from the sky in these same ships, and perhaps even in the terrible Herculaneum itself, blacking out the sun.

Stop it, she thought.

She limped across the deck and into the forest, passing through the rows of ships named after Roman territories on Hyacinth: the Dacia, the Epirus, the Hibernia, the Iberia, and hundreds of others. The names meant little to Sinistra, but she thought how ironic it was that these same ships might fire their weapons upon the very places from which they took their names.

Eventually, she emerged onto the vast plain of gray deck between the ships and the stern port, leading to open space behind the Herculaneum.

Ahead, a solitary dropship floated near the port. Its gangway descended from the dropship's waist to the cold deck below. On its side, the crew had painted the word ALBUS in bold Hyacinth characters.

Albus, Sinistra thought. It's the word for bright.

The small crew for the survey assembled at the gangway's base, each blowing steam in the cold air. Sinistra saw Chief Petty Officer Domitian, Marine Captain Ranant, Marine Lieutenant Vopiscus, and two armored marines with heavy blast rifles slung over their shoulders.

Then she saw First Lieutenant Flavia. Flavia stood beside Ranant, looking away towards the stern port, her shoulder almost touching Ranant's chest, her hands gesturing in the air, as if she were already saluting Captain Strahklan and the Parthia survivors.

Ranant noticed the new arrival first. His mouth opened. Then Domitian raised a hand. Vopiscus stood to attention and saluted. Flavia was the last to notice. At the touch of Ranant's hand on her arm, she turned, saw Sinistra, raised her chin, and put one slender fist on her hip.

'What exactly do you think you are doing here?' she said.

'Good afternoon, Lieutenant,' said Sinistra. 'Good afternoon, Chief.' She looked at Ranant and was about to speak when Flavia interrupted her.

'I said, what are you doing here, Second Lieutenant? The

doctor ordered you to rest.'

'Yes, Lieutenant, I know, but I have new orders from Captain Tiberius.'

'I don't believe you.'

'I have the orders with me.'

Sinistra reached into her uniform, brought out the document, and held it out to Flavia, who ignored it.

'What orders?'

'The orders only say to report to the Albus.'

Flavia turned to Domitian. 'Do you know anything about this?'

'No, Flavia, but, I'm glad the captain changed his mind. Lieutenant Sinistra is …'

Flavia cut him off. She turned to Ranant.

'What about you?'

Ranant held out one hand and raised his shoulders, then lowered them. He wasn't so talkative anymore. Flavia opened her mouth and growled in the native tongue. She snarled and barked the words 'my family,' then stopped, swallowed, and cleared her throat. After a several deep, open-mouthed breaths, she returned to the Hyacinth language.

'Whatever the captain said, you will not be coming on this rescue mission.'

'Ask him yourself, Flavia,' said Domitian. 'Here he comes.'

Captain Tiberius emerged from the dropship forest. Astronomer Manius and Petty Officer Triarius followed him. Advisor Cicero floated behind in his white Hyacinth senator's toga, rubbing his bare arms against the cold.

When they arrived at the dropship, Captain Tiberius smiled at the small crew. Cicero clasped his hands. Flavia said, 'Tiberius, did you order the second lieutenant here?'

Tiberius said nothing. He climbed the first two steps of the Albus's gangway. Then he placed one foot on a higher step and smiled at the small group on the deck. Standing like that, he looked just like the statues of Hyacinth emperors making speeches to actual Hyacinth creatures.

'At ease, everyone,' he said. 'I will be brief. Time is against us. That is certain, but the outcome of this short mission is not certain by any means. No, Flavia. Let me finish.' He drew a breath and cleared his throat. 'Your survey is to be brief—no more than three horae, which means you'll have one hora to cross to the object, one hora to survey, one hora to return.

'If you detect signals, do not proceed. We must first consider how any further action will affect our priorities: to reach Gordium, to find the Point of Acceleration, and cross the galaxy to Hyacinth. As much as we would like, we have no time for extraction of survivors. But I am keeping an open mind. Circumstances might prove otherwise. The survivors, if any, might be waiting for us.'

Flavia interrupted. 'Captain, what is Second Lieutenant Flavia doing here?'

'I ordered the lieutenant here.'

'Doctor Galen has ruled the second lieutenant unfit.'

'I overruled the doctor.'

'Why?'

'You have not heard the news, Flavia. Pilot Lepidus has fallen ill with this miseria affliction. That's why I want Lieutenant Sinistra aboard.'

'Lepidus can force himself to pilot the ship for an hour or two, can't he?'

'Yes, at the moment he can, and he will.'

Flavia considered for a moment, the steam coming from her nose in quick puffs.

'Why can't the second lieutenant take Lepidus's place? She can do anything, can't she? That's what they say. Why not order her to pilot the ship remotely?'

Advisor Cicero stepped forward. 'Captain, may I speak?'

The captain nodded. 'Of course, Advisor.'

Cicero gathered his robes around him and prepared to speak. Like Doctor Galen and the rest of the old-family officers, Advisor Cicero wore a family crest-pin over his chest. The crest depicted a red sickle bird, its wings spread, its sharp beak open wide.

'Lieutenant Flavia,' said Cicero. 'This decision was taken on the advice of the Senate. The Senate agrees you should lead this survey. There's no question of Lieutenant Sinistra commanding.'

'I should hope not,' said Flavia.

'However, the Senate also believes the people at home will approve of Lieutenant Flavia being aboard. Terrible eruptions are occurring from west to east. Any good news is welcome. The people are very interested in Lieutenant Sinistra. They consider her to be one of their own. A population that is pleased with their Senate will obey orders when the crisis deepens.'

Flavia's beautiful mouth twisted itself into the shape of a bow. 'We have thousands of pilots aboard who are not Lieutenant Sinistra. They also come from remote, deprived, horrible parts of the home planet, and they too speak with bizarre accents. Surely one of those can steer the Albus.'

'Even so, it is Lieutenant Sinistra who will join the mission, as the Senate commands. She also happens to have the most experience.'

'Since when does the Senate make operational decisions for the Navy?'

'Since our civilization became threatened with extinction.'

'But we need room for survivors, Cicero. We can't take any more people.'

Now the captain spoke. 'Lieutenant Vopiscus will stay behind. That will make room for Sinistra. In the unlikely event there are survivors, we will make a plan when the time comes.'

Flavia made the same expression of exasperation she used on the bridge. She held up her arms and looked up at the deckhead, as if beseeching it to spare her from so many fools. Then, she let her arms fall and slap against her legs. Then, she closed her eyes, raised both her hands, and pushed her lustrous hair away from her face and behind her ears.

'All right, so she's coming aboard as a dead weight.'

'I will not argue with you,' said Tiberius. 'No more talk. Let's get under way. Please, go forth, go well, and as Chief Petty Officer Domitian might say, "May Owanthan go with you."'

The small crew stood to attention and saluted. The captain stepped down from the gangway. He strode away, followed by the floating Cicero, Triarius, and the much-relieved Vopiscus. They disappeared into the dropship's white forest.

As soon as they had gone, the bell tolled. Then, the stern ramp's gravity warning lamp flashed. It was time to get moving. Everyone looked at Flavia, but it was Sinistra who spoke.

It was her first mistake of the mission.

22

'Should we get aboard, Lieutenant?' Sinistra said.

Flavia looked at Sinistra's feet, then her knees, then her waist, bust, and her oily yellow hair. Her mouth twisted itself into another new expression: one corner of her lips rose upward. 'Thank you for reminding me, Second Lieutenant,' she said, her voice as flat as the deck. 'Where would I be without you?'

She walked to the gangway and climbed the steps with exaggerated hip sway. Ranant watched this strange performance as if he'd never seen a female walk before. When he sensed Sinistra looking at him, he frowned at the Albus's bow cannons as if he'd never seen those before, either. Then he walked over to the two tall marines, reached up, and pushed their rifle straps higher on their shoulders.

Domitian boarded the Albus next, leaving Ranant and Sinistra alone.

Still checking the rifle straps, Ranant said, 'You're the ranking officer. You go first.'

Sinistra wondered whether Ranant would also watch her board the ship with the same interest he showed in Flavia. She didn't look to find out.

Inside the dropship, the four crew sat in chairs adapted to

Hyacinth creature body form. The two tall marines stood at attention at the sternmost bulkhead holding their large blast rifles. Newly installed brackets would hold them in place. Flavia sat in the pilot's chair before the bewildering constellation of lights, levers, and gauges. She looked at Sinistra.

'You do it.'

'Yes, Lieutenant.'

Sinistra sat stiffly in the co-pilot's chair. She flicked on the instruments displaying the positions of the Herculaneum and the object. Then she switched on the instruments to locate the Albus in Ilium. Next, she switched on the gravity pump and the atmosphere pump. She raised the gangway and closed the hatch. Finally, she fired the engines. The small ship shuddered. Flavia sat inspecting her red claws.

'Would you like me to contact the bridge, First Lieutenant?'

When Flavia said nothing, Sinistra said, 'Pilot Lepidus. Albus ready for …'

Flavia cut her off.

'I'll speak to the bridge. Lepidus?'

'Yes, First Lieutenant.'

'We're ready.'

They waited for Lepidus's voice to reply. Instead, they heard a cough, a wheeze, and a prolonged wet splutter.

Eventually Lepidus said, 'Aye, aye, First Lieutenant.'

While they waited, Sinistra sealed the airlock, and adjusted the atmosphere settings. Cold, metallic air flushed the cabin, which was now scented with Flavia's lavender perfume.

'Opening the stern port,' said Lepidus's voice. 'First Lieutenant, do you hear me?'

When Flavia did not reply, Sinistra said, 'Yes, pilot. We hear you.'

'Launching,' said Lepidus.

The Albus rose two passus above the deck, then drifted astern.

'Coming about,' said Lepidus.

Through the forward viewport, the forest of white dropships fell back and swung away. Then the great stern port slid into view, yawning open. The port was as wide as twenty dropships and twice as tall. It was like a giant rectangular mouth—the mouth of an enormous creature that had swallowed the Albus and was now breathing it out.

'Ye gods!' said Domitian.

'Owanthan protect us!' said Ranant.

Flavia said nothing. Instead, she stared through the forward viewport, her mouth falling open, and one hand sliding up her uniform toward her throat.

This was the moment things began to change.

The yawning blackness of space filled the forward view. It crept closer as the Albus passed by the massive port jambs and chains. Space seemed to reach for them, drawing them outside, pulling them from safety, and into the unknown. Then, silently, reluctantly, the Albus floated into the terrible immensity and the horror of the infinite void.

'Ye gods!' said Domitian once more. 'Ye gods! This must be what they mean by Owanthan's realm.'

'Keep your mind on the rescue mission,' said Flavia. 'Keep your mind on our cousins and our ...' but her voice trailed away. She blinked at the viewport and the terrible sight of space. She had never been exposed to it before, despite years of service in the navy.

Seconds passed. The cabin was quiet except for the hissing pumps, the engine burr, the sensors' bip, several sharp shallow breaths, and rampant, mounting terror.

'I never knew,' Ranant said. 'I never knew about this. Why didn't anyone warn us?'

No one replied.

In the rear viewport, the Herculaneum's stern port

receded, as if the ship were sailing away. The port's wide rectangle of light contracted to a small glowing bar. Now, the Herculaneum's black transom pushed into view from above and below, like the dark cliffs of a chasm, two milia high and deep.

Secunda by secunda, the Albus drifted away from the ship, into the infinity of space. A dimensionless realm surrounded them from the bow, the stern, aloft, and below. And now, the friendly stars in the far constellations looked friendly no more. Instead, they looked amused, delighted, and sinister, as if laughing at the tiny craft, alone and lost in their domain.

Everyone sensed their own vulnerability. Space could kill them, in both the Hyacinth form, and in their natural states. Everyone knew it. Everyone talked about it. Now, space was here. It was all around.

And it was horrifying.

The small crew, including Sinistra, felt their fragility and insignificance in the immensity of the cosmos. They might plunge into the abyss and never stop plummeting until they reached the end of the universe itself, and whatever waited there.

It was so totally different to the Herculaneum's bulkheads, boulevards, staterooms and holds. In the Herculaneum, with your ten thousand shipmates, you felt safe. Sometimes, you even felt at home, as if you weren't in space at all, billions of milia from your family. But the Herculaneum and its safe passageways and cabins soon fell away, and the four crew members of the Albus drifted in open space.

How quickly they would find themselves at its mercy.

Part Two: Grenda

OCTAVIA

"Cometh the hour, cometh the man."

A statesman from the Hyacinth planet

23

The Albus drifted to a distance of a half leuga from the Herculaneum's stern. Petty Officer Lepidus's spluttering voice spoke from the comms.

'Prepare to come about, First Lieutenant.'

Flavia said nothing. On the Albus's console, the bow thruster indicator lit up. In the viewport, the thruster's mist streamed out. Then, each of the crew felt a nudge and a twist as the starboard thrusters fired and the ship turned to port.

'What now?' said Domitian. 'Flavia, what now?'

But Flavia said nothing.

'We'll be looking along the Herculaneum's starboard quarter,' said Sinistra. 'Have you seen the ship from this angle before?'

'Never,' said Domitian. 'I came up from the home planet in a dropship with everyone else. I didn't see a thing until we disembarked on the ramp. Then, it was just like being on any other ship—except bigger, of course.'

'Well, beware, Chief Petty Officer. You too, Captain Ranant. The sight of a ship this size in space can be confronting,' she said. 'It's strange, but true. There's even a medical term for it. It means fear of enormous machines. Lieutenant Flavia, I'm sure you would you agree?

Lieutenant?'

Flavia stared at the viewport, her mouth now open and slack. She was totally still, hardly even breathing.

'I think the first lieutenant is experiencing that medical condition now,' Sinistra said. When no one answered, and the ship was totally silent, she turned to look at Domitian and Ranant.

Like Flavia, they stared at the forward viewport—no, 'stare' wasn't the right verb in the Hyacinth language. 'Gawk' was better, or perhaps 'goggle' or even 'gape.' Yes, all three gaped as the Herculaneum's immense starboard quarter loomed into view.

Domitian clutched his hands as if he were praying. Ranant's left hand covered his mouth. Flavia sat upright and rigid. Her red claws sank deep into the armrest cushioning.

'Are you all right, First Lieutenant?' Sinistra asked again.

Flavia said nothing. Neither did Domitian or Ranant. Sinistra guessed they had all expected to see the Herculaneum floating in space like a ship bobbing on blue water in the sunlight. But there was no sun and no light. The ship wasn't there. All that could be seen were the two circles of light cast by the Albus's bow lanterns against an immense black transom.

The scene changed again—for the worse. The two circles of light cast by the Albus's lanterns slid over what appeared to be entrance to the fires of the underworld described in the Old Book. The starboard exhaust funnel yawned like a black hole—immense, dirty and mysterious, leading not into the ship and its engines, but to furnaces and volcanoes of fire, torment, and terror.

Even Sinistra shivered at the sight of it. I hope, she thought, I am never called to float in open space at the ship's stern or go anywhere near those funnel rims.

'Is everyone all right?' she asked again. No one replied. 'Lieutenant Flavia, do you need anything? Lieutenant?'

Nothing.

Better not push it, thought Sinistra. I'll only embarrass her. Let her save face. She'll get used to things in her own time. Then she'll thank me. She'll see how valuable I am. She'll have to. She must.

But no sooner had the small crew relaxed after the sight of the exhaust funnels, when the next confronting sight slid into view: the two-milia-high slab of the Herculaneum's starboard side.

As the Albus pushed forward, dark rivets slid into view, like giant eyes leering through the viewports. Next came the huge black scales, their overlapping flaps casting shadows that stretched and withdrew as if they were part of a living, breathing creature, slithering past them in space.

And the flaps of metal were not clean nor smooth. Angry burns scorched their surfaces with dirty smears, and months of clattering space debris left them dented and pocked, like the surface of the home planet's dark gray moons.

'Won't be long,' Sinistra said. 'It doesn't get much worse.'

'What could be worse than this?' croaked Domitian.

'The object,' said Ranant. 'The object will be worse. It's still out there—somewhere. And we're going all the way across to it.'

Flavia spoke in a quiet voice. 'The Parthia survivors are aboard it. There's nothing to fear. There's …' but she said no more.

Sinistra watched Flavia's stricken profile until it seemed impolite to stare. She looked at the controls and gauges instead, and wondered about the questions that had bubbled in her mind from the moment she had come aboard the Herculaneum two Hyacinth months ago.

How could such a critical mission as this voyage to Hyacinth be such a mess? Why was the mission lead by so many incompetent, reckless officers? How could the officers be so inexperienced after so many years of service? Worse!

How could the Admiralty and the Senate appoint these officers at all?

It made no sense, unless all the admirals and senators were also incompetent, or blinded by the same unquestioning belief in the so-called example of history and the claims of the patrician families of Tiberius, Flavia, Gabinus, Decimus and the rest.

As usual, Sinistra didn't ponder these questions long. She didn't seek answers. To answer the questions might invite contempt for her senior officers. And what then? What would happen if there was no one from whom she could seek approval, validation, her reasons for trying so hard?

Yes, what then?

But Sinistra would never let her thoughts wander quite that far. Not yet.

The Albus pressed on along the Herculaneum's endless side, past each scale, porthole, scuttle, and gun port—past the viewing ports, at which the blinking eyes, open mouths, and raw necks of the crew were pressed, like stricken creatures dying in silence and agony.

Eventually, Lepidus spoke from the Herculaneum's bridge, breaking the tortured silence.

'Bow coming up, Lieutenant.'

Sinistra noticed he didn't mention Flavia's name. Did Lepidus also sense something was wrong with the first lieutenant?

'Do you see it?' Lepidus said.

The starboard side gave way to the bright light of the Herculaneum's bow lamps. The lamps drifted into view like the lights on a buoy on a dark sea, shining into an endless night.

Then, the bridge and its wide viewports appeared high above, as if they were atop a steep, black cliff face, and the Albus was a climber far below in the dark, forested foothills.

'This is a little better,' said Domitian. 'Sort of.'

Soon the bridge slid by and the Herculaneum was visible only through the stern viewport. The crossing to the object had begun, and the Albus pushed away from its mother ship, out into a lonely, enveloping gloom.

'I'm going to sharpen the lamp beams,' said Sinistra, 'with your permission, of course, First Lieutenant.'

Flavia said nothing. She stared straight ahead, blinking. Sinistra sent the instruction to Lepidus. Lepidus's voice replied, 'Aye, aye,' and then coughed deeply and wetly. 'Ignose,' he said. Pardon me.

On the Albus's console, the bow light indicator flashed.

'This will help,' said Sinistra.

'What will help?' said Ranant. 'Where are the lights? I can't see anything.'

'We can't see them because there's no atmosphere or dust to reflect the light.'

'But where's the object?' said Ranant. 'Why doesn't it show up?'

'It will,' said Sinistra. 'It's out there, just further away than it seems.'

'Yes, but where?'

'There,' Sinistra said.

In the furthest reach of the beams, a faint, gray shape waited. At the sight of it, Sinistra felt damp on the back of her Hyacinth-creature neck, and a new twitch began, this time in her withered right calf muscle. She turned to the rigid figure beside her.

'Lieutenant Flavia, do you see it?'

'Quid est?'

'Can you see the object—the Parthia wreckage? Should we inform the Herculaneum?'

Flavia blinked. 'Herculaneum, do you see … it?'

'Yes, Lieutenant,' said Lepidus, who then broke into more wet, deep coughs. 'Excuse me,' he said.

'It's there,' said Flavia. 'It's right there. It's … right …

there.'

The roles of object and ship seemed reversed. The object was coming for the ship, growing in size as it came towards them. Its dark columns stretched upward. The shadows on the porch behind them rose up and thickened and slid along the temple wall.

'I see it, Lieutenant,' said Lepidus. 'I'll take you to the object's port side, but first, a look at the front. Brace for the bow thrusters. I'll have to slow you up.'

'It's coming closer,' said Flavia. 'It's coming closer.'

Sinistra touched Flavia's arm. The arm was rigid, like a metal strut. Sinistra also noticed Flavia's red claws. They almost punctured the Goth hide on the armrest.

'Stand by,' said Lepidus.

Mist filled the forward viewport. The Albus slowed to a gentle drift. The object loomed. Up close, it looked different. It was taller and wider—taller than the Albus itself, perhaps three times its height and several times its width, and far more mournful, sinister, and mysterious. It looked more like a tomb than a temple.

The ancient writing they had seen from the probe appeared on the podium beneath the columns. 'May Owanthan save us. May Sirhain inspire us.'

'I still don't understand why it mentions Sirhain,' said Domitian.

'Lieutenant Flavia,' Sinistra said. 'Would you like to pause and examine the columns more closely? Lieutenant? Are you all right?'

'Quid est?'

'If you wish, Lieutenant, we could take control of the Albus ourselves. Then, I can respond faster to your instructions. Do I have your permission?'

Flavia's eyes flashed to life. Her red claws released their grip on the armrests.

'Did I ask you to take control?' Flavia snapped.

'No, Lieutenant.'

'Then don't. You will not pilot the ship while I am in command of this rescue mission. Your role is to stand by. That is all.' Her face contorted. 'Do you understand?' She barked some words in the native language. Then she clutched her throat and coughed in pain.

'Yes, Lieutenant,' said Sinistra.

'Do as I command!' said Flavia in the Hyacinth language. 'Do as I order. Nothing more. If I didn't watch you, you would take control of the entire mission.'

Sinistra said nothing.

When she calmed down, Flavia spoke with new confidence. 'The Parthia survivors are waiting. They know I'm coming to rescue them. They sense their beloved cousins are on the way. Together we'll write the history of our people.'

'But we've heard nothing from them,' said Domitian. 'I'm not saying there are no Parthia survivors inside. I'm saying this might be something we didn't expect. It might be something dangerous. I can't be the only one who thinks this way. Just look at it.'

Flavia ignored him. She was alert again, full of confidence. 'Petty Officer Lepidus, are you there?'

A series of deep, wet coughs replied. Eventually, Lepidus's wavering voice spoke.

'Yes, Lieutenant Flavia.'

'I'm ready. Take us to the object's port side.'

'Aye, aye, Lieutenant.'

Flavia sniffed. 'Captain Strahklan and the other survivors have waited long enough.'

The thrusters fired. The Albus nudged to starboard, then squared up to the dark gray wall.

'I don't believe it,' said Domitian.

On the wall, in the wavering circles of the lamplight, a new image waited.

24

As before, the image on the object's side depicted the object and the Herculaneum, with its fore-and-aft lanterns streaming. But now, the picture had changed. A teardrop shaped craft was also present, floating off the object's port side.

'Who's doing this?' said Ranant. 'Who's watching us? Who's drawing these things? And where are they hiding? Tell Lepidus to go back and look behind the columns.'

'It can only be the Parthia survivors,' said Flavia. 'They are not hiding behind the columns, Captain Ranant. They're inside, waiting.'

'Well, why the mystery?' said Ranant 'Why the pictures instead of messages?'

'It's not a picture,' said Domitian. 'It's a carving into the stone, or a bas-relief. Bas-relief—yes, I think that's the right term. But I think you can also say mural or maybe embossment.'

'Whatever it is, why don't they contact us?' said Ranant. 'Surely they can hear Telepathy's calls.'

'Perhaps they prefer not to hear,' said Flavia. 'Perhaps they want me to find them. Or perhaps they're incapacitated or weakened. Have you thought of that?'

The Albus floated beside the wall. No one spoke in the cabin. Then, in a soft voice, Sinistra said, 'The Albus has a mechanical arm, Lieutenant Flavia. We could test the consistency of the walls. They might not be solid. They might even be an illusion, a construction of light, not a building or temple at all. The whole object might be a signal pointing the way to the actual ship. We could do it, easily, Lieutenant Flavia.'

'No,' said Flavia. 'We will keep going.' She tossed her red hair over one shoulder and sat upright in her chair, her terror of open space fading. 'Pilot Lepidus,' she said to the comms. 'Move us to the stern.'

'Yes, Lieutenant,' Lepidus said. His voice was now a breathy wheeze.

'Are you all right, Lepidus?' said Sinistra. 'You sound sick.'

'I'll be all right,' said Lepidus.

'Then hurry up and move us,' said Flavia.

'Moving now, Lieutenant.'

The thrusters fired. The Albus lurched to starboard. The mural slid away and the object's rear quarter appeared. Then, it too slid away, and open space filled the screen. The thrusters fired again and the Albus squared up on the stern. A new image glowed in the lamplights.

This time, the carving depicted a scene on a planet. It showed a Hyacinth woman standing on a hilltop. Beneath her, in a valley, a multitude of Hyacinth creatures stood, raising their arms, as if saluting the woman.

Flavia spoke. 'Chief Domitian, who or what is that? It's not scene from the Old Book, is it?'

'No, of course not. Those are Hyacinth creatures. It's obviously a scene on the Hyacinth planet.'

'Is it from the future? Could the female on the hill be one of us?' said Flavia.

'Look how the creatures' mouths are open,' said Ranant.

'They're singing to her.'

'Or cheering her,' said Flavia.

Or worshipping her, thought Sinistra.

'But if this is another message,' said Domitian, 'what's it telling us? Is it supposed to be a scene from the Parthia's mission to Hyacinth, or is it a prediction of our visit? And who is the woman?'

'She might be a Hyacinth leader,' said Ranant. 'The leader of an uprising against our presence. This could be a warning.'

'Maybe, but we all know,' said Flavia, 'that if the Hyacinth creatures don't cooperate, we have a ship's hold full of ways to persuade them. Therefore, this can't be a vision of the future.'

'The crucial question then,' said Domitian, 'is who is that woman?'

'Petty Officer Lepidus,' said Flavia to the comms. 'What does Captain Tiberius think about this image?'

'The same as you, Lieutenant. The captain, the astronomer, and Advisor Cicero aren't sure what it means. They're consulting the Senate.'

'What about Telepathy? Has he heard any messages from Captain Strahklan and the survivors?'

'None, Lieutenant.'

'They obviously want us to continue,' said Flavia. 'Move us on, Pilot.'

'Moving now, Lieutenant.'

The port thruster fired. The stern image slid away. Space filled the viewport as the Albus left the object's stern and drifted to starboard. Then, for a moment, a terrible sight slid into view. The Herculaneum appeared in the distance. It was like a black leviathan with bright, tiny eyes, watching, waiting, considering. It was nothing like the secure, comfortable quarters they knew. It was a monster in space, a terrible master the size of a mountain.

The cabin was silent until the Albus squared up on the object's starboard side and a new image appeared.

'That's us again,' said Flavia. 'I can see ...' But her voice trailed away.

'Yes,' said Domitian. 'But what is it?'

'Something worse,' said Ranant.

The mural depicted three Hyacinth creatures, two males, one female—all holding their arms over their faces. Behind them, the two tall marines stood with rifles raised to their helmets.

And there was something else. A cloud or a mist floated before the small group. The mist concealed dark shapes resembling a thunder cloud heavy with rain.

Domitian spoke first. 'This time,' he began, 'it really must be a warning.'

'One rifle is firing,' said Ranant. 'See how the muzzle climbs.'

Sinistra kept silent. Flavia said, 'Pilot, any news from Telepathy?'

'None, Lieutenant.'

'Any Old Book significance, Chief?' said Flavia. 'You're the expert. What's that mist?'

'I'm no expert, Flavia, but I can't remember a scene in the Old Book like that.'

'From my memory of the Old Book,' Flavia replied, 'there is nothing but trouble and trauma, kings, queens, Owanthan, Sirhain, and the rest of them. Does that sum it up?'

'More or less,' said Domitian. 'The Old Book describes a tumultuous period in our history—and the history of the gods.'

'What now?' said Ranant. 'Do we go back?'

'Wait,' said Sinistra, then corrected herself. 'Lieutenant Flavia, I think the mural is changing.'

As they watched, one figure in the image disappeared. The two males and the marines remained the same, but the female Hyacinth creature reemerged in a new pose. Now, she lay stricken on the deck. Her right hand clutched her face.

No one spoke. There was hardly a sound. The atmosphere pumps sighed, the circuitry hummed, and fear crept into the cabin, like Gothi, the ship's mascot padding through the chair legs on the Herculaneum's bridge.

'It's us,' said Sinistra. 'That's us! But one of us has been hurt by whatever is in that mist.'

No one replied.

The comms came alive. Lepidus said, 'Lieutenant Flavia, Captain Tiberius doesn't like the look of it. He's ordered me to bring you back.'

Flavia waited before replying. Eventually, she said, 'But we haven't heard from the survivors.'

'Tiberius is right, Flavia,' said Domitian. 'Let's return. We can discuss what we've seen later.'

'What about you, Ranant?' said Flavia. 'Do you think we should return?'

'Me and my men are here to protect you,' Ranant said. 'We're not here to make navy decisions.'

'You're so noncommittal, Captain Ranant. Usually, you are more assertive.'

'That's the way it's always been,' Ranant replied. 'You make the strategy. We fire the guns. But if you really want my opinion, I also think we should get back to the Herculaneum before that thing out there does something we won't like, and which I can't stop.'

Flavia turned to Sinistra, then changed her mind, then changed it back.

'What about you? What do you think?'

Yet again, Sinistra faced the horns of a dilemma—a dilemma between performing her duty and her desire to please her touchy commanding officer. Her sense of duty said they should return to the Herculaneum immediately, then fire on the object, destroy it, and proceed to Gordium and Hyacinth as fast as the engines could shove them. But after all that had happened on this terrible day, her need for Flavia's approval demanded otherwise.

'Well, I …'

'Spit it out,' said Flavia.

Then, to Sinistra's relief, she found the answer she needed, one that was both unexpected but helpful, and most importantly, it told Flavia what she wanted to hear.

'Lieutenant, we haven't yet surveyed the object's underside. It's possible the Parthia survivors might be underneath the object. And, the underside might be a port into the interior.'

Flavia's eyes brightened. She actually smiled at Sinistra for the first time in a Hyacinth week.

'Yes, Lieutenant, of course! We haven't seen what's underneath. Why didn't I think of that? Pilot, please inform Captain Tiberius that we will survey the object's underside.'

They waited for the comms to reply. Then, Lepidus said, 'Beg pardon, Lieutenant. The captain wants your immediate return to the Herculaneum, but, if you wish, he says I can bring you back via the object's keel. You can view it as you pass by.'

Flavia said, 'All right. And if the Parthia survivors are there, we will halt.'

Nothing came from the comms but a wet cough, followed by a deep sniff.

'Pilot,' Flavia said, 'take us down.'

25

Down went the Albus. Up rose the object's starboard side, sliding away like a curtain rising, as if the object were staging a performance.

'Pilot Lepidus,' said Flavia. 'How will we see what's underneath when our view is only of what's in front?'

'Switching on the topside camera, Lieutenant,' came Lepidus's voice.

The forward viewport flickered. It came alive again, showing nothing but a rectangle of darkness pin-pricked with light.

'Are there any lanterns up top?' said Flavia.

'No,' said Sinistra, 'not on this generation of …'

'I'm asking the pilot, not you.'

'None, Lieutenant Flavia,' came Lepidus's answer over the comms. 'There are no topside lanterns on this generation of dropship.'

'Well, what use is that?' said Flavia. 'We won't be able to see inside. We will have to tilt to bring up the bow lamps.'

'Lieutenant,' said Sinistra. 'I advise against tilting. It will slow us down. It's also against the captain's orders.'

'I don't care what you advise. No, that's not quite true. I care slightly. Whatever you advise, I'm going to do the opposite. Pilot Lepidus, don't keep us waiting.'

'Yes, Lieutenant. Tilting the Albus now.'

They felt the thrusters fire at the Albus's stern and bow. The cabin tilted back. The viewport switched back to the forward view, revealing distant stars gazing down at them—watching, waiting.

Sinistra tightened her harness as the Albus settled onto its stern, and then, following a push from its port thruster, the ship slid directly beneath the object.

Everyone looked to see what the underside revealed. Perhaps the lamps would shine on the Parthia survivors, smiling and waving. Or perhaps there would be nothing but the insides of a hollow shell, or another blank surface.

But when the underside slid into view, it revealed nothing at all, except a square of blackness darker than open space.

'Herculaneum,' said Flavia. 'We can't see inside the object. Have the bow lamps failed?'

'The lamps are on,' said Sinistra. 'But there's nothing inside to reflect them back at us.'

'Then what's wrong?' said Flavia. 'Herculaneum, bring us closer. We must see what's inside.'

They waited.

'Herculaneum?'

Nothing.

'Herculaneum? Pilot Lepidus? Don't tell me this miseria has struck you down, too. Tiberius, if you're listening, please replace the pilot. We're waiting.'

But no answer came from the Herculaneum—not a cough, not a splutter, not a wheeze.

'Herculaneum?' said Flavia.

But no response came.

'Pilot, Lepidus?'

Nothing.

'Captain Tiberius?'

Nothing but silence.

'What now?' said Domitian.

'The sooner we get back,' said Ranant, 'the sooner we can turn the cannons on this thing. I don't believe there are any survivors in there. This is nothing but a waste of time.'

'No, Captain Ranant,' said Flavia. 'We must find out what's inside. You agree, don't you, Domitian? Captain Strahklan might be inside. They might all be inside. They might even be right in front of us—waving.'

'They won't be waving, Flavia,' said Domitian. 'They'll be in our natural form. If anything, they won't recognize us. They'll only see Hyacinth creatures. They might even be afraid of us.'

'Well, maybe that explains it,' said Flavia. 'They don't recognize us. That's why they're so coy. Herculaneum, take us closer. That's an order. I don't care what Tiberius says.'

But there was no response—not even an electrical crackle or a wet cough.

Sinistra kept quiet, but not for long. The balancing scale in her mind shifted. Duty and her desire for approval now weighed the same. The scales balanced. But at the sight of the object's black underside, the scales tipped.

'Lieutenant Flavia,' she said. 'I think you should break with protocol and send a telepathic message to the bridge. The situation allows it.'

'No,' said Flavia. 'There is no need to break with protocol, Lieutenant. Any moment, the pilot will be back.'

But as she spoke, something changed in the Albus: a shift, but not one propelled by the thrusters. It felt like a nudge by an unseen hand at the stern, or worse, a hand reaching out from the object's black hole to pull the ship inside.

The Albus rose. On the viewport, the black rectangle of the object's underside spread out, blocking the meagre starlight.

'See,' said Flavia. 'I knew the captain would agree with me. He has more relatives aboard the Parthia than I do.'

But Sinistra was not listening. She looked at the console, the sensors, the stern cameras, and the engine gauges.

'Lieutenant,' she said. 'The stern thrusters aren't engaged. The ship is not rising under its own power.'

'Upward into the object is where we want to go,' Flavia replied.

'Yes, but something is not right. Something is drawing us inside, or pushing us. I'd like your permission to override the bridge and take manual control.'

'Why?'

'To reverse us out. We need to be sure about what's happening before we go inside. We need to know what's in there first.' She almost said, 'Trust me,' but changed her mind.

'Not while I'm in charge,' said Flavia. 'Permission is denied—especially for you. You are an irritant, Lieutenant. When the scholars write the history of this rescue mission, they will describe you as a passenger, nothing more.'

But for once, the harsh words failed to sting. The scales had tipped too far. Flavia will disapprove of whatever I do, Sinistra thought, and she reached for control that would sever the link to Pilot Lepidus and the Herculaneum.

'Are you about to commit another act of insubordination, Lieutenant?' said Flavia.

'I'm sorry,' Sinistra said, 'but if we don't do something, we'll regret this. Pilot Lepidus. We're switching to control from the Albus.'

The comms remained silent.

'You've done it now, Lieutenant,' said Flavia, eerily repeating the words spoken by the dark voice in Sinistra's mind. 'You've really done it. Even Tiberius won't stand for insubordination.'

Sinistra wasn't listening. Instead, she pulled the Albus's helm, trying to tilt the ship to vertical. But the Albus did not respond. Worse, the bow lamps switched off. The view forward revealed nothing but darkness.

'Yes,' said Flavia, 'you've sealed your fate. Insubordination, disobeying direct orders, imperiling the Parthia survivors. You'll be locked in the brig for the rest of the mission, where you can't do any more harm.'

Sinistra wasn't listening. She fired the forward thrusters, trying to reverse. The Albus's joints creaked, and the bow shuddered. The chairs quivered on their racks. But the Albus kept moving up and up, into the object's dark base.

'What's happening, Sin?' called Ranant. 'Why can't you stop us? Where are the lights?'

'It's not me.'

'Then what is it?'

'It's the object. It's pulling us inside.'

'It's docking us,' said Flavia.

The darkness slid over the viewport. Shadow enveloped the cabin. The sobbing, twinkling stars disappeared completely.

Domitian recited some words from the Old Book. 'May Owanthan defend us and protect us from danger. May Owanthan protect us from those who would do us harm.'

Sinistra turned from the controls and looked at Ranant.

'Captain Ranant,' she ordered. 'Ready your marines.'

'What? Now? Inside the ship?'

'Yes, now, inside the ship. Unlock the braces and arm their weapons. I'll run out the cannons.'

Ranant looked at Flavia. 'That's a decision for the commanding officer, Sin.'

'I know it is, but just do it.'

Flavia looked over her shoulder at Ranant. 'Who is in charge here, Captain? Whose orders will you obey?'

Ranant said. 'I can't do anything unless Lieutenant Flavia orders it, Sin.'

Sinistra felt her arms swell inside their sleeves and grow hot and thick. 'You will address me as Second Lieutenant,' she said, 'just as the Navy's protocol requires, or you will find yourself in front of a military court. Then you will command nothing but the bacteria in the ship's brig. Understand, Marine Captain Ranant?'

'It's all right, Ranant,' said Flavia. 'Let the second lieutenant dig a hole from which she'll never escape.'

Ranant held out his arms, palms up, then let his hands flop to his knees. He turned and barked at the two tall figures at the cabin's rear bulkhead.

'Marines!'

'Sir!' they replied in their flat, electrical voices.

'Off braces. Arm weapons.'

The brackets holding the marines to the bulkhead sprung open and retracted. Then, the two giants unslung their heavy rifles. They racked the mechanisms on weapons' sides with a loud click and clack.

The big weapons squealed. Two small white lights blinked on each of the forestocks. Then, in unison, the marines twisted the weapons and held them diagonally across their chests in the port arms position. Their metal first-fingers rested on the fire buttons.

'Paratus!' the marines said in their electrical voices. Ready.

'Now what?' Ranant said.

'What kind of damage can those weapons do?' said Domitian.

'Extreme damage,' said Ranant. 'Astonishing damage. May Owanthan help anyone who gets in the way of a blast.'

'We might need them,' said Domitian. 'Lieutenant Sinistra, can't you get us out?'

'I'm trying,' said Sinistra.

'Try the cannons,' said Ranant. 'The blast might shove us back out.'

'Do not fire any cannons,' said Flavia. 'We might hit the Parthians.'

'It doesn't matter, anyway,' said Sinistra. 'The cannons

don't respond.'

And so, the Albus rose higher, and the object enfolded the ship in its dark, velvet grip. The forward cameras revealed nothing. The stern cameras showed a star field fading to black.

As the ship rose upward into the gloom, Sinistra sat in the co-pilot's chair with her Hyacinth-creature hand over her heart.

I caused this, she thought. Pleasing Flavia caused this. Ignoring my instincts caused this. Why does this keep happening to me? Why? But I know why. It happens because I'm bad. I've always been bad. I deserve whatever happens. But what else can I do? What else could I do?

She looked across at Flavia, at Flavia's strange smile. Illuminated by the console lights, the smile looked manic, unnatural, and unlike any Hyacinth-creature smile in the catalogue of expressions. It must be madness, Sinistra thought. She had never seen madness in the Hyacinth creature form, but this surely must be it.

'Don't worry, Lieutenant,' said Flavia in a surprisingly calm voice. 'We'll soon reunite with the Parthia survivors. It will be a glorious rescue. After we find them, I might be in a mood to pardon you. It's unlikely—very unlikely, but you never know.'

'May Owanthan protect us,' said Domitian again. 'May he protect us from dark forces. May he return us to the light.'

'Here we go,' said Flavia.

To where, thought Sinistra.

And to whom?

Or was it who?

Or what?

They would soon find out.

26

The Albus ascended.

The forward lanterns shone into darkness.

Inside the ship, the navigational instruments reported a world that couldn't exist. First, the sensors detected no dimensions. Apparently, there was nothing inside the object but limitless emptiness to port, starboard, stern, and aloft. Second, the Albus had been pulled upward for almost a mille passus, a Hyacinth mile, and yet it hit no ceiling or deckhead.

What was going on?

As she watched the instruments, Sinistra's digestive organs squirmed. Why had the Admiralty insisted on keeping them? The organs were like an internal enemy. They magnified stress. They intensified discomfort. So why did the Admiralty insist on them?

Probably, thought Sinistra, the organs were just another blunder, like appointing Flavia to the role of second in command.

When her organs settled down, Sinistra considered what to do? Options were limited. The engines wouldn't respond. The Herculaneum was out of contact. Not even the weapons responded.

She didn't dare to think of the most disturbing and baffling question of all: If there are no Parthia survivors, who or what had taken control of the Albus? And why were they doing it? And why now?

She scanned the console once more. At least the sensors and gauges still worked. She could measure every bizarre challenge to the laws of nature and common sense. But why the sensors and not the engines? Maybe it was all intended to intimidate, to amplify fear, and subdue the small crew.

Beside her, Flavia's beautiful face was calm, unlike the terrified rictus face she wore during the crossing from the Herculaneum. Now she looked almost serene. Her claws no longer sank into the armrests. Instead, she clasped her hands in her lap, as if she were enjoying herself.

'Lieutenant Sinistra?' Flavia said.

'Yes!' replied Sinistra, startled. She expected Flavia to say, 'I don't appreciate you inspecting me like a Goth sniffing rancid meat.'

But it wasn't Flavia speaking. The voice came from the rear of the cabin. It was Domitian.

'Sin! Did you hear me? What's going on?'

Sinistra turned to look at him. Domitian's face wore a Hyacinth-creature expression she'd never seen. His top teeth clamped down on his lower lip. Beside him, Ranant nodded over and over as if he agreed with something only he could hear.

Feelings, Sinistra thought. Hyacinth creature feelings! The Admiralty said they would give us empathy for the Hyacinth creatures themselves. Instead, they did something else. They confused us and rendered us incapable of action and clear thought. They made us afraid, lonely, offended, sexually aroused, paranoid, and irrational. And they made us crave attention from unworthy people such as Flavia, and, she conceded, from Ranant.

How much more effective the mission would be without

these feelings! How much better it was to think, move, and act without the distortions caused by fear, guilt, shame, sadness, desire, jealousy, and pride!

Hyacinth-creature feelings were dangerous. Look at the damage they had caused so far. Imagine what damage they might cause next.

'Sin?' said Domitian. 'Are you all right? You're babbling.'

Sinistra was about to answer, but Flavia spoke first.

'Quiet, Chief Domitian. We are in the good hands of our relatives and the other survivors.'

'Well, we're certainly in someone's hands,' said Ranant. 'Or their claws.'

The Albus had now travelled upward for a distance three times the apparent height of the object itself. Three times the height, thought Sinistra. How could that be? And what could she do? The answer was nothing. There was nothing to do but wait to see.

But then, Sinistra felt a jolt, as if the Albus's keel thruster had fired. Then, beside her right arm, the contact alarm flashed its small, insistent blue light.

She scanned the instruments. First, the sensors, fore and aft. The forward sensors now reported to barriers in the darkness: one straight ahead, one beneath the keel. How could that be? The contact light kept flashing. Now, the landing carriage suddenly engaged, and went down by itself. A thunk sounded below the deck, followed by creaks in the struts, joints, and hull, as the carriage took up the ship's weight.

So, now there was gravity, too.

Sinistra switched off the contact alarm. Then she turned off the thruster controls, just in case they reactivated and careened the ship onto its side.

When the various beeps, creaks, flashing lights and whirring motors had stopped, Sinistra closed her eyes, and searched for the right phrase in the Hyacinth language to describe this new situation.

Id est bonun, she guessed. It is all right.

But was it really all right?

Well, they had landed safely. That was all right. But everything else was definitely non recte. Not all right. The ship did not respond to manual controls. The Herculaneum was silent, and they were inside an object whose properties defied all experience of nature. Worse! They were also in total darkness and out of communication.

Sinistra checked the sensors once again. They still reported nothing above and nothing to the stern. But they had calculated the distance to the barrier straight ahead. It stood a half-milia away in the dark, out of sight.

The four crew members and the two marines were silent.

Then Flavia said, 'Well, we've arrived. Now, where are our kinsmen?'

27

'Our kinsmen, Lieutenant?' said Sinistra.

'Yes,' said Flavia. 'Our cognati. It sounds more appropriate than relatives. Our kinsmen will be coming to greet us.'

'What do the sensors say, Sin?' asked Domitian. 'Is there anyone out there? Is anyone coming towards us?'

'The sensors detect a deck or floor beneath us,' said Sinistra.

'We know that,' said Ranant.

'They also detect a bulkhead or wall a half-milia straight ahead.'

'No people?'

'No people, Chief. But that doesn't mean someone isn't out there. After all, someone must have pulled us inside, unless this object is running by itself on old instructions.'

'So what do we do?' asked Domitian.

'That's easy. We wait,' said Flavia.

'Is that it?' Domitian said. 'We wait for a welcoming ceremony?'

'At first, yes,' Flavia said.

Ranant said, 'Kinsmen or not, I'm going to keep my men armed—just in case.'

Both Ranant and Domitian unclipped their harnesses and stood up. Ranant inspected the two marines and their weapons. Domitian walked to the airlock hatch. He closed his eyes and mouthed silent words.

Sinistra sat at the console wondering about Flavia. The crossing had revealed new sides of the first lieutenant. Sinistra already knew all about Flavia's impulsiveness, her disdain, her irrational self-belief, and her temper. It was these aspects of her character that made Sinistra seek Flavia's approval so eagerly. Now, for the first time in the mission, she felt differently.

Flavia's abrasive personality now seemed like a liability. Her lack of awareness of her flaws displayed poor leadership. Her obsession with her family pedigree affected her judgment. There she sat, unconcerned, straightening the family crest pin in her lapel. The pin depicted some ancestor or other, skewering a giant Goth lying prone on its back.

Crisis reveals character, Sinistra thought. Hadn't Domitian said that when they stood beneath 'The Fate of The People'? And this mini crisis on the object had exposed Flavia's character to a harsh new light. Here in the darkness, Sinistra could see her plainly, or at least more clearly. Surely, it was not worth seeking approval from someone like Flavia.

'What are you gawking at, Second Lieutenant?' Flavia said. 'I don't need your advice, if you're about to offer it.'

'I was just thinking about what to do. With your permission, I'd like to suggest a course of action—just in case the Parthia survivors aren't here.'

But Flavia tossed back her hair, unclipped her harness, and said, 'Are there any mirrors on this ship? Before you say anything, I am aware that the captain has forbidden mirrors on the mission, but it's important we look our best—those of us who can, I mean.'

'No Lieutenant,' said Sinistra. 'There are no mirrors

Flavia called out to Domitian. 'Out of the way, Dom. Tell

Owanthan or whoever it is you're mumbling to that you'll get back to him later.'

Domitian backed away. Flavia took his place at the airlock and inspected her reflection in the small glass window.

Domitian said to Sinistra. 'Lieutenant, why did no one warn us?'

'Warn you, Chief?'

'About open space. About how things look outside—the ship's exhaust funnels and so on. It was terrifying. Flavia, you know about these things. Why didn't you warn us?'

But Flavia was too busy examining herself. She turned her chin one way, then there other. Then she dabbed at the lustrous curls of her hair. Finally, she flicked her eyes upward to see Ranant's reflection gazing at her.

'What did you say, Dom?'

'The terrible things we just saw: the ship's transom, the ship's sides, the scales. You saw them too. Why didn't you warn us?'

Before Flavia could reply, Sinistra said, 'It was my oversight, Chief. I should have spoken up on the Herculaneum. I mistakenly believed all of you had experience of …'

'No, I mean the mission trainers,' said Domitian. 'The Senate, the dropship instructors, Tiberius, even Manius—they said nothing. In all my years in the service, I've never seen anything like it. Most of us haven't.'

'I don't disagree, Chief,' said Sinistra. 'But I think now is not the time. There are still immediate dangers we must address. I would like to suggest …'

But Flavia cut her off.

'Dangers, Chief?' Flavia said, straightening the family crest pin once more. 'Hardly dangers. We aren't in hostile territory. We'll soon be among friends and family.'

'Even so,' said Domitian. 'Let us pray that Owanthan protects us and protects them, too.'

'Owanthan again, Chief?' said Flavia. 'Do you really think Owanthan is watching our mission? It doesn't seem like it. If anything, it seems like it's Sirhain who's watching it. Our entire planet is going to ruin and the gods don't notice a thing. Maybe they haven't heard. Maybe they're holidaying in another galaxy.'

'Don't be flippant, Flavia,' said Domitian. 'Not at a time like this.'

Ranant folded his arms over his chest. 'Well, where are they—these friendly family members of ours?'

'Have some patience, Captain,' said Flavia. 'Be useful. Make sure your marines are neat and presentable. They will act as my ceremonial guards.'

Sinistra saw Flavia use an expression she'd never noticed before. She winked at Ranant. Ranant saw it and smiled at her.

Instantly, she felt a stab of pain in her chest. This was yet another new feeling to add to the myriad emotions that emerged from her Hyacinth-creature mind each day. She didn't know the name for this new pain. She only knew she didn't like it, and didn't want to feel it again.

'Lieutenant Flavia,' she said. 'May I make my suggestions now?'

Flavia closed her eyes. 'If you must, Second Lieutenant.'

'While we're waiting, we should check the ship's systems to make sure they're functioning, especially the mechanisms for propulsion, communications, and navigation. We should also check the cannons.'

Sinistra expected a caustic reply. But Flavia simply said, 'Good idea. It will give you something to do.'

'Thank you. I also suggest we examine the wall or barrier that's ahead of the ship. There might be a carving or message there. It might explain where we are.'

'To be honest,' said Ranant. 'I would be happier if we got out of here. If this doesn't turn out to be the Parthia, we could knock a hole through that wall. These blast rifles could do it.'

'What are you talking about?' said Flavia, who was now smoothing a flesh-colored paste over the small, red lesion on her neck. 'We're waiting for the Parthians.'

'We can't leave, Captain Ranant,' said Sinistra. 'Not until we fix the engines.'

'So why not blast a hole? I know I'm the marine here, not navy command, but I think we need options. If there's a hole, the Herculaneum can send another ship. It could come right onto this deck and pick us up.'

'You are correct, Captain Ranant,' said Flavia, turning around. She showed him her new bright smile. 'You are not navy command.'

'With your permission, First Lieutenant,' said Sinistra. 'I'm going to try the bow lamps.'

When Flavia made no reply, Sinistra sat back down at the console and tried the controls. To everyone's surprise, the lamps came alive. Two beams shot forth from the bow and two distant circles of light revealed a milky gray barrier in the distance.

Sinistra switched on a small microphone on the console and said, 'Dilata.' On the viewport, the wall grew and advanced towards them. Ripples appeared on its surface, then grew into shapes.

'What are they—more murals?' said Ranant. 'More Hyacinth women on hills?'

'Maybe,' Sinistra said. 'Or something else—something that might explain why we were pulled in here.'

'Or a warning,' said Domitian. 'I don't see how you can be so certain this is friendly, Flavia.'

'Don't be foolish, Dom.' Flavia walked to the viewport. Her luscious hair bounced and her newly red lips glistened. 'I can't see anything,' she said. 'Can't you make it clearer?'

'Not without taking the Albus closer,' said Sinistra.

'Well,' said Flavia. 'The answer is simple. We'll have to see for ourselves. Come on, who'll go with me? Captain Ranant, why don't you and I stroll out there and see?'

Sinistra said, 'Lieutenant Flavia, I suggest we all stay aboard. It would be safer to send out the marines first.'

'That's right,' said Ranant, patting the shoulder of one of his men. 'I'll send out these two. They'll be like your advance escort.'

Flavia smiled. 'All right, Captain Ranant. That's a wonderful idea. Your marines might find a message from Captain Strahklan. No, Lieutenant Sinistra, whatever you are going to say, I don't want to hear it. Captain Ranant, send out your marines.'

28

Ranant shouted at marines in the growls of native language. Then he doubled up and clutched his throat.

'I forgot,' he rasped.

Then, he tried once more. 'Marines! Perge ad murus, lustra, nuntia. Ne sine licentia tua arma accendas.' Proceed to the barrier. Survey it and report. Do not fire your weapons unless I order it.

The two marines came alive. They saluted, slung the blast rifles over their shoulders, then clomped into the hissing air lock. The hatch closed after them.

'Testing comms equipment,' said Ranant. 'Marines, can you hear me?'

'Yes, Captain.'

'Good. On you go.'

The ship's outer hatch opened. The two marines stepped onto the gangway and down into the gloom. Their heavy steps shook the deck. Then the clomping ceased, and the marines dropped from sight until they appeared in the forward viewport. The bow lanterns turned their armor a dirty grey, and threw two long, writhing shadows ahead of them, as if the two marines were herding a pair of grotesque monsters.

'Dimidium half-milia ad aggerem, Capitaneus.'

'Perge,' said Ranant. Proceed.

'Nulla atmosphera,' added the metallic voice. No atmosphere. 'Gravitas eadem est ac navis principalis.' The gravity is similar to that of the main ship.

'Notandum,' said Ranant.

'Good,' said Flavia. 'As I expected. Ask if they sense any presences.'

'Presences? What do you mean?'

'Life force presences, of course, and intelligences—ones apart from ourselves. Can they do that?'

'Maybe.'

Ranant issued the command.

The metallic voice replied. 'Est aliquid.' There is something.

'Well,' said Ranant. 'What do you think?'

'The Parthia survivors,' said Flavia. 'We are getting closer.'

'But are they sure it's a presence from one of our kinsmen?' said Domitian.

'What else could it be, Chief? The gods, again? Owanthan? Another civilization? Don't make me laugh?'

'I hope you're right, Flavia,' said Domitian. 'I pray to Owanthan you're right.'

'Don't pray for me, Chief Domitian. Pray for our kinsmen.'

In the viewport, the marines clomped further away, herding their monsters. The lamps on their helmets bobbed in the gloom. After a quarter hora, two walking shadows rose on the distant wall. The shadows confronted the marines. The lamplight banished them. Flavia spoke to the console. 'Marines, show the view from your helmet cameras.'

A separate screen appeared on the main viewport. A bobbing view of the wall came up.

'Captain Ranant, tell them to stand still.'

Ranant sent the orders. The image of the wall steadied. It showed the two marines themselves standing before the wall with the Albus behind them.

'Not again?' said Ranant. 'This is becoming a joke.'

'Order them to scan left and right,' said Flavia.

Ranant issued the new order. The helmet lamps swung right. They picked out a series of images showing the Albus's passage from the Herculaneum to the object.

'Scan further,' said Flavia.

More images slid across the screen: the Herculaneum surrounded by stars; the Herculaneum standing off from a large planet that was attended by three moons—two small, one large.

'The home planet,' said Domitian.

Further along the wall, the next image displayed what looked like the Senate building.

'Stop,' said Flavia.

'What if we keep going?' said Domitian. 'Will the wall show our history all the way to the old planet?'

'It might,' Flavia said. 'The Parthia survivors have been here for centuries. They might have even created these murals to teach a new generation, born out here. Now, Captain, order your men to swing the light the other way.'

Ranant issued the order. The distant lights swung back along the murals. History advanced to the present. Then, the view displayed the same scene on the object's exterior: a female, two males, and two marines standing in what appeared to be a fog or a cloud or a swarm.

'What is it?' said Domitian. 'That mist—what can it be?'

'And why are there only three of us, not four?' said Ranant. 'One figure is missing. And is that you, Flavia, or Sinistra?'

'Order them to keep scanning,' said Flavia.

The scene changed. A new image slid into view: the same image as the one that appeared on the panel outside. A

Hyacinth woman stood on a hill. Beneath her, a multitude of Hyacinth creatures raised their arms to her with their mouths open.

But now, something was different. There were two figures beside the woman. One was a shorter female. The other was a Hyacinth male. The male wore a robe and a beard.

'Who is it?' said Domitian.

'Who is who?' said Flavia.

'The figure with the beard. Is it Cicero after he becomes governor of Hyacinth?'

'No. It might be Captain Strahklan. He was always a dandy,' said Flavia, 'long before he became famous.'

'But why is he in Hyacinth-creature form? His mission orders were to observe the Hyacinth creatures, not imitate them, and certainly not to meet them. And who is that tall female supposed to be?'

'It's Flavia,' said Ranant, smiling. 'It must be you, Flavia. There's only one person on the Herculaneum who looks like that.'

'Yes, Captain Ranant,' said Flavia. 'I think you might be right. This is wonderful. Order them to scan further.'

But the marines' cameras found only more blank, porous wall. The future was unknown, or the mural creators had stopped.

'Seen enough?' said Ranant

'More than enough,' said Flavia. 'I think it's now clear.'

'What's clear?' said Domitian. 'Do we wait for the bearded figure to show up?'

'No, we must be more enterprising. Captain Tiberius and the Senate will expect it.'

'Captain Tiberius and the senate don't know where we are,' said Domitian.

'When they know what I'm planning, they will approve it. They'll thank me.'

'And what's that?' said Domitian. 'What are you

planning, Lieutenant? A thought message?'

'More than that, Dom. We must go forth to greet them. Obviously, we've been issued with an invitation. The Parthians are cautious. They don't recognize us. They want us to make the first gesture of friendship.'

She turned and looked at Sinistra.

'And while we go to meet our kinsmen, Lieutenant Sinistra will stay aboard the Albus. Don't look so hurt, Lieutenant, and don't say a word. No, don't start talking about the mission priorities. I don't want to hear it. Not now. Just think. You'll have temporary command of the ship. If I were you, I'd make the most of it. It will be your last. Now, Captain Ranant! The airlock hatch, if you please.'

29

Flavia straightened the cuffs of her jacket. Then, she fastened her jacket's top buttons, covering over her famous Hyacinth-creature bust. Finally, she pushed the pin of her family crest deeper into her lapel, so that her ancestor pinned the writhing, prone Goth directly onto its back.

Then without looking at Sinistra, she said, 'Now, Lieutenant.'

The hatch slid open, and Flavia stepped into the airlock, smiling at Ranant, as he and Domitian followed. It wasn't necessary to go through the airlock routine. There was no air outside. Sinistra closed the hatch anyway, as if there were. She regretted it, and hoped Flavia wouldn't notice.

Flavia's face appeared in the small, round window, speaking silently and frowning at her. Sinistra switched on the comms.

'Lieutenant Sinistra,' said Flavia's voice. 'Don't contact us unless it's necessary. And I've warned you already about abusing thought messaging. I don't want the Herculaneum to hear—not yet. Now, Captain Ranant. Please place your firm hand on that lever and pull.'

Ranant pulled the lever. The airlock outer hatch unsealed. Flavia laughed and touched Ranant's arm. Domitian looked out at Sinistra with a facial expression she couldn't interpret. Later, she would understand what it meant. It meant 'I'm sorry.'

Sinistra sat by the console, alone. There she was: the withered shrub with the yellow hair, the blotched skin, uneven facial features, a lame foot, and threatened career. She had suffered rebuke and accusations of insubordination. She had endured humiliation and rejection. Now, she had to sit and watch Flavia court danger for the Albus and the entire mission. No, she thought. Things are definitely non est bonum. Not good. At all.

But could she stop Flavia and her recklessness? Possibly. She could send a thought message to Telepathy and the captain. She could try the cannons, too, blasting a hole in the wall, as Ranant suggested. But any of these actions would only condemn her further. Instead, she sent a secret to Nim, billions of milia away on the home planet. As usual, Nim did not reply. She never did.

Sinistra sighed in frustration. She sat back in the pilot's chair and waited for Flavia to come out from the gloom and go striding past the ship's bow. She could never have guessed that her own world was about to change.

As she watched the viewport, a small light on the console lit up. It blinked urgently in six double beats. Then it went blank. Secunda later, it lit up again, blinking its doublets six times before going out. The small light was a warning that the sensors had detected something outside the ship, and the something wasn't Flavia, Domitian, Ranant, the marines, or the wall.

For now, the 'something' was far astern of the Albus, at the limit of the sensor's range. But it would soon come closer.

Nim, thought Sinistra. Nim, old friend, old comrade. Surely things can't get worse than this.

But they could.

And they did.
And soon.

30

Solitude closed in.

The air pumps hissed, and the circuits hummed. Beneath the Albus's keel, the struts creaked as they resettled themselves to the reduced load. Otherwise, there was nothing but silence, solitude, and heavy defeat.

Sinistra looked at the forward viewport. The three figures came round from the Albus's port side and stepped into the glow of the bow lamps.

The lamplights exaggerated the differences in Hyacinth-creature locomotion: Ranant strode; Domitian stepped with stiff, unbending knees; and Flavia sashayed extravagantly. Sashay—was that the right word? It meant to walk in an ostentatious but casual manner. There was no equivalent word in the native language. The closest word was the name of a mating gesture.

A mating gesture! Ye gods!

Then Sinistra watched Ranant drop behind Flavia. Why? Wasn't he supposed to lead the way? Or was he trying to get a better view of Flavia's famous figure? Could he actually find Flavia's swaying hips more diverting than the darkness, the wall, the murals, the danger?

Apparently, he could.

Sinistra turned away and began her inspection of the ship. Before checking the engines, she reached for the weapons controls, and switched on the Albus's complement of cannons. She heard the portholes open with a satisfying clunk. So far, so good. But would the cannons actually fire?

Next, she checked the engines, the thrusters, the battery, the atmosphere pumps, the gravity pumps, and the Albus's small hold. The pumps were operating as normal. She knew that already. There was nothing unusual in the hold. What had she expected—a stowaway? The console signaled the engines functioned, too, and yet they didn't respond to any commands.

Sinistra flicked the switch to unlock the engine pit cover. Before she left her chair, she took a last look at the forward viewport. The three figures had receded towards the marines at the wall. The sensors showed they were a third of the way there. Ranant had moved forward to walk beside Flavia. Their shoulders touched. Flavia even pretended to stumble, so that Ranant had to put an arm around her shoulders and steady her. Sinistra guessed they were also using thought communication, not the comms devices.

Don't look, she thought, her feelings rising. Don't look. You'll see something you don't like. She didn't want to see anything to confirm her fear that her romance with Ranant—if it could be called a romance—was well and truly over.

Instead, she turned about in her chair, stood up, and limped to the engine pit. She knelt down and stared at the various hoses, fuel tanks, and exhaust pipes. But just as she leaned closer to examine the wires leading to the control panel, she noticed something at the edge of her sight.

A small light on the console was flashing. It flashed again, and again, in six bursts of rapid, blue, double beats, like a faraway beacon on the sea. She stood up and walked back to the console and examined this light. It was a very unusual light—one rarely called into action: the stern sensor light.

Sinistra sat down in the chair and squinted at the screen displaying the view from the stern. Until now, the screen had been blank and dark. Now it was not. Something had crossed over the sensor's outer limit.

But what was it?

She sat down in the co-pilot's chair and wondered. If she had to describe what she saw, Sinistra might have called it a wave or a tide. It wasn't an individual or an object, small and upright. Instead, it was wide, like the sea sliding up the sand on a beach. It looked flat, insistent, but benign.

She flicked on the Albus's stern lamps and cameras. They showed nothing but the pale, gray deck going away into thick darkness.

But on the sensor screen, the tide or whatever it was, had advanced an eighth of a leuga toward the ship. An eighth of a leuga! Whatever was out there moved faster than a Hyacinth creature could run.

Sinistra stood up from the chair. Something was wrong. Something was out there. True, it might only be the Parthia survivors. Many of them. But Sinistra's intuition warned her that whatever this wave or tide was, the Albus's officers should return to the ship until they could investigate it.

She reached for the comms device. She stopped and imagined how furious Flavia would be. Then she reached again.

'Lieutenant Flavia,' this is Albus.

The comms did not reply. No surprise there. Flavia would ignore her, even if she had bothered to fit her earpiece.

Sinistra thought about sending a telepathic message. Not yet, she thought. Not until it's unavoidable. Instead, she picked up one of Ranant's communication devices, and said, 'Marines!'

After a secunda, a metallic voice spoke over the ship's comms. 'Marines reading you, Albus.'

'This is Second Lieutenant Sinistra speaking. I have a

message for Captain Ranant and Lieutenant Flavia when they arrive.'

'Yes, Lieutenant.'

'The message is, "Unknown danger approaching from Albus's stern. Return to ship immediately. Danger." Have you got that?'

'Unknown danger. Albus's stern. Return to Albus immediately.'

'That's right. Return immediately, but ask them to speak to me first. The first lieutenant and Captain Ranant aren't wearing their comms.' She looked at the tide creeping across the sensor's screen. 'It's urgent, Marines.'

'Understood, Lieutenant.'

She put the comms device down and watched the forward viewport. Flavia, Ranant, and Domitian were still far from the wall—probably several minuta away. By the time they arrived, it might be too late. This tide or whatever it was might have swept all the way to the wall, knocking the party from its feet.

She wondered if Flavia could swim. Flavia was a navy officer, and therefore trained to swim like everyone else, but that was in her natural state, not her Hyacinth one. She also wondered whether Flavia would have paid any attention to the lessons. She probably thought lessons were beneath her, just as she thought navy protocol was beneath her, too.

Sinistra picked up the comms device once more.

'Marines! Albus.'

'Yes, Albus.'

'Shine your helmet lamp on the wall to your left, please.'

'The wall to our left. Yes, Lieutenant. Moving now.'

On the forward viewport, the tiny lights moved in the gloom. In the close up from the helmet camera, one mural had changed. It showed three Hyacinth-creature figures, the wall, the marines, and the encroaching tide almost upon them.

But there was one difference to the previous mural of the 'swarm' or 'mist', as Domitian had described it. Sinistra thought she saw a thick limb with long, raking claws.

'Marines! New orders.'

'Yes, Lieutenant.'

'I'm overriding Captain Ranant's previous orders. Leave your position. Leave immediately. Advance toward the Albus. Intercept Captain Ranant, Lieutenant Flavia, and Chief Domitian.'

'Leave the position ordered by Captain Ranant, Lieutenant?'

'Now, Marine! Leave immediately. Both of you.'

'Yes, Lieutenant. Immediately.'

'When you reach Lieutenant Flavia, tell her to return to the Albus. Then with your weapons raised, walk forward and aft of the officers in a defensive formation.'

'Yes, Lieutenant. Moving now.'

'And, Marines.'

'Yes, Lieutenant.'

'Arm your weapons, and run.'

She saw the tiny lights in the distance. The view from their helmets changed from a view of the wall to a view of the Albus's lights, and the three small figures coming forward like ghosts in the gloom.

The comms came alive. 'Moving now. Weapons armed and ready, Lieutenant.'

'Good. Report to me if you see anything in the dark other than the three crew members.'

'Yes, Lieutenant.'

She wondered if she should break protocol and send a thought message after all. Had it come to that? Had it come to where she could disobey Flavia's orders yet again? Could she risk another black mark against her career?

She cursed Flavia's recklessness—cursed her in the growls and barks of the native language. The pain in her throat was worth it. Flavia, the chief warrant officers, the chief petty officers, and perhaps even Captain Tiberius himself—all of them weren't up to their jobs. That was the truth. They were incompetent. Worse! They didn't even know they were incompetent. They were sentimental appointments and a danger to the mission, which meant they were a danger to the survival of the people.

She sat back in the chair, surprised at herself. The words made her feel a fresh surge of emotions. First, the usual shame and fear showed up. They lurked beneath the surface of her thoughts, waiting for their chance. But now she felt something more. She felt relief. She knew she had made the right decision. Despite the risk of rebuke and disapproval, she had allowed her sense of duty to win. Duty had long coexisted with fear, balancing the scales, but now duty had finally asserted itself. It had won, and for the moment, shame, fear, and self-loathing kept their distance, like creatures afraid of a dangerous foe.

Back on the screen, the mist or tide or swarm advanced. It was like a wave closing on the Albus from three sides. Worse! As in the wall image, it was no longer a formless shape. It rippled like the surface of a lake in a breeze. No, not rippled. That wasn't it. So what was it doing? Rolling? Undulating? No. A more terrifying description presented itself.

It writhed.

She turned to the Albus's weapons controls and flicked the switch to arm the cannons. The control panel lit up with blinking red lights and the words, 'Periculum. Telem ratio exercet.' Danger. System engaged.

Good, she thought. At least something is going right. I'll fire two blasts: one blast aimed high over the tide, and one to warn Flavia, Ranant, and Domitian. She set the stern cannons' elevation to forty-five degrees. Then she pulled the fire lever and gripped the chair's armrests, bracing for the recoil.

But there was nothing.

She pulled the lever again.

Nothing.

She tried twice more.

Nothing and nothing.

So much for the cannons.

She looked at the forward screens. The marines had not yet reached Flavia, Ranant, and Domitian. She turned to the stern screens, hoping the tide had gone. But the tide was closer. Its details were more distinct. Now, it wasn't a tide 'writhing.' It was many creatures moving—many enormous creatures. And they weren't just moving. They were galloping.

Her hand slowly rose to her blotched throat.

She saw rising snouts, arching backs, big triangular ears, driving limbs, flashes of long claws, and probing, questing snouts. They were familiar to her. She had seen them before, back in the remote, dark forests of her childhood, and on the artist's renderings of fauna from the home planet.

But never in such numbers.

These writhing, plunging shapes could only be one kind of creature. They were the large, terrifying animals of the Northern Forests, the ones with whom the people shared the home planet but rarely encountered or wished to meet.

In her own language, they were called a name that translated as forest giants. In the new Hyacinth language, they were named after one of the Romans' own list of hated enemies, the ones who waited on the empire's frontiers to attack, to sack, burn, and kill.

They were the Goths.

31

The Goths?
 Impossible.
 And yet.
 Sinistra froze the image on the screen and magnified the section at the edge where the 'mist' looked most ragged. Were those ears, paws, heads, flanks, snouts, and teeth? Sinistra rubbed her eyes and scratched her neck.
 The evidence was there.
 Goths.
 Not conceivable.
 But apparently true.
 Goths.
 The sensors even measured their heights—twice that of a standing male Hyacinth creature.
 As unimaginable as it seemed, a herd of Goths from the home planet rampaged in the object's dark vacuum, galloping their way towards the Albus, and towards Flavia, Domitian, and Ranant.
 Sinistra looked over her shoulder as if the silent creatures were about to burst through the stern bulkhead, or knock the Albus from its landing carriage, and tear open the hull.
 So now what?

Her first thought was of Flavia. How would she react to the news? What would she do? Would she believe it? Probably, she would say that Sinistra was mad, that's what she would do. She would also add that Sinistra was insubordinate, attention-seeking, and unfit for duty.

But if Sinistra did nothing, the situation would quickly turn dangerous. The Goths would do what Goths always did. They would overwhelm Flavia, Domitian, and Ranant. Then they would tear them to pieces, ripping them open, flinging about their entrails, just like in the early days of the home planet, before the clearing of the Southern Forests.

Sinistra felt her hated digestive organs squirm. Her Hyacinth-creature heart clenched in her chest. She stood and walked to the airlock, then walked back to the pilot's chair, caught between duty and fear, between her need to do something for the mission, and her need for the good opinion of her superior officer.

As always—just as it had been from the beginning of her career.

But this time, there was a difference. A quiet voice she had never heard before whispered in her mind, 'If you do nothing, you will never have to worry about Flavia's opinion again.'

She waited for the voice to whisper again. When it said nothing, she asked, If I do as you say, what then? What will happen after the Goths leave Flavia lying dead and silent on the cold deck?

The answer came: You will command.

Sinistra shook the thought away. She could never do such a thing. She wanted approval, not command, or at least not high command where there was no one left to impress, and where she would be alone with her shame and self-loathing.

Instead, she thought more about the Goths. How did they get here? What were they doing so far from the home planet? Who brought them and why? How did they breathe?

What did they eat? What did hunt in this dark void?

There were no explanations. The Goths could hunt nothing out there, and they couldn't breathe in the void, and it was impossible for them to be here. Who would even consider such a thing?

And yet, here they were.

She checked the forward viewport. Far ahead, the marines' helmet lamps bobbed towards Flavia. How soon would they reach her? Not soon enough?

On the stern viewport, the Goth tide was closer.

She took a calm breath and decided. She walked to the rear of the cabin, opened the weapons locker, and pulled out Ranant's spare blast rifle.

The rifle was shockingly heavy. The weight of it dragged her down to the deck. It was meant for the mechanical marines or powerful males, such as Ranant, not for withered shrubs. She tried again, lifting the sling strap over her left shoulder, and letting the shoulder stock rest on the deck, taking the weight. This was better, but not by much. How would she ever fire this weapon? How would she hold it steady? How would she even lift its heavy barrel?

Then she stepped to the airlock and opened the hatch, dragging the shoulder stock behind her. She wondered if this was the moment to break protocol and send a warning message using telepathic thoughts.

Not yet. I've got enough black marks against my name already. She stepped down the gangway, down from the safe, warm Albus, to the cold, hard deck and the airless gloom.

Damned if I do, she thought. Damned if I don't.

So, with her stiff legs, lame foot, and cumbersome weapon, she set off. As she limped along, she glanced behind, looking for eyes and teeth. Then she jogged a few steps before the rifle's drag and sway nearly pulled her over. She stopped, adjusted the strap, and limped on towards the darkness, the light, and her future.

32

As soon as she passed the Albus's bow, Sinistra felt fear slide up beside her like a silent companion. The darkness rushed at her. The glow of the lamplights pushed it away, but it regrouped, waiting for its chance to surge back in.

She changed her mind about using telepathy. She sent a thought ahead of her.

First Lieutenant. There's an emergency. An angry stampede of Goth is approaching from behind the Albus. Repeat. A Goth stampede. Overwhelming numbers. Three to five minuta till arrival at the most. Urge retreat to Albus. If there is no time to return, expand to natural form for defensive purposes. Extreme danger.

She'll thank me, Sinistra thought privately. When she sees them, she'll thank me.

She looked back at the Albus, expecting the worst: yellow claws about to strike; long, curved teeth wet with drool; dead, shiny eyes. Hundreds of them! Maybe thousands. But there was still nothing but the Albus's lantern beams streaming into the gloom, like the phosphorescent tentacles of a deep sea creature.

Meanwhile, no reply came to her telepathic message.

Two minuta later, she limp-jogged up to Flavia, Domitian,

and Ranant just as the marines clomped into view from the opposite direction.

To her surprise, Flavia sent a thought message of her own.

Leaving your post, Lieutenant? You don't know when to stop, do you? I'm reaching the point where I will ask Captain Ranant to arrest you and lock you in the hold.

Lieutenant Flavia, Sinistra said. The comms didn't work. You didn't reply.

Flavia smiled. We made a discovery. The earpieces don't work in a vacuum. It seems you're not the space expert you claim to be—either that or you're just forgetful. Which is it?

I'm sorry, Lieutenant, I …

Forgot?

No, I … beg pardon, Lieutenant, but we are facing an extreme situation. You saw the mural. You saw what it predicted about an attack on us.

I saw no attack.

The mural showed a fog or a swarm or a wave.

Yes, that was Dom's word: a swarm. Are you saying we're going to be attacked by insects—in space?

No. I mean a pack, a mob, a herd, a legion, whatever is the right word—but not of insects. The sensors imply we're going to be attacked by larger animals—much larger.

Goths, Lieutenant? That's what your message said. Which Goths—Equatorial Goths or Northern Forest Goths?

I know it sounds ridiculous, Sinistra replied, but that's what the sensors indicated.

Only indicated? You don't sound very certain, Lieutenant.

I've seen night-imaging of Goths before. The images I saw on the Albus are the same: the same ears, the same snouts, and the same gallop. I know it's impossible. How could they be here? How do they breathe? It's impossible, and it's ridiculous. I see that. But many things in here seem impossible. We must get back to the Albus where we can defend ourselves.

Flavia smiled even broader. You are not only insubordinate, Lieutenant, but you are also mad, just as Doctor Galen warned. And now you are hindering our search for the Parthia survivors. We will not indulge your insanity. You are ordered back to the Albus to wait until we return. So, if you please, take your rifle and hobble away.

Domitian interrupted.

Flavia. I think you should see something.

No, Dom. Whatever it is, I don't want to hear about Owanthan and his wife, or Angworn and his queen, or the other gods, and I certainly don't want to hear any defense of the soon-to-be ex-lieutenant.

It's not that. I think there's something back there.

He raised his chin at the Albus.

They all looked back at the tall ship standing on its landing carriage. The port bow lamps blinked. Then the other lamp beams flickered. Something flashed across them —once, twice, then again, and again. Within seconds, all the lamps blinked as if heavy rain were falling. Then the beams vanished entirely. Now, the only light came from the Marine's helmet lamps.

Not good, said Ranant's voice in their minds. Look around.

The marines' small lamps picked out a terrible sight. A front of hundreds of bulbous eyes gleaming in the dark; loping creatures twice the height of Ranant; curved white teeth as long as a Hyacinth creature's hand, and glistening black fur as far as anyone could see.

Your orders, Lieutenant Flavia? Sinistra said in her mind. Lieutenant?

No reply came. Flavia must be in one of her moods again. Sinistra could see her eyes flicking left and right at the Goths, and a strange sneer forming on her lips. Her right hand reached for the family-crest pin and straightened it on her lapel.

Ranant's voice said, I think Flavia's out again. What do you want to do?

No one replied. Then, Sinistra said, Captain Ranant. We can't outrun them. We'll have to confront them here. Tell your marines to raise their weapons. Tell them to fire into the snout of any creature that comes closer than a Hyacinth creature's body length. Otherwise, don't fire at all. A shot will antagonize them.

Sinistra unslung her own heavy rifle, and ignoring Ranant's outstretched hand, tried to raise the forestock to her chin. The weight was staggering, but she kept on trying until she could look down the barrel at the terrifying, writhing mass of fury at the end of the sights.

Captain Ranant, she said in a thought message. Order your marines to stand on either side of us. Domitian, please move into the middle, beside Flavia. Captain Ranant, do you hear me? But it was Flavia who answered. Her thought voice sounded toneless, flat, and strange.

I can hear you, Lieutenant. We can all hear you. The whole galaxy can hear you. But I disagree. We don't need to defend ourselves. We need to do the opposite. We must do as our ancestors would do.

We must attack.

33

Attack, Lieutenant Flavia? But we don't have the numbers.

So, you're an expert on Goths now too, as well as everything else?

No, Sinistra said. I grew up near the Northern Forests and saw the Goths regularly—from a distance, of course. I saw what they can do in large numbers like this.

In your orphanage?

Yes, First Lieutenant, in my orphanage. I've seen the Goths' behavior and can understand a few words of their language. I have seen them hunt and fight each other. We shouldn't believe the myths. Our folklore exaggerates. We're not invincible to them, not even in our natural forms—at least not when we're outnumbered.

You presume these shadows really *are* Goths.

Domitian's voice said, What else can they be?

They might be anything. They might be a light display staged by the Parthia survivors to show they're from home.

Now Ranant's voice spoke. If this is a light display, I'd hate to see the real thing. Look at their teeth.

No one said anything more. No one had seen real Goths except Sinistra. Now here they were in their hundreds or thousands. They surrounded the small group, baying and snarling in the darkness, lunging and retreating, or veering away at the last minute, like gang members on a street.

Lieutenant Flavia, said Sinistra's voice. It would be safer if you stood between the marines.

Flavia made no reply. Surprisingly, she didn't flinch as the Goths lunged from the darkness, tossing their snouts and splaying their nasal flukes as they sniffed the airless void.

Please, Lieutenant, step back. Lieutenant?

Then, Flavia's thought voice came deep and flat into everyone's mind. I'm not afraid. My ancestor, Colonel Krant, fought these creatures and killed them by the millions, including two Goth princes. In my family's house, there are Goth skins and Goth claws. There are also Goth heads mounted on the walls.

I urge you to be careful, Lieutenant, said Sinistra. You are in range of a paw swipe. The word swipe doesn't really describe what those claws can do. They can probably cut a Hyacinth-creature body in half. Then, there are the teeth.

Domitian said, And they're not shadows or light play, Flavia. See how their drool splashes on the deck? They're real.

So what are they doing here? said Flavia. What's the Old Book say about Goths in Hyacinth temples floating in Ilium?

I don't know, said Domitian. Like everything else here, it makes no sense, but there must be an explanation. Maybe the Parthia carried a Goth pair on their mission to Hyacinth. Now an army of them has bred over the centuries.

Why would anyone bring Goths to Hyacinth?

I don't know, but there might be a reason. The Herculaneum also carries strange sea-chests whose contents are unknown, even to the captain. Maybe the Admiralty ordered it as an experiment.

You can't be serious, Domitian.

I'm thinking aloud, Flavia. I might be wrong, but at least it's an explanation. If you have a better one, I'd like to hear it.

One of the Goths thrust its head at Flavia. Its snout, neck, and shoulders flashed in the lamplight. Its snout sniffed at her so vigorously that its black nostrils flared like the dark funnels on the Herculaneum's transom. Then the Goth reared on its hind legs, towering above them all.

This can't be real, said Flavia's voice.

Then, as if recognizing an old enemy, the Goth dropped back to all fours and swung a giant paw, with yellow claws extended as long as a Hyacinth creature forearm. The claws raked Flavia's blue uniform, tearing a yellow epaulet from her shoulder and slicing the blue cloth from her neck down to her hip.

The two marines swung their rifles at the Goth and prepared to fire.

Sinistra spoke to Ranant. Tell them to stop. Tell them not to shoot this Goth or any of the Goths—not yet.

What do you mean don't shoot? said Ranant's voice. You saw what it did.

It was a warning, said Sinistra. Firing the weapons will only make them more hostile. They'll stay away if we keep calm. They'll attack us if we provoke them.

Keep calm? said Ranant. That's it? How long should we keep calm?

Can you see any Goths behind us? Sinistra asked. Are there any Goths between us and the wall?

Hard to say, replied Ranant. I can't see anything.

Then, we'll just have to take a leap of faith. With Lieutenant Flavia's permission, we should retreat slowly towards the wall.

And then what?

We can defend ourselves better with the wall at our backs.

Why don't we try to reach the Albus? said Domitian.

Can you see the Albus, Chief Warrant Officer?

Domitian looked back towards the ship. There was

nothing there. The horde blocked the lamplight beams entirely.

Then, as if reading everyone's thoughts, two more Goths reared onto their hinds legs. Their terrible, open maws, and bared teeth, rose into the darkness. Their bodies blocked the way. There was no way back to the Albus.

Lieutenant Flavia, Sinistra said. Permission to move towards the wall.

Flavia's thought voice replied in the same, strange, flat tone. I'm not moving anywhere.

But you can see they're in a frenzy, said Ranant.

I'm in a frenzy, too, said Flavia. I'm going to do what my ancestors did. I'm going to teach these filthy creatures a lesson.

Wait, please, Lieutenant, said Sinistra. Don't do anything. Let me try something first.

She sent a thought out in the few words of Goth she knew. Friends, she thought in Goth tones of growls and barks. We not fight. Not fight. Friends.

She waited. Then she heard a reply.

Get back! came the growled Goth voice. Get back or die. Get back or die. Die by paws, claws, and teeth. Get back or die by paws, claws, and teeth.

Get back? Sinistra replied. Get back where?

Back, came a growled thought. Get back!

Get back where? Wall? Ship? Home?

Get back, came the reply. Or die by paws, claws and teeth.

What do you want? Sinistra said.

The words 'get back' growled in Sinistra's mind once more, followed by a word she didn't recognize. It sounded like the Hyacinth word 'strain.'

Get back, the Goths said. Get back. Get back. Strain. Strain. STRAIN!

What? What is strain?

Strain said the Goths. Strain.

Do you mean Sirhain?

No explanation came, except the words Get back! Get back! Or die by paws, claws, and teeth.

Sinistra stood, thinking. The marines stood waiting with their rifles raised. The small forestock lights blinked, waiting. Beside the marines, Ranant stood with his fists balled. Domitian stood behind him, silently mouthing a prayer. Flavia stood in the semi-dark. Her beautiful face rippled like the dunes in the desert on the Domum Deck. A vein throbbed in her slender neck.

And then Sinistra heard Flavia's voice once more, this time with a nasty edge.

How dare you! How dare you! You filthy creatures. How dare you!

Flavia, please don't, said Ranant, but Flavia ignored him, just as she ignored Sinistra and anyone else who disagreed with her.

In the weak light, Flavia's uniform tightened. The sleeves fattened. The pants legs bulged. The three rips in her jacket gaped wide, and the figure beneath them—so admired by the crew—was red, angry, and swollen.

Lieutenant Flavia, please don't, said Sinistra.

You said we should expand to our natural form, Lieutenant.

Yes, I know, but I was wrong. Now, I think it will only antagonize them. With your permission, we should stay in Hyacinth form, and fall back to the wall.

But it was too late.

The left sleeve of Flavia's uniform burst apart. A scaly forelimb glinted where the cloth ripped. Then, Flavia's shirt split completely, revealing her chest bubbling and gray. The shirt and the family-crest pin fell down beside Flavia's Goth hide boot. The stitching split open, revealing red skin and scales.

No, Lieutenant. Please don't.

Why in the galaxy not? came Flavia's reply, but not in her usual singsong voice. Instead, she barked and growled the native language. Someone, she said, has to teach these creatures some manners.

Get back! came the growls in Sinistra's mind. Get back! Strain. Get back. Strain.

A Goth thrust its head in front of Sinistra's face, its nasal flukes splaying, its two enormous eyes wet and glistening.

Dark friend, Sinistra thought. Please. We not attack. Not fight.

For a moment, the eyes softened as if the beast understood, but then they swung away towards Flavia, who now stood a head taller. Get back! Strain. Strain. Get back!

Sinistra heard Flavia's voice bark in her mind. Get that snout away from me or you'll feel it. Do you hear me?

How suddenly Flavia had changed in body and attitude! She didn't even care about her nakedness. The red mist of anger blinded her. What little self control she possessed was gone.

And then, everything became worse.

Much, much worse.

34

First, the Goths dropped to all fours and sniffed so hard at Flavia that their snouts bucked upwards like rifles after a shot.

Then they unsheathed their long yellow claws. Once fully extended, the claws fringed the small circle of light, like the exposed roots of a terrible garden. The Goths nearest to Flavia stalked forward, their snouts low, their eyes glistening.

Flavia stood before them, glaring back. She planted her own claws onto her scaly hips. She spread her feet apart and stood defiantly, challenging the Goths to attack.

Non est bonum, Nim, Sinistra thought. Most definitely non est bonum.

Steady, Flavia, said Domitian. They look like they're going to swipe at you again.

Let them, barked Flavia's voice.

Please, Lieutenant Flavia, said Sinistra. The Goths are confused. They don't recognize our Hyacinth forms. To them, we're just new creatures. But if you if you expand any further, they'll recognize us. They'll see you as the old enemy, even without smelling you. A pile-on will follow. You see that, don't you?

Absolutely not, Flavia growled. Our people, my people stand up to Goths. We always have. We never retreat. Our ancestors, my ancestors, drove these things far away. We banished them to the forests, killing them to make sure they understood. Now, I intend to follow my ancestors' example.

Sinistra began a thought message, then stopped. The singsong of the Hyacinth language sounded wrong. It didn't have the gravity she wanted. So, she thought in barks, snarls, and growls.

This time, she said, it's different. This is not the home planet. We are not an army and we have only two weapons. The Goths outnumber us by hundreds if not thousands. We cannot defeat them, whatever they are. We won't survive if they attack. The only thing to do is to keep calm. You must think of the mission, of our future on Hyacinth. Think of the Parthia survivors. They must know about these Goths. That's why they're hiding. They know the danger. They've seen it before. They have lived with it for centuries. Please, Lieutenant!

Too late, came Flavia's reply. There's nothing to do but teach these Goths a lesson, a good old-fashioned lesson about who is the dominant people in our world.

Then Ranant's voice spoke. Let my men do the fighting, Flavia. Don't risk yourself.

Brave talk, Captain, but what do you suggest? Do you want me to creep away? To cower? To obey them? My ancestors would never run. Neither will I.

I have prayed for Owanthan's help, said Domitian's voice.

No one replied. Flavia raised her chin high, as new scales slid down her stomach and back.

Sensing the change, the Goths stood on their hind limbs, forming a barrier like the dark edge of a thick forest at night. They faced Flavia in a standoff: the beautiful aristocrat and monstrous beasts.

All was still. No one spoke. Everything waited.

Then, just as Sinistra had feared, the last shreds of Flavia's uniform ripped from her arms, legs, and chest, and dropped to the deck. Flavia exploded outwards and upwards, rising into the darkness, twice the girth of the bulkiest Goth and three times his height.

As she grew, her own claws slid from her fingers. The scales thickened and locked together on her flanks. The muscles bubbled on her calves, chest, and arms. She grew so tall and so fast, her head was soon high in the darkness. Only her legs and waist remained in the weak light.

But her furious thoughts were all too present in everyone's minds.

I will teach these Goths who rules in this galaxy, she growled. I will show them who are the conquerors and who are the conquered. I will make them pay for their insolence at the battles of Grath and Kulawao—and here.

Lieutenant! Sinistra thought. It's not too late. But she stopped. A second thought flashed into her mind—a thought speaking in the same insidious voice that whispered to her in the Albus.

Leave her, the voice said. Let the Goths kill her and tear her up. It will be better for the mission, better for the new world on Hyacinth. And better for you, Sinistra. Better for you.

But Sinistra shoved this thought away, stealing a glance at Ranant and Domitian in case they had overheard.

But they said nothing.

Don't do it, Flavia, said Ranant's voice. Sin's right. Stop.

But Flavia kept on swelling and growing. The sight of her was even more astonishing in the silence. She was a giant rising and congealing, a colossus of the gloom, a nightmare figure even to those used to the natural form.

The Goths tilted their heads upwards, sniffing. Their great maws opened. Their tongues lolled, obscene and red. For a moment, they almost looked friendly, like giant pets, but soon, their maws clamped shut, and the claws twitched in their sheathes.

Undaunted, Flavia glowered down from the darkness. You filthy beasts, said her voice with all the venom the native tongue could inflict.

Then the first Goth attacked.

It exploded from the mass with astonishing power and leaped at Flavia's right knee. The long, yellow claws raked the knee's scales, scratching but not piercing them. The Goth's hind claws gauged the unprotected skin along Flavia's shin, plowing red and white furrows. Then the Goth toppled backward, its fore-claws raking at nothing. As the Goth fell, Flavia's fist swung down and struck its snout. The Goth dropped into the baying mob and was lost in the darkness.

This, growled Flavia's voice, is how we reassert dominance. It's how we establish the natural order. This is how planets are won.

By then, a second Goth launched itself at Flavia's knee. And this time, the yellow claws hooked into the gap between two scales. Flavia tried to kick it away, but the Goth hung on.

But not for long. The great fist swung again, this time down and up, knocking the creature away into the dark. The Goth's eyes closed and its chin lifted, as if it were asleep. Its four limbs flopped. No one saw where it dropped into the waves of fur and teeth.

A third Goth leaped, this time from Flavia's rear. It hung onto the softer flesh of her right calf muscle. Then, a fourth Goth jumped from the mass, then a fifth, then more, until as many Goths as could reach her began climbing the backs of Flavia's legs, straining to tear at the unarmored regions of her thighs.

Flavia swung a fist at each one, knocking them back down. But as soon as one fell away, another leaped from the mob to take its place. And after that, a thousand more waited their turns.

Captain Ranant, said Sinistra's voice. It's time.

Time for what, Lieutenant? I'm staying as I am. Look what they're doing to her.

No, I mean for your men. Order them to fire.

Only Flavia can order me to fire.

Just do it, Captain.

Aye, aye, said Ranant. He turned to the two marines. They waited with the big rifles pressed to their helmets. The small lights still blinked on the forestocks.

And Captain, said Sinistra, returning to the Hyacinth language.

Yes?

Remember. Aim for the maws not the bodies.

Their maws?

Yes, their maws—their ora, their rostra, their naso. I don't know the right word. You must hit their maws. No matter how powerful these new rifles might be, they won't do any damage against the Goths' flanks.

You haven't seen the rifles.

Just do it, Captain.

I still think we should wait for Flavia.

Sinistra found herself speaking words she never thought she could utter aloud.

Lieutenant Flavia is not competent, Captain. She is a danger to us and to the mission. She's not rational, and neither are her orders. Hurry, Captain. You are wasting time. The Goths will soon topple her, and then turn on us.

Ranant held out his hands and tilted his head at the rifle slung on Sinistra's shoulder.

Hand it to me, Sin.

So I'm Sin again?

Just give me the rifle.

Why? Will it knock me off my lame foot?

That's not what I mean.
Will my twisted up face smash into the deck?
What's come over you? Of course not.
The answer is no, Captain. The rifle is staying with me.
Don't be stupid. It's too heavy for you.
I'll manage.
You might hit something you shouldn't.
Just get your marines firing before it's too late.

Ranant closed his eyes, exhaled the non-existent air, turned away and gave the signal to his men.

Sinistra raised the rifle at the horde.

35

The beams from the marines' helmet lamps moved up Flavia's legs. The light revealed a glistening, shimmering nightmare: a tower of contorting fur, dripping claws, scales pried apart, and shredded, bleeding flesh.

Then, the lamplights steadied on two Goths biting the tops of Flavia's calves. As the light shone on them, the Goths' ears flicked upright. One Goth stopped biting and raised his head to stare dumbly into the light, his maw wet with black blood. The other Goth concentrated on the wound he had opened, sinking his teeth into the flesh, then twisting and yanking, until he tore the wound apart.

A secunda later, the huge rifles flashed in the silence. The muzzles climbed, the stock butts shoved into the marine's shoulders, forcing each back a step. Smoke drifted down to the deck.

Back on Flavia's legs, the two Goths found their lower jaws missing. A micro secunda later, a second set of blasts knocked them away completely. The impact was so great that their claws ripped from Flavia's legs and the Goths dropped out of the light with their claws scrabbling.

Once more, the heavy guns flashed. Two rabid Goths were hit in the shoulders and knocked sideways. Once hit, they turned to bite their own wounds until the next blasts ripped their snouts off, leaving only bone, gums and teeth. They too fell down into the throng.

Sinistra stood with her own rifle—not yet fired. She planted her boots far apart on the deck. Then, she aimed the quivering barrel at one Goth among the many on Flavia's knee.

But the rifle was too heavy. Sinistra could barely hold it steady, let alone aim it. She also didn't have a helmet lamp. She had to follow where the marines' lamps shone. One moment she could see the Goth climbing, the next, the darkness rushed in to conceal it.

It's time, Sin, said Ranant. Hand it to me.

Not yet. I've had a thought.

What thought?

But she was already transmitting to Flavia.

Lieutenant, can you see the Albus?

Flavia did not reply.

Can you fight your way there? We could follow—if the Goths let us.

I am not moving, Flavia said. All of you, return to your natural forms and help me. I order you.

I can't expand, Lieutenant.

Can't or won't?

Can't, Lieutenant.

Ranant, Domitian?

I don't know, Lieutenant, said Domitian.

Do it! said Flavia. Now!

Sinistra tried one last time. Lieutenant, I request permission to retreat to where we can defend ourselves.

No, Lieutenant, Flavia hissed.

Lieutenant, you're going to get us all killed.

You would like that, wouldn't you? Well, listen to me, Second Lieutenant …

But she didn't finish. Sinistra soon saw why. One Goth

had avoided Flavia's swinging fists, and pulled itself up her thigh, then her flank. Finally it pulled itself up to her shoulder, it sunk its claws into the hated flesh just above Flavia's collar bone.

Ranant pointed up at the Goth atop the swaying giant, and waved at his men to shoot it.

'Non patet, Capitaneus,' came the reply in the comms devices. The shot is not clear.

Meanwhile, Flavia grabbed the Goth by the neck and tried to wrench it free, but the Goth hung on by its claws and now its teeth, tearing her flesh. She staggered out of the light, draped in Goths who tore at her scales, gouging at her flesh. A second Goth tore a deep wound in her arm, exposing bone. There were so many Goths climbing on her she looked like a bizarre new creature, a thick, fur-covered giant whose fur was alive.

Then, three things happened in rapid succession.

First, a lone Goth broke from the hysterical mob, turned its ears and eyes to the source of the lights, and leaped at Domitian. The nearest marine saw it coming, and stepped in front of it, rifle in one hand, the other hand extended to fend the Goth away.

Next, a great flash of light exploded at eye level, stunning Ranant, Domitian, and several Goths. Then, Flavia's head snapped backwards as if she had struck her own chin with her own fist. A plume of black mist rose above her. Then she reeled in the dark with eight Goths still aboard.

The Goth at her throat seized the chance to bite even harder, to push its long, curved, yellow canine teeth between the Trapezius muscles and the Sternohyoid muscles, and into the vertebrae. Flavia released her grip on the Goth's fur and flung out one arm to steady herself as she fell.

But it was too late.

She toppled backward into the mass of Goths on the deck and disappeared into darkness. She only became visible again when one of the marine's lamps swung down at her.

The lamplight illuminated a terrible scene.

Surrounded by the carcasses of shattered Goths, Lieutenant Flavia Tatius, the First Lieutenant of the navy ship Herculaneum, the granddaughter of the famous Admiral Guern, lay stricken and toppled. One of her great claws clutched her throat; the other clutched her face, where the blast had struck. Her legs flailed and kicked at nothing.

Then the claw at her throat seemed to give up. Her arm fell to one side, her face turned away, the hand still clutching it, and Lieutenant Flavia moved no more.

36

For several secunda, nothing happened.

Time stopped.

No one moved or sent out a thought. No one made any gesture at all. Everyone looked at the terrible scene revealed in the half-light.

They saw Flavia's huge, clawed feet and shredded legs. They saw the ruin of her thighs and the deep furrows on her sides, stomach and chest, each glistening with blood and crusted with pried-apart scales.

Then they watched the small circles of light travel upward to reveal Flavia's neck. The Goths had torn away a flap of gray flesh. Red girders of muscles glistened beside obscene white bones.

The lamp light moved on. Tentatively, it climbed up to Flavia's jaw. There, it found Flavia's left hand planted over her face. Her red claws dug into her cheeks the way they had once sunk into the armrests on the Albus. Black blood oozed between her fingers, streamed down her cheeks, and puddled on the deck beside her left ear.

The lamplight moved to one side of Flavia's stricken body, then the other. It illuminated a tide of Goths retreating. The Goths' triangular ears were erect. They tossed their snouts to inhale deep drafts of the non-air, just as they would do in their native forests where the air was rich and thick.

Five Goths struggled underneath Flavia's back. Their yellow claws scrabbled at the deck, dragging their bodies out from under the massive weight. Once free, the Goths loped away. A few Goths remained behind, sniffing the spreading lake of blood. Then, they too galloped into the dark, as if someone had called them away.

As the Goth horde retreated, the bow lamps on the Albus flickered into life, shooting their beams into the gloom.

Ranant pointed to the darkness behind him. One marine turned his helmet lamp about. The light found Domitian. He was staring at Flavia with a hand over his mouth. The lights swung further round. It showed the second marine in the grip of an intense, silent struggle with a red furred Goth. The marines held the Goth around the throat. The Goth's fore claws and hind claws scratched furiously at the metal legs, chest, and helmet, gouging the paint. Its eyes bulged with panic. Ranant raised a hand. The marine released his grip. The writhing Goth dropped to the deck, turned, sniffed at Ranant, then fled.

Then, under Ranant's instruction, the lamplight swung deeper into the darkness. At first, it found nothing. Then, it searched further away until it revealed the pale, blotched face, and yellow hair of Lieutenant Sinistra.

She was several passus away along the deck. The blast had flung her off her feet. The giant weapon lay on the deck beside her. Its barrel pointed at Sinistra's back, like an accusing Hyacinth-creature finger.

No one said a word, and no one moved. They didn't even offer to help—not even when Sinistra tried to climb to her feet, staggered, and fell down again.

37

Sinistra tried to stand once more, but her knees would not bend, and her legs would not obey. She fell back onto her bony pelvis and sat there, blinking.

A terrible thought formed in her mind. A senior naval officer had been shot, possibly killed. The senior naval officer was the granddaughter of an admiral—the famous Admiral Guern—and descended from a line of military heroes and Senators.

And there were four witnesses to the incident.

Non est bonum, Sinistra thought, and then added, Nim, if you can hear me, I've really done it now.

Neither Ranant nor Domitian had moved. Their voices did not speak in Sinistra's mind. They didn't ask if she was hurt, or if needed help. They were silent.

Eventually, Sinistra climbed to one knee, then onto two feet. She stood up and looked at the two faces staring at her. Both were blank with shock or astonishment, or with revulsion.

One voice spoke, but not to her.

How bad? said Domitian.

Let's take a look, said Ranant. He signaled the marines, then pointed at Flavia. The marines swung their lights away from Sinistra, abandoning her to the dark.

She reached down and picked up the heavy, accusing rifle. The barrel was too hot to grip. She let it drop to the deck, then pulled it up by its strap.

Ranant's voice said, She's not moving.

Sinistra walked over to them, dragging the rifle behind her. She said, Captain Ranant, tell your marines to bring the light onto the First Lieutenant's face.

Ranant didn't move, didn't obey, as if he were staging a silent mutiny. A few secunda passed, then he signaled the order. The beams swung onto Octavia's neck. Sinistra limped closer, casting a long shadow over the ruined giantess.

As she watched, Flavia's body contracted. The muscles in her legs rippled and shrank. Her scales softened and reformed. The claws retracted into Hyacinth-creature fingers and toes. Eventually, the famous Hyacinth-female figure returned, except for one shocking detail: its skin was gray, mottled, and slack. Flavia's skin now matched her age.

Something was also wrong with the wound in Flavia's neck. It hadn't healed. It remained deep, black, and oozing. Meanwhile, her rigid fingers covered her facial wound from her jaw, on one side, to her ear on the other.

Once the contraction had ended, Flavia sent out a word in the native language: Fas. That was all. Fas—a word with several meanings, including right, law, and duty. Sinistra said her name several times, but Flavia said no more.

Is she dead? said Sinistra.

Ranant knelt and looked into Flavia's gaping neck.

Her Hyacinth creature heart is still pumping, he said. I guess that means she's alive.

Thank Owanthan, Sinistra said, but regretted it. It sounded insincere. Ranant and Domitian said nothing. They remained behind in the dark. Sinistra wondered whether they were about to seize her and arrest her? Ranant could do it. He had his men. He had a reason. There were four witnesses.

Sinistra stood a little taller and dragged the rifle closer to her knee. I'm the senior officer now, she thought. I'm the senior officer. No matter what has happened. I'm the senior officer.

To assert herself, she said, Chief Domitian, Captain Ranant. Gather up the First Lieutenant's uniform and cover her. She shouldn't be naked.

Sinistra waited: one secunda, two secunda, three. Then, to her relief, Domitian came past and stepped over to Flavia's body. He picked up the shreds of blue uniform and spread them over the pale, scratched, naked limbs. Sinistra sent another thought, as softly as she could think. Captain Ranant, please order your marines to lift and carry the lieutenant to the Albus. Lay her across the three seats at the cabin's rear bulkhead.

Then, she then sent another thought. Chief Domitian, please attempt to contact the Herculaneum by thought message. The captain will approve of its use.

Ranant came up beside her. He stood apart from her with his arms crossed. His thought voice said, What just happened, Lieutenant?

Sinistra breathed imaginary air—slowly in, slowly out.

What do you mean, Captain?

What do you think I mean?

I know that many things just happened. The Goths attacked us; Lieutenant Flavia attacked the Goths in return. Your marines defended her and prevented her from being killed. I defended her, too.

I saw what happened, Sin. So did the chief. So did the marines. We all saw it.

Sinistra suddenly disliked Ranant's use of Sin.

You'll have to be more specific, Captain.

No, I don't. You know what I mean.

I don't know what you're talking about. All I hear from you is the beginning of insubordination. Will you order your men to carry the lieutenant back or not?

How about showing some remorse?

You talk as if I killed her, Captain Ranant.

Did you see her head wound, Lieutenant? It's a miracle she has any head left.

Sinistra stood as tall as her awkward posture would allow and said, Now is not the time for Hyacinth-creature emotions, Captain. You, of all people, should know that. Despite what happened to Flavia, we must remain calm. The mission depends on it. Remember where we are. So please have your men carry the lieutenant back to the Albus while Chief Domitian and I survey the wall.

You're going to hang around here? With all those Goths?

I think they've made their point. They won't be back.

How can you be sure?

I can't, but we won't take long. We'll scan for messages, then we'll return. That's what Lieutenant Flavia ordered.

I thought you wanted to get out of here.

I do, but the Albus is still disabled. The Herculaneum can't reach us. There's nothing we can do. I also want to talk to Chief Domitian about something.

Nothing we can do? We can use my plan. We can blast a hole in the side of this thing with the rifles. They'll see the blasts from the Herculaneum.

I will consider it, Captain Ranant. At the moment, even if we make a hole in the side of this object, it's no good if the Albus's engines won't fire.

They might send a rescue ship.

We'll consider all options when Chief Domitian and I return, Captain Ranant. It won't be long.

Ranant scowled at the deck as if about to say something. But then, he looked up and pointed at one of the marine's helmet lamps. Is he arresting me? thought Sinistra. But no, the marine detached the lamp from his helmet and handed it to Ranant. Ranant passed it to Sinistra. Then he pointed at the rifle. What about that?

I'll keep it for now, Captain.

Domitian's voice spoke: No response from Telepathy, Sin.

Then it's settled.

Ranant looked up into the darkness. His voice said, No good is going to come of this. No good at all—not for Flavia, not for the mission, not for you, me, the chief, nor anyone else. Tota mala est. It's all bad.

Yes, thought Sinistra. It's all bad, and I'm to blame.

'Yes, you're to blame,' whispered a voice in her mind. 'You're bad. You've always been bad. You couldn't help yourself, could you? You wanted to kill her, didn't you?'

No, replied Sinistra in a silent thought. You're wrong. I didn't mean to shoot her. Then, she added, But I don't regret it.

38

The marines clomped away towards the Albus's distant lights. Flavia lay slumped one of the marine's thick, metal arms. Ranant sent a message as he walked beside them. Don't take too long, Sin.

Sinistra watched them go. Then she sent out a thought to Domitian. Let's move, Chief.

But Domitian was not ready. It was his turn to let Sinistra know his thoughts.

I saw what you did, Lieutenant.

Sinistra ignored him. We'll stick with the plan. We'll go left along the wall, forward into the future, ad sinistram, as they say.

Did you hear me, Lieutenant? I saw what you did.

Sinistra caught the chilly edge in Domitian's tone. The easy friendliness was gone.

Not now, Chief Domitian. You'll have your chance later. There'll be an inquiry. The captain will hear the testimonies, both yours and mine.

And I will to tell the inquiry what I saw.

Noted, Chief. I will also speak and tell the truth about what happened.

They stood in silence, watching the marine's helmet light

bob away until the tension faded.

Eventually, Domitian said, Do you really think there are Parthia survivors on this object?

No, do you?

No. That was just Flavia's wish. We're only here because the captain insisted we indulge her.

Right, said Sinistra. I'm glad we agree. So, let's complete the orders while we have time.

I think we should follow Captain Ranant back to the Albus. He's right about the Goths.

Don't worry, Chief. We won't be long. There's something I want to know about.

You saw the wall was blank, Lieutenant. There's nothing more to see.

No, it's something else. When the Goths attacked, I heard their thoughts.

So did I. Grunts, growls, and barks, and maybe their word for 'gone' when they retreated.

No, said Sinistra. I'm talking about something else: a word they were thinking while they attacked, like they were chanting it to themselves.

You can speak Goth, Lieutenant?

A few words.

And what did they say?

Sinistra shone the light towards the wall.

Let's get moving, Chief Petty Officer, and while we walk, I want you to tell me something, if you don't mind.

Tell you what?

I want to know about the mural of 'The Fate of The People,' but not the one in the captain's stateroom. I mean the one in the passageway.

What about it?

The Goths spoke a word that sounded like the name of one figure in the painting.

What figure?

The same figure whose name is written on the podium outside: the demon god, Sirhain, Chief Petty Officer. The demon god, Sirhain.

39

They began their survey, moving left along the wall, *ad sinistra*.

The lamplight pushed no further than ten passus into the dark, a distance equal to ten Hyacinth-creature strides.

Sinistra limped behind the light. Domitian shortened his step so as not to overtake her. Each watched the frontier between light and dark. On the wall, only one mural appeared and no more: the Hyacinth woman on the hill addressing a multitude of Hyacinth creatures below. As before, two other figures stood behind her: a shorter Hyacinth female and a figure wearing a robe. After that, the wall to the left was blank.

Let's keep moving, Sinistra said.

And they carried along the wall into the dark, further and further from the Albus.

Chief, said Sinistra. You are supposed to tell me about Sirhain.

Is this really the best time, Lieutenant? I think we should be more concerned about ourselves out here.

You're not nervous, Chief, are you? Aren't you a man who believes in the Old Book and in Owanthan?

Yes, but now we can barely see the Albus. What if the

lamp fails and we're lost in the dark?

Tell me about Sirhain, Chief. I'll keep an eye on the wall.

Are you sure that what the Goths said? Sirhain? Could it have been a growl, a snarl, or their word for enemy?

Maybe, but I want to know if there's a connection between all these events. Is there a link between Sirhain, the Goths, and the object? A religious connection?

You sound as if you have had a change of heart, Lieutenant? Has the mission made you reconsider the old faith? Isn't it strange that someone in danger always turns to higher thoughts?

It's not that, Sinistra said. Let's just say I've discovered an interest in the faith's prominent figures—Sirhain in particular. Why would the Goths shout his name, especially while attacking?

You mean, *if* they shouted his name.

Let's assume they did.

As it happens, Domitian said, there is a connection. I don't really know much about Sirhain. He's not a prominent figure in the Old Book, except for the story of the migration from the old planet.

Just tell me what you know, Chief.

They probed further along the wall, following the circle of light. No more murals appeared, only the wall's porous stone.

After a few seconds, Domitian said, First, Sirhain wasn't a demon. 'Demon' in the Hyacinth language implies that he was a force of evil. That wasn't the case.

Well, what was he?

He was more like one of Owanthan's ministers, like one of our senior Senators. Sirhain didn't agree with Owanthan, but he wasn't a demon.

So he was an advisor?

Yes, he had responsibility for a part of the old planet.

Responsibility for what?

Well, some gods handled war; others handled the seas, and some were responsible for the arts and the afterlife.

And what was Sirhain's responsibility?

He was the god of nature, Lieutenant. He took care of the planet, the animals, the birds, the trees, the insects, and possibly the volcanoes. The volcanoes—now that's an interesting thought. Sirhain was in charge of keeping them dormant.

Was he in charge of the Goths?

Well, the Old Book story took place before our ancestors reached the home planet. So we didn't know about Goths until we arrived. And then, of course, the Goths repelled us. Everyone knows that story—about the years spent fighting the Goths. But yes, I guess so. The Goths are animals—intelligent ones, but animals nevertheless. So they would have been Sirhain's responsibility.

And how did Sirhain come to be known as a demon god?

He fought with Owanthan.

Over what?

Over destiny. He didn't want to move our ancestors to the home planet. He said it would lead to our deaths. He said if it happened, Owanthan would not be able to save us.

But he was wrong.

Yes, but given what's happening now, you could claim he was correct.

Why did he care?

Care? He's a god? He's supposed to care.

But why do the gods care at all? What's in it for them? What do they gain from caring?

That's simple. They want something from us.

What—what do they want?

Tribute, adoration, gratitude—perhaps even entertainment.

You mean, they're not benevolent gods?

Well, this is only what the scholars say. The gods

themselves don't mention their motivations. The scholars say that they're like us, but powerful and immortal. They have very mortal drives, including vanity. So mostly, they wanted adoration. That's my guess.

What kind?

The usual kind: prayers, monuments, festivals, submission, sacrifices, and other expressions of fear of their power.

The gods seem very shallow. They don't seem worthy of respect let alone adoration.

I didn't write the Old Book, Lieutenant Sinistra.

So why do you worship Owanthan?

I don't worship him. I acknowledge him. I ask him to help us. I believe he has our interests at heart.

All right, so what happened? How did Sirhain acquire his evil reputation?

Well, Sirhain didn't just disagree with Owanthan. He was ambitious, and he wanted power. But since the gods are immortal, Owanthan would never die. There would never be a succession. Even if there were, the next in line would be Owanthan's son.

Owanthan mocked Sirhain for even suggesting he take power, and Sirhain hated to be mocked—absolutely hated it, like most people in power hate it. Think of our laws prohibiting mockery of the Senate and the old families. It's the same.

And so what did Sirhain do?

He took action. He got support from several other gods and led a rebellion to seize power.

And he lost?

Yes, he lost and Owanthan banished him.

Banished where?

I don't know. Just away. Another part of the galaxy, I suppose.

Banishment—is that all? Did he stay away?

No. He took others with him. He weakened Owanthan's court. But even when he was banished, he still wanted to play a role in the destiny of our ancestors.

And did he?

Yes, but in a terrible way. This is the part of the story in which he earned his reputation.

How?

He did something that might be called an unspeakable act.

What unspeakable act?

To weaken Owanthan's resolve, he perpetrated a terrible crime that would hurt Owanthan as much as possible. He committed a massacre.

A massacre, Chief? Killing in large numbers? I thought you said the other gods were immortal.

Domitian said, In some cities, the blood rose to knee height. So the Old Book says.

What? The gods have blood?

Not the gods, Lieutenant. He massacred our ancestors.

Our ancestors? He killed our people?

Yes, in his lust for revenge and power, he killed nearly a third of the old planet's population. Some historians say this act is the real, unspoken reason we fear ambition in our leaders so much, and why we revile the dictators and kings in our history. It's why we have our Senate. The lust for power, Lieutenant, it …

But Domitian could not finish his thought.

Stop! said Sinistra. Stop, please Chief!

Domitian walked into Sinistra's back, knocking her forward. The heavy rifle swung on its strap, tangling in her legs, so that she fell to one knee.

Sorry, said Domitian. What is it? What's happened?

Look at this, Sinistra replied, climbing to her feet. Domitian stepped out into the gloom and came around to the other side of the lamplight.

See it? Sinistra said.

Domitian leaned towards the wall. The light revealed a small crack or gap between two sections, as if stone masons had tried but failed to join two enormous slabs.

It might mean something, Sinistra said.

Or it's just shoddy construction.

Sinistra shone the light into the gap, and then onto the walls either side. There was nothing there. So, she shone the small circle of light upward, following the gap until it disappeared into the gloom.

Wait, said Domitian. Shine it back to just above your head.

The circle of light slid down.

There!

That?

Yes, that?

But what is it?

It was two words—one word on either side of the slim opening.

Sinistra squinted. I can't read it.

That's because it's the Old Book language again.

And what does it say?

I'll only be guessing.

Then guess.

Domitian stepped closer to the wall and began mouthing the words.

40

You sound drunk, Chief.

That's how you pronounce these words, Domitian said. You say them with a slow lisp.

And what are they? There are only two of them.

On the right side of the crack is the old language for the word 'past,' and on the far side is the word, 'future.'

Past and future—that's it? We know that out already from the murals.

Well, that's all there is.

So what's the significance? Are the words supposed to imply that the crack in the wall lies between past and future? This Old Book isn't very profound, is it?

She shone the lamplight back onto the gap. Something had changed.

Are you sure that's what the words say, Chief? Past and future?

Domitian looked again.

It's changed, he said.

To what?

Domitian leaned in closer and once more Sinistra heard the strange, slurred words.

It says, 'All can be yours if you speak my name.'

Is it from the Old Book?

I don't know.

So, whose name does it mean? Could it be Sirhain's?

I don't know, Lieutenant.

Well, let's try it. Let's speak the name. Maybe the gap will open. You speak it, Chief.

How can I speak it when there is no air to form the word and no atmosphere to carry it?

Just pretend, Chief.

Domitian hesitated. I would prefer not to speak the name, if you don't mind—not in such a formal way.

'Don't tell me you're afraid, Chief.'

I'm a religious man. I don't want to chant the names of Owanthan's enemies.

Then, I'll speak the name.

I don't think you should, Lieutenant. I know that sounds strange, but think of all we've seen so far. This kind of action should only be taken with the captain's endorsement.

Then, I'll just think it.

So, they stood in the total darkness while Sinistra thought the name. Sirhain, she thought to the darkness. Sirhain.

But nothing happened.

I'll try mouthing it, Sinistra said. This time she imagined filling her lungs with air. When her chest swelled, she was about to open her mouth when a message came from Ranant aboard the Albus.

Sin.

Yes, what is it?

Flavia's looking bad.

How bad?

Her heart rate has slowed. We've got to get the ship started.

Do any of the controls respond? The propulsion? The weapons?

I'm the marine, not the pilot.

What about the Goths? Any sign?

If there were, you'd have seen the blasts.

Anything from the Herculaneum?

Nothing.

All right, Captain Ranant. Stand by. We're about to return. There's just one last thing to examine.

Sinistra stood to her full height in the dark. Once again, she filled her lungs with imaginary air. Then she stated the name, 'Sirhain. Sirhain. Sirhain!'

Instantly, something changed. She heard the name, but not in her mind. She heard it even though there was no atmosphere.

Her own Hyacinth voice had spoken. She heard it through her ears. She heard the flat, close echo from the wall. Then she heard another echo coming from far away in the gloom. 'Sirhain. Sirhain. Sirhain. Sir—hain.'

She shone the lamp onto Domitian's face. She saw an expression she guessed meant horror. Domitian's mouth was open wide as if he'd been stabbed in the back.

'What's the matter?' she asked, but not as a thought. She spoke the words aloud. 'What is it, Chief?' But Domitian didn't move.

Sinistra felt a vibration beneath her feet. She shone the light down at the gray deck, then onto the wall. It was opening up at the point where the gap had been. Two great slabs withdrew from each other like stone curtains. Thick darkness lay beyond them.

Ranant's voice said, Sin, you'll never guess what. I think the console just lit up. That's a good sign, right? Sin? Can you hear me? Are you there?

But she didn't hear him. Instead, Domitian's voice spoke in her mind. No, Lieutenant. Whatever you're thinking, don't do it. Don't go there. Don't go inside.

But Sinistra had already disappeared from Domitian's sight.

41

On the other side of the wall, it was dark, empty, and silent.

Chief? Sinistra said. There's nothing here but darkness, deck, and desolation.

But Chief Domitian did not reply.

Keeping the wall at her back, Sinistra took four steps inside. There was nothing to see or hear. What had she expected—the Parthia survivors and a pathway of guiding lights?

Chief, she said. I'm coming back before I get lost. Chief?

She was about to turn around when something strange happened: her Hyacinth-creature senses, starved of stimulation since she left the Albus, now came vividly alive.

Her ears popped—first one, then the other. They registered external sounds: the rasp of the uniform on her legs, the comic squelch of her boots on the deck, the creak of the rifle strap, and the nudge of the rifle stock on her hip. She also heard the beat of her Hyacinth-creature heart.

Next, her feet suddenly carried more weight and the rifle strap pulled harder on her shoulder. Even her head seemed to weigh more heavily on her neck.

Then her sense of smell returned. Cool air surged in through her nose and down her windpipe, filling her lungs, swelling her chest. She detected familiar odors: the reek of wet leaves, the decay of damp bark, and the mineral scent of coming rain.

After months in the Herculaneum's artificial atmosphere, this was a dramatic change, a cornucopia of sensuousness far richer than the Domum Deck's artificial world. It was thrilling, fresh, and heady.

It was also frightening.

'Dom,' she said aloud and in thought. 'There's air, and something else, too, like grass or wood. It's amazing. For all its faults, the Hyacinth-creature form is a wonderful thing. It might be weak and useless, but its sensory organs are strong.'

The sensory rush triggered recollections of other sensory pleasures, of bright mornings on the home planet; of navy ships on the sea; the touch of Ranant's hand on her waist; the wind in the forests of her childhood; Ranant's lips on her throat.

No, she said to herself. Now is not the time. Here is not the place. And then, to Domitian, she said, 'I'm coming back, Chief. Don't move. I'll be there after I try one more thing. It's going to hurt my throat, but I have to try.'

She drew a breath and called 'Hello!' in the growl of the native language. Then she clutched her neck. 'Hello!' she growled a second time. No one replied.

She turned around and retraced her steps back to the wall, or what she thought were her steps. But after only ten paces back through the darkness, her lamplight found nothing. The wall wasn't there.

She swung the lamp left, right, up, and down. The weak lamplight probed a void where nothing reflected it back. Meanwhile, the cornucopia of sensations grew. She heard fresh sounds: a bird's squawk, a plop like a stone tossed into a pond, a mournful sigh high above. She felt other sensations, too. A breeze stirred the lank hair from her ears, and something scurried over her left boot. Then she heard a deep, long growl that could only have come from a large animal.

'Domitian!' Sinistra said. 'Chief, put your head through the crack and shout something. I can't find my way out.' She repeated the words as thoughts. Chief? Are you there? Chief? Put your head in the gap and shout.

But the Chief made no reply.

Sinistra stood with the lamplight in her hand wondering what to do and which way to turn. And then, like the dawn at the end of a long, winter night, it happened.

There was light.

Someone had spoken the actual word light, but not in Hyacinth. The voice said, 'light' in the growls of the home planet's language. The blast of sunlight was so sudden that Sinistra turned her face away and shut her eyes till she could squint at the blue buttons on her cuffs.

When her eyes adjusted, she could see that the wall was gone. In its place, a forest had risen, dark, and forbidding. There were blue trees with trunks as thick as three Hyacinth creatures, standing side by side. Each tree trunk ascended to a leafy canopy and a soft blue sky.

She turned about. She was standing in a crescent-shaped clearing with the forest pressing in on three sides. On the fourth side a lake glittered in the sunlight. On the lake's distant shore, more forest ascended, blue and green, with flocks of birds passing over the thick canopy.

Sinistra felt as if she had wandered onto an elaborate stage on which performers would soon take their places. But this stage was unlike the artificial world of the Domum Deck. It was far richer, more colorful, fresher, and vivid. It was real.

'Salve!' she called, forgetting to use the native language. 'Salve!'

No one replied. Everything carried on as if Sinistra had

barely made a sound. The lake sparkled, the forest brooded. Small birds flitted over the canopy and over the rippled water. Her hair stirred on her neck, and a red beetle pushed through the obstacle course of her bootlaces. She raised her foot and flicked the beetle away. Then, she called out once more. This time in the native language.

'Hello!' she called. 'Don't be afraid. I'm a friend from the home planet. I'm an officer from the ship Herculaneum, previously known as the Grankasar. Is Captain Strahklan here? I can help you. My name is ...' and she spoke her name—the one she used before the Admiralty re-named her Sinistra. Then she clutched her throat in pain, retching onto the loamy soil where the red beetle was picking its way back to her boot.

As before, no one replied. The forest, the lake, the sky, and the creatures were busy with their own concerns, calling, swooping, twittering, growing, grazing, and decaying. Beneath the lake surface, they might even be swimming—all of them, oblivious to her.

I'm going back to get Chief Domitian, Sinistra thought. I need a witness or they'll never believe me.

But that was when she heard a branch snap. Something had moved in the forest depths. It wasn't a bird, but something large and lumbering. She heard a rasping breath, a deep belch, and the rhythmical crackle of heavy, padded tread on twigs and leaves. Something, or someone, was approaching.

Finally, it came into view. A beast lumbered from the gloom. Sinistra saw the gleaming eyes; the thick snout; the triangular ears; the massive quivering flanks; glossy fur; and shoulder blades alternately rising and falling as the creature padded forth on enormous paws, each fringed with long, yellow claws.

No, she thought. Not again.

'Gwah,' the Goth growled. That strange word again—this

time it sounded like a warning. Sinistra placed a hand on the rifle strap and slid it from her shoulder. 'Gwah!' growled the beast. Soon more Goths emerged from the depths. There were ten, twenty, fifty of them. They were a tide of Goths flowing from the forest and into the clearing by lake's shore.

As Sinistra held the rifle unsteadily on her chin, the first Goth padded by her without turning its head or even sniffing at her. It reached the lake's edge and stopped, but instead of lapping at the water, it turned about and stood panting with its obscene red tongue, drooling onto the sand.

The other Goths came forward. They too lumbered past Sinistra, then turned and stood by the first Goth, forming a barrier to the lake.

Next, a commotion began. The trees filled with birds. There were glistening ravens, mournful scavenger birds, and curved-beaked sickle birds. All of them were species from the home planet. They settled on the branches, side by side, as if gathering to watch a performance.

Or a trial, thought Sinistra.

Or an execution.

Then Sinistra saw small creatures coming forward. Moles, rats, deer, and forest boars crept, hopped, scurried, and trotted from the forest and settled between the enormous Goth paws, as if there were no danger from the scything claws, and the long, curved teeth.

Sinistra tried listening for the Goths' thoughts, but she heard nothing—not even the usual thoughts of hunger, sex, violence, and their god, Gwanta. Their minds were as silent as the cosmos.

Then, as if hearing a secret command or signal, every creature bent its forelimbs and lowered its head. Down went the Goth muzzles, followed by the smaller heads of the rats and the moles. Down went the beaks of the birds into their plumages.

They're bowing, thought Sinistra. They're bowing like the

people in the days of the dictators. But they're not bowing to me. They can't be doing this for me, or can they?

But then another figure came forth from the forest. The figure was in Hyacinth-creature form, riding high on the back of a tall, red-furred Goth. As this strange rider came into the sunlight, the circle of Goths parted. Each Goth nudged the next and shuffled along to make room. Meanwhile, the creature and his terrible mount swayed closer.

Sinistra backed away, clutching the rifle.

The big Goth stopped. It bent its back legs, lowering its rump. Then, it shuffled its forelimbs out until its shaggy stomach rested on the wet ground.

On its back, the Hyacinth creature smiled at the assembly of beasts and birds. Then, he gripped his robe and swung one leg over the Goth's back and slid down the glistening flank. His boots thumped into the soil and his dark robe flopped around him.

Sinistra raised the heavy rifle to her cheek and centered the sights on the Hyacinth creature's chest. The creature smiled. Sinistra would later describe the smile as a wicked little grin.

Keeping the rifle up, she slowly backed away.

The Hyacinth creature spoke in a deep, rumbling voice that seemed to come from all directions at once—from the forest, from the lake, and from the sky.

'Lieutenant Sinistra,' the creature said in the growls of the native language. 'Don't you recognize me?'

42

Sinistra pressed the trembling rifle to her chin.

'I know you can hear me,' said the strange Hyacinth creature. 'But, I'll ask you again. Don't you recognize me? Or would you prefer me to speak in Hyacinth? Non me cognoscis? Isn't it a wonderful language?'

Sinistra kept the rifle level. 'Should I recognize you?'

'My, my,' said the creature. 'You speak with a pronounced accent from the Northern Forests. It's so pure, so totally authentic.' He looked at the terrible creatures around him. 'I like to think that's how these fellows here would sound if they could speak our language. But yes! Most definitely! Of course you should recognize me. Apparently, you do not. If you *did* recognize me, you would lower your weapon and emulate my children.'

He raised his arm again, sweeping it over the bowing Goths, the prone moles, the worshipful birds, the sprawling worms, the kowtowing moths, beetles, and bugs.

'Your children?' Sinistra said.

'Yes, my children—figuratively speaking, of course. If you recognized me, you would bow your head to the ground. You would certainly not threaten me with that enormous weapon. It looks so heavy, Lieutenant. Why don't you put it down?'

'Why should I act like your … like these animals?'

Sinistra looked closer at the bizarre Hyacinth creature's face. His age appeared to be about forty Hyacinth years. His hair was red like the fur on his Goth mount. He wore a shiny broad-brimmed hat with a green feather rising from it like a military standard. The hat tilted so far that it concealed his right eye. It looked as if it might slip from his head onto his arm.

On his face, hair grew on his top lip. The hair curled out and up his cheeks like the wings of a small bird. Beneath his lip, more facial hair grew in the shape of a triangle. The creature's smile was unfamiliar, too. It was subtle. She never seen anything like it aboard the Herculaneum. The little smile seemed to mock her, as if the creature knew her secrets, her most private fears, and desires.

His clothes were bizarre. He wore a thick coat or cloak, embroidered with swirls and symbols, some of which looked like birds; others looked like stars. On his legs, he wore wide pants that plunged into tall black boots, turned over at the knees, forming a wide cup. These certainly weren't Roman robes or tunics, so what were they? And despite their lavishness, the clothes looked old, faded, and soiled. One sleeve was torn at the elbow.

As she looked at this bizarre male, Sinistra kept the rifle level.

'Why?' she repeated. 'Why should I do anything you say?'

'Because,' the man continued, raising both his eyebrows. 'Because of who I am. That's why, dear Lieutenant. And because of one other reason.'

'What other reason?'

'Because I will make you.' One of the creature's eyebrows rose, intensifying his mockery.

'Make me?' Sinistra said. 'I am an officer of the Senate Navy ship Herculaneum and I hold this rifle. No one makes me do anything.'

'Is that your answer? You're an officer of a navy ship. You only follow the commands of your captain. No one else?'

'Only the Senate Navy can make me do anything.'

'Interesting!' said the strange creature. 'But I believe I can change your point of view.'

The creature raised one puffy sleeve and snapped his fingers. At the forest's edge, the first row of trees shook. Birds exploded from the canopy. Then the trees were suddenly alive with squirrel monkeys. The branches dipped and flicked upwards as the monkeys dropped from their perches and swung their way down the ladders of branches all the way to the roots. Then, screeching and laughing, the monkeys leaped over the prostrate Goths and loped sideways across the sand.

Sinistra swung the heavy rifle down, but the small creatures were unafraid. They soon surrounded her. They climbed her legs, her belt, her shirt, the rifle itself. They pulled her fingers apart until the forestock slipped from her grip. Then, they shoved the backs of her knees until she fell level with the snouts and paws of the Goths. The monkeys yanked the rifle away and dragged it across the sand and into the forest.

'Now, you may rise,' said the Hyacinth creature. Sinistra climbed to her feet, brushing the mud from her wet knees. The Goths and other creatures rose, too.

'And now we can talk.'

'Who are you?'

'You have asked me that already, Lieutenant.'

'Are you a survivor from the Parthia?'

'A survivor? Yes. From the Parthia? No.'

'Are you from the home planet? Or are you from Hyacinth? You're obviously not one of my people. You must be a Hyacinth creature who returned with Captain Strahklan.'

'You're not even close, Lieutenant. But I think it's fair to say I am from the home planet if I'm from anywhere.'

'Did you place this object in the Herculaneum's path?'

'That is obvious.'

'Not to me. So did you?'

The creature placed one arm by his side and the other across his chest. Then he bent at the waist, performing a low bow. As he did so, he removed his hat, and, holding it by the brim, flourished it in a downward arc, and then brought up again to his chest. Then he settled it back on his head at the same ludicrous tilt.

'What about the Parthia? Did you do the same to it? Did you make its crew come about this … this temple? Or did you simply blow the Parhia up?'

'Not I, Lieutenant. The Parthia's demise resulted from Captain Strahklan's incompetence and some bad luck with his ship's engines. The engines!—they're so fickle, aren't they? So fickle, so troublesome, and so very dangerous.'

'Are you a Hyacinth creature?'

'You keep using that term, Lieutenant. It's very disrespectful.'

'I don't care. Are you a Hyacinth creature—a member of the dominant species from the planet Hyacinth?'

'The dominant species! That's an interesting term.'

'Are you or aren't you?'

'If I were a member of the species that dominates Hyacinth, I would look like more like these creatures.' He held out a clenched fist, then opened his palm. A cloud of moths flittered over the still surface of the lake.

'Insects? They are the dominant form on Hyacinth?'

Sirhain smiled. 'I have many forms, Lieutenant, but I chose this one to match your own, to put you at ease. And, as you see, the form is not unpleasant.' He raised a hand to his mustache and took one wing of it between thumb and forefinger.

'You still haven't told me who you are.'

He lowered his hand to his hip and looked up at the soft blue sky with the same pained expression with which Flavia and Engineer Gabinus looked at the deckhead in the Captain Tiberius's cabin.

'That's because you already know who I am,' he said. 'You simply don't want to say my name, do you? You don't want to acknowledge what that would mean. Am I right? You are skeptical, modern, a military creation. You mock and sneer at old traditions and beliefs. All your generation does, except for one or two.'

'Where is my weapon?'

'Over there.'

Sinistra looked to the forest's edge. The rifle leaned against a tree. One squirrel monkey crouched beside it, glaring at her, its teeth bared. She turned back to the Hyacinth creature and his mocking smile. The creature raised a hand, and she felt the rifle strap pull on her shoulder.

'Don't bother raising it again, Lieutenant. You can't do any harm with it.'

She ignored him and leveled it at the creature's abdomen.

'Go on,' he said and spread his arms wide. 'Shoot me.'

Sinistra raised the weapon and sighted down the barrel at the robed chest. She remembered the damage the rifle could do. Then, she lowered the barrel.

'Thank you,' the Hyacinth creature said.

Sinistra breathed the cool, sickly air and thought, I'm trapped in here with a madman—just as I am trapped with mad men and mad women aboard the Herculaneum. Then, she said, 'What is it you wish to talk about?'

The creature smiled and clasped its hands.

'You, Lieutenant Sinistra. I wish to talk about you.'

'Me?'

'Yes, about you, but also me, and our futures. Oh, your

poor throat! It's red raw from speaking the home planet language. There, that should fix it. You feel better, don't you?'

Sinistra felt the sharpness in her throat vanish. She coughed and said, 'Why have you blocked the Herculaneum from reaching Hyacinth?'

'That,' said the creature, 'is what we are about to see.'

43

'First, our names,' said the Hyacinth creature. 'You are Lieutenant Sinistra, the second officer commanding the navy ship, Herculaneum. Am I correct?'

'The second lieutenant.'

'But you are called other names, too, aren't you?'

'What names?'

'Well, there is your original name, the very old-fashioned Grenda—the name given to you by your guardian.'

Sinistra winced. 'Don't!' she said. 'Don't call me that name.'

'Then there is your Goth name. The Goths call you Lanalan.'

As he said this, several Goth ears flicked upright.

'You are also called Lavinia and Octavia. And, by your detractors, you are referred to as The Lovelorn.'

'The Lovelorn? Lavinia? Octavia? I've never heard of these names.'

'Even so, they exist, or, to be more precise, they might exist in the future. Come now, Lieutenant! Don't pretend to be baffled. Please don't frown. Don't shake your head in that unappealing way. You always imagined that a conversation like this might take place, didn't you—back there in the

Northern Forests?'

'You know nothing about me.'

'That is not true, Lieutenant Sinistra. I know everything there is to know about you and your past. I also know everything about your future.'

'No one can know that much.'

'I am not no one.'

'Then who are you?'

'I'll help you this one time.'

She waited. The strange creature waved a hand over his animal subjects. They shrank from it. The birds flinched in the trees.

'I am beloved by all creatures. I am the lord of all nature on what you call the home planet.' He looked at Sinistra with his eyebrows raised. 'Once, I was even beloved by creatures such as you.'

'You are claiming to be some kind of god.'

'Exactly! Why else would the Goths and these other creatures behave this way?'

'You're not a king?'

'No, not a king.'

'Don't the Goths have their own god named Gwanta?'

'Who is to say I am not him as well?'

'Are you?'

'Nature is only one of my responsibilities. It is merely the beginning of my power, my entitlement, my magnificence. Observe!'

He thrust out his arms. Then he expanded upward and outward. His head and shoulders rose as high as the treetops, with a dreadful squelch and snap. His robe and trousers stretched with him until he was a giant version of himself. He put his fists on his hips and looked down at Sinistra with a giant, mocking smile.

At the sight of him, the forest creatures fled. They hopped, galloped, or flapped away. Even the big Goths turned and lumbered into the trees.

Sinistra backed away with the rest of the creatures. Then, seizing her opportunity, turned and ran towards the way she had entered the forest. But a shadow soon overtook her. A giant boot planted itself in the mud in front of her. The mocking face, now huge, came down and smiled.

'Say my name,' it said.

'I don't know your name.'

'Say it. Just once.'

'You are a creation of my mind—my perverse, Hyacinth-creature thoughts. You are not real. I am not here. I have fallen into a trance brought on by exhaustion.'

'Come now, Lieutenant. I don't have all century. Or do you need help? What if I showed you something: the painting in your ship's Great Passageway? Would that help?'

Sinistra lowered her eyes to the muddy soil and said, 'You are the fallen god.'

'Fallen? Who says so?'

'You fell from Owanthan's favor. That's what Domitian said.'

'Not fell,' the face continued. 'I resisted the tyranny and incompetence of a tyrant. I proposed a better plan, and the tyrant didn't like it.'

'You are what the Old Book calls the demon.'

'Demon? Oh, come now! The Old Book was written by my rivals. Naturally, they call me names. But I'm more worthy than a demon. Demons are servants—resentful servants. Quick now, Lieutenant. You're almost there. Say my name.'

Sinistra drew a breath. 'You are Sirhain.'

'Bravo, Lieutenant! I am Sirhain.'

'All right, I've said it. Now will you let me go? My comrade and shipmate, Domitian waits outside. The crew of the Herculaneum expects our return from this … place. The people on the home planet are desperate for us to complete our mission. We are running out of time. If you are who you say you are, you must know all this already. And you must want us to succeed, not imprison me here, delaying the ship.'

But Sirhain wasn't listening.

'Domitian—who is he to call me a demon?'

'You aren't listening. The people are waiting. They're your people, too, aren't they?'

'They cannot wait if time stops.'

'Stops?'

'I am losing my patience, Lieutenant. We must talk.'

'Talk about what?'

'I have explained already. About your future.'

'I'm just a navy lieutenant. I serve the people.'

'Oh, Sinistra. You are more than that.'

'What do you want from me?' she said. 'Why did you create so much chaos? Why this temple—if that's what it is? Why the mysterious messages and murals? Why the Goth attack? And why the theatrics with these animals?'

'Simple, Lieutenant! It's all to prepare you. If I'd just shown up in your stuffy little cabin, you wouldn't have believed me, would you? Also, I like a thrilling performance as much as the next man. The more thrills the better, I say.'

'What about the attack by the Goths?'

'Ah,' said Sirhain. 'That was so that you should show your real potential—perhaps for the first time in your life. And just look at what you did!'

He was before her again: a male Hyacinth creature of Ranant's height, a head taller than herself. He smiled. 'And now I'm going to show you some things—things from the past and from the future.'

'The future again! Are you going to show me the mural of the crowd and the figure on the hill—the figure of Lieutenant Flavia? Or are you saying that the Hyacinth female is me?'

'There, Lieutenant! You are already picturing yourself as a

great leader. But I don't want to talk of that particular image —not yet. A little more preparation is required. I must show you something else first.'

'And what's that?'

'The thing you fear most in all the world, and in all the cosmos.'

He waved a sleeved arm. Instantly, the sky darkened, the trees sighed, and the lake vanished. Sinistra found herself in another forest, an older, damper, thicker, winter forest under snow.

And far more sinister.

'Do you know where you are?' said Sirhain.

'Please,' Sinistra said, 'not here.'

'Take your hands from your eyes, Grenda. I won't keep you long. But you must see what I have to show you if you are going to make your choice, with all options before you, as they say.'

'Not this. Please, not this.'

'Quiet now. Here she comes.'

44

'There!' said Sirhain. 'Do you see?'

'Please,' said Sinistra. 'Take me back. I'm not who you want.'

'You are familiar with this forest, aren't you? You know who that is, too, don't you? And you remember this very day. It's the day you relive in your dream, isn't it, Grenda? But you never allow yourself to see what happens, do you?'

Sinistra stared far ahead into the forest's shadows.

'In our measurement of time, you were still young,' Sirhain said. 'You were so young that you couldn't understand. You were confused. No, don't hide. Take your hand from your face.'

'I can't watch,' Sinistra said. 'Let me get back to the Albus. Let me go. What good will this do?'

'Watch, Grenda. Watch it till the first blows.'

'No.'

'Trust me. Watch. The truth will free you from your torments. It will give you relief—the relief you have wanted all your life. Look! Go on. Look!'

Sinistra lowered her hands from her face. She saw the panicked figure running through the trees. It was Sinistra in her natural form, as she was in the orphanage.

'Good,' hissed Sirhain. 'Good. One way or the other, painful or not, it will only be good for you. Watch!'

The child Sinistra hid behind a tree, shivering, her face twisted with fear, unaware of the two creatures watching her.

'See how your form changes, Grenda. First, you have thick scales. Now you have fur and claws like a Goth. And what is that now? Some shape of your own invention? What a pity you couldn't expand into the treetops and defend yourself.'

'I couldn't think,' Sinistra whispered. 'I was still learning about expanding, about adults, about the world, and about … that woman.'

'You never mastered it though, did you—expansion, I mean? Just look at you now. Surely, you could do better than that.'

'I was terrified. I couldn't fight back. I can't expand even now.'

'You were terrified of your guardian, weren't you? Listen. She's almost here.'

'Please stop it. I've seen enough. I know what happens.'

'Yes, but you never allow yourself to see it in your dream. And now, you can't make your choice unless you watch.'

'Why?'

'Because destiny can't wait.'

Sinistra stepped away from Sirhain to a tree on her right. She put her arms around its trunk, and pulled her face closer until her skin chafed against the frozen, jagged bark.

In the forest, the pursuer appeared, a tall female in the natural form. She came from the young Grenda's blind side. She caught her hind limb and upended her, spinning her onto her back. Then she placed a clawed foot on young Sinistra's chest and pressed her into the snow.

'You never learn,' the pursuer growled in the native language. 'You never learn.'

'But I haven't done anything,' growled the child Sinistra.
'What is her name, Sinistra?' said Sirhain. 'Say her name.'
'No. I can't.'
'You will feel relief if you do.'
'I can't. Stop. Please make it stop. Please, Sirhain.'
'You'll regret it. Trust me.'

Then, the beating began. The nameless pursuer carried a metal rod called a brak. She raised it above her head. Down on the forest floor, the young Sinistra squirmed and pleaded.

'Don't look away, Grenda,' said Sirhain. 'Don't hide your face. Don't cover your ears. Watch and feel. It's the only way to free yourself. Imagine! No more nightmares and no more compulsions from deep in your mind, driving you on, or should I say, driving you *from* a repeat of this memory.'

'I can't. I won't.'
'Then, I will make you.'
'I didn't do anything,' pleaded the young Sinistra. 'I didn't do anything. I didn't do anything.'
'Is it true?' said Sirhain.

'It was always true,' said Sinistra, watching the blows land on her young self, seeing the flesh split, the black blood ooze, and worst of all, hearing the deep animal yelps and growls from the childish face, like a Goth cub, caught in a trap, and howling for help.

'It's interesting,' said Sirhain. 'Your guardian prefers that weapon over her own claws and teeth. Was it to intensify the pain, or to amplify the humiliation?'

'I never did anything wrong,' Sinistra said. 'And she never explained why. But she did this over and over.'

'It's unfair, isn't it?'
'Yes.'
'And she was your guardian, wasn't she? A protector appointed by the Senate to educate and care for you.'

'She never explained why,' Sinistra sobbed. 'Never.' The Hyacinth-creature tears fell to her uniform collar. 'She never explained.'

'And yet you didn't hate your guardian.'

'She was all I had.'

'You loved her?'

'I don't know. Love is a Hyacinth creature concept.'

'But you wanted her affection?'

'I tried hard at everything. I did all I could. It never worked. She never explained. She just said, "You are bad. Do better."'

'Yet all you did was never enough.'

'Never.'

'And you did everything you could in your studies, your behavior, everything.'

Sinistra sobbed and looked away. She felt no relief, none at all.

'And is this why you are the way you are?'

'What do you mean?'

'You are still trying to do better, every day, and in every way, although you don't see it, do you? You are still trying to win this woman's praise—or rather, you are still trying to avoid another beating. The memory of it is so traumatic, your mind won't allow you to think of it.'

The young Grenda lay on the forest floor, her claws over her face, the black blood glistening in the white snow. The figure above her rubbed her limbs, then she bent down, grabbed a forelimb, and hauled Grenda to her feet.

'It might be a consolation to you,' said Sirhain, 'that I have punished this so-called guardian. She can't hurt you anymore.'

Sinistra looked down at her feet.

'Do you forgive?' said Sirhain. 'Do you feel relief?'

Sinistra made no reply.

'To be free of this, to be at peace, you must forgive her. You must let your fear go.'

'But I never think of this.'

'Deep in your mind, you are never *not* thinking about it.'

Sinistra said nothing.

'I will give you some time, Lieutenant, but only a little. Then, I'll give you your choice.'

'What choice?'

'Perhaps the better description is offer or proposal.'

'A proposal for what?'

'You'll know soon enough. Now stand up and wipe your face. You're a naval officer. You should only be seen at your best, not in that state.'

'Please. I've had enough. Let me out. Let me go. Whatever it is you want to propose, I'm not the one you want.'

'Not yet, Sinistra. Be patient. It won't be long.'

Sirhain raised his arm.

And they were gone.

45

They reappeared in a bright, dry, alien land beneath a clear, soft sky.

Sinistra smelled a salty breeze from an ocean out of sight. She felt the warm, dry air on her hands, face, and neck. It was a pure air, a scented air, a healing air.

Sirhain had brought her to a round hilltop overlooking a shallow valley. In the distance, on another hilltop, a lone female Hyacinth creature stood wearing a long robe. In the valley beneath this figure, a multitude of Hyacinth creatures looked up at her.

'Where is this?' Sinistra said.

'Do you like it, Octavia?'

'Octavia?'

'Yes, Octavia.'

'But why that name? Are you going to give me a different name for each place we visit?'

'In this future, Octavia is what you call yourself.'

'This is like the image on the wall.'

'More or less.'

'So who are those creatures? Who is that female?'

'You don't need me to tell you, do you? You know already.'

'But this land, these hills—they don't look like any impression of Rome or Hyacinth I've seen. Where are the white buildings? Where are the stadia?'

'This is another part of Hyacinth—a region that your expeditions did not survey.'

'What are the Hyacinth creatures wearing?'

'They're called smocks.'

'I've never heard the word.'

'That is what they call them.'

'But where are we?'

'This is a different continent. It lies several thousand milia from Rome. We are also in another age.'

'What age?'

'It's two thousand Hyacinth years since your first missions visited.'

'So, what has happened to the home planet? Are our people safe? Are they here? What about the Herculaneum?'

'You must limit your questions, Octavia. We don't have much time.'

Sinistra looked at the slender figure on the hilltop.

'Will you tell me her name?'

'False modesty again. You know very well who she is.'

But Sinistra didn't know. The woman looked like Flavia but with fairer hair.

'So she survived the rifle blast?'

'Come now, Lieutenant. You know that woman is not your commanding officer.'

Sinistra scoffed. 'Well, if you're suggesting she is supposed to be me, why does she look so different, so …'

'Tall? Slender? Healthy? Beautiful? Everything you are not? Is that what you're trying to say—that she looks like the statues of the Roman goddesses?'

Sinistra looked down at her feet. Then she looked up. 'Why does she stand like that. Why is her posture so …'

'Languid? Confident? Assertive?'

'She looks so at ease, so at peace with herself. So composed.'

'That is because she has acquired a graceful bearing, as the powerful do. It is power, Octavia. Power mixed with beauty is intoxicating. It's irresistible. See how it becomes you.'

'Me? I don't want power. I don't seek it.'

'You are correct. You don't want power. You crave relief from the fear of what we saw in the forest.'

'What about that woman? Is she both powerful and at peace?'

'Tyrants never find peace, but sometimes they find relief in the adoration of the many and the subjugation of their rivals.'

'I don't believe you.'

'If you make the right choice,' said Sirhain, 'that woman really will be you, and the adoration will be yours. So will her sense of relief. Just look at the faces in the crowd. Look at the enchantment. You can almost feel it.'

'They look mad.'

'Madness and enchantment are not dissimilar. Let's move closer.'

Sirhain raised his arm again. The warm breeze ruffled his puffy sleeve. The sleeve was now clean. The embroidery was richer, as if this grand display invigorated Sirhain, from his moustache to the threads in his clothes.

Then, he lowered his arm, and for a moment, the world disappeared. Then it reappeared. Sinistra found herself standing behind the female figure, looking up at her slender neck, and her beautiful earrings glinting in the sun. Over the woman's shoulder, she saw the multitude of Hyacinth creatures below. They were chanting a name.

'Octavia, Octavia, Octavia!'

Now, it was the turn of the woman to act. She raised a hand. As soon as the rings on her long fingers flashed, the chanting ceased. The crowd was silent. Their upturned faces waited. When there was complete silence, the woman spoke in a full, round voice.

'What is she saying?' Sinistra said. 'I can't understand.'

'It's a new language. It is not the language of ancient Rome. Wait a moment. There!'

'I can't believe this beautiful woman is unhappy,' said Sinistra.

'Yes, remarkable, isn't it. But she has other consolations, too, besides her power.'

'What are they?'

'For one thing, she controls two worlds. Therefore, she controls everyone in the galaxy.'

'That's just more power.'

'She also has something else. She also has a lover.'

'A lover?' Sinistra said. 'That is another Hyacinth concept.' After a moment, she added, 'Who? Who is the lover? Is it Ranant?'

'No, not him. He's an opportunist, a flit bird, pecking at whatever he sees. No, Octavia, your lover is someone more courageous and more moral. But he is also like two edges of a sword.'

'What do you mean?'

'Quiet. Your future self is speaking.'

'Before I begin,' said the woman, 'I ask you to join with me in thanking the one who brought our two worlds together.'

The woman tilted her face to the soft blue sky. Then, she mouthed the words, 'We thank thee. We thank thee.'

And as she did this, the people in the valley repeated the words, 'We thank thee. We thank thee?'

Sirhain leaned closer. 'You know who she means, don't you?'

But Sinistra wasn't listening. 'Why are you offering to make me this woman?' After a moment, she added, 'How do I become her?'

'I offer it to you for one reason: so that you will thank Sirhain. Haven't you guessed? I want you and these people to thank Sirhain—to thank him every morning, and to thank him every night. You will be like a messenger. You will be Sirhain's prophet.'

'Why do you need my help? Why don't you just make them fear you?'

Sirhain smiled. 'You don't know much about your religion, do you, Lieutenant?'

'But you say I will be unhappy?'

'Everyone is unhappy to some extent.'

'Everyone? Even you?'

'Even me.'

'But look at this wonderful scene. Look at the people. How could I be unhappy?'

'Oh, for various reasons. For example, you will be unhappy when your transport ships arrive and the planet-altering equipment deploys. You'll be unhappy about churning up all those forests and boiling all the blue oceans. The destruction will be terrible. Most terrible! Those people down there.' Sirhain pressed his manicured fingers to his eyes.

'Why now?' Sinistra asked. 'Why are you doing this on our mission?'

Sirhain took his hands from his eyes. He was smiling.

'The people are rediscovering us,' he said. 'Your people. Haven't you heard your crew asking for the Old Book? It's the same on your home planet. As the volcanoes erupt, everyone seeks answers. They also seek salvation. Your Senate and the patrician families can provide neither. They're too old and inept, as you are discovering. But the Old Book! Well, what a story! Our time has returned, Sinistra. Or should I say, my time? Owanthan had his chance. Now he's too weak. He daydreams about his so-called days of glory. The old fool! But I'm still here. Now, you will help me, Sinistra. Soon, you'll have a new painting on your ship. It will be called ...'

But Sinistra interrupted. 'Can I choose another path?'

'What?' said Sirhain. 'What did you say?'

'Is there a different path—different from this?' She looked up at the beautiful woman and the adoring the multitude.

Sirhain's brow creased. He blinked several times. 'Yes,' he said. 'You can choose to return to the forests of your nightmares and heal yourself. With luck, you'll find relief and perhaps even some serenity.'

'But not something like this.'

'No, nothing like this. The navy will arrest you. They'll find you guilty by a court martial, and you'll spend decades languishing in a navy prison.'

'What if I choose nothing? What if I let things go as they are?'

'Then you will be at the mercy of hazard, in which case there could be many futures, some of them very unpleasant. If you ask me, it's better to choose this future and learn to love and worship.'

'Please, show me one of these other futures—the ones that will result if I choose nothing?'

'Nothing? Don't you want to be this woman? If you like, I can make you her for just a moment, so that you will know how she feels, and how magnificent it is.' He smiled a shrewd, wicked smile. 'I'll also show you what a relief it is—a complete release from the terrible grip of your torments.'

'No. Please show me the other way.'

'But you like what you have seen?'

Sinistra watched the beautiful woman clasp her slender hands and smile as the crowd returned to chanting 'Octavia, Octavia, Octavia.'

'Yes,' Sinistra said. 'Yes.'

'For now,' said Sirhain, 'don't worry about how all this will come about. I will see to that. The future, as the

Hyacinth creatures say, will take care of itself—with my help.'

Sinistra looked one last time at the healing sky and the friendly round hills. Then her eyes lingered on the astonishing woman standing perfectly upright, poised, and aglow with the adoration of the people.

Then, the woman, the multitude, and the hills all vanished, and Sinistra found herself floating in cold, lonely space.

46

Sirhain floated beside her. The rifle strap drifted on her arm.

Before them, at a distance of two milia, the enormous Herculaneum floated, immense and silent. But the lights of its portholes and bridge were dark and blank. The topside beacon was out, as were the lanterns. All of which meant that the great passageways, staterooms, cabins, and holds must also be in darkness.

'Why are you afraid?' said Sirhain.

Despite the absence of atmosphere, Sinistra could hear his voice.

'Open space can kill us,' she replied. 'Everyone knows it.'

'Not this time, Lieutenant. Calm yourself.'

When the invisible rays of space did not burn her to ash, Sinistra said, 'Is this the Hyacinth solar system?'

'No,' said Sirhain. 'Far from it.'

'Then where?'

'It's what I call the Horse Latitudes.'

'Horse Latitudes? Is the Herculaneum lost?'

'Lost and worse.'

'Did the Acceleration fail?'

'Yes. The ship stopped halfway through its crossing. Then it drifted, unable to steer. The engines could not restart.'

'The crew—are they alive?'

'Not any more.'

'How did it happen?'

'How do you think it happened? It was many things: incompetence, lack of preparation, arrogance, poor training, ancient machinery, petty squabbles and, of course, poor leadership. But it was other things, too—bad luck, for example.'

'If the hull is intact, the crew can survive until they fix it, can't they? There are spare engines and reserve engineers.'

'It wasn't a hull breach that killed the crew, Lieutenant. That happened after.'

'Then what was it?'

'Breakdown of discipline, panic, mutiny, fighting, madness, a befouled atmosphere, and an insidious malady.'

'Is there anybody left alive?'

'Yes, Lieutenant. One crew member.'

'And who is that?'

'I'm not going to tell you.'

'Why not?'

Sirhain slowly shook his head.

'Can we leave this future?'

'Of course! If you like, I can show you something more. I can show you the families on the home planet. They suffer terribly—most terribly.'

'Can you show me my friend, Nim?'

'No, Lieutenant. I cannot show you Nim.'

'Why are you doing this? Why do you need to be worshipped at all? Aren't your powers enough? If you want to help, why don't you act unseen?'

Sirhain looked far away at the throbbing stars.

'In some ways, we are mortal gods, Sinistra. We have mortal flaws. Even Owanthan is mortal, with mortal yearnings, the pompous fool. We are jealous, we are vain, we are vengeful. If you had read the Old Book, you would know. Only one god is pure and incorruptible, but He is not here.'

'Tell me how to become the woman on the hill.'

'You saw for yourself. You must first choose to accept my help. Look at the poor Herculaneum. The choice is not a difficult one, as you can see.'

Sirhain turned to look Sinistra's bewildered profile, waiting for her response. But Sinistra was silent. Meanwhile, the Herculaneum drifted and the stars flickered.

'Why me?' Sinistra said. 'Why not Flavia? Why not choose her?'

Sirhain smiled. 'I have hinted at this already, Lieutenant. You have not understood.'

'Then tell me again.'

'Flavia is vain and reckless. Her lust for power is a way of complementing her vanity. She would choose without hesitation. But you, Sinistra, you are different. You struggle to make this choice. To me, that makes you far more worthy, and your allegiance more desirable.'

'This is too much,' said Sinistra. 'It's too much. I can't choose.'

'But you must.'

'I'm dreaming,' Sinistra said. 'It's the Hyacinth-creature mind again. 'I'm in a dream that feels like reality, aren't I?'

She looked across at Sirhain, expecting to see his small little smile, but something had changed. The smile-smirk had gone. Sirhain's forehead creased. His mouth opened in a very Hyacinth-creature gesture of distress. He tilted his head, listening for something. Then he straightened up and stared into space.

'Sirhain? Is something wrong?'

'I have to go.'

'Go where?'

'He has begun,' he said. He's started already. He must have found out what I was doing. The silly fool has been spying on me. Now he's making his move. I knew it would happen. I knew it! But I never thought it would happen this fast.'

'What would happen?'

'Owanthan is making his move to stop me. And now I have to go. I have to prepare. I have so much to do.'

'Go where? You can't leave me here? You can't show me all these things and then just leave. Sirhain? Sirhain?'

But Sirhain wasn't there. He had vanished.

Sinistra was alone.

'Sirhain!' she called, but suddenly, her voice made no sound. Sirhain, she thought.

But there was no reply. There were only the stars and infinity, and the terrible, dark Herculaneum, black and lifeless.

Sirhain! Sirhain!

Nothing.

So, she floated in the emptiness of space, two milia from the starboard side of the stricken, lifeless Herculaneum. What now? she thought. Will I have to swim over to it? How will I get inside? Will I have to crawl through its darkened passageways where the dead crew members collapsed and died?

Suddenly, Sirhain reappeared, flustered and irritated. 'All right,' he said. 'There's no need to panic.'

This time he was in front of her, and he was different. His clothes were shabby again. He was impatient. He looked like he'd been in an argument. One wing of his mustache drooped and there was a tear in his jaunty hat.

'I forgot,' he said.

'Forgot what?'

'To bring you back.'

'But wait? What do I do about Hyacinth and the woman?'

'Oh, you'll work it out.'

'Work it out? That's your answer? But what will I work

out?'

'I have to go. I'm in the middle of something.'

'But I have more questions.'

'Sorry, it's not the time. I have bothered you unnecessarily. Please accept my apologies. As a consolation, I have a small gift for you.'

Then Sirhain was gone again. Sinistra felt the weight return to her Hyacinth-creature legs, and she stood in the soft evening light of Sirhain's domain, between the forest and the dark lake.

She felt confused, shocked, afraid, and betrayed. She also felt exasperated and annoyed. She decided that she had been dreaming after all, and anything she saw in the dream should not be believed.

But this wasn't quite true.

She had glimpsed something she'd never seen before. She'd tasted something forbidden. She had seen futures both wonderful and terrible. Also, she had seen that the gods—if they existed—could be as vain and inept as the leadership of the Herculaneum and the Senate. Most of all, she had also seen a glittering path for herself, a vision she could never have imagined.

Was this vision possible to achieve, even without the help of a god?

She looked at the sparkling lake and wondered.

47

In Sirhain's forest domain, the master was absent. And now, the domain itself was in turmoil, as if it needed its master to control it, order it, and perhaps even discipline it.

The forest churned. The trees writhed in the breeze. The clouds boiled, and thunder growled over the hills. On the far side of the lake, the sun smoldered on the horizon.

This sensual cornucopia within the object was no longer a wondrous place to be. It had grown threatening, and dark.

Where was Sirhain? Why has he abandoned me? Is there something I'm supposed to do? Wait for him? Search for him? Go into the forest shouting his name? Or should I shout my choice? That's if it isn't too late. That's if it ever existed.

Or is this a new and elaborate test? Does Sirhain want me to beg for his return, to plead with him? To make the first gesture of worship? Could he actually be observing me from the forest gloom?

She looked at the forest's dark interior. She heard the wind hissing through the leaves and saw the swaying branches warning her to stay out.

I'm not going in there, Sinistra thought, but then said aloud, 'Unless I must. Unless that's what you want. Is it? Is that what you want? Is this the first step?'

No answer came. Sirhain did not reappear. There was no glorious return, no blaze of sunshine, no raising of the embroidered sleeve to calm the storm. Nor was there any hint or signal of his intentions.

And so, Sinistra stood on the lakeshore with her boots sinking into the sand and her mind too full, too afraid, and too exhausted to do anything but wait.

However, Sirhain's domain had other plans for her.

The first raindrops plopped onto the shore. Out on the lake, each droplet cast small circles that spread and collided, like tiny galaxies spinning through the cosmos.

Sinistra looked down at the troubled water at her feet. The sky reflected up at her. She saw clouds swirling beneath the lake's surface. She also noticed something else: the reflection of a face looking back at her.

She leaned closer. There was something strange about this face? What was it? The nose? The eyes? The tiny cleft in its chin? Its hair, neck, and mouth? Then she realized. It was her own face, frowning back, but not as she'd ever seen it before.

It was beautiful.

But how? Had the small glimpse of power 'become her' as Sirhain said? Or was this another of Sirhain's displays? Or was it an unfinished gesture, the first step in transforming her into the woman on the Hyacinth hill?

Beneath the ripples, the beautiful eyes narrowed. One eyebrow rose, posing a question. What are you going to do? Who are you going to be? What do you want to happen? Who are you going to tell?

Sinistra closed her own eyes. Perhaps if she waited a moment, the domain would restore itself. The wind would calm to a breeze. The sun would rise, and the sky would clear.

But when she opened her eyes, the face in the water was still there. The eyebrow still posed its question over one glittering, bright, cerulean eye.

It must be a dream, Sinistra thought. All of it. It's too bizarre, too extreme, too illogical. I'm a navy officer. I don't believe in gods or visions or even in this forest and lake. It's an illusion, a trick of my mind, just like Sirhain must be an illusion.

Her senses disagreed. They knew reality when they found it. The forest reeked too much of decay and damp. At her feet, the sand sucked too eagerly at her boots. The raindrops smacked too hard into her uniform collar and felt too cold on her neck. Dreams weren't like that.

'Sirhain?' she called. No one replied.

She stood up. The face in the water sank beneath the ripples, the questions still in its eyes. She turned and looked at the dark forest once more, at the small ferns at the edge. They contorted in the wind, as if trying to uproot themselves and escape—or worse—trying to pull themselves free so that they could reach the alien creature at the lake's edge.

Sinistra also sensed something beyond the ferns—something hiding in the trees. It watched her from just beyond the point where the blackness pushed back the light. Is that where Sirhain waited? Was he observing her with one hand twisting his mustache? Was this his way of forcing her to make a choice—by demonstrating a world without his presence?

The rain fell heavier. Cold droplets hit the crown of her head. Her shoulders felt damp. Time to get moving. She lifted one boot and then the other. The sand made a comical sucking noise.

Once free of the shore, she ran for shelter at the forest's edge, where the ferns waved. She didn't notice that her right foot no longer dragged or that the heavy rifle was no longer a burden.

She reached the first rank of ferns and the first knotty roots of the trees, then stopped and looked into the depths.

Sirhain was not there. Instead, big, dark Goths crept forward on their giant paws. Their heads were still, their ears were flat, and they tossed their black snouts at her with deep, searching sniffs. The reek of wet fur preceded them like an advanced force.

'Sirhain!' she called, and then, seeing the Goths' enormous ears flick upright, she covered her mouth. 'Sirhain,' she whispered. 'Where are you?' But the only reply was a hiss as the rain rushed across the lake and into the clearing.

Sinistra backed away from the forest, back towards the lake. But sensing the Goths would trap her against the water's edge, she veered to her left toward the way she had entered the domain several hours and a lifetime ago. 'Sirhain,' she whispered again. 'Sirhain.'

No one replied.

The Goths spread into a crescent of shining eyes and yellow claws. Sinistra tried to listen to their thoughts but heard only a low, menacing rumble. She spoke the Goth words for 'friend' and 'not fight.'

The words only made the Goths' ears flattened even further.

So she turned and ran. Her new, long legs drove her forward through the yielding soil. She ran faster than she had ever moved in Hyacinth creature form.

She ran along the forest edge. Surely the place she had entered was somewhere near. If she just kept running, she could reach it. She could escape before the first Goth paw tripped her up, and then, the teeth, the weight, the smell!

Instead, she fell into a cold, dark nothingness. There was no more reeking forest, no more rain, no thunder, no thrashing trees, no Goths, no wind, no sound, no smells, and no light.

There was only silence, a cold hard deck, and overpowering, solid darkness.

Part Three: Flavia

OCTAVIA

'What in me is dark illumine'

A Hyacinth poet

48

Someone spoke in Sinistra's mind.

It was Domitian speaking the music of the Hyacinth language.

Tarn cito? His voice said. Back so soon?

He spoke his next words with an edge of caution.

It's you, isn't it, Sin? I can't see you, but I felt you come past.

Yes, Chief. It's me.

Why don't you shine the lamp?

The lamp?

Yes, where is it?

I lost it.

You were running. What happened?

I wasn't running.

You were. I felt you. The rifle hit my knee. Scared the life out of me. You're not still running, are you? I can't see where you are.

No, I'm just here. I fell.

Where?

Here—just here.

Are you all right?

Yes, Chief. I'm all right. There's no need to keep asking

questions.

I disagree. There is every need to ask questions. Did you see anything? Hear anything? Meet anyone? Did you see any Parthia people? What's inside?

Sinistra made no reply.

Sin? He waited. Can you hear me? Did you see anything in there?

All was silent for several secunda. Eventually, Sinistra said, Nothing, Chief. I saw nothing.

Just darkness and nothing else? The same as out here?

Yes. That's it. Just darkness. Nothing else. The same as out here.

No more words from the Old Book? Nothing about Sirhain or the future—nothing like that?

No, nothing. Nothing at all.

And yet you lost the lamp. So, something must have happened. Are you sure you're all right?

Yes, Chief.

If only you had the lamp, we could see writing on the wall. I've been running my fingers over it. It's definitely changed, but I can't tell what it says.

Sinistra wondered too.

Domitian said, I'll take a quick look inside for the lamp.

No, Chief! Don't go in there.

Why not?

You won't find anything. It's just more darkness.

I'll only put my head inside. Don't worry. I won't be a moment.

Chief? Dom? Are you there? Chief? There's nothing in there. Chief?

Instead of Domitian's reply, Ranant's voice sounded in her thoughts.

Sin, did you hear? I said the comms are working again. So is the console. It's all lit up and flashing.

What? When?

Just now. That's what I've been trying to tell you. Didn't either of you hear me?

No. Who contacted you? Was it Telepathy?

No. It was the comms—the regular comms from the bridge. They had a recording sending out the same message over and over: Albus, this is Herculaneum. Report or return to ship immediately.

And did you report? What did you say?

Well, I'm the marine here, but I sent a reply. I said that you and Domitian were exploring the object's interior. I also said we'll try to restart when you're back. That's still the plan, right? A half hora?

Right, Sinistra replied. Right.

She was still stunned by all that had just happened. It took a few seconds for the reality of the exterior world to reassert itself.

Eventually, her memory returned, like a loathed enemy resuming a fight.

What did you tell them, she said, about Lieutenant Flavia?

Nothing, Sin. I'm leaving that to you. I just told them Flavia was injured and that they should have a medical team meet us on the stern ramp. They know about the other things, though.

What other things?

You know. The things on the way over. They listened to recordings and heard Flavia accuse you of insubordination.

So, what now? Are they going to arrest me?

They didn't say.

Tell them Chief Domitian and I are on the way back. Once I'm there, I'll send a report.

They want you back soon, Sin. They said to return with all possible dispatch. What about your lungs? Time's almost up, you know.

We've lost the lamp, so we'll have to take our time. Why the hurry, anyway?

They want to get under way for Gordium. That's what they said. Time's ticking, Sin. I think the plans must have changed. No one wants to miss the Acceleration and sit around for six months.

Domitian's voice sounded in her mind.

I'm back. Did you hear me?

No. Not a thing. Where are you?

I'm here. I've been sending messages from the other side.

Sinistra answered slowly and carefully.

And what did you find, Chief?

Just as you said. Nothing but darkness. It's even darker in there than out here, if that's possible. I didn't take more than a step in case I couldn't find my way back. Owanthan and the gods work in strange ways, you know. One minuta, they're guiding you, the next you're on your own. So I kept one hand on this side of the wall.

Sinistra wondered whether she should have done the same.

Did I miss anything? said Domitian.

Sinistra told him about the Albus.

Owanthan be praised, Domitian said. Captain Ranant, how is Flavia?

I was just about to ask, Sinistra said, too late.

I think she's the same, said Ranant.

Are the engines working?

We're going to find out.

We better get moving, said Domitian. We can feel our way back, like old sailors on the sea at night.

Sinistra did not reply.

Sin? Did you hear me?

Yes, Chief. I heard.

But Sinistra didn't move, didn't take a step. She waited in the darkness. It felt better to be here, unseen, away from the ship, away from the consequences of firing the rifle at Flavia, and the confusion she felt about choices and the future.

Do you want to take the lead, Sin? said Domitian. I'll keep within touching distance. We don't want to lose our way. Sin, are you sure you're all right?

Before Sinistra could reply, a bright light flashed in the distance.

Ranant's voice spoke. Sin, I've sent out one of my men. He's going to fire a shot every half minuta so you can find us. You probably saw the first flash just now. Don't worry. He's firing straight up not at the wall.

Thank you, Ranant.

So, it's Ranant again?

Domitian said, Something's different, Sinistra. Your thought-voice sounds, I don't know, rounder or something.

Does it?

What aren't you telling me, Sin? What did you really see in there?

Nothing.

They started walking back. Each kept their left hand on the wall's rough surface.

After a while, Domitian said, Well, this was a strange little mission. We'll never know the truth about this object, will we? And now Decimus will have his way with his guns. He can finally blow all this to pieces. But it's Flavia I feel for. She really believed the Parthia people survived.

Light flashed away to their right side. It was closer.

Good, said Domitian. I've had enough of all this darkness. Don't you agree? Sin?

But Sinistra did not reply.

49

A half hora later, Sinistra climbed the Albus's gangway. Ranant waited just inside the hatch. Sinistra stepped past him and walked to the console. Then she walked to the back of the cabin. Flavia lay prone on the deck.

She was a revolting sight.

She lay beneath Ranant's jacket. Her gray right hand clamped itself over her face, concealing the wound beneath. The wound on her neck was open and deep. The skin on either side of it was gray and loose. Sinistra could see the white jawbone and a pulsing red pipe as thick as her thumb. She put a hand to her own throat, repulsed.

'Has the lieutenant spoken?' Sinistra said. 'Does she remember anything about what happened?' When no one replied, she added, 'Let's hope it's not too late for Doctor Galen to save her.'

Then she stood up.

'What's the matter?' she said. 'Why are you two looking at me like that? What did she say about me?'

'Nothing,' said Ranant. 'She said nothing about you, Sin. She hasn't woken up. She hasn't even moved.'

'Then what's the matter? What happened?'

'Your face,' said Domitian.

'What about it?'

'It's changed,' said Ranant.

'Changed how?'

'It's more … You're more …'

'More what?'

Domitian said, 'What really happened on the other side of the wall, Lieutenant? It can't have been nothing. You're taller, and your face has changed. It's …'

'It's what?'

When neither replied, Sinistra stepped across the cabin to the console. Ranant and Domitian stepped aside as she passed. Ranant almost bowed to her.

At the forward viewport, Sinistra leaned towards her reflection. The beautiful Hyacinth-creature face came closer. The large, glittering eyes watched her, and she saw the question posed by one fine eyebrow, the same as the reflection on the lake's surface in Sirhain's domain.

Her body had changed, too. The blue uniform was loose at her waist and tighter on her hips, and she was taller. Her wrists showed at her cuffs. A strip of skin showed above her boot collars.

Then Sinistra saw the reflections of Ranant and Domitian, watching her from behind.

'I don't know what happened,' she said.

'But it's so strange,' said Domitian, 'that you changed in such a definite way. You now have a face like one of the Hyacinth statues.'

'Do I?'

'In fact, you're not unlike Lieutenant Flavia. You have different hair coloring, of course, but in some ways …'

She looked at Ranant. His eyes were on her hips. 'Do you agree, Captain?'

'Oh, yes. I agree.'

'How much do you agree?'

'Completely. You're like the statues.'

The comms system came alive.

'Albus. Your status?'

Sinistra reached out a languorous arm and flicked the switch.

'We're about to make last checks.'

'No need, Albus. We've checked the instruments already. They're functioning.' The voice wasn't Lepidus's. It was someone she didn't recognize.

'Any explanation for what happened?' Sinistra asked.

'None yet, Lieutenant, unless you have one.'

'No,' said Sinistra. 'We're still in the dark.'

The voice said, 'Doctor Galen would like to know the status of Lieutenant Flavia.'

Ranant said, 'She's unconscious, but her heart is still beating. Is that a good sign?'

'The doctor would like to know the details of the accident.'

'We'll explain once we're aboard,' Sinistra said. She leaned back from the beautiful reflection and lowered herself into the helmsman's chair.

'Stand clear of the hatch,' said the comms. 'Take your seats. Fasten harnesses. 'We're bringing you back?'

'But you don't know the way out,' Sinistra said.

'We're going to find it. We're going to take you up and monitor the sensors. Once we detect a port or hatch, we'll take you out to open space.'

'That's your plan?'

'Yes, Lieutenant. That's the plan.'

'Whose plan?'

'Third Lieutenant Cadmus's plan.'

'But do you or Lieutenant Cadmus know how big the interior is in here? Our stern and top sensors don't register any dimensions. There's only the deck beneath us and the wall or bulkhead.'

'We have to try something, Lieutenant.'

'Then, with all respects to Lieutenant Cadmus, I think it's time I took control.'

'No, Lieutenant. The plan requires control from the bridge.'

'The plan didn't work on the way over here, did it?'

'Lieutenant Flavia approved it.'

'Let me speak to the captain.'

'The captain is unavailable.'

'Why?'

'I don't know, Lieutenant. His steward said no one could disturb him.'

'Well, given the captain's unavailability and Lieutenant Flavia's condition, I'm now the senior officer.'

She reached to the console and switched off the remote control the from the bridge. Then she turned off the communications.

'Let's get under way,' she said. Then she reached for the helm and switched on the engines.

The Albus coughed, growled and shook itself awake. The bulkheads creaked, the deck quivered. Flavia groaned at the back of the bridge.

Seconds later, the gangway retracted. The Albus rose from the deck and hovered at a height of five passus while the landing carriage clicked into place beneath the keel. The bow lanterns shone out into the gloom towards the wall.

'So,' asked Ranant, 'which way from here?'

Sinistra urged the Albus onward. 'For now,' she said. 'We'll work that out as we go.'

50

'There isn't a way out, Sin,' said Ranant, 'not through a port or a hatch. We've got to use the weapons. We've got to blast our way out.'

'That's not entirely true,' said Domitian. 'We could ask Owanthan for help. There's no shame in asking. It's what our ancestors did during the crossing to the home planet. And Owanthan answered them with miracles.'

Ranant scoffed, 'Come on, Chief. Not now.'

Sinistra made her decision. 'All right. We'll use the cannons.'

She fired the keel thrusters. The Albus rose to a hundred passus above the deck—more than twice its height.

'Why so high, Sin?' said Ranant.

'I want to be above the murals when we fire.'

'What does it matter now?'

She ignored him and set the stern thrusters to counter the blast recoil.

Before she fired the cannons, she waited for a sign from Sirhain—a sign of approval, a port opening in the wall—anything. When nothing happened, she said, 'Brace the first lieutenant. This might toss the ship about.'

Light flashed. The blast silently shot away. The Albus

rocked back until the stern thrusters caught it. Flavia groaned.

On the screen, the dust cleared, and a crater appeared in the wall. The sensors measured its diameter at half the height of the Albus.

'Brace again,' Sinistra said. The light flashed, Flavia groaned, and the stern thrusters caught the ship a second time.

'One more,' Sinistra said.

Now the hole in the object gaped wide and tall, like a wound.

'We're going,' Sinistra said.

She engaged the forward thrust. The ship advanced. As they neared the blast hole, the twinkling star fields appeared. Once outside, they could see the Herculaneum in the distant gloom.

But back inside the object, down where the wall met the deck, to the left of the image of the woman on the hill, a new image had formed. It showed a slain giantess, burst and broken on a street between the tall buildings of a city very different to the artist's impressions of Rome. Beside this fallen giant, a lone Hyacinth male stood wearing a uniform similar to that worn by the Herculaneum's crew. He carried a weapon that was almost as tall as himself. He stood with his head bowed, as if he were paying tribute or grieving a slain adversary.

'What did you say, Chief Domitian?' said Sinistra. 'Or were you praying aloud?'

'It wasn't a prayer, Lieutenant. It was a quotation from the Old Book. I chose something that seemed appropriate.'

'What quotation, Chief?'

'I'm only paraphrasing. Some scholars say this passage is a mistake because it's at odds with all the stories about worshipping the gods.'

'What's the quote say, Chief?'

'It's the quote about the difference between fate and destiny.'

'And what's that?'

'It's something like "Fate misleads the weak of mind and the fearful. It is submission to past failures, a giving in to them. But destiny is created by will and intention. It bestows hope, allowing one's future to be created." No, that's not right. I'll have to look it up later.'

Behind the Albus, the object receded and vanished in the dark. In the forward viewport, the Herculaneum waited.

What will happen when we return? Sinistra thought. What will happen when I descend the gangway? Who will be waiting for me? What will be my fate, or my destiny?

She would soon find out.

51

A half hora later, the Albus passed the Herculaneum's stern quarter, tacked to starboard, then tacked again until the cliff face of the transom appeared. Then it entered the leviathan's stern port.

Sinistra brought the ship to a halt on the ramp and began the shutdown routine. She sent down the landing carriage. Then she switched off the engines, turned off the fuel pump, the atmosphere pump, the gravity pump, the lanterns at the bow and stern. Then she sent down the gangway and waited until the joints extended and locked. Finally, she unsealed the outer hatch.

It was time to meet the future.

In the forward viewport, the dropship fleet stood in silent ranks. As before, the fleet resembled a mournful white forest, still and desolate. At the sight of it, Sinistra shivered—a new Hyacinth gesture—and she thought to herself, I've had enough of forests for the moment.

There was movement between the white ships. Mechanics came forth with their cart for the post-mission inspection. Then a detachment of twelve masters-at-arms, dressed in their dark blue uniforms and carrying light rifles on their shoulders, marched out and overtook the mechanics.

'What are they doing here?' said Ranant.

'Probably just a precaution,' said Sinistra.

'But what are they expecting? Stowaway Goths?'

'We've been to a strange place,' Sinistra said, 'And we've been out of contact. Captain Tiberius is just being cautious.'

'No. I think it's something else, Lieutenant,' said Ranant. 'Someone saw you on a monitor.'

At the rear of the cabin, Domitian leaned over Flavia's stricken body. He peered into the carnage of her neck and pulled at the fingers clamped over her face.

'Well?' said Sinistra.

'Still unconscious. Her heart beats—just, but that's the only good sign. It would have been better if she stayed in her natural form.'

'Have her eyes opened?' said Sinistra.

'I can't see them. Her fingers are like iron.'

'Is she breathing again?'

'Maybe.'

'Thank Owanthan,' said Sinistra, aware of the lack of emotion in her voice. 'We all want her to recover as fast as possible.'

She walked to the airlock and unsealed the inner hatch. She turned the wheel and pulled the lever. The hatch released its grip on the jamb. Sinistra swung it open. The usual smells rushed in: metal, oil, paint, and the smoke from engineering. There were other things, too: the reek of order, authority, and power.

Down on the deck, the masters-at-arms stood to attention. Someone shouted, 'Salutate!' The small detachment stamped their boots and saluted. Sinistra stepped from the hatch and stood on the gangway's top step and looked down at the assembled men. A medical crew of four had joined them.

Sinistra saw the covert glances, the blinks, the sudden jerks of thyroid cartilages in each neck, and in one case, a backward step. For a second time, the commanding officer shouted, 'Salutate!' The confused MAs stamped their boots and saluted all over again.

Sinistra descended to the lowest step.

'Welcome back, Second Lieutenant.'

'Thank you, Sergeant Marcus. That's your name, isn't it? Marcus?'

'Why yes, Lieutenant.'

'Are you all right, Sergeant?'

'Yes, I'm just … your appearance, it … I thought you were …'

'Tell me, Sergeant, why the masters-at-arms?'

'Captain Tiberius's orders, Second Lieutenant.'

'Did the captain state his reasons?'

'I wasn't present when he issued the orders, Second Lieutenant.'

'Make a guess, Sergeant Marcus.'

'I heard it was something to do with First Lieutenant Flavia and yourself.'

'Lieutenant Flavia's injury is not a reason for an armed escort, is it?'

'No, Lieutenant.'

'There's no need for any iron rings, Sergeant Marcus. I don't plan on expanding.'

'Iron rings, Lieutenant?'

'Aren't rings required when you make an arrest?'

'Lieutenant, we aren't here to arrest anyone. We're here to escort you.'

'Escort me?'

'Beg pardon, Lieutenant. We must hurry. Doctor Galen is waiting to treat First Lieutenant Flavia, and we are ordered to take you directly to Captain Tiberius's stateroom.'

'Of course,' Sinistra replied, standing up straighter. 'Of course. Lieutenant Flavia is in the cabin. Chief Domitian is caring for her.'

Sergeant Marcus saluted and pointed at the medical crew.

The crew came forward and hurried up the gangway, smiling shyly as they passed. Sinistra turned to Sergeant Marcus. He beamed a smile back at her.

'All right, Sergeant. Let's get it over with.'

When Sinistra and the escort arrived at the captain's forward stateroom, Sergeant Marcus ordered the detachment to stand at attention all over again. Sinistra saluted, and the detachment marched away. She lifted a comradely chin to the marine sentry and at Frumentius, the captain's steward. Then she knocked and entered. Now there is going to be an arrest, she thought, a formal arrest in front of the captain.

But inside, there was only one person waiting for her. Advisor Cicero stood in his white and purple toga beneath the painting of 'The Fate of The People.' When he saw Sinistra, he straightened the toga's folds over his shoulders and shifted the family crest pin so that it rested over his heart.

'Yes. What is it?'

'I am here to see Captain Tiberius, Advisor Cicero.'

Cicero frowned over Sinistra's shoulder at the retreating masters-at-arms.

'I'm here as commanded, sir,' Sinistra said.

'Yes,' Cicero replied. 'So, I see.'

'Is the captain on his way?'

'First things first,' said Cicero, straightening his robes once more. 'Who in the galaxy are you?'

For a fraction of a secunda, Sinistra did not know the answer.

52

'It's me, Second Lieutenant Sinistra, Advisor Cicero. Where is Captain Tiberius?'

Cicero stared at her. Like the navy officers and senior warrant officers, he was descended from the old patrician families. The Admiralty had assigned him a Hyacinth form appropriate to his status, though definitely not representative of his advanced age and poor health.

In Cicero's case, the Hyacinth-creature form was based on a statue of Marcus Tullius Cicero, a Roman statesman. The statue depicted an old, bald man, but the Admiralty had made Cicero young, tall, handsome with a head of golden curls and square shoulders.

The slight crease in Cicero's forehead deepened as he blinked at Sinistra, making him look young and old at the same time.

'But you have changed your appearance, Lieutenant.'

'Yes, Advisor Cicero. Is the captain on his way?'

'I'll get to the captain in a moment. Please, answer my question.'

'I didn't change my appearance, Advisor. Something happened on the object.'

'And you have changed your voice.'

'I hadn't noticed, Advisor.'

'If I didn't know any better, I might have said you were Lieutenant Flavia. It's extraordinary.'

'I am still unaccustomed to it myself.'

'How did this change come about?'

'I don't know, Advisor.'

'You have no idea?'

'The object's interior is full of inexplicable forces. I will explain our findings to Captain Tiberius when he arrives.'

But Advisor Cicero straightened his robes once more.

'Lieutenant, you know the Admiral has forbidden changes to your form, don't you?'

'Yes, Advisor.'

'You are aware of the importance of maintaining the traditional hierarchy. Am I correct?'

'Yes, Advisor. I'm aware of all the requirements.'

Sinistra felt her impatience rising. Cicero only ever spoke to the captain. Why was he speaking to her as if he were now part of the navy command?

'Doctor Galen will want to examine you and make the change back to your original form as soon as possible.'

'Yes, Advisor. Of course.'

'It's nothing personal, Lieutenant. It's only to maintain the natural, traditional order. You can't just change your appearance whenever you like. I'm sure you understand.'

'Yes, Advisor. Of course. But may I ask why you are here, not Captain Tiberius?'

Cicero looked at the deck for a moment. Then, he said, 'In a way, it's a pity. Your new appearance might have been helpful.'

'In what way, Advisor?'

'Take a seat, Lieutenant.' He raised a bare forearm at a chair. When Sinistra sat down, he said. 'There has been some terrible news, both from home and aboard the ship.'

'What news, Advisor?'

'New eruptions have occurred, violent ones near the city of Ashtagron, where the captain's family has a home.'

'Is the captain's family all right?'

'We don't know. No news or messages are getting out of the city, not even telepathic ones.'

'And Captain Tiberius?'

'Patience, please, Lieutenant.'

'If it's about Lieutenant Flavia, I can explain.'

There was a knock at the door. A medical staff member stood at the entrance. He seemed unsure what to do—to salute or not? When he saw Sinistra sitting in a chair on one side of the room, he stood upright, looked at her, looked at Cicero, then looked back at Sinistra. Finally, he placed his fingertips to the side of his head.

'Surgeon's Mate Cordinaus, sir.'

'Yes?' said Cicero

'A report on the condition of Lieutenant Flavia.'

'Yes?'

'Doctor Galen says the lieutenant is still unconscious and unresponsive to attempts to wake her.'

'Why didn't the doctor come here himself?'

'He sends his apologies, sir. There has been a new influx of lurgy. Beg pardon, I meant the new miseria disease. There's a fresh crop from the hold. The doctor is also attending to the other patient, sir, the very important one.'

'All right, Cordinaus. Is that all?'

'Yes, sir.'

The surgeon's mate left. Advisor Cicero drew a long breath, looked at Sinistra and said, 'This makes what I have to tell you more urgent and grave.'

Sinistra made no reply.

'Captain Tiberius is unwell, Lieutenant. You won't have heard the news, but the captain is also suffering from this terrible miseria. After he received the news of his family, he fell unconscious. He has not woken since.'

'Oh, no. That is terrible news.'

'Yes, the worst news, the very worst. Naturally, I have informed the Senate about it, and also about the first lieutenant.'

'But what can the Senate do?'

'Well, first, a replacement is necessary. The Senate is sending Captain Dranta, just in case.'

'A very experienced officer, Advisor.'

'Yes, he's from one of the oldest families. The Admiralty has named him Captain Agrippa for the mission. Unfortunately, he will not arrive before we accelerate. He can only rendezvous with us in the Hyacinth solar system. This is where the news concerns you, Lieutenant Sinistra.'

Sinistra leaned forward in her chair.

Advisor Cicero continued. 'With the captain and our first lieutenant unwell, you are the most senior naval officer on active duty. Active duty—is that the correct term?'

'Close enough, Advisor.'

'In other circumstances, I would congratulate you, but in this awful situation, it's only appropriate to ask if you are you ready to assume command of the Herculaneum. As acting captain, you must guide the ship to Gordium, through the Acceleration, and to the Hyacinth solar system. If Captain Agrippa does not arrive in good time, you might be required to command the marines and the crew for our first descent to Hyacinth itself. You will also accompany me to the first meetings with the Hyacinth leaders.'

Sinistra said nothing. Instead, she stood up and walked towards the painting of 'The Fate of The People.' Cicero frowned. 'Are you all right, Lieutenant? You have commanded large vessels before. Am I correct?'

'Yes,' said Sinistra. 'Many. In fact, I have commanded the Herculaneum before on several cruises.'

'Oh, really? I never knew. Why did no one mention it?'

Sinistra walked to the captain's table and gazed at its

varnished top. The beautiful face gazed back at her.

'There really is no other option, Advisor, is there?'

'It's an enormous responsibility, I agree, Lieutenant.'

'Thank you.'

'Don't thank me, acting Captain. The mission cannot wait. If we're to play a part in saving the people, there's no other option.'

And it was done, just like that. She was captain of the Herculaneum, a ship the size of a city, with a crew of ten thousand, a hold full of terra-forming machines, and enough weapons and marines to mount an invasion.

Cicero said, 'I assume you know what to do next. You must enter your new rating in the ship's log, meet with the senior officers, and so on. Then you must deal with this object and get us under way. There isn't much time, Captain Sinistra. We have only a few days to reach Gordium.'

'I thought we had a week.'

'You have been gone at least two Hyacinth days, Lieutenant. A few days is still enough time to reach the Point of Acceleration, is it not?'

'Yes,' said Sinistra, 'if Engineer Gabinus strains the cruise engines.'

'Good. I leave it to you.' He raised the white fold of his robe to his mouth and coughed. 'Beg pardon,' he said, and walked towards the door.

'Advisor Cicero?'

'Yes?'

'Has the Senate approved the plan to fire on the object if necessary?'

'Of course,' said Cicero. 'I forgot to mention it. The Senate has approved the use of the cannons.'

'Thank you, Advisor.'

'One last thing. I have asked Doctor Galen to examine you. The Senate expects it, and your new promotion might depend on the doctor's opinion.'

The door closed, and Sinistra was alone with 'The Fate of The People.'

'Thank you,' she said to the painting, even though Sirhain did not appear in the captain's version. 'What now?' she said. 'What now?'

Someone knocked.

Frumentius stood in the doorway.

'Do you require anything, acting Captain Sinistra?'

'Yes, thank you Frumentius. Pass the word for Astronomer Manius, Chief Gunner Decimus, Chief Engineer Gabinus, and Chief Purser Seta.'

'Yes, acting Captain.' He turned to go.

'And Frumentius.'

'Yes, acting Captain?'

'Pass the word for Lieutenant Imbrex of the Marines. Tell him to bring four of his men. Tell Imbrex I want the men armed.'

Frumentius saluted and closed the door.

Sinistra was alone again.

If I am to do this, she thought. I must remove any obstacles from the Herculaneum's path, and from mine.

53

The bell tolled.

Frumentius knocked on the stateroom door.

In came Decimus, Manius, Seta, and Gabinus, chatting as if they were entering the officers' club on the home planet. Decimus cursed to Manius about the damage done to his family home by the eruption in the province of Traxta. Seta spluttered to Decimus about Flavia. 'Her face!' she said. 'Have you heard about her face?'

As usual, each officer wore the special dark uniform, epaulets, and chest pin displaying their various family crests.

Watching them stride through the stateroom door, Sinistra detected the scent of lavender, Flavia's scent, the one she had worn aboard the Albus.

The commotion only died down when Seta, seeing someone else in the stateroom, tossed her chin toward the starboard bulkhead. Then, each of officer turned to the lone figure standing beneath 'The Fate of The People.'

Sinistra said, 'Thank you for coming. With Captain Tiberius and Lieutenant Flavia both gravely unwell, Doctor Galen has declared them both unable to perform their duties. And so, while the captain and Lieutenant Flavia recover, someone must assume command.'

Sinistra looked from one blank, hostile face to the next. No one replied. She went on.

'Today, Advisor Cicero, the Senate, and Admiral Drack, have appointed me as acting captain of the Herculaneum until further notice. They have ordered me to command the ship to Gordium and through the Acceleration to Hyacinth. If necessary, I ...'

'I don't believe it,' interrupted Gabinus.

'Don't believe what, Chief Engineer?' said Sinistra.

'I heard about it, but I didn't believe it,' Gabinus said. 'Now I see what the fuss is about. It's convincing—a genuine fake, you might say. It looks like us. It also sounds like us.'

'Yes, amazing. Isn't it,' said Seta, 'considering how it looked before.'

'The question we must ask,' said Gabinus, 'is not *how* it did it, but *why* it did it?'

Sinistra felt the burn of disrespect, but she kept her voice calm. 'I will address the change in my appearance after I speak to you about the mission.'

The senior officers looked at her. They seemed surprised she was speaking at all.

Astronomer Manius said, 'Why not tell us now, Lieutenant? We all want to know how it happened?'

'Hear, hear!' said Gunner Decimus.

Manius continued, 'Why is it only you, Sinistra? Domitian doesn't have a new appearance. Neither does Captain Ranant. He looks the same. Flavia looks the same, too, except that someone shot up her face. So tell us. Why are your face, body, and voice the only ones to change?'

'And who fired the shot at Flavia?' said Decimus. 'That's what I want to know. Who pulled the fire button? Surely that should mean an arrest. Why isn't Cadmus commanding instead of you?'

Sinistra watched their faces. Like her new ability to walk

freely, her skill at reading Hyacinth-creature expressions had improved. She could see the faces ranged before her expressing a mixture or curiosity, disdain, and hostility. They glared at her. They sneered. They scowled.

'At the right time there will be a hearing,' she said, 'and if necessary, there will be a court martial.'

'And when will that be?'

'Captain Tiberius will decide once he recovers, but as you know, a court martial requires six captains to be present and that won't …'

'When is the relief captain arriving?' said Manius. 'I heard someone was coming.'

'Captain Agrippa is on his way,' said Sinistra. 'You know him as Captain Dranta.'

'Dranta? Isn't he a cousin of yours, Manius?'

Before Manius could answer, Sinistra said, 'In the meantime, nothing is more important than reaching Gordium and then accelerating to Hyacinth. As acting Captain, I want to make sure that …'

'Reaching Gordium,' said Gabinus. 'That's what you're telling us—something we already know?'

'No,' said Sinistra.

'Well, don't keep us waiting, Second Lieutenant? What do you want to say?'

'I'm asking for your cooperation and support, and I also want to know that you are ready for …'

The door opened. Frumentius was there. A young male wearing a green engineer's uniform bobbed behind him.

'Beg pardon, Captain,' said Frumentius, 'but he wouldn't wait.'

'Not now,' said Sinistra.

'Chief Gabinus,' said the young male over Frumentius's shoulder. 'It's Apollo. It's that noise again.'

'Apollo, eh?' said Gabinus. 'Always Apollo.' He looked around the room at everyone except Sinistra. 'I'll be off.'

'But you'll miss its explanation,' said Seta. 'The explanation for its striking new appearance.'

'Tell me later,' Gabinus said, stepping towards the door.

Sinistra sensed a shift in the already tense atmosphere.

'Chief Gabinus,' she said. 'What do you think you're doing?'

'I'm going,' Gabinus said over his shoulder.

'Chief Gabinus!' Sinistra said. 'The engine can wait until we're finished.'

But Gabinus kept walking.

Sinistra drew a breath, and said, 'Chief Engineer, I order you to stop.'

She immediately knew a line had been crossed—perhaps two lines. She had never dared to speak this way to the senior officers. Not even the captain spoke this way.

Gabinus stopped. Then he turned slowly to face Sinistra across the stateroom. The other officers watched him.

'Order me?' said Gabinus. 'You order me? Is that what you just said, you little upstart? You order me?'

'You are a critical part of this mission, Chief Engineer, and I haven't finished what I have to say to you.'

'Just so you know,' said Gabinus, 'because clearly you don't understand, I play my part every day keeping this ship pushing through the galaxy.'

He turned to go and took two steps to the door. Sinistra felt herself at a mental crossroads. She had to act decisively, now or never.

'Lieutenant Imbrex!' she called. 'Bring in your men!'

In the doorway, Frumentius disappeared. A powerful arm in a dark sleeve pulled him out of the way. The same with the young male from engineering. They vanished from the doorway and the bright buttons on Lieutenant Imbrex's uniform appeared.

Imbrex pushed his way inside, followed by four armed men. They crossed the floor and stood at the far end of the stateroom. One Marine stood in front of the door, blocking the way.

Gabinus said, 'Don't tell me you're going along with this, Imbrex?'

Imbrex glared back at Gabinus but said nothing.

'Tell your man to get out of the way, or you'll know about it.'

He carried on towards the door, but Imbrex shouted a command and the marine at the entrance shoved Gabinus back into the stateroom.

'What do you think you are doing, Sinistra?' said Manius. 'This is unacceptable. It's outrageous enough that Cicero put you in command, but this is intolerable.'

'The situation has changed,' said Sinistra. 'What ever you think of me, you are bound by the articles of the navy and the dictates of the Senate. So am I.'

The officers smiled. Manius said, 'It's not as simple as you think.'

'It's perfectly simple, Chief Astronomer. I am in command until either Captain Tiberius or Lieutenant Flavia is fit for duty.' She turned to Gabinus. 'Now, Chief Engineer, you will wait a little longer until you hear what I have to say.' She looked at the other officers. 'This includes all of you, too.'

She waited till there was silence.

'Astronomer Manius, I want to see your charts for the course to Gordium.'

'The captain has already approved the course,' said Manius.

'I would like to see it today and approve it myself.'

She turned to the gunner.

'Chief Petty Officer Decimus, we will test your cannons.'

'We tested the cannons while you were on your little expedition, Lieutenant.'

'Good, then you'll have no problem testing them a second time now that I'm back from my little expedition. And in the future, all of you will address me as Captain or acting Captain.'

'But nothing has changed since the test,' said Decimus. 'The guns are fine.'

'Then, nothing will go wrong, will it, Chief Gunner?'

Sinistra looked at Seta. 'I will also want to see your plans for removing the foul smell I detected when I came aboard.'

'I've agreed my plan with Tiberius already.'

'Well, the plan is not working, is it? The Great Passageway reeks of something it shouldn't.'

She turned to Gabinus. He glared back at her, shook his head, and said, 'No one touches engineering. Not even Flavia.'

'That would explain why were are still in Ilium and not on Hyacinth, Chief Engineer. We will have a test of the great engines both idling and at near-Acceleration speed. Have them ready at six bells.'

'You aren't the captain, missy. You aren't one of us, either, if that's what you're trying to be.' He stood to his full height and pushed out his chest and its pin.

'Who shot Flavia?' he said.' Was it you? I wouldn't have believed it three days ago, but now I can see what a dangerous little upstart you are. You shot her, didn't you?'

'You'll have to wait until the inquiry, Chief Engineer.' She looked across at Imbrex.

'Marine Lieutenant.'

'Yes, Captain.'

'Please withdraw your man from the door and permit the officers to leave.'

The marine stood aside. The scions of the great families shuffled toward the door.

'Wait!' Sinistra said. 'You have forgotten to salute.'

The officers looked at each other, then with mock formality, they raised their fingertips to their temples, and then stormed through the door.

Sinistra looked at Lieutenant Imbrex. He was already looking back at her.

'Was I excessive, Imbrex?'

Imbrex cleared his throat. 'It is unwise for leaders to make enemies of senior officers.'

Sinistra was about to reply, but she had just discovered a new idea. It had come to her while Imbrex stammered through his words. The thought was this: It is better to be feared than to be liked. Yes, she thought. Why I haven't I ever thought this before?

Cadmus knocked and entered. After congratulating Sinistra on her promotion he said, 'It's Doctor Galen, Captain Sinistra. He wants to see you on the Domum Deck immediately.'

'Immediately, First Lieutenant Cadmus? Why did he contact you to bring this message. Why didn't he go through Frumentius?'

'I don't know, Captain, but he said Admiral Drack requires his personal endorsement for your promotion. He said you knew that.'

'But did he actually use that word: petitiones?'

'He used a more emphatic word.'

'A command?'

'More emphatic.'

'More emphatic than a command?'

'More like an order.'

Sinistra turned to the marines.

'Lieutenant Imbrex.'

'Yes, Captain.'

'Don't dismiss your men. I would like you to escort me to the forward-aft shuttle and then the Domum Deck.'

'Is that necessary, Captain?' said Cadmus.

'Yes, First Lieutenant. It's necessary if I say it is.'

54

Gordium. Accelerate. Hyacinth.

These became like three guiding stars in the sky.

And Sinistra added a fourth: And whatever waits in the future.

But first, she had to overcome Doctor Galen and his questions. She felt like some old warrior in a furious melee who, having defeated one opponent, must turn and fight the next.

With the next bell approaching, Sinistra ordered Frumentius to make her a captain's uniform by the end of the afternoon watch. She ordered Cadmus to prepare the bridge for clearing away the object.

Once the orders were issued, she said, 'Follow me, Lieutenant, and bring a notepad.'

'Aye, Captain.'

She swept from the stateroom with her new, upright, Hyacinth-creature stride. Imbrex and the four marines marched behind.

In the Great Passageway, Sinistra ignored the appraising glances of the female crew members and the furtive leers of the males, but one crew member leered so long, that she stopped.

'Cadmus,' she said. 'Take this man's name.'

'Take his name, Captain?'

'Yes, for insubordination.'

'I'm just wishing you well on your promotion, Captain,' said Ensign Candida.

'You're not writing anything, Lieutenant Cadmus.'

'Are you sure about this?' said Cadmus. 'I know this man. He has made an honest mistake. That's all.'

'Well, now he won't make the mistake again, honest or otherwise.'

'Yes, Captain.'

'You are dismissed, Ensign Candida.'

Candida slunk away into the traffic.

Sinistra raised her beautiful chin and frowned.

'There's that smell again. I noticed it coming up from the stern. Why hasn't Seta done anything about it?'

'It's a new smell, Captain, a fouling in the scuttles.'

'What fouling?'

'From the suicides, Captain.'

'Suicides? How?'

'The crew members who receive bad news about their families—they climb into the vents and go out into space. Some of then try to climb back in again, but of course, by then, it's often too late.'

Sinistra looked at the streaming crew. Each crew member seemed affected by either disease or bad news. The sailors, petty officers, electricians, stewards, and marines all wore faces that were pulled about, stretched, and aged. Many also suffered lameness, hair loss, and the usual weeping rashes on their necks.

'Tell Chief Seta I want to see her as soon as we are under way.'

'Yes, Captain.'

They walked on. The marines followed. On the way to the shuttle station, they passed the large version of 'The Fate of

The People.' Sinistra looked up at Sirhain, glaring at the back of Owanthan's head. The Sirhain in the painting looked nothing like the Sirhain in the object. Even so, Sinistra sent him a message in her thought voice.

Are you making this easy or difficult for me? she said. Are you making it anything at all? Did I even meet you? Yes, I must have. How else could I be in this body with this face? And do I have a new future? You didn't say it, but surely you implied it: a new future if I just carry on, if I take command.

But Sirhain did not reply.

At the forward-shuttle station, there was a crowd pushing to get to the newsroom for the latest from the home planet. Cadmus ordered them to stand aside. The acting captain took a shuttle for herself and her escort.

When they reached the Domum Deck, two stewards were on duty—the same two stewards who had reported Sinistra for using unnecessary force. As Sinistra approached, the stewards stood to attention, and, once again began their curious exchange of cryptic remarks.

'Hail, Lieutenant Sinistra!'
'Hail, the captain of the Herculaneum!'
'Savior of the mission.'
'Savior of the people.'
'Bringer of hope.'
'And of despair.'
'The doctor awaits.'
'Destiny awaits.'
'Salvation awaits.'
'Two paths diverge.'
'Which will you take?'

Sinistra looked at their faces. 'First Lieutenant Cadmus,' she said.

'Yes, Captain.'

'Take these stewards' names. Then, order the Master-at-arms to report here and take them into the brig.'

'Yes, Captain, but what is the charge?'

'Insubordination.'

'Insubordination again?'

'Did you not hear me? Are your ears blocked?'

'No, Captain, but …'

'But what, Lieutenant Cadmus?'

'But the stewards have said nothing.'

Sinistra stiffened. 'What?'

'They haven't said anything, insubordinate or otherwise. They saluted. That's all. They know they may not speak until the captain speaks first.'

Suddenly Sinistra felt the burden of her new role: the Acceleration, Hyacinth, the destruction of the object, the threat of the object retaliating, the senior warrant officers, the senior petty officers, the doctor's examination, Flavia waking and denouncing her, the vision of the Herculaneum adrift and lost, the mission failed, her own failure, and the punishment that must follow.

Cadmus said, 'Any other orders, Captain?'

'Yes,' Sinistra said after a few moments. 'Tell Engineer Gabinus I'll see him as soon as I've spoken to the doctor. Tell him to start the Acceleration engines. I want them warm and idling. All three of them: Jupiter, Mars, and Apollo.'

'Aye, Captain.'

'And tell Imbrex to post sentries here till I return. No one is to enter.'

Then she strode past the two penitent stewards, through the doors of the Domum Deck, and into the realm of deserts, lakes, fields, and forests.

And to fate, thought Sinistra, but then she remembered Domitian's quotation from the Old Book. No, she thought. To destiny! To duty!

Destiny through duty, she thought. Yes! It was another discovery along with 'It is better to be feared than liked.'

Why had these ideas never occurred to her before? It was wonderful. She already felt herself walking a path to the woman on the hill.

But first she must overcome the doctor.

55

The Domum Deck was not the same.

After the rich, sensory world of Sirhain's forests and lakes, the deck's elaborate simulacrum of home planet regions was stale and underwhelming. The colors, the textures, and scents were all there, but there was no freshness, no vitality.

Sinistra stepped into the lavender field and waded through the calyxes and stems, wondering about the doctor. Why did he choose the Domum Deck again? Why not the medical deck? Will he want to re-test my ability to expand? Would he differ from the other warrant officers and put the mission first? No, thought Sinistra. He is an old family member, and last time we met, I soiled his robes with mud.

As she waded through the lavender, Telepathy raised his giant head. Sinistra listened for his growls in her mind. But this time, he said nothing. There was no warning, no advice on what to say to the doctor, no hints about her destiny and her 'role' in the people's future. By the look of his bent back, more terrible news was surging in from the home planet. Sinistra walked past him without speaking.

After trudging through the desert dunes, she entered the forest's cool dark. Doctor Galen waited in the same clearing as before. His hands were clasped, and he wore the white physician's toga (now laundered and snowy white again) and the same smile. This time, however, Sinistra could read that his smile was not sincere.

The doctor waited by the large log.

'Salve, Doctor!' she said.

'Salve, Lieutenant. I hope you don't mind me asking you here again. The medical deck is so noisy at the moment with all the miseria patients.'

'No, Doctor. I don't mind,' Sinistra said, forcing a smile of her own.

'Good,' he replied. 'It's much nicer here, anyway. The ship is so hectic lately.'

'Yes, Doctor. It's very calming.'

'Well, then.' He smiled. 'Admiral Drack has asked me to examine you.'

'Yes, Doctor. So I heard. However, I don't think it's necessary. I feel as fit as ever. And if I may be candid, with so much to do before the Acceleration, I am very short of time. I hope your examination won't take long. Or, if it's possible, we might postpone it.'

At this change in tone, the doctor raised his noble chin.

'I'm sorry to hear that, Lieutenant, but my examination must take as long as I think is necessary. Please, sit down.' He opened his palms towards the log.

They sat at opposite ends.

'First,' said the doctor. 'Have you rested after your mission?'

'No, Doctor.'

'But it's been seventy horae.'

'I feel fine, Doctor.'

'You must sleep, Lieutenant. Without sleep, your Hyacinth physiology will deteriorate. Unhealthy chemicals will accumulate in your brain. They will affect the clarity of your thoughts.'

'I'll sleep once we're under way to Gordium.'

'Are you suffering any ill effects from the object? I heard from Cicero you encountered strange phenomena.'

'No effects, Doctor, except that I am concerned about Lieutenant Flavia. How is she?'

'We will come to Flavia. Before that, I want to ask about your changed appearance and altered speech. How did they occur?'

Here it comes, Sinistra thought, but she kept her gaze on the doctor's handsome face and calm green eyes.

'I don't know,' Sinistra replied. 'As I explained to Chief Petty Officer Domitian, I passed through a gap in a wall and lost consciousness. When I woke, I was different.'

'Did you feel nothing, see nothing?'

'Nothing. It was totally dark.'

'Why do you think you transformed into this appearance and not something else?'

'I don't know, Doctor. The object is a place of strange forces. I can only think it was one of those.'

'Did you expand? Perhaps you fell unconscious. Your unconscious mind made you into the image it desired.'

'No, Doctor.'

'Are you sure?'

'Yes. My uniform was intact. There were no tears, no missing buttons. I remained the same size.'

'Have you tried to reverse the transformation?'

'I've had no time.'

'But it is important for your health, and especially the natural order. Cicero should have mentioned it.'

'Advisor Cicero thought this altered appearance might help while I am in command.'

'Advisor Cicero is not a doctor, Lieutenant, nor is he a naval officer.'

'I agree, Doctor, but the circumstances are extraordinary. For the mission, I propose we make an exception.'

The doctor's chin rose higher still. 'Then you must

propose it to the admiral, not to me. For now, if you remain in this form, you cannot be captain.'

For the briefest of moments, they examined each other, not as doctor and patient, but as adversaries appraising each other's strengths. One of the forest sickle birds made its plaintive cry, as if agreeing with one of them and not the other.

'So, please, Lieutenant. Here and now. Let's reverse the change. First, expand as high as you can and then I will give you the instructions.'

The doctor offered his insincere smile.

'I can't expand, Doctor. You've seen that already.'

'Even so, it is necessary to try.'

When Sinistra made no reply, the doctor mistook her silence for agreement.

'Don't forget, Lieutenant. You must remove the uniform in order to create the right frame of mind.'

Sinistra considered the doctor's youthful face. She noticed the slightest upward curl at one side of his lips—a mix of triumph and lechery.

'I can't expand, Doctor,' she said. 'But I will try again after my Hyacinth-creature sleep.'

'Sleep is no substitute for expansion, Lieutenant. You can't stay as you are.'

'Well, I'm sorry Doctor, I can't transform, not to my old appearance and not to my natural form. I might never transform again.'

'Well, if that's the case, I cannot give the Senate my endorsement of you as acting captain. It's as simple as that.'

Before Sinistra could object, the doctor added, 'And there is something else I must ask: this shooting incident.'

'There will be an inquiry, Doctor. This is not a medical matter.'

'I disagree. The circumstances of the shooting will help me form my medical opinion of you—or rather, your fitness for duty. Why did you fire at Lieutenant Flavia?'

Sinistra drew a breath and straightened her back. 'I protected her from an attack by … strange creatures on the object.'

'The two of you did not like each other.'

'In the military, liking someone is not important. It's duty that matters most. For what it's worth, I liked Lieutenant Flavia. I admired her.'

'You said liked not like. What do you mean? You no longer admire her?'

'I mean, I like her. I admire her.'

'And yet you shot her. You remember our conversation, don't you, the one about the danger of ambition and the lesson of the dictators in our history?'

'Yes, of course.'

'You are angry.'

'No.'

'Sit down, Lieutenant!'

'My rank is Captain, Doctor.'

'Not until I conclude you are fit to command.'

'I have commanded this very ship, the Herculaneum, several times before this mission. Did you know that, Doctor?'

Someone walked out of the forest. It was Cordinaus, the surgeon's mate.

'Doctor Galen,' he said. 'Doctor Lentinus sent me.'

'I am with a patient, Cordinaus.'

'But it's about Lieutenant Flavia and Captain Tiberius.'

Sinistra stiffened.

'What is it?' Galen said.

'Doctor Lentinus says you must come now, sir. Something has happened.'

'Yes, but what has happened?'

Cordinaus looked at Sinistra, then back at Doctor Galen. 'Doctor Lentinus said he must discuss it with you alone.'

'You are not listening, Cordinaus. I asked you what has happened? Is it the captain?'

'No, sir. Just one thing, sir. Lieutenant Flavia woke briefly and then she spoke. Then she fell unconscious.'

'She woke?'

'And spoke, doctor. Lieutenant Flavia woke, then Lieutenant Flavia spoke.'

Doctor Galen said, 'Are you all right, Lieutenant Sinistra? Your back seemed to spasm. Are you in pain? '

But before he could finish, the Herculaneum shuddered and a low moan roared across the desert, over the treetops, and came rumbling back like thunder.

'What was that?' said the Doctor. 'What made that noise? Lieutenant, did you hear me? What was that?'

'It's the Acceleration engines, Doctor,' Sinistra said, holding her stomach. 'I have asked Chief Gabinus to test them.'

'But why do they sound like wild animals?'

'They sound the same as usual, Doctor. You are simply hearing them at close range, not from forward at your Acceleration station.'

'Well, they are terrifying. Truly terrifying! All right, Cordinaus, let's get away before this noise damages our hearing.'

Sinistra shouted after him.

'Doctor Galen!'

'Yes?'

'Your endorsement. Please! I must have it to command the crew and the senior officers.'

But Doctor Galen only offered her a tolerant little smile, and then was gone.

56

Sinistra stood alone in the clearing.

Flavia woke, and Flavia spoke. But what did Flavia say? Did she accuse me of attempted murder? Are the masters-at-arms and Sergeant Marcus coming to arrest me? Will they lock me in the brig for decades—after only one watch as captain?

She thought of all that had gone well for her so far: the encounter with Sirhain; the object releasing the Albus; her astonishing change from shrub to beauty; and her promotion to captain. They had all happened suddenly, one after the other.

Then, there were the powerful new ideas, like unseen helpers waiting their moment—ideas that gave her the courage to face down the old-family warrant officers.

Surely these things were meant to be. There was an order to them, a logical progression that if followed might lead to the woman on the hill, and to the adoring multitude, and to relief and validation at last.

True, she couldn't imagine exactly how it would happen … and yet!

She listened to the Acceleration engines. How they moaned! In three days, they will take me across the galaxy to

Hyacinth itself. I will stand with Cicero and greet the Hyacinth leaders, and glimpse the adoring multitudes. T o walk any other path seemed foolish.

But the Acceleration was still two days away. In the meantime, Flavia had woken, and Flavia had spoken. If Flavia recovered from the blast, she would become the new captain and she would take her revenge, and then her recklessness might end the mission entirely.

Sinistra's viscera churned. Her heart thumped. Could everything be about to come crashing down—the mission, her promotion, her dream? Suddenly, it felt inevitable. How foolish and indulgent she had been? How rash and careless!

Now, the masters-at-arms were on their way with the iron rings. She was bad after all, and she always would be bad. Look what she had done. She deserved whatever was coming.

Someone stepped into the clearing. She looked up, expecting to see the rifles, the rings, and Sergeant Marcus no longer smiling.

But it was only Cadmus.

'Yes, First Lieutenant?' Sinistra said.

'Beg pardon, Captain. Gabinus says he can only spare you a half bell. Captain, are you all right?'

57

Sinistra walked aft along the Great Passageway towards engineering and the confrontation with Gabinus. As she walked, she recited to herself that it was better to be feared than liked. Cadmus walked beside her. Marine Lieutenant Imbrex and the escort marched behind.

A group of seven crew members came forward from the stern ramp. Each wore a gray uniform soiled with paint. Each also suffered from an ailment, a limp, clawed fingers, a facial twitch, a glistening lesion on their wrists or necks.

'Who are they, Cadmus?'

'Beg pardon, Captain. What did you say?'

'I said who are they—those seven men?'

Cadmus turned and looked at the gloomy, slouching group.

'They are from the last watch on the stern, Captain.'

'Why are their uniforms like that?'

'The have been painting new livery on four dropships. Advisor Cicero wanted the ships renamed after the Senators who nominated him for the Hyacinth governorship. Then he wanted a fifth ship named after himself.'

'Why are these men so downcast?'

'Beg pardon, Captain. Why are they what?'

'So gloomy. So angry.'

'I don't know. But I can guess. They had family members killed by the eruption at the capital two days ago.'

'I sense something other than mourning.'

'Something else?'

'Something dangerous.'

'You mean they are distracted from their duty by grief?'

'No, I mean their thoughts—disobedient thoughts, perhaps mutinous thoughts.'

'Mutinous thoughts? I don't think so. There are no rumors of anything like that. Most of the crew likes your appointment.'

'Take their names.'

'More names, Captain?'

'Yes, Lieutenant Cadmus. More names.'

Cadmus turned and walked back along the Great Passageway. Sinistra walked on. The words in her mind kept repeating: Flavia woke. Flavia spoke. But what did Flavia say?

A voice interrupted her thoughts.

'Permission to speak with the acting Captain,' said the voice. Despite the noise from engineering, the voice was distinct and soft. It came from her left, near the starboard bulkhead.

Sinistra turned and saw a tall, open-faced seaman with fair hair and a slight smile.

'I shall take only a moment of your busy day, Captain,' the seaman said. 'I hast something you crave to hear.'

'No,' said Sinistra. 'Step away and return to your station. Imbrex! Bring two of your men and seize this man.'

Imbrex and the marines came forward.

But the tall seaman stood his ground, and the marines came no closer. He spoke again in his firm, quiet voice.

'It's about the woman on the hill.'

Sinistra looked at the man's face for traces of the wicked,

mocking smile, the amused eyebrow, and the twinkling eyes. Was this Sirhain?

'Imbrex,' said Sinistra. 'You may stand down.'

'Aye, Captain,' said Imbrex. The marines backed away.

Sinistra turned back to the tall figure by the bulkhead.

'Mine master?' the seaman said. 'Did you say mine master?' He spoke in the native language, but it was a version from centuries before, a mixture of old and new grammar in an accent Sinistra had never heard.

'Master,' he repeated. 'I hast no master.'

'Then who are you? Aren't you from him?'

'I'm a friend.'

'Whose friend? His friend? Are you one of his followers? I might have expected a mole or a monkey rather than you?'

'No, Captain Sinistra. I am thy friend, here to give thee advice. I am not a stranger. Thou hast seen me oft.'

She looked at his name patch. It read 'Navita Merula.'

'You were on the stern ramp before the mission.'

'Yes, I was, and other places, too.'

'Where?'

He smiled. One of his front teeth was chipped. 'In the great painting, pointing the way. Thou knowest whom I mean.'

'You?'

'Aye, Captain. Me.'

'I don't believe you.'

'Do thou believest thou met the traitor, Sirhain? Do thou believest thou walked in his forest among his so-called children?'

Sinistra said, 'If you are who you say you are, what do you want?'

'I crave thy ear, thy attention, and thy trust. I say again, I hast advice.'

'I have enough advice already.'

'Doth thou truly? For someone with so many problems,

thou should seek advice—good advice.'

'I am doing all I can to save this mission before the Acceleration. You, of all people, should approve—if you are who you say.'

'Saving the people? Such a lofty claim for one mortal to make.'

'It is the truth.'

'Don't misunderstand me. I want thou to save the mission. I want thou to save the people, just like Sirhain wants thou to save the people, but there are things I want not.'

'What things?'

'I don't crave thou to become this vision of which thou dream, this woman on the hill.'

'Who says I am dreaming of it?'

'The vision is alive in thy mind. It is like the sun in the mornings. Thou canst not hide it—not from me.'

'What if it is? What's it's to you?'

'Sirhain hath no plan for this, yet thou still believe it. Thou labour to save this mission to make the vision real.'

'I'm only doing my duty,' Sinistra said. Navita Merula looked briefly at the deckhead as if summoning patience.

'If thou succeed,' he said, 'thou shall do great harm—harm to the home planet people, harm to the Hyacinth people, and to this ship's crew. And thou shall harm thy neighbors the Goths.'

Sinistra almost laughed. 'Oh, really! So what do you recommend? Should I step aside? Hand the ship over to Cadmus and hide in my cabin?'

'No. Save the mission. Command the ship to Hyacinth, then withdraw. Heal your mind. It is the better path—for thou and thy people.'

Sinistra scoffed. 'Why do you care? Sirhain told me about you and the rest of them. It's all just vanity. None of you are divine; you aren't even moral. You're like spectators watching a contest, hoping the contestants will thank you for watching. You're no better than the old families.'

'Is that thy answer?'

Suddenly, Cadmus was shouting to her over the engine noise.

'I have the names, Captain!'

'What?'

'I have the . . .'

But Sinistra heard only Navita Merula's hissed words. 'Sirhain offered a choice. Now, so do I: him and darkness; or me, you and your people.'

'Are you all right?' said Cadmus. He looked at the uniform swelling on Sinistra's back. 'Would you like to go back to your cabin? I can speak to Gabinus, if you please.'

Sinistra's anger flared. 'You would like that, wouldn't you?'

But Cadmus only said, 'Beg pardon, Captain. I didn't hear you.'

'No,' said Sinistra. 'No. There isn't time. We have to fix this now or never.'

58

Cadmus knocked three times on the heavy black door. The door remained shut, so Cadmus knocked again. The door did not open. He tried the lever. It wouldn't budge. Then, Cadmus pulled back his hand. The door was hot to touch.

'They can't hear us, Captain,' he shouted over the howling engines. 'With your permission, I will send a thought message to the Chief Engineer.'

'No, they can hear us,' Sinistra said. 'Gabinus simply wants to make us wait.'

Suddenly, the heavy lever swung upward. The door opened but no further than the width of a Hyacinth-creature arm. Out rushed smoke, heat, the acrid smell of hot machinery, and something else: the scent of lavender.

Then, a young, disfigured Hyacinth-creature's face leered through the crack. His appearance was so bizarre that he could have been a creature from the underworld described in the Old Book.

'Etiam?' the creature shouted. Yes?

Cadmus filled his lungs and said, 'Tell the chief engineer that Captain Sinistra is here to inspect the Acceleration engines.'

'What?'

'You heard me. Tell the chief engineer.'

'Tell him yourself,' the face shouted, and then the door slowly opened.

Cadmus stepped aside. Sinistra walked past him into Gabinus's noisy, dirty realm. The face at the door ogled Sinistra's legs.

Inside, the engine room was a vast hall almost as tall as the Herculaneum itself and as half as long as the Domum Deck.

In its center stood the three great Acceleration engines. Each engine was shaped like a tree trunk, with several branches splitting away up to the deckhead far above, and leading to the terrible exhaust funnels at the stern. The effect of these tree-trunks, funnels, and pipes, made the deck appear like a decrepit temple with nightmarish monuments to gods of fire and violence.

Aft of the Acceleration engines, a bank of smaller cruising engines idled in their pits. All the engines were fussed over by Gabinus's hand-picked crew of mates. Like many of the Herculaneum's crew, the engineers suffered from deformities of the Hyacinth-creature body: hunched backs, facial tics, short limbs, and the usual suppurating rashes on their necks.

All the mates turned lecherous gazes on the tall, beautiful, acting captain as she strode through the steaming pipes, oil-caked work benches, and smoke. On the bulkheads, the crew had drawn obscene images in the grime. The images were mostly of naked Hyacinth-creature males.

Gabinus stepped forward. He had an arm around two younger, shorter mates. Compared to them, Gabinus was healthy and young. His skin was clear and his posture was upright, even though in truth, he might be three times the ages of his crew.

Sinistra said, 'Chief Engineer,' but Gabinus held up a finger. Then, one of the disfigured mates held out what looked like seashells, each the size of a Hyacinth-creature hand. The mate pointed at his ear, then at Sinistra's and Cadmus's ears. Once the shells were in place, the engine noise faded to a burr and Sinistra could hear Gabinus's disdainful voice.

'You're late, Lieutenant,' Gabinus said through the shells. 'We have more important things to do than wait while you brush your hair and manicure your claws.'

'It's Captain, not Lieutenant, Chief Engineer, as you well know.'

'Not yet it isn't.'

'Are your crew always so hostile to senior officers?'

'Yes,' said Gabinus. 'They don't like female officers. Sorry, but that's the way things are. They're used to males.'

Sinistra looked at the drawings on the bulkheads. 'So I see.'

'How long will this take?' said Gabinus. 'We don't like the noise either, you know.'

'It will take as long as I need it to take.'

'I told you. There isn't any need. You're just wasting our time.'

'Well, if there's no need, you'll have nothing to worry about, will you?'

'You like saying that, don't you?' Gabinus said.

'I do if it fits the circumstances. Are the engines ready?'

'I don't like straining them simply for the whim of just anyone.'

Sinistra ignored him. 'I'd like to trust you, Chief Gabinus, but we can't have the engines fail again.'

'The engines didn't fail. Not Jupiter, not Mars, nor Apollo. It was the object that caused the trouble.'

'Then let's check and make sure.'

'As I keep saying, there's no need. Tiberius approved them already.'

'I want to see for myself. It's not personal, Chief. There's no need to make things awkward just because you don't care for authority.'

'Don't care? Is that what you said? Don't care! Well, listen to me. Many of my crew lost family members last week. I myself lost a cousin in the Garantar eruption. Are you saying I don't care?'

They stared at each other while the noise raged around them.

Cadmus broke the silence. 'Captain, we're due on the bridge.'

'Don't let me keep you,' said Gabinus.

'We will inspect the engines first,' said Sinistra. 'Proceed to the test, Chief Engineer.'

'Everything was going perfectly before you stuck your nose in, Lieutenant.'

'I disagree. The Acceleration failed. The mission is now dangerously delayed. And you will address me as Captain or acting Captain.'

'You shot Flavia, didn't you?'

'Chief Engineer, we are running out of time.'

Gabinus scowled. Then he raised his chin and looked across at the mate standing at a panel on which various levers, dials, and gauges flickered—all beneath a large drawing of a reclining Hyacinth male.

'Stand back,' said Gabinus. 'Or the heat will burn your fair new skin.'

Sinistra walked away from the engines. Cadmus joined her.

Gabinus smirked at them. 'Here comes the thunder.'

The howling increased in volume. The three great engine-trees writhed as if hit by strong winds. The grimy deck shook beneath Sinistra's boots.

'Satisfied?' said Gabinus.

'This isn't Acceleration speed.'

'Of course not.'

'Bring them up to Acceleration level.'

'Can't do that. Too dangerous.'

'If it's not too dangerous during Acceleration, it's not too dangerous now.'

'Can't do it. They'll shake themselves loose.'

'I insist you do.'

'Insisting is not ordering. Are you ordering me?'

'Just do it, Chief Engineer, and yes, that is an order.'

'All right, but if something happens, you explain yourself to the families at home.'

Gabinus turned to the leering engineer's mates at the controls and rolled his eyes at the deckhead. The mates giggled, but then their faces became very grave as they adjusted the controls. The engines responded. The whine became a shriek. The deck shook as if it were suffering a volcanic eruption of its own. Debris spiraled down from the deckhead. It stuck to the bulkheads and melted into bubbles.

Meanwhile, the trunk of Jupiter glowed red, then orange, then white. The trunks of Mars and Apollo joined it until the three engine trees shone as bright as stars.

'Seen enough?' said Gabinus, but before Sinistra could reply, one engine failed with a loud bang. Sinistra, Cadmus, and Gabinus clutched their ears and ducked. When they looked up, spouts of flame shot forth from a red wound in Apollo.

Gabinus yelled something to the mate at the controls. The shrieking descended in pitch to a whine and then a low, unhappy growl punctuated by sick clangs.

'I warned you,' said Gabinus.

'What's happened?'

'Didn't you see the fire? You've broken Apollo.'

Sinistra thought for a moment. She kept her voice level. 'Better to damage Apollo now than in Gordium, Chief Engineer. Can you repair it?'

'We'll have to, won't we?'

'I'd say it was a good thing we made the test.'

Gabinus's handsome face flushed red. 'I know what you're doing, missy. But it won't get you anywhere. You won't replace Flavia, and you won't be standing beside Cicero, waving to the people on Hyacinth. The sooner they court-martial you, the better.'

'If I find out you are delaying the mission so that Captain Agrippa can take command, it will be you who faces a court-martial, not me, Chief Engineer.'

'It might be both of us,' said Gabinus.

'Just repair the engine, Chief. Repair it before we reach Gordium or there won't be any Hyacinth, and there won't be any home planet or families.'

She pulled the shells from her ears, dumped them with Cadmus, then turned and swept from the hall, past the grinning faces of Gabinus's crew.

Waiting for her in the passageway was a young midshipman. His name patch read En. Nerva.

'What?' snapped Sinistra.

'A message from Sixth Lieutenant Cephus, Captain Sinistra.'

'What message?'

'It's from Doctor Galen, about Lieutenant Flavia.'

Sinistra felt her organs sink to the bottom of her abdomen, like sacks of home planet seeds flung into the ship's hold.

'What about Lieutenant Flavia?'

'Her condition, Captain Sinistra.'

'What about her condition?'

'She is awake again. She opened her eyes this last bell. The doctor just sent word to Advisor Cicero. He asked Lieutenant Cephus to tell you.'

Sinistra waited a moment too long before replying. 'Owanthan be praised,' she said in a flat voice.

'Yes, Captain,' said Nerva. 'The doctor said it was a miraculum.'

'And is the lieutenant all right?'
'I don't know, Captain Sinistra. They didn't say.'
'Did she speak?'
'Yes, Captain, but it was only a few words.'
'What words?'
'The report from the doctor didn't mention them, but in the wardroom, people said they'd heard about it in the Great Passageway.'
'What did they hear?'
'They said the lieutenant's first words were your name.'
'Captain Sinistra,' said Cadmus. 'The bridge is ready for you.'

As they walked towards the forward-aft shuttle, Cadmus said, 'Wonderful news about Lieutenant Flavia, isn't it?'

'Yes,' said Sinistra, flatly. 'Wonderful. I was expecting the worst.'

'I never thought I'd say this,' said Cadmus. 'I was not raised in a religious family, but Owanthan be praised. It really is a miracle. From what I heard, Lieutenant Flavia was close to death.'

They passed beneath the painting of 'The Fate of The People.' Owanthan pointed the way to sanctuary. Sirhain glowered at the back of Owanthan's head.

'Yes, said Sinistra. It's like the gods are on Flavia's side,' but in her thoughts she said, Are they on mine?

59

Sinistra entered the forward stateroom. She was flustered at her sudden change of fortune. If Flavia had spoken Sinistra's name, what else had she said? Now, the master-at-arms would be waiting with the iron rings. 'Deprehensus es,' they would say. You are under arrest.

But why had Flavia woken at this exact moment, just when Sinistra was making progress? Was it due to Owanthan, Sirhain, or simply the effects of hazard? If only she had time to think, to work it all out! Instead, she was swept along by the torrent of events and the pressure of time, like a ship in a storm blown across the mouth of a mighty river. Also, she hadn't slept for several days, and couldn't focus her thoughts. Her feet were heavy. Her eyes ached.

Soon, Hyacinth-creature sleep would demand its rest.

To her relief, the master-at-arms was not waiting for her at the bridge. There were only the usual pair of marine sentries. Once she was through the door and into the familiar atmosphere for darkness and bright screens, she relaxed, but not much. Destiny through duty, she thought. Keep thinking that thought: Destiny through duty. For now, it's all I have.

'Captain on the bridge!' came the shout.

The bridge crew stood up from their various stations and saluted. Sinistra stepped to the podium on which the two chairs waited: the chair of the officer of the watch, and the chair for the captain. She sat down in the captains's chair and for the first time, assumed command of the Herculaneum's course.

Around the bridge, the most senior crew members were on duty: Corvinus, the helmsman; Consus the quartermaster; Manius, the astronomer; Cossus, the gunner's mate; and three technical officers monitoring the ship's port, starboard, and top sides. Domitian was also present as communications officer. Two mechanical marines stood to attention at the rear bulkhead, commanded by Captain Casca, not Captain Ranant.

The bridge was silent. The only sounds were the atmosphere pumps, the humming circuity, and the bip of the sensors. Everyone watched their screens. Everyone waited for the acting captain to take charge and clear the way.

When everyone sat down again, Sinistra said, 'Astronomer Manius, bring up the image of the object.' Manius closed his eyes in forbearance, but the object soon appeared on the main screen, luminous and gray.

'A closeup of its front base, please, Astronomer—as close as you can.'

'Why?' said Manius, then softened his tone and said, 'For what reason, acting Captain?'

'To see if there are any more predictions written in the old language, Astronomer Manius. That's why.'

Manius opened his mouth to speak, but then closed it and brought up a blurred image. It wasn't a message in the old language. Instead, it showed the Herculaneum pointing at the object, like one great sea creature meeting a smaller one.

'Do you see that, Astronomer?'

Manius concentrated on his screen and said nothing.

'Gunner's Mate Cossus?' Sinistra called to the comms.

'Yes, Captain?'

'Is the gun deck ready?'

'Yes, Captain. Chief Decimus has trained the weapons on the object's bow.'

'Good. Tell Decimus to stand by.'

'Aye, Captain.'

'Good,' said Sinistra. At least she still had this, the pleasure of commanding the ship. Arrest and incarceration might be waiting, and Flavia's vengeance might end her career, but at least she had this moment.

She called out, 'Engineering?'

A sneering voice spoke on the comms system. 'The cruise engines are idling, Captain.'

'Good,' Sinistra said. She turned to the technical officer. 'Port, starboard, top and keel sensors?'

'Nothing out there, Captain,' came the reply. 'No objects approaching.'

'All right. Let's get under way. Helmsman!'

'Yes, Captain,' said Corvinus.

'Let's see if the object will let us pass. Take us along its starboard side, if you can. Gently now.'

'Aye, Captain.'

Corvinus reached for the lever to signal engineering. Then, for the first time in four and a half Hyacinth days, the Herculaneum gained way. On the forward viewport, the object slid to starboard, almost as if nudged out of the way. Distant stars now filled the screens. The way to Gordium, the Acceleration, and Hyacinth was clear.

The bridge crew almost cheered. Corvinus stood taller at the helm. Consus actually turned to Sinistra and smiled. Even Manius seemed pleased, scratching his neck while he looked at his charts. And, there might even have been an actual cheer coming from deep in the ship.

Yes, at least I have this, Sinistra thought again. If Sirhain was displeased, he hasn't shown it—if Sirhain even exists.

But almost as quickly as the mood had brightened, it once turned dark. Manius said, 'Lieutenant ... Captain Sinistra?'

'Yes, Astronomer?'

'It's coming back.'

All eyes returned to the forward viewport. On the starboard side, the object's gray face pushed itself across the screen till it reached the centre. There it stopped, dead ahead, blocking the road once more.

'Your orders, Captain?' Manius said.

Sinistra ignored the tiny mockery in his voice. She knew there could be only be one set or orders: to fire on the object and clear it away. But would this finally provoke Sirhain's anger? It might, if he was paying attention.

Nothing to do but my duty, she thought. I'm sorry, Sirhain, but this time, there's no choice.

'Gunners Mate,' she said.

'Yes, Captain Sinistra,' said Cossus.

'Fire a single shot.'

'At the object, Captain?'

'No. Send a beam over its top. Maybe we'll warn it away.'

Cossus spoke into his console. Then he looked up. 'Firing, Captain.'

On the screen, the beam streaked out, blue and straight, over the object's slanted roof. Everyone waited, hoping for an explosion, or some kind of retreat, a stepping aside, a withdrawal.

But the object remained where it was, gray and obstinate.

Sinistra wondered if the image on the object's front had changed to a warning.

'Helmsman,' she said. 'Alter course by ten degrees to port.'

'Aye, Captain. Ten degrees to port.'

The wheel turned, the object slid from the screen once more, but then, just as before, it returned and stood defiantly in the Herculaneum's path.

'Gunner's mate. Send a beam at the object's bow. Five secunda.'

'Five secunda,' Cossus replied.

'Wait,' she interrupted. 'Check with the gunner for the debris blast range.'

Cossus lowered his head and spoke to the gun deck. Then he looked up.

'Chief Decimus says that if there is any danger of the Herculaneum being in the blast range, he would have alerted you. He said you should know that.'

'Thank you, Gunner's Mate. Tell the chief to proceed.'

Then she sat back in her chair and waited. She expected Sirhain's voice to whisper in her head or for some sign to appear in space: a beam of light, a herd of Goths, anything. But nothing appeared. No voice spoke in her mind. No thunder rumbled through space. For all intents and purposes, Sirhain was nowhere to be seen.

The beam went forth in the viewport. It smashed the object's colonnade, like a punch to a face.

Then a curious thing happened.

Silently, the object seemed to draw in on itself, as if it were gasping in shock and looking inward to check the damage to its own organs.

A quarter secunda later, it exploded. The Herculaneum shook with the blast. The view on the screen turned to snow. Debris showered the hull, clattering against the metal like a hailstorm. Some of the crew flinched and raised their forearms over their heads. Sinistra put a hand to her heart.

Eventually, the screens cleared to reveal a gray mist, the pin-prick lights of distant stars, and nothing in the road.

'Helmsman Corvinus,' Sinistra said.

'Yes, Captain.'

'Port helm, please. Proceed gently around the blast site. Then, once we are a thousand milia along, correct the course for the Point of Acceleration in Gordium.' She turned to

Domitian. 'Chief Communications Officer?'

'Yes, Captain.'

'Alert engineering. Tell them to stand by to bring the engines to cruising speed.'

'Aye, aye.'

'Cadmus.'

'Yes, Captain.'

'At eight bells tomorrow in the afternoon watch, issue the order to clear for Acceleration. In the meantime, the bridge is yours.'

'Aye, Captain. Thank you.'

'Captain?' said Chief Domitian.

'Yes, Chief.'

'Telepathy just received a message from the Senate.'

Sinistra placed her hands on the arms of her chair and held tight. 'Yes, Chief. What does the Senate say?'

'The Senators say, "Congratulations and may Owanthan speed you and the Herculaneum to Hyacinth."'

Sinistra relaxed her grip on the chair. Around the bridge, the mood lightened again. Consus, the quartermaster, turned and smiled. Then, in a gesture she had never seen before, he raised his hands and clapped them together several times. Two technical officers did the same. So did Domitian, and even Manius, though only briefly.

This was one of the happiest moments of Sinistra's career.

'Thank you, Chief. Thank you, everyone.' She turned back to Domitian. 'Please broadcast the Senate's message to the crew.'

And then she stood, feeling lighter in spirit but still heavy in fear. The Flavia threat still remained. Flavia had woken, and surely she would have said more by now. She might have even ordered someone to wait outside the bridge door with iron rings and a warrant.

Keeping her composure, Sinistra stepped over the threshold and out of the bridge, expecting to face the masters-at-arms. Instead, it was Cordinaus, the surgeon's mate, who stood waiting for her with a message.

60

Cordinaus saluted, then stood at attention, waiting for Sinistra to speak. He waited a full ten secunda while the pumps in the deckhead sighed.

'Yes, Surgeon's Mate,' Sinistra said.

'A report from Doctor Galen, Captain Sinistra.'

'Yes,' she said, not wanting to hear whatever came next.

'It's about Lieutenant Flavia's condition.'

'I had a feeling it would be,' Sinistra said.

'But the report is for your ears only, Captain.'

Sinistra looked at the marines and back at Cordinaus. 'Come over here,' she said, walked to the far side of the stateroom. 'What's the news?'

'Doctor Galen wishes to inform you that the lieutenant's condition has changed.'

'Changed again, Surgeon's Mate?' Sinistra said, examining the stitching on her own sleeve. 'She was speaking not one bell ago.'

'Yes, Captain. The doctor regrets to report the lieutenant has once again fallen unconscious.' He lowered his voice. 'He says her condition is now serious. He thought you would want to know.'

'More serious than before, Surgeon's Mate?'

'Very serious, Captain. Her Hyacinth-creature organs have deteriorated, and because she can't expand, recovery is difficult if not impossible.'

Sinistra drew a slow breath, affecting a gesture she had seen Captain Tiberius perform: a measured, thoughtful nod indicating a solemn appreciation of grave new information.

She looked up, keeping her mouth slack, and her forehead creased. 'May Owanthan watch over Lieutenant Flavia,' she said, 'and return her to …' she almost said 'duty,' but caught herself and said, '… health.'

'May Owanthan watch over her,' said Cordinaus.

'And what about Captain Tiberius?' Sinistra said.

'He is unconscious, but stable.'

'Thank you, Cordinaus. 'Please send my thanks to the doctor.'

'Doctor Galen also said he wishes to examine you again, Captain.'

Sinistra had expected this. 'Yes,' she replied. 'As soon as I have time.'

'Doctor Galen says it must be sooner rather than later.'

Keeping her fury down, Sinistra employed the slow, thoughtful nod once more. 'When I have time,' she said.

Cordinaus saluted and left. Frumentius entered, carrying a new captain's uniform. He came over to Sinistra and held it up, smiling with pride. 'Here it is, Captain.'

Sinistra saw the rich blue cloth, the glowing brocade of stripes, the dazzling epaulettes.

'Do you like it, Captain Sinistra?'

She was delighted, and yet, in this small moment of celebration, her tiredness weighed heavier, and she felt overwhelmed by all that was in play in her role as captain and in her private, solo quest.

Ever since she had stepped from the Albus, some things had gone well (her promotion, her browbeating of the senior officers), but others had not (Doctor Galen, Gabinus, the

Acceleration engines). But after the news about Flavia, things, on balance, were tiling in her favor.

Nevertheless, it suddenly felt all too much. She felt that if she stopped fretting, even for a bell, all the events in play would collapse and she would wake up with her hands in iron rings as the ship hurtled to its destruction.

She drew a long breath. This time the breath was sincere. It ended in a long, wide, overpowering, Hyacinth-creature yawn.

'Thank you, Frumentius. The uniform is magnificent. I will try it on the moment I have rested.'

'As you wish, Captain.'

Yes, she thought. Rest. It's time. It's necessary. And this moment is as good as any.

And, after all, didn't she command five capable lieutenants who would control the ship while she was gone? So, what could possibly happen if she were away for just a few hours?

Yes, what could possibly happen?

61

Sinistra might have been entitled to wear a captain's uniform, but she was not free to use Tiberius's cabin while Tiberius still breathed.

So, she walked solemnly down the Great Passageway to her own cabin, past the grave salutes, the slow nods of encouragement, and the furtive leers. She traveled the entire length of 'The Fate of The People' without looking up. She didn't want to see Sirhain's image so soon after destroying the temple.

At her cabin, she waited while Lieutenant Paetus and the marines took up their sentry positions outside. Frumentius hung the new uniform in her locker. Once she was alone, she leaned against the bulkhead, put a hand to her forehead, closed her eyes, and tried to direct her thoughts away from the ship, the mission, Flavia, Sirhain, and the woman on the hill.

When she felt calmer, she walked to the shiny metal bulkhead and examined her new Hyacinth-creature form. The change was astonishing. The withered yellow shrub was well and truly gone. Instead, a tall woman gazed back at her —a woman with level shoulders, lustrous hair, and upright posture—the image of a Hyacinth goddess.

She walked to the closet, lifted the new captain's uniform and was about to try it on when she changed her mind. She put the uniform and its hanger back on the rail. Then she walked to the cabin door.

'Lieutenant Paetus.'

'Yes, Captain Sinistra.'

'I've changed my mind. I'm going aft.'

'We will escort you, Captain.'

'No need. Please wait. I won't be far away.'

Sinistra walked down the passageway, returning the salute of a smiling midshipman along the way. She entered the section of the Marine officers' quarters and found the door she wanted. The name plate read, 'Capitaneus Ranant.'

She knocked. Then, without waiting for a reply, tried the door handle. The lock opened. The door yielded to her gentle push. She entered the cabin. Ranant was at his desk again, admiring himself in his hand mirror.

'Sin?' he said as she entered. 'What are you doing here?'

62

Sinistra raised her chin at the mirror.

'I ought to issue you with a code violation for possession of a prohibited object, Marine Captain Ranant.'

Ranant put the mirror down.

'And then, I ought to order the master-at-arms to arrest you, put an iron ring on your leg and take you to a dark cell in the brig where all you can see is your Hyacinth-creature feet.'

'I heard the object is gone,' said Ranant. 'Congratulations, acting Captain.'

'Yes,' said Sinistra. 'And now the mission continues.'

She closed the door behind her, but she didn't walk any further. She leaned against the bulkhead. Then, placed one foot over the other, and put a languorous hand on one hip.

'You seem nervous, Captain Ranant. Were you expecting someone else?'

'No, it's just that ship captains don't show up in the cabins of the Navy's Marines.'

'This captain does—for this marine.'

'I'm also still getting used to the way you look. Ten horae ago, you looked … you know … not like that.'

'Forget about how I looked ten horae ago. Ten horae ago is

ten Hyacinth-creature lifetimes ago.'

'That's not very long.'

'The world was different ten horae ago. So was the future. So don't tell me how I looked then. Tell me how I look now.'

She waited for him to stand, but he didn't move from his chair.

'To be honest,' he said, 'I thought you'd be busy with the Acceleration. Everyone's worried about it. My men don't believe it will happen. One of them said we're going to die like the Parthians.'

'I don't hear you saying you're glad to see me, Captain.'

'I'm serious, Sin. They're worried.'

'The Acceleration will be fine, now that I'm in command. Things are going to be better.'

'How can you be so certain?'

'For one thing, I'm going to push Gabinus until he fixes the engines properly. I won't allow him any slack.'

'Not even Tiberius could manage that.'

'Don't change the subject. We were talking about me. You've hardly spoken to me since the object. All you've done is sneak a look at my tergo finis. It's my duty to warn you, Captain Ranant, that if someone in the Great Passageway looked at me like that, they'd be joining you in the brig, where you could both stare at your strange Hyacinth-creature toes.'

Sinistra peeled herself from the wall and took two, three steps towards him, swaying as Flavia had done climbing the Albus's gangway. Now Ranant stood up, pushing the chair away. He reached out a hand to her waist. Sinistra intercepted it.

'What about Flavia?' she said.

'Flavia who?'

'I've got eyes, Marinus Capitaneus. I saw you on the Albus.'

'What did you see?'

'I saw you smiling at her, and winking at her.'

'The cabin was cramped. I couldn't ignore her.'

'You liked her, didn't you?'

'Liked? That's past tense, Sin. Flavia is still alive. She's breathing. I heard she woke up.'

'Yes, but then she fell unconscious again. '

'You should have more compassion, Sin. Flavia is your shipmate, your senior officer.'

'She was a danger to the mission, as you well know.'

'She's still alive, Sin.'

'Is she alive in your heart?'

'What in Owanthan's name does that mean?'

'Did you like her the way she liked you?'

'Like is a Hyacinth-creature concept, Sin, not one of ours.'

'Did you lust for her? Is that the right word?'

'I noticed her, if that's what you mean.'

'How did you get such good looks, Captain? Why do you have that chin? You're from the wrong side of the home planet, the same as me. You ought to look like the crew in engineering. Why do you look the way you do?'

Ranant smiled. 'A technicality. I have old family relatives. They're distant relatives, but they're close enough for the Admiralty to notice. That's why I have this chin, and this face.'

'But they didn't give you a Hyacinth name.'

'Marines don't need Hyacinth names. Hyacinth names are for the diplomats. Marines are the bad men. We have bad-man names, like Ranant.'

'Do you like me, Captain Bad Man?'

'A little.'

'Only a little?' She released Ranant's hand. 'Don't spoil the mood. Things are just starting to going well for me.'

'So, I heard, Sin. It's great news—about the object.'

'For the first time on this mission,' she said. 'I'm feeling better, more hopeful.'

'It's your new form. Your limp! That neck rash! They're gone, and you're … well, look at you.'

'No, it's not that. It's something else. I don't have the usual … I don't know. Let's just call it bad feelings.'

'What bad feelings?'

'If I had to name them, I'd call them formido.'

'Dread, Sin? Dread of what? Of the eruptions on the home planet? Dread of the Acceleration failing? Dread of what we have to do on Hyacinth? Most of the crew has that kind of dread.'

'No, not that. It's my personal dread of … I don't have it now—not as much. And if things keep going well for me, it might be less … dreadful.'

'You're not making sense, Sin.'

'I know. I'm tired.'

'But what do you mean?'

'At the moment, I only know how I feel. Don't look at me like that. Just come here.'

She reached for Ranant's hand.

Later, in the dark cabin, she lay beside Ranant on his narrow bunk. The scales on his arm chafed the soft skin on her neck. His claws scratched the delicate skin of her ankles.

'I knew you would choose me,' she whispered. 'I knew it.'

It's only been a few horae, Sinistra thought. A few horae! How much difference they can make! The Herculaneum, the Acceleration, Captain Tiberius, Flavia, and even the home planet catastrophe—they all seemed far away. And they also seemed … what was the word? Was it manageable? Yes, that was it. Or did she mean that she, Sinistra, was now better at managing herself? Yes, that might be it. She didn't even feel the old craving for approval—not when there was the adoration of an entire planet waiting in the future.

Perhaps I can do anything, Sinistra thought. No, I *will* do anything. I *will* do everything. Everyone will adore me.

And for the first time in four Hyacinth days and two

Hyacinth months since coming aboard the Herculaneum, she fell into heavy, restful, Hyacinth-creature sleep.

And in that sleep, she dreamed she stood on the Hyacinth hill in the warm sunshine. Ranant stood beside her, smiling, while the multitude chanted her name. Octavia! Octavia! Octavia!

It was the happiest she would ever feel again.

63

Someone knocked on the cabin door.

'Captain Ranant!' called a voice. The tone was not deferential. 'Captain Ranant, we know you are in there.'

Ranant blinked himself awake.

'Send them away,' whispered Sinistra.

'I'm off duty!' shouted Ranant. 'Speak to Lieutenant Tiburs. He's the Marine officer of the watch.'

The voice persisted.

'Can't do it. Open the door.'

'What do you want? Who's knocking?'

'This is Lieutenant Lupis.'

'Never heard of you.'

'I'm from the Master-at-arms.'

'What does the Master-at-arms want with the Marines?'

'Open the door, Captain. This is not a request. We are ordered here.'

'Ordered by whom?'

'I'll tell you when you open the door.'

'Is this about the fight in the viewing room? Well, sorry. I'm not your man, Lupis. I told your C.O. to keep away from the Marines. Ask him about it. I'm off duty.'

'We're not here for you, Captain. We're here for

Lieutenant Sinistra. She was seen entering your cabin.'

Until this point, Sinistra had smiled in silence. Now her smile faded. She pulled Ranant's scaly forelimb from her waist and sat up on the hard berth. The voice at the door spoke again. 'Captain Ranant? Is the lieutenant with you?'

Sinistra pulled on her uniform and boots. Ranant, with a series of cracks and snaps, reverted to Hyacinth-creature form and reached for his shirt.

'Captain, we have Chief Steward Seta's permission. We have a key and a battering ram.'

'Tell me your name again,' called Ranant, buttoning his shirt.

'Lieutenant Lupis, from the Master-at-arms.'

'Go away, Lupis!' called Ranant.

'Not this time, Captain. I'm here with an armed detachment. We're ordered to stay until we've seen inside. Open the door, Captain. If the lieutenant is not with you, we'll leave you alone.'

'Why don't you try the acting captain's own cabin?'

'It's guarded by marines.'

'Did you try knocking?'

Lupis made no reply.

'What do you want with the acting captain, anyway?'

'Last warning, Captain Ranant.'

Sinistra was ready. She stepped to the desk, wrote a quick note, and handed it to Ranant. He put the note in his pocket. Sinistra stood by the desk and he walked to the door and opened it.

Outside, Lieutenant Lupis waited in the light blue uniform of the ship's MAs. Sinistra noted the iron prisoner rings weighing on his belt. Behind him, stood no less than twelve men. They wore side arms; two held a small battering ram. Most had lesions on their necks ranging from dry, crusted pink to bright, wet, and red.

Ranant said, 'I'm in a meeting with the captain. Take a

good look, then go away.'

Lupis ignored him. 'Beg pardon, Lieutenant Sinistra.'

'It's acting Captain,' Sinistra said.

'Beg pardon, Lieutenant,' Lupis said. 'I have an order for your arrest.'

'No one's arresting anyone,' said Ranant.

'Who gave the order?' said Sinistra. 'Was it Captain Tiberius?'

But Sinistra already guessed who it must be. Tiberius would never humiliate her in this way. So, it could only be one other officer, the one most likely to send someone like Lupis.

'The order was issued by First Lieutenant Flavia,' Lupis said.

'She's still unconscious.'

'No. She's awake, Lieutenant. The medical deck says she opened her eyes not one hora ago, which was when you were seen entering this cabin. They say it's a miracle, like something from the Old Book.'

'Surely she is not fit to issue orders yet. What did Advisor Cicero say?'

'I know nothing of Advisor Cicero. The first lieutenant is now in command.'

'She is not in command. I am authorized by the Senate to be the acting captain. I have the documents.'

'We know nothing about documents, either, Lieutenant. We're just here to arrest you.'

A passing technical crew stopped to listen.

Sinistra said, 'Captain Ranant, please send a message to Cicero. Tell him what's happened.'

'I'll try,' Ranant replied.

'Do more than try. Tell him to cancel Flavia's order and make her stand down. Obviously she has not yet recovered her wits. She's not fit for duty, and not fit to command.'

Sinistra turned back to Lieutenant Lupis.

'As for you, I'm not going anywhere till you read me the charge.'

Lupis pulled a blue document from his pocket and read. 'Insubordination, three incidences of refusal to obey orders, and one incidence of attempted murder of an officer.'

'Those are old charges. They will all be dealt with at an inquiry, and, if necessary, at a court martial.'

'There is one more charge.'

'And what's that?'

'Fraternization with a Marine officer,' he said. 'Fraternization, including Hyacinth-creature intimacy.'

Sinistra said nothing, just blinked at Lupis's face. She thought she saw the slightest smile. Then, she said, 'I'm not going anywhere.'

'Don't make it difficult, Lieutenant. There's only one of you. We'll have to grab you and pull you along. Surely you can appreciate how undignified that would look in front of the crew.'

In the passageway, even more people gathered to watch. Some stewards and marines had joined the technical officers at the back of the detachment, craning their necks like creatures from Sirhain's forest.

'All right, Lieutenant Lupis,' Sinistra said. 'I'll come with you. Then we can clear this up. In the meantime, send your men away. Tell them to take those rings with them.'

'No, Lieutenant. Our orders are for all the men to accompany you.'

'Then bring one of the cars.'

'No cars. Orders of First Lieutenant Flavia. No cars, no shuttle.'

'You don't expect me to walk all the way forward?'

'Those are our orders, Lieutenant.'

'Why?'

But she knew why. An image of Flavia flashed in her mind: the old Flavia with her chin held high, her full hair, and curling disdainful lip.

'Where is Lieutenant Flavia now?'

'No idea.'

'Have you seen her? How does she look? What about her face?'

Lupis ignored her. 'We've been patient long enough, Lieutenant. It's time to come out.'

'Or what?'

Lupis raised the iron rings. 'Or we'll make it worse for you.'

When the awkward detachment began the long journey to the Great Passageway, Sinistra said, 'Don't take me to the brig. Take me to see Flavia so that we can discuss these charges.'

'We're not taking you to the brig,' Lupis said.

'Then, where? The forward stateroom? To Advisor Cicero?'

'No. We're taking you to the chain locker.'

'What? Why?'

'Lieutenant Flavia has ordered you to be keelhauled.'

Sinistra felt a shift in the world, as if the Herculaneum had hit a towering ocean wave in space, and careened onto its side.

'She ordered you to do *what*?'

'To keelhaul you.'

'Keelhaul me? She can't be serious. Are you sure that's what she said? I'm surprised she even knows the word. It doesn't make sense. It isn't even legal.'

'That's what she said.'

'But you see how ridiculous it is. No one has been keel hauled for centuries, and never in space. It's the most barbaric punishment in the Navy code.'

'That's what she said, Lieutenant.'

'I don't believe you. Tell me her exact words.'

'Her exact words, Lieutenant Sinistra, were, "Keelhaul

her. Keelhaul her from the ship's bow to the ship's stern. Make sure the rope is not too long. It must be short enough so that when the hauling begins, she comes face to face with every keel plate, pipe, box cover, and bolt.'"

64

In the Great Passageway, the detachment of MAs created a spectacle. They forced the foot traffic to make way. The crews from the hold stopped pulling their loaded carts and stood open-mouthed. The seamen rushing to the newsroom saluted, then lowered their hands to their chests.

Most kept their faces blank, but some smirked. Engineer Gabinus, walking aft with two of his 'boys', sneered before feigning concern with a deep frown. Astronomer Manius came out of the map room, his face like a stone. For a moment, his eyes met Sinistra's. There was no smile, no salute.

But many crew members disapproved. Glycias from the dropship maintenance crew actually called out, 'We're with you, Lieutenant,' before Petty Officer Tegula ordered him to shut up or he'd be joining the lieutenant in the brig. And on it went for four horrible milia from officer's quarters abaft the beam to just aft the forward stateroom.

The detachment reached the elevator leading to the lower decks. They descended, past the gun decks, past the crew's quarters, past the holds, down to the orlop. It was the very last deck, almost a milia down, just above the longitudinal girders, the keel plates, and open space.

The elevator door opened. Then they walked forward to the chain locker.

In the chain locker, there was no air to carry words, engine noise, or screams. It was the remotest part of the Herculaneum. No one ever went there except the hull maintenance crew, who visited for less than five minuta once a month. There was nothing in the chain locker to speak of. The Herculaneum needed no anchors and therefore no chains.

However, there was one aspect of the chain locker that was very much in evidence: the hatch opening out onto space.

Lupis marched Sinistra to the edge of this hatch, which was open for the first time since launch. Beside the hatch, a tall pulley stood waiting loaded high with a long thin rope. The rope ran from the pulley's wheel out of the hatch and into the black void.

Sinistra looked at the pulley, the rope, and the black square of space.

'Flavia is not serious,' she said. 'She can't mean to do this. It's too ridiculous, too insane, and almost certainly against the Senate Navy Code.'

Lupis smiled with one eyebrow raised—one of Flavia's favorite Hyacinth creature expressions. 'What's there to smile about?' said Sinistra. Then she realized there was no atmosphere. She sent out a thought message instead.

She's not serious, she repeated. She can't be.

Lupus replied with a thought of his own. Those are her orders.

Keelhauling hasn't been used for centuries. If she must disobey the Navy Code, why not inflict a punishment that's —she searched for the word—but could only think of one: humanus. Humane.

Our orders, Lieutenant Sinistra, are to use this old punishment, just like the captains of the past.

But we're in space, not on the Saran Sea two thousand years ago.

As she thought these words, Sinistra realized how foolish they sounded. Flavia's actions rarely made sense. And where Flavia's vanity was concerned, her actions made the least sense of all. Now that Flavia's jealousy of Ranant was pricked—and pricked by someone such as Sinistra—Flavia could be capable of anything.

Lieutenant Lupis shook his head and smiled.

Keelhauling is still in the Code. The lieutenant said it's one of the few punishments an acting captain can administer without a court-martial sentence.

She's lying. I know the Navy Code. You can bet Lieutenant Flavia doesn't. She barely knows it exists.

Nevertheless, those are her orders.

But surely Flavia realizes what open space can do. She's seen it herself. And if she doesn't know she must surely guess what keelhauling will do the Hyacinth-creature form.

It's never been proven that space can kill us, Lieutenant, even in the Hyacinth form.

It's never been tested either.

Lupis smiled. Then consider yourself a pioneer, a boundary pusher who endures danger for the benefit of her people.

Sinistra said, What is it, Lupis? Why are you going along with this? Did Flavia promise you a promotion? Or is it something else?

You're wasting time, Lieutenant. He turned to his men, and said, The rings.

Two of the MAs came forward, carrying the heavy rings. Each grabbed one of Sinistra's arms while a third pushed the rings over Sinistra's wrists, and clipped them shut.

Why? said Sinistra. Isn't the keelhauling enough? Why the rings?

Captain Flavia doesn't want you to grow scales, said

Lupis.

I can't expand. She knows that.

Those are her orders.

You'll regret this, Lupis. When I'm back in command, I'll make you regret you ever knocked at Captain Ranant's cabin.

Oh, I almost forgot, Lupis said. We'll have to take off your clothes. You three! Remove her uniform.

That's not in the Navy Code, sir, said one of three MAs.

You're right, said Lupus. It's not in the code, but Captain Flavia wants to make an exception.

Sinistra stood with her eyes shut as her shirt came off. She raised one leg, then the other as the men pulled off her boots.

Once the disrobing was complete, Lieutenant Lupis said, Now the rope.

The men circled the rope around Sinistra's waist and tightened it. The harsh fibers scratched Sinistra's vulnerable skin.

Meanwhile, the hatch yawned open.

May Owanthan have mercy on you, said Lieutenant Lupis.

If you want me to feel mercy, Sinistra said, you'll order whoever is on the stern to haul as fast as they can.

Lupis looked past her to the men and said, Hold her over the hatch.

Now four MAs surrounded Sinistra. The grabbed her arms lifted her over the black square. Two of the men averted their eyes and looked down at the deck. The other two looked up at the deckhead.

Lupis said, A piece of advice, Lieutenant Sinistra. Don't grab the hatch on the way out. You'll only delay the inevitable, and we'll have to break your fingers. Also, don't hold the rope. It will burn your hands when it tightens.

Sinistra looked down through the hatch at the distant stars. She would soon be out there, pulled beneath the ship as it rushed through space.

And she was naked.

She was about to beg Lieutenant Lupis one last time when a familiar voice hissed in her mind. You've really done it, hissed the voice of her orphanage guardian. You've really done it this time. You thought all this was over, didn't you? So sorry, Grenda, but it's not. Now, take your punishment.

No! Sinistra shouted.

Now! shouted Lupis.

The four men shoved her down, out, and into the blackness.

65

Only open space can kill us.

That's what everyone said, but was it true? Can it kill us? Will it kill me?

And exactly how did space kill? Did the radiation burn your skin and organs to ash? Did the cold freeze your blood? And how much worse would it be when you were naked? Despite all the voyages into space, no one had tried to find out. Everyone believed the old tale, just as they believed the tales about eating some types of fungus.

But was it true?

Sinistra was about to find out.

She plunged feet-first down from the bow, out into the Herculaneum's shadow. Then, the shadow slipped away, and she was far below, where the weak light of the Gordium star shone.

The rope around her stomach plunged alongside her. The coils drifted at her shoulder, like a sleeping serpent. This snake-rope would soon wake up. It would rush upward. It would jerk Sinistra's head up, bend her spine, and cut a stripe across her naked back, or her stomach. Worst of all, it would yank her along like a flailing corpse under the ship's keel, tearing her flesh, breaking her limbs, crushing her new cheek bones.

And smashing her teeth.

But at first, all was calm—the calm before the terrible storm. She was going down into the light, into infinity, towards the winking stars, falling so silently she forgot all about the Herculaneum traveling above her at a speed approaching that of light.

So what to do?

Better not think too much. Better to calm my nerves. Better to stop the hammering in my chest. Better to stop what's happening to my knees. Better to thank the god Owanthan that space isn't freezing cold like everyone said it would be. Not freezing?—how can that be? No atmosphere, no thermal conductivity—that must be the reason, right? And what if the radiation burns my skin to black flakes? Better not to think about that either. I have to control my wild Hyacinth-creature mind.

But Sinistra failed.

She couldn't stop her mind from showing her images of the worst things of all: terrible burns, her ruined body, her ruined career, a brown hill on Hyacinth on which no one stood. And then she felt a tingle on her neck. She felt it spread down the creamy skin of slender new arms, and down her spine, over her back. Then she felt it on her legs and at the backs of her knees. Was it burns or fear?

And then, silently, gently, just as she feared, the worst thing happened.

The sleepy rope woke up, expanded its coils as if it were yawning, then it straightened out and fled upward—up and away from her, as if it realized what was about to happen and couldn't bear to watch.

Sinistra looked one last time at the cold beauty of the distant stars. She tried to draw a breath to steady herself for the worst, but of course, this time there was nothing to breathe.

A second later, the rope tightened around her waist. The fibers tore across her delicate skin, bending her spine. Sinistra bounced and then tumbled. Her naked feet pitched over her swirling fair hair. Her long legs spun up and tangled in the rope itself as she bounced along.

And then the hauling began.

The rope jerked her towards the ship's stern so far, far away. Then, Sinistra caught her first glimpse of the horrible sight: the enormous black ship, the size of a city, rushing down at her from above. How terrible it looked! How horrible to be so close to it. It was like creeping up on a monster. But down, down came the ship, heavy, immense, and jagged.

Slower, Sinistra thought, sending a message to the crew hauling in the stern. Haul slower, not faster. Please!

But the ship's keel rushed towards her.

Lieutenant Lupis was right, of course. The Herculaneum's keel wasn't smooth, like the underside of a seagoing ship. Instead, it was studded with gun turrets, spiked with sensor arms and scuttles. There were pipes, hatches, chocks, elbows, and hooks—all sharp-edged and dangerous. There were also exhaust funnels for the never-used landing engines. From a distance, the keel looked like an open draw into which an armful of knives and spare parts had been dumped.

Sinistra raised her arms as the first pipe swung at her. It was an angled pipe, shaped like the bend in a Hyacinth creature's elbow. She even knew the pipe's function. It was a pressure exhaust for the atmosphere pumps.

She reached up with her burning red hands. The pipe smacked the iron rings on her wrists. The impact hurt far more than she expected. One of her wrists might have broken. She heard it snap from inside her body. But by then, she was tumbling again and could see only space, then twisted metal, then space, then metal again.

And, as her head came up for what seemed like the sixth time, she saw the next torment: a box with sharp edges. What was this box? Was it some kind of landing gear? Of course not. The ship never touched land. It spent its life in space. So what was the box?

Then she remembered.

It was the outer casing of a crane motor in the hold. That's what it is: the outer casing. Then, just before the cover of the box eluded her flinging hands and struck her straight white teeth, she thought: On the stern, when they pull me up, they're going to see me naked and wrecked. Oh, Nim! It's terrible.

A secunda later, she could no longer see which sharp corner broke her ribs, or which pipe a snapped her left shin. Even if she could raise an arm, she didn't know where to place it to protect herself.

When the torment couldn't seem any worse, the sinister voice whispered in her mind once more. It was the same deep female voice from her nightmares. You deserve this, hissed the voice, You're not good enough. You thought you were, but you know the truth. You never are. You never were. You're bad, and you know it.

Later, at the stern, when the traumatized, breathless seamen, pulled her from space, her nakedness would be the least of her concerns.

'Just cut it away,' she heard someone say before she fell unconscious. 'I can't tell what's rope and what's ... whatever that is.'

66

The Herculaneum's bow lamps pushed through the gloom towards Gordium two days' sailing away.

At the stern, in engineering, the cruise engines hammered away in their pits, watched by the chief engineer's mates. Meanwhile, two of the giant, tree-like Acceleration engines hummed on their mounts.

However, the troublesome engine named Apollo stood inactive and silent. Its trunk was split open. Four of Gabinus's mates were inside it, while Gabinus watched from a chair.

Straining together, the engineers dragged a broken part out onto the deck, spreading ash and oil. 'Non bonus, Dux,' they said to Gabinus. Not good, Chief. 'Habebimusne tempo?' Will we have time?

Gabinus slid his hand from his chin where it had been stroking his neck. He sat and thought for a moment. When Sinistra was in command, part of him wanted the engine to fail. But now that Flavia was back, he was as eager as the rest of the crew to reach Hyacinth and its great cities, and its people.

'Get the spare from the hold,' he said. 'Quick now and move your behinds, or you'll be sitting on them down here for another six months.'

On the bridge, Corvinus stood at the helm. Beside him, stood the quartermaster, Consus. Astronomer Manius sat with his charts. The officer of the watch, Lieutenant Cadmus, surveyed the bridge from his chair. We will not make it, Cadmus thought. We will not make it. My family flees the volcanoes and we will not make it to the Acceleration point on time.

Around the Herculaneum, the crew prepared. In the passageways, gun decks, holds, armories, map rooms, staterooms, ramps, and the cold, loneliest reaches above the keel, the crew tied, strapped, weighed, tightened, and bolted every dropship, cannon, rifle, terraforming machine, tank, pipe, seed sack, and the disassembled stacks of pre-fabricated huts.

The crew had never taken so much care, checking and rechecking, tying and re-tying, weighing and re-stowing, mostly to relieve anguish and grief over the news from home, but also to make sure that, this time, they really would accelerate across the galaxy.

When the crew's watches were over, everyone went to the viewing room for the latest news from home. Last night, another dormant volcano came horribly alive and threatened Ranator, the capital city. This had never happened before. The Senate had ordered the people to evacuate.

'But to where?' said one of the astronomer's mates. 'Where can they go? There's nowhere left.'

On the Domum Deck, in his compound, tethered by his chains, Telepathy sprawled on his great back, clutching his head. The never-ending news of devastation, destruction, maiming, and loss of life through scalding, poisoning, burning, and crushing, frazzled his mind and hurt his heart.

Just until the Acceleration, he told himself. Just until the engines fire. After that, I'll be free—free from the news, free from the chains, free to swim in the blue Hyacinth seas.

When they were not on their watches or in the news viewing room, the crew looked for ways to keep up their spirits. They returned to their happiest subject: Hyacinth. They imagined the clean air, white cities, high mountains, and the friendly, smiling creatures who would welcome them, and want to share their planet—just as the Senate said they would.

However, everyone avoided the sensitive subjects. They didn't discuss the number of their mates who had mysteriously vanished, never to be found. Nor did they talk about the wet, itchy lesions on their own necks and backs, and how the ship's artificial light might be the reason they felt so sick.

They also stopped talking about the incompetence and ill health of the ship's senior command. Suspicion was rife from bow to stern, but no one said a word. If someone overhead a discussion about the senior officers, the senior officers would hear about it, and take disciplinary action.

On the medical deck, the cases of miseria increased to over fifteen hundred. There weren't enough beds for them all. Worse! The crew now suffered new illnesses that afflicted the Hyacinth-creature mind. There were raving crewmen, mute crewmen, unconscious crewmen, and crewmen who believed themselves to be animals. At the end of every watch, there were more.

Meanwhile, despite the aerosol disinfectant sprays ordered by Chief Petty Officer Seta, the foul odor in the Great Passageway intensified from a smell to a reek and finally, to a stench. It was so bad, some crew members wore face masks. Others dabbed lavender perfume on their upper lips. When confronted about the smell, Seta said, 'As soon as we clear one body from the scuppers, another three take its place. They never seem to learn.'

Some of the ship's more humorous crew members quipped that if things continued, there would no one left aboard when the ship reached Hyacinth except Telepathy and Gothi, the ship's mascot. The joke met with brief, thin, Hyacinth creature smiles.

There were also calls for the Domum Deck to be opened to all crew members so that everyone could heal themselves through expansion and access to sunlight. But acting Captain Flavia (whom no one had seen) had been definite. Except for senior naval officers, warrant officers, and senior petty officers, no one could enter the Domun Deck.

Nor was anyone below senior officer rank permitted to expand to their natural form. A suitable location would be found on Hyacinth, Captain Flavia said. In these new Hyacinth locations, everyone would be able to expand as much as they liked. She added it wouldn't be long until the ship actually arrived in the Hyacinth solar system, and the crew could bathe in the light of the planet's small but powerful sun.

Then, there was the recent interest in both old superstitions and religion. The crew talked about bad omens and unlucky behavior. And some crew members gazed at the painting of 'The Fate of The People,' drawing strength from it. They believed Owanthan would save them, just as he saved their ancestors.

Still more wondered about the Old Book. Were the old stories true after all? If so, where was Owanthan now? Was he just hiding until they needed him again? And what about the rest of the gods? Where were they hiding? If the gods cared at all, surely they would return. If not now, then when?

In the meantime, the crew depended for their existence on the ship and its technology. This offered little comfort. The technology didn't seem very reliable any more. Everyone secretly doubted the Chief Engineer would get them through the Acceleration. A few of the engineer's mates has whispered in secret, 'We're as good as doomed as safe.'

Finally, there was the question of Lieutenant Sinistra. She had been the officer who remembered everyone's name. She was 'one of us,' having made her way up from the Northern Forests to third in command of the ship. In the crew's opinion, she was also the most competent officer, too.

Most crew members liked Sinistra—or at least, they liked her until she came back from the object. After that, 'she didn't seem like one of us anymore.' She had turned into one of 'them.'

Then, there was the subject of Sinistra's punishment.

Everyone had heard the terrible reports from the stern. Some of the stern crew had actually seen Sinistra after the keelhauling. They'd seen the shattered bones, the red, bubbling flesh, the ruined teeth, the smashed face, and the rest of it. 'Such a waste of beauty,' they said. 'A tragedy. A mess.'

But what would any of this matter if the Herculaneum never made it to the Point of Acceleration? What if the ship never reached Hyacinth at all? And what if the crew never saw the famous blue oceans and the shining white cities? How would it be if they never breathed the clean air or smelled the fresh fields? What if they never even saw the beautiful, real Hyacinth creatures?

Worst of all, what if the people on the home planet were all killed by the volcanoes and planet quakes? And what if out here in space, the Herculaneum and its crew died too, wasting away from Miseria, a trillion milia from their destination?

Best not to think about it. That's what the oldest crew members said. Best to think happy thoughts whenever something unhappy comes along. But the reasons for being happy were fewer and fewer.

'You think old Gabinus will fix the engines properly this time?' said one of the hull technicians after another watch spent clearing bodies from the scuppers.

'Gabinus!' said his mate. 'That old pervert! He couldn't fix his own bootlaces.'

'But will he fix the engines?'

'He'll have to, because if he doesn't fix them and we get stuck out here for months, he's going to be the first one tossed outside.'

Time passed. The Herculaneum cruised on. The bad news kept coming. The crew worked tirelessly to cope with it.

There were one and a half Hyacinth days to go.

67

In the Herculaneum's brig, Sinistra languished in agony, confusion, and fear.

On her narrow, hard bunk, she drew her mangled legs up under her chin and stared through the cell bars. Her right hand gripped the heavy iron ring on her ankle to stop it from chafing her burnt skin. Her left hand, with its smashed fingers, tentatively hugged her broken knees.

Beside her, small lamps in the bulkhead radiated a dirty green light. The light turned Sinistra's fair hair the color of dead grass, and her raw skin the color of slime.

No one else was in the officers' brig. Sinistra was the only prisoner. She was alone with her shredded skin; her shattered bones; her smashed, bloated face; her bitter disappointment; and her crippling self loathing. Her moans and sobs echoed back to her from the bulkheads, mocking her.

'Ow,' she said as the ring on her ankle slipped onto the oozing skin below it. 'Ow,' came the echo, mocking her. She reached down and lifted the ring onto the dark blue cloth of her uniform, but it instantly slipped back down again. 'Oww!' she said. 'Oww!'

Pain and misery. Incapacitation and loss. Shame, and

guilt, and despair.

What am I going to do? she thought. No one answered—not the sentries, not the gods, not Nim, and not even the hissing voice of her childhood tormentor. Everyone had abandoned her—even her enemies. Apparently, she wasn't even worth tormenting. Instead, she was alone, defeated, irrelevant, and without hope.

The brig door opened. It was Corporal Heva of the Masters-at-arms. The thrum of boots from the Great Passageway came with him. Corporal Heva locked the door, shutting them out.

Sinistra raised her blotched and streaming face from her knees. 'Any news from Lieutenant Flavia?' she asked, but through her torn mouth, dented throat, fat lips, and broken teeth, the words sounded like, 'Ah newf tear a Fah?'

Corporal Heva never spoke. He shone his toro at the iron ring on Sinistra's ankle and the iron ring on her wrist, then he noted something in his log, turned about and walked away.

As usual, he carried the same type of blast rifle Sinistra had carried on the object. It was ridiculously oversized for use inside the ship, let alone the brig. Sinistra guessed it was due to Flavia playing a joke on her former second lieutenant.

She tried again.

'Corporal Heva, I have to speak with the first lieutenant and Captain Tiberius. We have to avoid a catastrophe. We have to stop the Acceleration.'

Corporal Heva stopped and turned around. He was thinking. This time, he seemed to understand her. He looked her in the eye, as if waiting for her to go on.

'Thank you, Corporal,' Sinistra said. 'Do you have pen and paper? I can dictate the message for Lieutenant Flavia, and a second one to Tiberius.'

Heva replied in a short, irritated tone. 'Captain Flavia has ordered me to gag you if you keep this up.'

'But the Acceleration!' said Sinistra, trying and failing to stand. 'She has to know about the engines and the danger. She has to watch Gabinus.'

Heva shook his head. 'I don't understand any of that gibberish—not a single word. It's your last chance, Lieutenant. Speak that nonsense again and I'll gag you. I have the gag ready at my station. No, don't try a thought message, either. If you do, I'll order the medical deck to put you to sleep.'

Corporal Heva waited, watching for a reaction. 'Cogitesne?' he said. Sinistra blinked several times, (she couldn't nod) and slumped back against the bulkhead.

Corporal Heva was soon gone again. The brig's door opened and closed. The ship's sounds surged and faded. The latch bolts rammed through the lock's strike plates. Sinistra was alone once more, with the sighing atmosphere pump, the sickly green light, her agony, and her misery.

'What can I do?' she whispered. It sounded like 'Wah fah do?' and her face shrieked with pain, from her jaw to her throat, and even to the backs of her eyes. Speaking the Hyacinth language was painful, just like speaking the native language, which, given her crushed larynx, she could no longer attempt.

So, she asked herself the same questions she had asked ten, twenty times already. Can you escape? Can you get out of here? The answer was obvious. She looked at the iron rings preventing her from expanding. Then she looked at the mashed up and mangled limbs. She couldn't even stand, let alone walk. And what would she do, anyway? Force her way out of the brig and lead a mutiny?

What about Sirhain? Could he help? She looked at the deckhead as if he were hovering there, watching. Yes, she could call to Sirhain. She could ask him to restore her body and her looks. Then, she could ask him to free her from the brig. She could even ask him to fix the Acceleration engines.

And she could say, 'Just make me the beautiful woman on the hill, whatever it takes.'

But after the keelhauling, she wondered whether Sirhain was real. She suspected that her meeting with him had simply been the product of her treacherous Hyacinth-creature mind. Perhaps it was same with everything else, too: the forest on the object; the vision of the woman on the hill; the promises; the meeting with Owanthan; everything. They had all been vivid daydreams brought about by exhaustion.

The only thing that still seemed real was the danger of a failed Acceleration and the Herculaneum either destroyed or drifting in space forever while its crew languished, fought, and died.

She slumped against the bulkhead. Her wounds shrieked. She sat up. The wounds shrieked again. No, there was nothing she could do. Nothing! She would have to sit and wait and let it all happen. She was now a spectator, removed from history, doomed to watch others act, sentenced to reflect on how fast she had risen in rank and how swiftly she had fallen.

The ring on her ankle slipped again. 'Oww!' she said. 'Oww!' The echoes mocked her all over again. And then she heard the hiss of that same voice from her childhood. It seemed she was worth tormenting, after all.

'You deserve this,' the voice hissed. 'You've always deserved it. Now, it's finally caught up with you.'

Sinistra slumped further against the bulkhead. Yes, she deserved this, just as she'd always known. And now it was worse than any beating in the forest. She didn't even know who she was anymore.

The bell tolled. The rings slipped. Warm tears fell onto her knees. Dark, wet patches spread on her uniform. She had never felt more wretched.

But worse was to come.

The bolts in the cell door shot back. The door opened. Corporal Heva appeared in the light, then stepped outside.

Four marines marched in. They halted in front of Sinistra's cell and stood at attention. Then, they did a strange thing. They each turned and faced the bulkhead so that they could not see the door, nor could they see the centre of the deck.

Then, someone entered the brig, limping with sharp intakes of breath, as if astonished at how much pain a single step could cause. Whoever it was supported themselves on a metal stick, and one of their feet dragged like a sack of meat.

Then, like a ghoul crawling from a cave, First Lieutenant Flavia, now Captain Flavia, slouched into the dirty green light.

68

Flavia stood swaying in the shadows.

The Marine lieutenant said, 'All clear, Captain.' Then, with a small toss of her head, Flavia said, 'Out.' The marines turned and left the brig.

After Corporal Heva bolted the door shut, Flavia limped up to the bars of Sinistra's cell.

Sinistra tried to climb from the bunk and stand to attention. It was impossible. The iron ring chafed her ankle. The ring on her left wrist slid down her red, raw hand. Her legs could not bear her weight. She slumped to the bunk.

She looked at Flavia, but not for long. It took only a secunda to see it all: the empty eye socket; the ruined nose; the smashed left cheek; the drooling mouth; the torn lips; and the blotched, gray skin drooping like an old, dirty cloth.

The rest of her was worse: the lustrous red hair grew in patches and tufts; her forehead was dented like a pale egg shell; a bulbous cyst or goiter swelled on her neck. It squirmed when she raised her chin.

'Stand up properly when you address the ship's captain,' said Flavia.

Without thinking, Sinistra responded to the old need to please. She tried to stand on her unbroken right shin, but fell back onto the bunk.

Flavia watched her struggle, then said, 'Before I say anything about your crimes, let me make one thing plain: you will never see Captain Ranant again. Have you got that?'

Sinistra couldn't nod.

'Did you hear me, Lieutenant?'

'Ita.'

'And from the way you look, Ranant won't want to see you. I'd say he won't want anything to do with you, nor will anyone else.'

Flavia let the barbed words wound and stick.

'Next, as soon as a quorum of captains is present, you will be court-martialed. You will be found guilty of attempting to murder an officer. That is certain. Then, you will be sentenced and imprisoned far, far away, where you can do no more harm. In the meantime, you will be incarcerated here, even during the Acceleration. When we establish ourselves on Hyacinth, I will move you to a land brig in the remotest part of the planet.'

Sinistra said nothing.

'Furthermore, while you are here, you will not receive medical attention. The doctor is busy enough with miseria patients. There aren't any beds and you don't deserve one. Don't quote the Navy Code to me, if that's what you are about to do.'

When Sinistra didn't reply, she said, 'Do you have anything to say for yourself?'

Sinistra's eyes flicked to the squirming goiter. At least I don't have that, she thought.

She rasped the words, 'Machinae.'

'The what? It's hopeless,' Flavia said. 'Speak in thoughts. I'll allow it for the next three minuta.'

Sinistra repeated her question.

'The engines?' said Flavia. 'What about them?'

The Acceleration will fail unless Gabinus repairs Apollo, Sinistra said. It failed when I tested it. I don't think Gabinus is trying. Either that or he is incompetent.

Flavia shook her head. 'No, Lieutenant. Gabinus was obviously playing games with you, for his amusement. Apollo is fine, as are the other engines.'

But it failed the test.

'I trust Gabinus's judgement. He's one of us. That's enough.'

You must order another test.

'I'll order no such thing. I do what my judgement tells me to do. And now my judgement advises me not to listen to criminals who put their lust for high rank ahead everything else, including the lives of their superior officers.'

'Captain Tiberius?' Sinistra said aloud.

'Captain Tiberius—is that what you said?'

He would want to test the engines.

'Captain Tiberius is dead.'

'Dead?'

'He died of Miseria—or a combination of Miseria and frailty. Yes, that's right, Lieutenant. The captain is gone. Yes, your lone supporter is dead. The Senate has already appointed me as captain of the Herculaneum. I've promoted Cadmus to first lieutenant. Captain Agrippa is out of contact but he will return to the home planet—if we reach him in time. He will command a transport ship when the time comes.'

Flavia pulled a cloth from her pocket and dabbed at her crooked, drooling mouth.

Please, Flavia, Sinistra said. Whatever you think of me, you must order Gabinus to retest the engine. Hoping it will work is irresponsible.

Flavia stopped dabbing and looked up. Her face distorted. The goiter squirmed. Her arms swelled. The epaulettes tilted. Her hand, now a three-pronged claw, shot through the cell's bars and gripped Sinistra's own wet neck. It lifted her from the deck. The broken bones flopped beneath her.

'How dare you tell me to do anything!'

I'm trying to help. The engines will fail and then who knows what will happen? We could drift for months. It's not fair to the crew.

'You are very high minded all of a sudden. You weren't so high minded when you beat the two stewards at the Domum Deck, were you? Yes, I know all about it. And you weren't so concerned when you dismembered your former comrade and friend, Lieutenant Nimark.'

Nim? I don't … I have never …

'Come now, Sinistra. Don't act like you don't know what I'm talking about. I ought to flush you into space through the scupper and leave you there, burning up with your rings on. I ought to pull you apart myself and toss you to the void. You'll float in agony for days before you die.'

I didn't hurt Nim. I didn't fire the rifle to hit you.

'You didn't fire the rifle to hit me. Is that what you said? Don't make me laugh. No one believes you, not even Domitian. You'll never be acquitted. Never. Oh, don't look so sad. There might be a good side. You can finally stop trying so hard to impress everyone, except the jailers.'

I didn't mean to shoot you, said Sinistra's voice. I was aiming at the Goths. They were about to kill you.

Flavia shook her head and said, 'The most disgusting thing is that you probably believe that.'

It's true.

Flavia smiled and said, 'I don't care what you think.' She turned and shouted over her shoulder. 'Corporal!' Then she turned back to Sinistra. The goiter squirmed. 'Oh, I almost forgot. I have something for you.'

She reached into her uniform pocket and pulled out a disc the size of her hand.

'Here.' She tossed it onto Sinistra's bunk. 'Go on, pick it

up.'

Sinistra reached out a broken, oozing wrist and lifted the object as high as she could.

It was a mirror.

'Take a look,' said Flavia. 'You have my permission to use it, just this once.'

Flavia's lopsided eyes gleamed as Sinistra tilted the mirror upward.

'As you can see,' said Flavia. 'I'm not the only one with ruined looks. Ooh, are those what I think they are, Lieutenant? At your age, too! I've always known that you are mentally deranged, but I never thought you were weak. You surprise me.' She turned and shouted once more. 'Corporal, where are you? I've seen enough. I don't think my stomach can take any more.'

Corporal Heva opened the door. Flavia limped from the room, holding her head as high as her squirming neck would allow.

Once Flavia was gone, and the door re-bolted, Sinistra cried alone on her bunk. The tears irritated the wounds on her cheeks. They fell onto the sheets and mixed with the bloodstains and the slime. Self pity overwhelmed her. So much had happened. Her career had climbed so high, so fast, like a meteor. Its end had been so swift, so devastating, so final.

She was so deep in misery that she barely noticed the dark presence in the brig's far corner. She looked up, wiped her face with her sleeve and squinted into the gloom with her hurt eyes.

'Who's there?' she said. It came out as 'Hur air?'

No one replied. Sinistra squinted and sniffed. She squinted harder. Yes, someone or something watched her from the dark.

69

But who was it? Who watched from the dark?

The air thinned. The pressure dropped. Sinistra could feel the change in her burns. Then she heard a voice.

'I've just been listening to you,' the voice said.

'Who are you?' Sinistra tried to say. There was no reply. Then the voice spoke again.

'At first, I thought you were praying. I thought you were asking for salvation from your distress. It's funny. Long ago, I used to hear so many prayers—millions each night. Some of them might have come from your ancestors. Imagine that.'

The voice paused as if fondly recalling the pleasure of so much worship from so many souls so long ago. Then it spoke again.

'Of course, I realized straight away that you weren't really praying. You were talking to yourself. That's all. You were talking to yourself in your native language, and in a strange voice. You weren't even aware, were you? That's not healthy, Sinistra. No, not healthy at all.'

'Is it you?' said Sinistra. 'Are you real?'

'In the old days,' said the voice, 'I would insist that you get up and bow your head low, or get down on your knees and press your face to the deck, but from the look of you, I don't think you're capable of it. You can't even stand up. My, my! You look worse than you did when I first saw you—and that, my dear, is saying something.'

'Are you here to save me?' Sinistra said. 'Have you changed your mind about . . .' She chose the words carefully. 'Hyacinth? About me speaking to the people?'

'My goodness! How thoroughly Flavia has ruined your voice. You can barely speak. Fortunately for you, I can understand. No, don't start coughing and snuffling like that. Don't wave your hands. I don't want to see them.'

'Are you here for me?' Sinistra repeated. 'To take me away?'

'No. I'm just passing through.'

'Are you here to gloat?'

'Gloat?' said the voice. 'I'm many things, but I'm not cruel —at least, not all the time, and I'm certainly not like your childhood guardian whose voice you were growling. Yes, I heard that too. It was very unsettling, even to my ears. Believe me. These ears have heard it all. It's no wonder you're tormented. I wonder if I was wrong about you.'

'Why are you here?'

'I didn't plan to come here. It's because your cries of agony and despair were so … what's the phrase? Cor scindens? Yes, that's it. They were so heart-rending.'

'Why don't you show yourself?'

'Brace yourself, my ruined dear, and I will.'

Sirhain stepped from the shadow into the light. He stood there with one hand on his hip. The wings of his mustache curled upward with new vigor. Unlike the last time Sinistra had seen him, he looked strong and healthy.

But it was his new clothes that stood out. The lush robes were back, but now he also wore a shiny metal breastplate. It was embellished with a crest of two standing goths guarding a shield. At his waist, a sword glowed silver and green in the lamplight. The sword was so long, its point scraped the deck.

'These are symbolic,' Sirhain said, raising the sword, 'but the war is very real, Sinistra. Oh, yes. Just imagine. Two enormous armies will clash in the cosmos: Owanthan's and mine. It's going to be a dreadful sight, truly awful. So much carnage before I triumph.'

'Free me, please, Sirhain,' Sinistra said. 'Restore me.'

Sirhain looked at the deckhead. 'No,' he said. 'I cannot.'

'Is it because "Religion is not like that" as you said, and because I have to make a choice? Well, Sirhain, I've made it. I want to be what you offered. But there's a problem. The ship might not survive the Acceleration, and, well, you see my wounds.'

'Listen, Lieutenant Sinistra. You must understand something. I'm not here to save you. Don't expect to walk around your ship looking tall, beautiful and confident again. All that's over.'

'Why did you abandon me? Why did you show me Hyacinth and the woman on the hill and then abandon me?'

'It wasn't my intention. Owanthan's declaration of war was unexpected. He's never been that devious before. Usually, he's obvious and foolish. He's never used spies, either. My only guess is that, like myself, he sees the people need us again, and he wants all the glory to himself. Well, this time, he won't get it.'

'Did you hear me? I said you abandoned me. Aren't I one of your people, too?'

'I didn't abandon you, Sinistra—not entirely. No. I helped you—up to a point. I made you beautiful. I released you from my realm and sent you back to your comrades. You left my temple without harm. I didn't even retaliate when you fired your weapons at it. Surely that's something.'

'But you turned the senior officers against me. You woke Flavia from her sleep at the worst moment. Why did you kill

Captain Tiberius and stop me from saving the mission and the people on the home planet? Why have you brought the mission and me to this state? Don't you want me to succeed?'

Sirhain looked at her with his head on one side. 'Is that all? Are you finished?'

'No. Why did you allow Flavia to keelhaul me? Look at my legs. Look at my face? My face! My poor face! Now Flavia is in command of the entire mission—the most reckless, the most dangerous ...'

She broke into a series of wet, painful coughs.

'Sorry to disappoint you once again, Lieutenant, but it wasn't me. The events happened by themselves. Other people make choices, too, you know. Not just you. Yours is a complex world, Sinistra. It's crueler than you imagine. And when you assert yourself in that world, you risk incurring your superiors' displeasure—the displeasure of the status quo. Now, it's too late. It's over. But don't feel too bad. Look what you achieved by yourself.'

'What's over? My life? My destiny on Hyacinth?'

'All those things, my sad lieutenant. The powerful will crush you. They're crushing you already. There's nothing more for you. Believe me.'

'So that's it? I'm to live my life as a wretch in a cell?'

'Not exactly. You can still choose to heal your mind. That's not nothing.'

'Please do me one last service.'

'And what is that?'

Sinistra tried lowering herself to one knee. Then she bent her shattered leg so that she could slowly push her face to the cold, slimy deck.

'No, don't do that,' said Sirhain. 'Not now.'

'Release me from this horrible life,' said Sinistra. 'If not by freeing me, then by sending me onward.'

'Sending you onward? What do you mean?'

'To whatever is waiting after this life, to wherever the sailors go who throw themselves into space from the scuttles, to wherever Tiberius and Lieutenant Commodus have gone.'

Sirhain sighed. 'Sorry, Lieutenant. I can't do that. Ending lives needlessly is one point on which Owanthan and I agree—one of the few.'

'You killed people in the past. Domitian told me about the massacre—the one in the Old Book.'

'Different times call for different measures. That was a long time ago. I've put it behind me. I can't say the same for Owanthan. He can't get over how I one-upped him.'

'Please, Sirhain. I can't live like this. I can't end my life by myself. You've got to help me. To leave me like this is inhumanus.'

She tried to raise her arm to show him the ring, but her broken bones could not bear its weight. 'Look, Sirhain,' she said. 'Look at what they did.'

But Sirhain was neither looking nor listening. He cocked an ear to the forward bulkhead.

'I've got to go,' he said. 'I'm late, and to be honest, I don't think my help is required. This other world you mention, this afterlife—it's not far away.'

'Please,' said Sinistra, looking up from the deck.

'No,' he said. 'I have to go.'

Sinistra's head sunk to her chest. She felt as wretched as it was possible to feel.

Sirhain looked at her pathetic, broken state, and said, 'Listen, Lieutenant. I can't send you on to the next world, but I can offer you something else instead.'

'Only death can help me.'

'Stop crying and stop making those noises. Listen to what I have to say. You'll learn something.'

And what he said changed her life.

70

When Sinistra didn't reply, Sirhain hurried on.

'All your life, Sinistra, you have lived in fear. It's fear that makes you to try so hard. It's fear that makes you grovel for approval—yes, grovel—even from those you should despise. You know who I mean. You convince yourself that these people are noble, but you are wretched. "I'm evil. I'm bad," you say. "I cause the pain. I hate myself. My only relief is to win approval, to try hard, to distinguish myself. Flavia, I've done well, haven't I? Captain Tiberius, I'm very capable, aren't I?"'

'Yet despite your efforts, despite your achievements, all this running from fear has brought you nowhere but here to this miserable brig and that horrible bunk. This mission and my intervention just sped everything up.'

He cleared his throat, then, after tilting his ear to the bulkhead again, he went on.

'You are far more powerful than you imagine—in mind and body. Yes, even here, even now. So, since you seem incapable of acknowledging this truth about yourself, here's my advice.'

He stood to his full height, drew a deep breath of the rancid air, and said, 'It's all right, Sinistra, to be bad.'

Sinistra stopped sobbing. After one long sniff, she raised her head and looked up, her mouth open, blinking. It was like she'd just heard a voice calling her name from far away. The voice had been calling all her life, and yet she had only just heard it, here under the brig's sickly green light. She opened her bruised lips and spoke.

'What did you say?'

'I said, it's all right to be bad. You could say that it might even be good to be bad—in some circumstances. Yes, that's a better way of describing it. It's good to be bad. "Brevity is the soul of wit." Some Hyacinth poet will say that one day.'

'Did you say it's good to be bad?'

The words seemed to relieve her pain and the shame she'd carried since the orphanage and the forest and through every day in the navy.

'I don't have time to explain it again,' said Sirhain. 'But a word of caution. If you follow this advice, it won't make you happy, but then happiness isn't everything. I think I told you that before.'

He paused, raised a hand and twisted a wing of his mustache.

'It might even be a source of strength,' he said. 'Convincing yourself every day that you're worthless is very draining, Sinistra. True, it has taken you far in your career, but it has also taken a toll. Now, I'm offering you a better idea: to be bad and like it. So make use of it.' He smiled. 'I'll say it again. It's good to be bad, Sinistra.'

Sinistra had pulled herself back onto the bunk. Her broken body felt stronger. Her mind felt unbounded, lighter, even hopeful.

'Isn't it better to be good?' she said.

Sirhain laughed. 'I'm going to paraphrase some words from a Hyacinth-creature of the future: "It's better to reign on Hyacinth than to serve the Senate as a slave." That's my conclusion.' He waited, watching. 'Don't you think that's good?'

Sinistra slurred the words. 'It's better to reign on Hyacinth than to serve the Senate and be a slave.'

'Exactly.'

'And it's good to be bad.'

'Right again.'

'Does that mean I can create my own woman on the hill?'

'My dear, with your talent and energy properly directed, anything is possible. Are you listening?'

Sinistra's eyes had closed. The torrent of foul thoughts coursing through her mind dried up. The exhaustion, which she'd kept at arm's length for days, now seized its chance. Her chin slumped to her chest. Her head flopped to her shoulder.

Sirhain took a last look at the crumpled creature on the bunk. He sniffed. 'A little gratitude wouldn't hurt, you know.' Then he pulled at his robes, adjusted his sword, and walked into the shadows.

Soon after Sirhain had vanished, the bolts in the prison door shot back. The door opened. The ship's sounds surged inside. Corporal Heva entered and walked to Sinistra's cell.

He took out his log and recorded his observation: 'Scnd. Lt. Sinistra, prisoner, asleep, or unconscious.'

'Lieutenant Sinistra?' he said.

There was no response. Sinistra lay slumped and still. Her terrible wounds were exposed. Her chest was still, not rising and falling. Corporal Heva raised his pen and added to the entry in the log: 'Comatose. Possibly dead.'

He pushed a tentative hand at her bruised ankle to check if her Hyacinth-creature heart was pumping, then drew his hand back and wiped it on his uniform leg.

If she doesn't wake up by the next bell, he thought, I'll send a message to the captain. Let her decide what to do. I don't want any part of it. He turned and left. The door bolted shut. The darkness and silence returned.

Sinistra was alone. When the ship lurched to starboard, her foot slipped from the bunk, and, propelled by the iron ring, hit the deck with a sickening crack as the broken bones crunched across each other.

Then, all was quiet.

But deep in Sinistra's mind, there glowed the embers of a red dawn.

OCTAVIA

Part Four: Octavia

OCTAVIA

"Our torments also may, in length of time,
    Become our Elements."

A Hyacinth poet

71

Sinistra fell into a swirling dream.

The cell and its weak light vanished, and she was suddenly far away.

She was aboard the Krast, the cutter that rushed her from the Admiralty to the Herculaneum three months earlier. In the dream, she saw herself as she was back then: bent, small, odorous, and unable to walk properly or speak the Hyacinth language.

The Krast's commander, Lieutenant Ashtar who was also from the Northern Forests, said, 'Good luck, Grenda. You'll need it. The Herculaneum officers aren't like the rest of us. They won't like you, and you'll probably end up in personal battles with all of them. I've seen it before.'

To Sinistra's surprise, her former self replied, 'I'm the third in command. It doesn't matter if they don't like me.'

Next, she saw her former self limping into the Herculaneum's stateroom. She greeted the elderly Captain Tiberius. His appearance surprised her. He was young and healthy. So were the other senior officers, and yet all of them had been in service for as long as anyone could remember.

She felt the warmth in the communication officer's greeting as his smooth, strong hand closed her small, weak fingers. 'We're glad you're here,' Domitian said. 'We can certainly use you.'

'Thank you,' Sinistra had replied. 'It's good to be aboard.' Then, she turned to greet the other officers, but was met with only hostile, silent, and expressionless nods from Decimus, Gabinus, Manius, and Seta.

Then she met the tall first lieutenant, whose appearance was even more striking than the captain's. Sinistra held out her hand to this beautiful woman, but Flavia ignored it and then ignored Sinistra herself. She turned to Lieutenant Cephus and said, 'I heard she would be bad, but not *this* bad.'

To her astonishment, Sinistra witnessed a remarkable occurrence. Instead of cringing away, stung by Flavia's words, her former self stood her ground and replied. 'I'm here to make up for your lack of skill, First Lieutenant. Yes, that's right. I said your lack of skill, but now that I've met you—or almost met you—I see I must also make up for your lack of courtesy.'

Sinistra watched her former self, amazed. The scene was wonderful. Why hadn't she spoken this way at the time? Why hadn't she ever put Flavia in her place?

Then, the dream scene changed. Sinistra saw herself in the stateroom three months later. She was the Herculaneum's acting captain. Her new self stood before the bellicose senior officers. As before, Gabinus sneered and said, 'You little upstart.'

But as soon as Gabinus's mouth shut, Sinistra turned and ordered marine Lieutenant Imbrex to arrest him. Imbrex ignored Gabinus's shouted 'How dare you!' and grabbed his arms, fixed rings on them, and dragged his smug face out of the stateroom to the brig.

If only she actually ordered this!

Then she saw herself back inside the object. The Goths attacked in their frenzied hatred of Flavia. Over the sights of the heavy rifle, Sinistra watched the claws tearing at Flavia's scaly neck. As before, the Goths flashed in and out of the wavering lamplights.

When the light flashed over Flavia's face, the rifle bucked, and the blast blew Flavia's head away into the dark. She staggered backward, dragging five Goths with her.

Why hadn't Sinistra done this, too—with intent?

The vision faded away, scurrying from her mind like the shadows behind the object's forward columns. And then, the dream was gone, too. Sinistra was back on the hard berth with the sickly green light, the shattered bones, the agony of her burnt, suppurating legs, and the slime on the sheets.

But something was different.

While she'd been dreaming, she had expanded. Her body had ballooned into the bulkheads, bulging through the prison bars, like sacks of home planet soil bound up with rope. The iron rings choked her wrists and ankles, but they hadn't stopped the emergence of scales, claws, and bones, surging to expand and to heal themselves.

Two voices argued out of sight. One sounded like Corporal Heva. The other like the Surgeon's Mate Cordinaus.

'The rings! Look what they've done. They were supposed to stop her from expanding, not tear off her hands.' This was Cordinaus speaking.

'It's not my fault,' said Corporal Heva. 'Captain Flavia said she wanted the rings.'

'Well, look what happened!'

'You don't have to shout. I can see what's happened.'

'Will she live?'

'I'm not the doctor, just an assistant.'

'So you keep saying, but what do you think? Will she live?'

'Not without treatment.'

'I've got to tell the captain. She wants to know

everything.'

'It's better if I ask for Doctor Galen.'

'We can't ask the doctor first.'

'Why not?'

'Because it's not worth my career. That's why.'

'Well, do something. If she keeps going, she'll crack the hull and then where will we be?'

And then Sinistra fell back into the dream's swirling world. Now she was in the dark forest of her childhood. She stood in a clearing, waiting, listening. Her younger self appeared. Her guardian pursued her from behind, like prey and predator.

The guardian carried a thick metal rod called a brak. She swung the brak at the child's legs. The rod tripped the young Sinistra at the clearing's edge. She fell on her face in the snow. The guardian seized her ankle and spun her onto her back.

'I warned you,' she said. 'I warned you. Didn't I warn you?'

The terrified young Sinistra replied, 'What have I done?'

Sinistra saw the kicking legs, flailing arms, and terrified face. The guardian jabbed and prodded until the rod slipped past the flurry of limbs, and found the soft flesh. Then, the stabbing began. The beating and clubbing followed.

'I warned you,' said the guardian. 'Didn't I warn you?'

'But what have I done?' shouted the young Sinistra. 'I've been good.'

And then, amid the beating, the older Sinistra saw a shocking sight. Her young self looked up while the guardian struck at her back. For a moment, the young Grenda looked directly into the eyes of the older Sinistra. The past had seen the future.

'Make it stop,' the young Grenda pleaded. 'Make it stop. You can stop it all, can't you? You can stop everything—everything that's happening, and everything that will happen. Make it stop. Please, please, make it stop.'

Sinistra stared back. The girl's face implored her. 'What are you waiting for? Make it stop. All of it. Make it stop!'

'No,' Sinistra said. 'I won't make it stop.'

'Why?' called the stricken child. 'You are me. Why don't you make it stop?'

Sinistra's face hardened. 'Because you deserve it. You've been bad. You *are* bad. You always will be bad. Haven't you heard? It's good to be bad.'

The young child blinked in confusion and pain, and covered her face as she sank beneath the blows. The older Sinistra turned away. She could hear the whip-whip of the rod, the thwack on soft flesh, the flinty sound of metal on scale, and the un-natural deep growls of the tortured girl.

But instead of feeling revulsion, she smiled and looked up through the forest canopy to the wintry sky.

Then, at the forest edge, she stepped onto the dry, brown earth, and the warm, fragrant air. In the distance, the woman on the hill stood waiting, tall and beautiful in the sunlight. Beneath her, in the valley, the adoring multitude raised their arms and called her name. 'Octavia! Octavia! Octavia!'

It's good, thought Sinistra. It's good to be bad, and it's better to reign on Hyacinth than to serve the Senate and the likes of Flavia.

This time, Sirhain did not appear beside her. She was alone on the hill with the crowd below her. But out of sight, high in the clouds, a terrible, black sky vessel appeared, with hundreds of gun ports ranged along its sides like dead eyes. The great ship dragged its heavy shadow over the land, preparing to discharge its weapons, preparing to wage war, preparing to poison the fields, smash the hills, and drain the oceans.

And then, far away, on the other side of the galaxy, in the sickly light of the Herculaneum's brig, Cordinaus, the surgeon's mate, said, 'There's no pulse and no breath.

There's nothing.'

'Pulse?' said Corporal Heva. 'Pulses are just for Hyacinth creatures. They don't matter. What about her real self?'

'I'm not the doctor,' said Cordinaus, 'but as far as I can tell, all of her is gone.'

'All of her or just the Hyacinth part?'

'All of her—her old self, her new self. All of her.'

Sinistra moved no more.

72

She opened her Hyacinth-creature eyes.

Then, she closed them again, opened them, squinted, and, after a few secunda, she blinked at a changed world.

She sniffed the air. The usual scent of metal was there, but now there were additions, a chemical smell and a rank, sweet odor, like the reek of a decaying forest.

The sickly green light was gone. Instead, a pale blue glow illuminated the deckhead, but it wasn't a healing light, like sunshine. It was a sterilizing light—like a blue disinfectant.

She listened for the engines. Yes, they were there, softly groaning—the cruise engines, not the howling Acceleration engines. The ship had not yet reached the Point of Acceleration. Or maybe it had accelerated and succeeded without the engines failing.

Which was it?

She lay naked beneath a blue sheet reaching up to her chin. She didn't want to move—not just yet. Instead, she scanned her body with her mind. Her skin felt cool, as if the burns had exhausted themselves. Her ribs no longer shrieked when she breathed, and her broken fingers extended without quivering. She could clench them into fists. What about the iron rings? She raised each limb. Her left wrist was heavy. So was her right ankle.

She sat up. She wasn't in the brig. There were no reinforced bulkheads or cell bars. Instead, she was in an open space many times the size of the captain's stateroom.

And she was not alone.

On either side of her, metal tables streamed in rows, running fore and aft. On these tables lay the bodies of at least fifty crew members, each covered by a blue sheet. She could see white hillocks of their heads and the ridges of their feet and noses. None of their chests rose and fell. No one rolled onto their side to make themselves comfortable. No groan or sigh escaped from any mouth, and no one reached a hand out to scratch a lesion on a neck.

Then, she realized: she was on the medical deck and this room was the camera mortuorum. The mortuary.

She raised her left hand and felt her face. Her fingers found firm cheekbones and a straight nose. The terrible gashes in her forehead and cheeks were gone. Her eye sockets were round and firm. Her skin felt smooth. The eruptions of blisters and cysts had subsided and healed.

Next, she felt her hair. The arid patches on her scalp were now lush with recent growth. All of her head felt this way, as if her old hair had been harvested and a new crop had sown, cultivated, and left to flourish.

As far as she could tell without siting up, her legs and arms had healed completely. There were no bone shards protruding from her thighs and shins, and her back no longer throbbed where the keel's sharp edges had sliced.

So what had happened?

She remembered the fever dream in the brig: the forest, the beating from her guardian, her first day aboard the Herculaneum, the woman on the hill. And most of all, the new ideas: it was good to be bad; it was better to reign on Hyacinth than be a slave to the Senate. The thought of them made her draw a breath. Her Hyacinth-creature heart beat faster. The ideas invigorated her mind. 'Bad' felt better. 'Bad' might have healed her. And bad might take her a long, long way.

She would find out how far.

A door creaked open. It was Cordinaus, the surgeon's mate, the one who spoke to Corporal Heva while Sinistra's body burst through the cell bars, and the one who pronounced her dead.

She watched him blunder into the tables, sending two rows of corpses out of alignment. Then he stood up, rubbed his hip and stared at her across the hillocks of blue sheets.

'Expergiscus nunc?' he called. You are awake? 'But you were dead, Lieutenant. You should be dead.'

Before her arrest, Sinistra might have answered with an officer's courtesy to avoid courting disfavor from the crew. Now she knew that courtesy mattered no more.

'Yes, Surgeon's Mate. So it seems. But now, I'm alive.'

73

'Alive?' Cordinaus said. 'But you were …'

Sinistra interrupted him.

'What bell is it? What day? Who is the officer of the watch?'

'You can't get up,' Cordinaus said, wading through the sea of blue tables.

'Why not?'

'Because you can't.'

'Because I can't? That's not much of a reason, Surgeon's Mate Cordinaus. Who says I can't?'

Sinistra's pronunciation had changed. Each musical word was now spoken with round, assertive vowels.

'Stay where you are,' said Cordinaus. 'Stay on that table and lie back down.'

'Why?'

'Doctor Galen is coming.'

'That is also not much of a reason, Surgeon's Mate.'

'Please, just stay where you are.'

'Why would I do that? So you can take me back to the brig? So you can put rings on my wrists and ankles? Don't even think about it.'

'No, it's not that. We're not the masters-at-arms. It's just that I recorded you as dead.'

'Did you? Well, that makes sense. Why should incompetence limit itself to the ship's captain and chief engineer? Everyone must have their turn.'

'But your Hyacinth-creature heart had stopped. Brain activity ceased. They're the major signs of death in the Hyacinth-creature form. I've seen it with the miseria cases.'

'Well then, I guess you're right. I was dead. Now, tell me: have we accelerated or are we still in Ilium? Also, where is the acting captain? I'd like to speak to her. And, while you're here, I'd like these rings removed.'

But Cordinaus seemed not to hear. 'You don't understand. Doctor Galen is coming to confirm my opinion. Then he's going to sign the deceased officer's form, and he can't if you're … '

'Not dead?'

'Yes. I mean no.'

'Well, you better tell Doctor Galen that his signature is no longer required.'

Sinistra inspected her bare legs, arms, and naked stomach.

'Where is my uniform?'

'What?'

'I don't like the way you look at me, Surgeon's Mate. You're like a Goth panting in heat. Close your mouth and tell me where you put my uniform.'

'It ripped when you expanded. We stripped it from your … look, please don't get off the table.' He held up his hands. The fingers splayed wide.

'I will borrow a uniform from one of these,' said Sinistra, looking at the tables on either side of her. 'They're dead, aren't they—actually dead, I mean, not your version of dead?'

'Of course they're dead.'

'So was I, Surgeon's Mate.'

'Listen. Please wait for Doctor Galen. He'll want to know

about your case. The expansion in the brig has healed your limbs and heart, and also your face. It's unusual and it might be important for the miseria cases.'

Sinistra ignored him. She lifted the sheet covering the female body beside her. The corpse's neck glistened with lesions. Its small black tongue probed the edge of its lower lip.

'Who is this, I wonder?' She read the name patch. 'Petty Officer Bursio, purser's assistant. All right, she's about my size, and look, she's still clutching her cap.'

'No,' said Cordinaus. By now his splayed fingers were patting something invisible in the air. 'Please, Lieutenant. No.'

'Did you say no, Surgeon's Mate? I'd say she's a close fit— a little large, a little short, but close enough for now.'

Cordinaus said, 'No, I mean you can't touch the bodies. I'm going to call the master-at-arms. We need to sort this out.'

Before he could finish, Sinistra raised her ringless right arm. She closed her eyes and concentrated. Can I do it? she thought. Should I do it? It isn't really necessary, so should I? I could simply leave here and Cordinaus won't try to stop me. So, should I? What would somebody named Octavia do?

She closed her eyes and concentrated, recalling the feeling of expansion she wanted: a very precise feeling of strength, length, and speed.

'I can,' she said aloud. 'I will.'

Her right arm telescoped away from her. It squelched and cracked as it thickened and stretched. Cordinaus flinched. He ducked and turned his face. The three claws hit the back of his neck, knocking him to his knees. The claws enclosed his throat, squeezing the slight bump known as laryngeal prominens.

'Stop!' gurgled Cordinaus. 'What are you doing?'

'Experimenting,' said Sinistra, 'but also defending,

restraining, and coercing. And do you know what? It's marvelous.'

She lifted Cordinaus from the deck. His legs flailed. His hands shot to his neck. Sinistra flattened his throat towards his spine. In panic, Cordinaus expanded. His uniform ripped open at the legs, exposing swelling calf muscles.

'First,' said Sinistra, 'you will address me by my rank. I'm the captain of this ship—the only legitimate captain. Next you will tell me what happened to me between the brig and here. Then you will tell me whether or not we have accelerated, and the location of Lieutenant Flavia. Then you will remove these two rings.'

She eased her grip. Cordinaus spoke in a breathy, strained voice.

'When you expanded in the brig, I went to see her—acting Captain Flavia.'

'You mean Lieutenant Flavia.'

'Yes.'

'And?'

'I told her what happened.'

'What did she say?'

'She was on the Domum Deck with Captain Ranant.'

'The Domum Deck. Makes sense. How did she look?'

'She was angry. She expanded right up through the trees till she hit the deckhead. Then she said to keep you alive. She was very specific.'

'Then what happened?'

'When I got back to the brig, you had contracted again. I examined you. By then, your bones were just shards. Your tongue was black. Your pupils were open wide. One eye had popped from its socket. Your brain electricity was barely there.'

'Nice to know.'

'Then we moved you here on a trolley with four MAs, but Doctor Galen was busy with the miseria patients and then you ...'

'Died?'

'Your signs of life were all gone. That's what I measured. But somehow you healed your Hyacinth form on the table. The expansion must have caused it.'

'And my mind?'

'I don't know, Lieutenant. Your brain was inactive for several hours. It might be . . .'

'And the two rings?'

'Your wrists and ankle were just threads. I didn't even need keys for two of them. The others have to be removed by the MAs.'

'Where is acting Captain Flavia?'

'I don't know.'

'Guess.'

'She might be on the Domum Deck.'

'Doing what?'

'Trying to heal herself.'

'How many sentries are here on the medical deck?'

'Corporal Heva is here, but I think he's gone now because . . .'

'I'm dead.'

'I don't know. He's an MA, not medical crew.'

'Thank you,' Sinistra said. 'Thank you. I see I have little time. Now, don't move. Don't struggle like that. Look what you did. You kicked three rows out of alignment.' She squeezed his throat tighter.

'Stop,' said Cordinaus. 'Please.'

'Where are the keys to these rings? They're not with the MAs, are they? They're in here, aren't they?'

'No,' Coridinaus wheezed, his hands swimming in the air. 'I can't.'

She squeezed tighter.

But Cordinaus had finally found his courage.

His legs swelled and extended. He kicked backwards

through the scattered tables. His boot sole struck Sinistra's naked chest, knocking her sideways. The second blow forced her hip into a table corner. The third knocked her to one knee.

Then, when a boot stamped at her face, Sinistra squeezed Cordinaus's throat until his tongue slipped from his lips and probed the air like a worm, and then his head lolled to his shoulder, and dropped to his chest. Sinistra pulled the head free to prevent Cordinaus from reforming. The head fell to the deck and rolled underneath the nearest row of tables. Then it settled face up, an expression of horrible surprise in its eyes.

'Practice,' said Sinistra. 'That's what I need. Practice.'

She undressed Chief Petty Officer Bursio's corpse and pulled on her uniform, then she settled one iron ring on her boot collar and one on her new shirt cuff. Then, she wiped Surgeon's Mate Cordinaus's black blood from her hand onto the uniform of a corpse with the patch reading Able Seaman Asina. Then she stepped towards the exit.

But before she could reach the door, it opened. Corporal Heva stood in the jamb. He blinked. His eyes widened. He opened his mouth to speak. His hand reached for the ridiculously large rifle dangling on its strap.

'Hello, Corporal,' said Sinistra. 'Oh, so now you finally want to talk to me!'

The claws struck Heva's throat, knocking him backwards through the door. His hands shot up and grabbed Sinistra's wrist. With her free hand, Sinistra unclipped the rifle and let it fall to the deck.

'You were kind to me, Corporal,' she said, 'and you have a family on the home planet, so I'm only going to disable you. I'm going to let you keep your head. No, don't struggle. Don't make the same mistake as Surgeon's Mate Cordinaus.'

But as Corporal Heva scratched at Sinistra's wrist and kicked out at her legs, a voice spoke behind her.

'Put the corporal down, Lieutenant.'

Sinistra turned to see a tall, mournful figure standing among the corpses, as if he might be one of them come back to life. 'I said stop, Lieutenant. Let the corporal go.'

Sinistra recognized this soft, inoffensive voice. It wasn't Doctor Galen's voice. It wasn't a warrant officer's voice, either. It was Navita Merula.

There were less than two Hyacinth horae to go until the Acceleration.

74

'What do you want?' Sinistra said.

'First,' said Navita Merula. 'I want you to put the corporal down.'

'Where's your old-fashioned accent? Where are your thees and thous? Or were they just to impress me?'

'Put the corporal down, Lieutenant.'

'No.'

'I can make you put him down.'

'Yes, but you won't, will you? You don't interfere in our lives anymore. Isn't that what you said?'

Navita Merula waded through the tables, then stood between Sinistra and the door. Corporal Heva writhed beside him.

'Please, Lieutenant. I have something to ask you.'

'I don't have time. We're almost in Gordium. Haven't you heard?'

'This won't take long. Then you can be on your way to whatever you're planning to do. Please.'

'If I let him go, he'll inform his commanding officer that I've risen from the dead. Then, a hundred Corporal Hevas will be at the door.'

'He won't do anything,' said Navita Merula. He raised a

palm. Corporal Heva stopped struggling and closed his eyes.

'Go on, Lieutenant. Put him down. He won't move.'

Sinistra set Corporal Heva down against the bulkhead. She retracted her arm, straightened her sleeve, and took a longer look at Navita Merula. He no longer wore a blue navy uniform. Instead, he had draped himself in a shabby robe made of dirty brown cloth. Beneath the robe's hem were pale shins and sandals made of dried leather. On his chest, he wore a breastplate, just like Sirhain, except that Merula's breastplate was dull, scratched, and bare of any coat of arms.

'What do you want?' said Sinistra.

'Is that any way to speak to me? Once upon a time, you would have thrown yourself to the deck and worshipped me. Then you would have begged me to save you and your family.'

'I don't have a family, unless you are talking about the navy, and I'm tired of stories of how I would have worshipped someone. I'm also tired of saluting and respecting people who haven't earned the right.'

'You know what I mean, Sinistra. You know who I am, and what I did in the former age.'

'In the former age, you looked like the figure in 'The Fate of The People.' You acted like him, too. You were a leader. You found the home planet and saved the people. Now, you hold the rank of a purser's mate in the ship's hold.'

'I conceal myself for a reason.'

'Yes, I remember. I saw you wielding your powers to command a broomstick in the passageway.'

'I still guide my people,' he said. 'But in this era, it is they who choose their destiny. I don't show my face anymore.'

'You're showing it now.'

'To you. No one else.'

'Why me? Why not Flavia? Why not show your face to the entire ship's company in a blaze of light. Why not cure everyone of miseria? They'd appreciate it. Haven't you heard? The crew is rediscovering you.'

'I am not here to intervene,' Merula said. 'I am here to protect the people through counsel and guidance. There is a higher power above us all. The same power is even above me, and above Sirhain. It is the higher power that commands me not to intervene.'

'Well, forgive me if I am skeptical. Your counsel and guidance have exposed us to the worst of things: volcanic eruptions, planetquakes, the deaths of millions, the incompetence of Flavia, Gabinus, and the old families, and now you expose us to mission failure. If we keep following your advice we'll be extinct.'

'My guidance also brought something else.'

'And what's that?'

'It brought you, Lieutenant.'

'Me? Now, you're sounding like Sirhain.'

'My guidance brought you to this medical room on this ship at this very hour.'

Sinistra looked at the soft face before her. It was not a god's face, but the face of an aging Hyacinth creature, careworn and tired.

'Well then, Owanthan. Please step aside and let me pass.'

'No, Lieutenant. Not until you make a choice.'

'Another choice? Haven't you got a battle to fight? That's what Sirhain told me. The winner gets to be the god of the year. Meanwhile, I'm running out of time. If I don't do something about this Acceleration, and the leadership of this ship, there won't be any more choices to make.'

'Then make your choice now, Lieutenant. Here and now.'

'I'm not going back to the brig, if that's what you mean. Nor am I going to heal my soul or whatever you and Sirhain call giving up and hiding in some cave.'

'You talk as if you were trying to help the people, but we both know you act for yourself, Sinistra. Choose to help the people for their own sakes, not yours.'

'It comes to the same thing, Navita Merula. My aims will fulfill the mission's aims too. That's more than you can say about the new temporary captain and whatever she is planning—if she plans at all.'

'I'm talking about the future, Sinistra, the distant future.'

'So am I.'

'Don't do it, Lieutenant. Or if you must, save the people and withdraw yourself. Stop pursuing this insincere vision Sirhain has planted in your mind—this dream of power and adoration.'

'No.'

'Are you so sure of the outcome? This woman on the hill is just a fantasy, as unobtainable for you as the senate leadership. Flavia and other powerful individuals stand in your way.'

'Even so, I'll find a way. The fact you try to stop me means you know it's possible. As for Flavia, well, let's find out how dangerous she really is.'

'Did you say you'll find a way? Are you sure? All you have is that rifle and your wits. You will fail. Surely you see that.'

'Not true,' Sinistra replied. 'I also have an idea. Haven't you heard? It's better to reign on Hyacinth than be a slave to the Senate.'

'Are you so sure you can reign on Hyacinth? What if the Senate recaptures you?'

'I'll take the risk. I'll die trying.'

'There's more than the Senate to fear. There is Sirhain. He won't be content to play a guiding role from afar. He will demand you obey him, constantly interfering and threatening.'

'I don't care.'

'Please listen, Lieutenant. Make the right choice for everyone, including yourself.'

Sinistra looked at Owanthan, the once mighty god, now a poor Hyacinth creature in old robes, a scratched breastplate, and pale, vulnerable feet. How typical it was, after all that she had seen of the old families and now the old gods, that the chief god should be this way: an unimpressive daydreamer.

But what was his concern, anyway? That she would become an autocrat, like the cruel dictators of the past with their police and their torturers and their oppression of the people? She wouldn't be like that? Would she?

'Well, Sinistra?' said Owanthan.

She bent down and lifted the heavy blast rifle. She looked at Owanthan.

'Out of my way,' she said, 'if you please.'

After a slow shake of his head and a long, exaggerated intake of breath, the great god of the Old Book stepped aside.

Sinistra pushed past him, over the prone body of Corporal Heva, and into the medical deck passageway.

Outside, an announcement sang over the address system.

'Attention. All crew move to Acceleration stations.'

Sinistra stopped. She slid the cuff of her right pants leg over the iron ring. Then, she tugged down the cuff of her left sleeve over the ring on her left wrist, and pulled down the peak of Petty Officer's Bastia's cap.

But she needn't have bothered. The passageway was empty. Sinistra didn't see a single person and the only sounds were coughing, and the Acceleration engines with their slowly climbing pitch.

So far, so good.

But just before she left the medical deck and turned into the Great Passageway, she stopped and stood with the rifle bumping against her hip.

Now what? she thought. What exactly am I going to do?

75

It was a good question.

After all her bravado in the mortuary, she hadn't thought through her next steps. All she had were ideas, a vision, and no time. It's good to be bad, she thought. It's better to reign on Hyacinth than to serve the Senate. I can be the woman on the hill. Yes, but what can I actually do?

She was like a ship accelerating with no map and no helm. How would she ever bring about the hill, the chanting of her future name, the adoration? The one thing she knew for certain was that there was no way back, not in reality and not in thought. To go back, to surrender, was worse than death. That ship had sailed. The gate had closed.

So what to do?

The door leading to the passageway opened. Engine noise surged inside, followed by one of the medical deck crew wearing a helmet. He looked at the name patch on Sinistra's uniform, at the dangling blast rifle, said something about weapons, and hurried away.

If I go to engineering, thought Sinistra. I could force Gabinus at gunpoint to shut the engines down, or I could shut them down myself. The rifle can see to that. I could save the ship and the crew. But that would lead to arrest, the brig, the court-martial, and imprisonment on Hyacinth.

Or I could find Flavia and finally have it out with her. With Flavia out of the way, I could claim the right to be captain, and then order the Acceleration to halt. Yes, she thought. But would anyone go along with it? What about the old-family warrant officers and petty officers? What about the Senate, the Marines?

So what to do?

She didn't know. Her only thought was to get moving and trust that the way forward would reveal itself. The door to the passageway opened again. It was a female crew member wearing a surgical mask covering the lower half of her face. Her eyes opened wide at Sinistra and the huge rifle hanging on its strap. 'What's happened?' she said. 'Is there trouble?' But before Sinistra could answer, the female waved her hands as if flinging 'the trouble' away and ran down the passageway.

Sinistra pulled the rifle strap higher on her shoulder and walked to the door and the Great Passageway. Forward, to the left, lay the bridge, where Cadmus and possibly Flavia would be. To the right, going aft, lay the Domum Deck, engineering, Gabinus, and also the possibility of Flavia still trying to heal her face in the forest.

The door opened once more. Yet another female crew member rushed inside. She mouthed the words 'Acceleration Stations!' Sinistra raised her one free hand at her, as if to say, 'I know. I'm going.' Then, when the crew member had disappeared around a corner, Sinistra got moving. She opened the door, stepped through it, and collided with a male rushing from the stern.

'Watch your step, Petty Officer.'

The voice belonged to Domitian.

76

The Great Passageway was empty. For the moment, there was no one about, except Domitian and herself. Sinistra hadn't spoken to him since disembarking from the Albus— except to issue him a command on the bridge.

Now, here he was, hurrying forward, a wad of documents bound in red string under his arm, and a strange expression on his face—one that could mean annoyance or embarrassment, or guilt. They had been friends before. What were they now?

Sinistra spoke first.

'Hello, Chief Domitian.'

'Lieutenant Sinistra? Where are you going? And how is it you are …?'

'Alive? I don't think you'll want to know, Chief.'

Without thinking, she walked aft, then stopped. Then she turned and began walking forward.

Domitian said, 'Why are you carrying that?' His pointed at the rifle. 'And where's your uniform? And, if you don't mind me asking, how is it that your face is …?'

'Let's just say I've healed, Chief.'

'Whatever you're thinking of doing, Sin, don't. There's another way. Go back to the brig. Please. Wait till we're on

Hyacinth.'

Sinistra stopped and faced him. 'Wait till we're on Hyacinth? Is that what you said, Chief?'

'It will be better for you,' Domitian replied. 'Flavia is distracted today. She's not herself. She'll calm down once the Acceleration is over.'

'Have you seen her? Where is she?'

'On the bridge, of course.'

'Forgive me if I don't believe you, Chief. After all, you're the one who is going to testify against me at the court martial.'

'I saw what I saw, Sin.'

'So you said.' She pulled the cap lower over her eyes. She looked forward along the empty passageway, then aft. Which way would lead to Flavia? Of course, the bridge was the obvious place, the responsible place for the captain during an Acceleration. But would Flavia be responsible?

'Sin,' Domitian said, 'don't make another mistake. I know Flavia did a terrible thing to you, but think of what will happen if you take revenge. Think of the mission.'

'But that's exactly what I'm doing, Chief. I *am* thinking of the mission.'

Sinistra looked at the documents Domitian carried. On one of them, she could see Flavia's curling, assertive signature.

'Where have you just been, Chief? You were coming from the stern. Who did you just see?'

Domitian waited too long before replying. 'I was in the hold. Why?'

'The hold? Does your duty normally take you so far below decks?'

'I went to see Seta.'

Sinistra looked at Domitian's feet. The toe of one boot pointed towards her. The other boot pointed towards the forward-aft shuttle station. She looked at his right arm, the way it clutched the documents to his chest, and the way it pulled the documents away when he saw her looking at them. Domitian's Hyacinth-creature body spoke louder than his voice.

'You're lying, Chief. She's not on the bridge.'

'Sin, please. This is not your fate!'

'I agree. It's not my fate, but it's going to be my destiny, just as you said.'

'You know what will happen, Sin. The MAs will be called out. So will the marines. They'll be ordered to fire on you. You could die. Sin, listen to me!'

But she was already walk-limping aft, towards the Domum Deck, towards Flavia, towards destiny.

There were one and three quarter Hyacinth horae to go.

77

Before the shuttle station, Sinistra reached the painting of 'The Fate of The People.' She walked past the images of ancient stragglers, the crippled, the young, the frightened, and the old. They slid behind her as if she, too, were in the legendary migration, pushing forward to the head of the throng.

But when she reached the section depicting the gods and the king, she kept her eyes on the deck. She didn't want to see the supposed ancestors of Manius, Gabinus, and Flavia. And she didn't want to see Sirhain.

At the Domum Deck entrance, the usual two stewards were on duty. Normally, they would be at an Acceleration station, but they were still at their desk. All of which could mean only one thing: an officer was still inside.

The two stewards stood and saluted as Sinistra approached. They shouted over the engine noise surging up from the stern.

'Beg pardon, Lieutenant Sinistra. The Domum Deck is closed.'

'I don't care. Is Captain Flavia in there?'

'The deck is closed, Lieutenant. Also, no weapons are permitted inside.'

Sinistra looked at the blank face of the steward in front of her. 'Are you trying to stop me?'

'Begging your pardon, Lieutenant. We are here to help. That is why we suggest you find another way.'

'What other way? What do you mean?'

And then, both stewards began yet another strange sequence of exchanges.

'Control is gained when blood is cool.'

'Not hot.'

'The good captain acts when the crew needs him to lead.'

'He does not rampage alone.'

'Less is more.'

'More is less.'

Sinistra felt her anger rising and her arm swelling.

'What are you?' she said. Are you from him?'

'We are here to help, Lieutenant.'

'Really? Well, tell Sirhain I make my own destiny. Now get out of the way.'

The stewards stayed put.

'Advice from the divine should be heeded.'

'Rash confidence is never needed.'

'Well,' said Sinistra. 'Where is this so-called divine? Does Sirhain even exist? Or are you here serving Owanthan?'

'For those who believe, the gods exists.'

'Really? Then where are they?'

'In serried ranks, they wait for the battle of the ages to begin.'

'Gibberish!' said Sinistra.

She pushed past them and entered the Domum Deck.

78

Inside, it was dusk. The sun was low in the deck's west.

She expected Flavia to be there, expanded to the sky, and throwing a shadow over the lavender plain. But there was nothing but a light breeze breeze rippling the field.

She could see Telepathy behind his enclosure's bulkhead. His hulking silhouette was hunched in concentration, transmitting and receiving as many messages as possible before the Herculaneum accelerated out of range.

A great engine howl rolled up from the stern, and Telepathy flinched. Sinistra ducked down into the lavender, her hands cupped to her head. She could discern Zeus's howl from Mars's high-pitched snarl. She waited, listening for Apollo to take its turn. But no sound came. Had Gabinus fixed it or not?

There was no time to check.

Instead, she sent a message to Telepathy?

Where is Flavia?

But Telepathy did not reply.

She stepped into the lavender and waded towards the orange desert. The heavy rifle stock bumped her side. The ankle ring chafed her new skin. She barely noticed. Beyond the desert lay the dark wall of the forest. In the evening light, the forest appeared even more sinister than usual. It would be difficult to see inside. She would be at a disadvantage.

But that's where Flavia must be, so that's where she must go.

Sinistra dragged her ringed leg across the desert's shadowed dunes, then limped into the woods. Inside, it was a changed world. The air was cool, the tree trunks were thick with shadow. It was quiet, too. The engine growls couldn't penetrate inside. All was hushed. Sinistra's careful boot steps crunched too loudly on the forest floor.

One hundred passus in, the night descended. In the poor light, Sinistra's Hyacinth-creature eyes were too weak to see the trees twenty passus ahead. In a few minuta, she would hardly see at all. And, if Flavia were in her natural form, there would be no hope of evading her, let alone creeping up on her.

Something had to be done.

She unslung the rifle and leant it against a tree trunk. Then, she stood and tried to transform herself—not her feet or her legs, which always turned out uneven in both girth and length. She only wanted to transform her head.

But what if I can't transform it back? My beautiful face—what will happen? She pushed this thought aside and drew a breath, imagining the change she wanted: from small eyes with round pupils to large, night-eyes with slitted apertures, like the eyes of a Goth or a reptile. Then, she pictured large ears with triangular flaps. Finally, she imagined a sense of smell that could detect a Hyacinth creature's odor a hundred passus away.

Then she waited, reaching out her free hand to a cold tree trunk.

But nothing happened.

Nothing.

She stopped, breathed slowly, and imagined how it would feel to be the woman on the hill standing in the sunlight.

Then she tried again. This time, she felt a shift. The bones on either side of her eye sockets bent. She slapped her hands on her temples and pressed inward in case her skull cracked. Then a snapping noise broke out all over her head—from her eyes to her chin, and the back of her neck. Her eye sockets expanded; her inner-ear parts writhed; and her nostrils widened as olfactory glands spread.

When the snapping ceased, she touched her ears, her face, and her scalp. They had not only changed shape, but expanded far more than she imagined. After she calmed down, she removed her hands from her temples, opened her eyes, and blinked at the gloom.

It was a strange world that appeared—one of grainy shapes of blue, green, yellow, and gray. She could see through the trees for fifty passus at least. Her sense of smell had changed, too. The bark on the tree beside her reeked of decay. The sap inside smelled sweet, and the forest floor radiated the odors of rotting leaves, wet soil, and bark.

But she couldn't smell the scent of Flavia's uniform nor the rancid body sweat of 'natural' Flavia, the one who menaced her after her first meeting with Doctor Galen.

But her new ears could hear something.

She tilted them one way, then the other. She heard faint words growled in the native language: the word 'no,' and then 'nothing' and then the words, 'hideous' and 'never.' Then she heard a snap.

The growls came from deeper in the forest, deeper to the 'east.'

She re-slung the rifle, adjusted the rings on her foot and wrist, and crept through the trees towards the noise. Eventually, she reached a clearing and could see a blurry image colored dark blue. A tall, naked, Hyacinth female with long, thick hair stood holding a flat object in front of its face.

The Hyacinth creature put down the object, then threw up its arms and drew a deep breath. Then, with much snapping, cracking and long inhalations, the creature expanded outwards and upwards into the trees, blocking out the moonlight.

This colossus stood still for a half minuta, breathing hard, gazing at the artificial stars, its arms spread wide, the scales on its flanks slithering around. Then, the cracking, snapping and heavy breathing repeated as the creature shrank back down.

Once it had returned to Hyacinth-creature size, and Hyacinth-creature form, the tall female picked up the object and gazed at it. Then she scowled, shook her head, looked to the sky, as if beseeching the old gods for help. When no one answered, she put a hand to the goiter on her neck and dropped her gaze to the forest floor.

'Once more,' the woman growled in the native language. 'Once more.' Then she rose again, up towards the night.

Watching on, Sinistra quietly slid the rifle strap down her arm. She flicked a small switch on the rifle's forestock. She heard the tiny squeal and saw the small light blinking.

She raised the rifle to her chin and looked down the barrel to the sights. How easy it was to hold the muzzle steady compared to her days as a withered shrub, and compared to the last time she had fired a rifle, back on the object during the Goth attack—back when she wasn't sure if was aiming at the Goths or her first lieutenant.

Now, with murderous certainty, she looked through the sights at the gray and blue giant. The creature's scales would deflect most of the blast. Even a headshot wouldn't kill her—not if Flavia stayed in expanded form. To end Flavia's life, Sinistra had to wait until the giantess shrank back to Hyacinth-creature form and all the vulnerability of the thin skin, the eggshell skull, and the easily severed neck.

So, Sinistra waited in the shadows, whispering comforting phrases to herself. 'It's good to be bad. It's better to be feared than liked. It's better to reign on Hyacinth than serve the

Senate. Come on Flavia! Shrink.'

But Flavia did not shrink. Instead, she suddenly tilted her head like a Goth, and sniffed deeply. Her snout flicked daintily up and down, taking its time, making sure of something—something it had just detected.

Finally, after one deep inhalation, Flavia stood tall and spoke the native language in a deep, bass growl that sent the nesting birds fleeing into the night.

'I know that smell,' it said. 'It reeks of traitor.'

79

Flavia's voice boomed down from the canopy.

'You!' she said. Her blue nostrils flared as she sniffed deeper, seeking Sinistra's hiding place.

'What I don't understand,' said the booming voice, 'is that you are here at all. You should be dead—as dead as your career, decaying on the medical deck, or burning up in space with the suicides. And yet, here you are, yet again. What happened? Was Galen was mistaken or did you rise from the dead?'

Sinistra kept quiet. Flavia lowered her head and sniffed the clearing's edge. 'What do want from me, anyway?' she said. 'To whine about how you were only following Cicero's orders when you stole my command? Is that it? Or, are you here to explain about Captain Ranant? Well, save your breath. Ranant told me how you threw yourself at him. You are so pathetic, but what else can anyone expect from you?'

Flavia stepped closer. Sinistra crouched lower.

'So what is it?' she said. 'What's this all about, hmm? Why have you followed me here? Tell me.'

The clawed foot sank into the soil a mere four passus away. Sinistra held her breath. She knew she had missed her chance. Flavia wouldn't risk shrinking back to Hyacinth-creature form. She would stay expanded with her hard scales, thick bones, night eyes, and sense of smell. A new plan was required. But how would Sinistra ever trick Flavia into shrinking again?

'You disgusting little upstart,' came Flavia's voice.

Sinistra lifted a tentative boot and stepped back. But even the gentlest touch of her heel on the soil alerted Flavia's ears. It was as good as shouting 'Here I am!'

Instantly, Flavia's colossal head pushed through the leaves. The cavernous nostrils flared. The slits of her pupils dilated, and the great snout probed left and right.

'I'm close, aren't I?' Flavia growled. 'And you are alone.'

Sinistra assessed the danger she was in. She knew there could be no escape—not by fleeing. The slightest movement and Flavia would instantly pin her down with her claws. Then, she would probably tear Sinistra apart. That left only one option: she would have to risk a shot at Flavia in her expand form—and take the consequences. The rifle's tiny light blinked beneath her left hand. The fire button waited beneath her right. But how could she get into position without making a sound.

'Why don't you say something, Lieutenant?' Flavia growled. 'Why are you so silent? It's so unlike you. Where is your usual fawning self, so eager to please me, to show me respect? Or is this the new, assertive Sinistra, the one who wanted to arrest Gabinus?'

Still crouching in the shadows, Sinistra decided to take a risk. She spoke, and as she did, she lifted the rifle and lowered her head.

'If you must know,' she replied 'It's something else. I've discovered that you don't deserve respect. None. Not as a navy officer, not as a comrade, not as anything. You have never deserved respect. And you never will.'

Flavia's head jerked five degrees. The nostrils flared. The ears flicked up, and the eyes narrowed. She smelled the metal and machine oil. She saw the dull gleam of the rifle's barrel, the slender hand on the forestock, and the bulging head lowered to the sights. Her forelimb came up, claws bared. She swung a fist down at Sinistra's bent head.

Before it struck, Sinistra pulled the fire button.

The blast flash was so bright, it bleached the trees green and white. The astonishing boom crashed away through the forest, scattering the birds in the canopy. The forestock leaped from Sinistra's grip, and the rifle spun away. The sling strap pulled Sinistra onto her back, and the blast rumbled over the desert like a storm till all was quiet except for the anger of the distant engines.

On her back between the trees, Sinistra was in shock.

In the blinding glare, she had glimpsed terrible sights: Flavia's gleaming black claws scything the dark; the scaly forelimbs huge and bulging; the riot of bleached and writhing branches. Then, she had seen and the most terrifying sight of all: Flavia's astonished, recoiling face with its eyes squeezed shut, and its teeth clenched, as her reflexes flinched at the blast.

But there was more.

Sinistra had suffered her own blast shock. She had crossed a line—no, not just a line. With a clear mind and open eyes, she had crossed a frontier into a new galaxy where only the irredeemably bad people dared tread, the ones who shot their commanding officers, not by accident in the frenzy of a Goth attack, but in cold, black calculating blood.

The old self-hatred in her rose like the tide. It was worse than ever. With it came the urge to do something. Anything would do—anything at all to make amends. She wanted to apologize. She wanted to dress Flavia's wounds, to stand five watches in a row, to clean the scuttles of suicide bodies. Anything.

She sat breathing hard, on the soft wet soil, where the recoil had flung her. Then she came to her senses. It was better to reign on Hyacinth than to serve Flavia and the Senate. It was all right to be bad. There is a woman on the hill in the sunshine, a multitude below her, adoring her. And there could be no other way to think.

She picked herself up and crept forward to the clearing's edge. She pushed aside the leaves and gazed upon another terrifying sight.

She had missed.

80

Yes, she had missed, but not completely.

Across the clearing, Flavia staggered with one claw at her neck. Sinistra raised the rifle, but she was still too flash-blinded to see her target: Flavia's left ear. When she saw Flavia's head turn in her direction, she fired anyway.

The sequence repeated: the white flash, the astonishing boom, the hysterical muzzle, the rolling thunder over the deserts and fields, and the ten secunda wait till her eyes could partially see the devastation.

She held her breath and listened.

In the clearing, there was no stagger, no heavy crash to the ground, no agonized moan, no last words. Sinistra had missed her mark again. And now Flavia had found her feet. With astonishing speed, she stomped across the clearing.

Sinistra climbed to her knees and scrabbled for the rifle. The strap had come free of her arm. The rifle had flung itself behind her. She sniffed in a circle for traces of metal and smoke, but she was too late.

The branches shivered above her. Flavia's voice spoke with a wet slur. 'Now, we don't need a court martial, do we, Lieutenant?'

Sinistra climbed to her feet and ran. The rings on her left

arm and right leg bit and scraped. Behind her, the trees thrashed as giant Flavia bludgeoned her way through the branches.

What now? thought Sinistra. Where now? But she knew the answer.

No rifle, no plan.

She ran-limped towards the desert. Behind her, Flavia's stomps were heavy but halting. She was too big to barge her way through the trees with any speed. Sinistra could outrun her.

At the forest edge, Sinistra stopped and surveyed her options. Dusk was gone. Night was here. The desert loomed gray and black, like a choppy frozen sea.

I've come the wrong way, Sinistra thought. I should have gone deeper into the forest, not back here. She looked closer at the desert. The shadows between the dunes might provide cover for a while. Or she could hobble into the forest, doubling back on her track. That might confuse Flavia's nose.

Yes, but what about Flavia's ears? And how long could Sinistra run, anyway? Till morning? Till the Acceleration began and the engines failed? What would be the point of evading Flavia but losing the ship?

'Come out now,' slurred Flavia's voice from deep in the forest. 'It'll be easier for you. I won't kill you. Not yet.'

Sinistra didn't reply. Without the rifle, she realized a desperate act was required. She turned and re-entered the forest and found a tree with thick, exposed roots. She slipped off her boots, shirt, and pants and dropped them at the tree's base. Naked, she limped back to the forest edge. Then, she closed her eyes and imagined herself as tall as the trees themselves.

'Concentrate,' Sinistra said. She pictured herself expanding outward and upward into a creature of height, power, scales, claws, and teeth—bigger than Flavia, as big as

Telepathy. Somehow, she would get round the restrictions of the two rings.

As before, nothing happened.

And then, something.

Pain surged in her spine, followed by hot spikes in her arms and stomach. Her legs grew first. They expanded so fast that she lost her balance and lurched onto the sand. The ring on her right leg bit into her ankle. Her Hyacinth creature calf muscle ballooned above it. Her left leg swelled out and telescoped down.

When all the expanding ceased, Sinistra was on all fours with one long leg, one long arm, and two grossly swollen, painful limbs. When she tried to take a step, she tipped over, face first, down into the sand with her rump in the air. Failure.

Flavia's voice spoke in her mind.

Remember how everyone says only open space can kill us? Well, there is one other way we can be killed, Lieutenant. No, I'm not referring to rifle blasts. I'm referring to something else. Can you guess what it is?

Sinistra didn't answer.

The voice said, It's called dismemberment. I'm going to dismember you, Sinistra, out on the sand. I'm going to pull you apart. Then I'm going to toss you into space alive. Your legs and arms will drift with you in the void. They'll keep drifting, long after we accelerate away. Then, you'll be alone, which I think might cause the greatest agony of all

Flavia stepped from the forest edge and stomped towards the ridiculous Sinistra-creature with its uneven limbs. Flavia's moon shadow swam ahead of her, gliding over the rippling dunes. It took her only ten steps to overtake Sinistra, who staggered like a wounded spider.

Flavia's scaled calf thumped into the sand in front of Sinistra's face, barring her laboured progress onto the desert. Then, a fist struck the back of Sinistra's skull.

Before I dismember you, said Flavia's voice. I'm going to disable you.

Sinistra felt Flavia's heavy claw on her back. Then she felt Flavia's teeth sink deep into her neck, seeking the gaps in her spine. The pain was astonishing. The thought of Flavia's teeth prying apart her vertebrae was almost as unbearable.

Not since her childhood had Sinistra experienced violence so close, and so personal. Outmatched in strength and hatred, there was nothing she could do except fight back with the few defenses available: her two free limbs, and her own teeth.

With the pain hot in her neck, she hooked an arm around the ankle of Flavia's leg. Then, with the scales cutting her soft skin, she pulled.

In response, Flavia shook Sinistra's neck, like a Goth shaking a forest deer. But Flavia's claws slipped in the sand and Sinistra was able to pull Flavia's horrible claw close enough to bite down on it so hard one of her teeth separated the scales and pierced the soft flesh beneath.

Flavia shrieked and released Sinistra's neck. Then, she beat her fists on the back of Sinistra's head until she unclamped her teeth.

Then the both of them looked at each other, reappraising strengths and weaknesses. Flavia's mouth dripped dark blood. Sinistra's head wobbled on the top of her spine.

'Shouldn't you be on the bridge, Lieutenant?' Sinistra said.

Flavia ignored her and said to herself, 'This is more difficult than I imagined. I'm going to need help.' Then she sent a thought across the desert.

Telepathy! she called in the Hyacinth-creature language. Telepathy!

At the far end of the desert, the slumped figure raised its head.

That's right. I'm calling you. Yes, Telepathy. You! I know

you can hear me. I need your help to hold this creature down.

As Flavia joked, Sinistra tried to run.

But she didn't make three lopsided lunges before Flavia's shadow slid over her and caught her by the ankle. Then Flavia spun her over, just as Sinistra's guardian had done decades before, and stomped her clawed foot into Sinistra's face, pinning her in the sand while her ludicrous, uneven limbs flailed.

Come on, Telepathy. Hurry up! Don't worry. I won't keep you long. Just a few minuta.

Beneath the heavy claw, Sinistra made a desperate plea

Sirhain! Sinistra said in a thought shout. Can you hear me? Sirhain! And when there was no reply, she said, Are you just in my mind? Were you always only in my mind?

And then Telepathy's shadow arrived.

81

Flavia was impatient.

We haven't got all night, Petty Officer!

'Yes, First Lieutenant,' shouted Telepathy over the engine noise. Sinistra noticed that when he spoke aloud, he had the same northern forest accent as her own.

Speak in thoughts, Petty Officer. I can't hear you.

'Beg pardon, Lieutenant Flavia, but on this mission, thought messages are restricted to communications with the Senate.'

It's Captain Flavia, Petty Officer. And don't be smart with me. We all know you use thoughts outside of navy business. So use them now.

Beg pardon, Captain Flavia, but I must be at my post for the Acceleration. Lieutenant Cadmus has ordered me there.

I don't care where you have to be. Take this creature's leg. Stop it thrashing around like that.

May I ask why, First Lieutenant?

No. You may not. Seize her leg.

Sinistra felt a second set of claws clutch her left ankle with hard chafing scales. Now there was a monster at each end, both about to pull against each other.

Flavia's voice sounded almost flirtatious. Before you came

aboard, Petty Officer, you were a murderer, were you not?

Yes, Captain, a long time ago, in my youth.

And you were in prison on Danraath Island. Is that right?

I was in many prisons.

Your real name is Malawg, isn't it? You committed murders on behalf of a criminal organization.

A long time ago, Captain.

Murders are rare on our planet, aren't they, Malawg?

Very rare, Captain Flavia.

Why is that?

Because people don't know how to do it.

They don't know how to commit murder?

No.

But you know how to do it, don't you?

Yes.

Is dismembering someone an effective way of killing them? That's what I've heard.

Not always.

Why not?

The person might be quick enough to reshape themselves before you can disjoint the limbs—and remove the head.

I don't think we'll have to worry about any sudden reshaping from this criminal. Just look at it. See?

Yes, Captain. I see.

All right. Good. Let's begin. Are you ready? No, don't listen to Lieutenant Sinistra. She's sick, and she's mad. Our ship's own doctor says she's dangerous. Just grab hold of the other leg and pull. That's an order, Malawg.

Sinistra pleaded in thoughts to Telepathy, but he didn't reply. So she said nothing and braced herself for the agony. She felt Flavia pull hard, then yank at her leg, digging her hind claws into the sand. Yet, to her surprise, she didn't feel any force from Telepathy.

You're not pulling, Petty Officer Malawg.

No, Captain Flavia.

Are you disobeying an order?

Yes, Captain Flavia. I don't wish to harm Lieutenant Sinistra.

She's a traitor, who tried to murder me—twice!

She is the only officer who is courteous to me.

This isn't a social club, Malawg. This is the navy. If I say pull, you pull, or else you'll also float in open space. Now pull.

No.

No? Did you say no, Petty Officer?

Now Sinistra sensed something else. She felt Telepathy release her leg. She felt him stomp forward. His claws tossed sand onto her stomach. She heard Flavia shout, 'What do you think you are doing?'

And then Flavia also released her grip. Her claw rose from Sinistra's face. Sinistra instantly pulled herself up and crawled away across the sand, like a bleeding wounded arachnid, fleeing to the forest. But just before she entered the trees, she looked back at the desert. The two giants were in a clinch. Telepathy locked Flavia's neck in the crook of his forelimb. Flavia's claws were sunk in his eyes, forcing back his head.

Thank you, Sinistra said in a thought message to Telepathy. Thank you. She heard no reply. By now the two were squaring off against each other. Telepathy's arm and face dripped black blood. Flavia stood tall and strong. She could see. Telepathy could not. Flavia would defeat him.

Then, Sinistra turned away and lumbered into the forest gloom, wondering what to do next.

There was less that one hora to go. Before that, Sinistra would have to expose herself to the danger of the unimaginable.

82

I'm bad, Sinistra thought. I'm no good. I'm bad. I've always been bad. Now, I've killed Telepathy. Now, I'm going to fail. When Flavia catches me I'm going to die, and the Acceleration will fail, and the ten thousand crew will perish, and the people on the home planet will die before they can escape the volcanoes.

And there will be no woman on the hill.

Unable to move in a straight line, and dazed by Octavia's cruelty, she staggered into one tree after another, falling over and climbing to her four uneven legs, then trying again, until she tripped, knocked her head on a tree truck, fell again, and sprawled on the damp soil. Then she lay breathing, trying to stem the torrent of thoughts.

How foolish it had been to expand. She had panicked after missing the shot in the clearing and couldn't think straight. That was why. While she wore the rings, she had better stay in Hyacinth-creature form. Then she would return to the only plan that made sense. She would find the rifle and try again. But was there still time? Were the engines howling louder than before? She couldn't tell, and she hadn't heard a single bell. But the Acceleration must be near. It must be no more than an hora away.

She got to her four ridiculous limbs and snuffled the air till she sensed cloth, leather, and detergent. After she found her uniform, she dropped to the forest floor again, and focused her mind, shutting out the horrible shrieks and snarls drifting in from the desert.

She imagined herself in female Hyacinth-creature form with its legs, arms, waist, breasts, neck, hands, and lustrous hair. Soon, her bones contracted, the forest darkened, the reek of decay faded. She became a Hyacinth creature again—naked, vulnerable, limited in sensory perception, but mobile and agile.

She stood up and felt her face, hair and limbs. They seemed the same as before. But what about her face? Was she still beautiful, like a Hyacinth goddess? She would have to wait to find out. Meanwhile, she pulled on the uniform, and settled the rings on her shirt cuff and boot collar, and hobbled towards the clearing and the rifle, as fast as her right leg could swing.

Halfway to the clearing, she saw something standing ahead in the gloom. Whatever or whoever it was leaned against a tree. The forest was too dark to see clearly, but yes, someone was definitely there in Hyacinth-creature form, stroking its face in the dark.

She crouched and waited. After a few secunda, the figure spoke in a male voice using round vowels and singsong tones, just like Flavia used to do before the blast wound made her slur her words.

'You never know,' said the voice.

Sinistra waited.

'You never know,' the voice said once more, 'who you'll meet on a dark night in the woods.'

83

'Come out from there, Sinistra.'

Sinistra watched and waited.

'Notice I'm calling you Sinistra,' said the figure, 'not your other names. That's because the future—your future—is not what it used to be.'

'Are you here to help?'

'Are you here to help?' the figure said, mocking Sinistra's breathy plea. 'Is that any way to speak to me? I'd show more respect if I were you. Consider your situation. You are outnumbered. You are unarmed. You are over matched for size, and you lack the speed and sensory perception to evade your determined and angry pursuer.'

The figure stepped away from the tree. Sinistra saw the robe, the thin legs, the puffed sleeves, the jaunty hat, and the right hand fiddling at the upper lip. The moonlight glinted on his breastplate.

'Are you here to help me?' said Sinistra. 'Or to mock me?'

'Neither.'

'So why are you here?'

'To bid you goodbye.'

'What?'

'You heard me. I'm here to say farewell. You might not see

me again. And last time we met, you fell asleep on me. It was so disrespectful, especially when I was making such a good speech.'

'Why? Where are you going?'

'As I told you, I have a battle to fight, a battle to win, and an old enemy to defeat. The old goat has brought his entire force across. He even brought along his general, Galanthan, another old goat. What a struggle it will be—a struggle for the ages! And then, after I've won, you and the rest of the people are going to need a New Book to replace the Old Book.'

'Owanthan told me. I saw him.'

'It seems we've all paid you a visit. Who'd have thought you would gain such attention, Sinistra?'

'He also told me about you and the rest of the gods.'

'Did he now?'

'He said there was a higher power, and it demanded that you both stay out of our lives.'

'Sanctimonious old goat—Owanthan, I mean.' He looked up at the moon.

'What will your battle mean for me, for us, for the mission, for the home planet? What about the promise you made to me?'

'Promise? I promised you nothing, Sinistra. Your mind is strained. Your memory is flawed. There was no promise made by Sirhain.'

'You said it would happen. I'd be the woman on the hill if I found a way to control the mission. You said the Hyacinth people would follow me and adore me. My own people would follow me, too.'

'Things have changed. Give it up, Sinistra.'

'But you said I could make it happen if I chose to.'

'I have a war to fight, and if you must know, my own future is at stake. I don't have time for yours.'

'But you can help me. You know you can.'

'Help you how?'

'Bind Flavia in ropes. Kill her for me. Suspend time so that I can stop the Acceleration. Or if you won't do that, fix the engines so they won't fail. Then help me win the support of the crew. That's a start.'

'You ask a lot, Sinistra, especially when you offer nothing in return.'

'For your information, Owanthan thinks I can do it. He thinks I can be the woman on the hill. He must. Why else would he warn me not to try?'

Sirhain drew a long, ruminative breath.

'You really crave the adoration, don't you? Or is it the power you want?'

'Aren't you the exactly the same? Isn't power what you crave and what Owanthan craves, too? You are seizing your opportunity just like I am, aren't you? Admit it.'

Silence as Sirhain's hand fingers twisted one end of his mustache.

'I see I have a corrupted your soul, Sinistra.'

'Maybe, but you also opened my eyes. Now my corrupted soul might also save the crew. Does that make a difference? If you help me, you also help them, and all the people on the home planet. They, we, me—we're your people too, aren't we? And if it isn't me who saves them, who will it be? Flavia? Cadmus? They're not the ones called to greatness. You said so yourself. I'm the one. It's me. It's only me.'

'I never used the word greatness.'

'You know what I mean: to lead in a crisis, to see a glorious future others can't imagine, to bring them to it, and yes, to enjoy the praise. What of it?'

Sirhain looked at the moon. It had risen over the canopy and shone a soft light, dappling the forest floor. 'It's too late, Sinistra.'

'Why—why is it too late?'

'Your comrade, Lieutenant Cadmus, will soon issue his

Acceleration orders. Your commanding officer, Flavia, will hunt you, find you, and kill you. Fate will take its course.'

'Then do something simple. Stop the clocks. Stay the bell. Give Flavia a stomach ache. Anything would help.'

'No.'

'Why not?'

'Must I say the word in your native growls and grunts so that you understand? It's clear to me you have received too many knocks to your head. They have damaged your faculties and your sense of reason.'

'At least take off these rings.'

'Listen, if I were you, I'd save myself the trouble. Stay as you are. Beg Flavia to spare you life. She might spare you because of the dreadful keelhauling. Even I can see it was a step too far. And you never know. The ship and crew might survive. Then, you can find peace. It will be better in the end. Believe me.'

'Really? Then why don't you do it? Why don't you live by your own advice? Why don't you find peace instead of fighting a war for power?'

Sirhain's hand ceased twirling his mustache and hovered in the dark.

'Well?' Sinistra said.

Eventually, Sirhain replied. 'You want to defeat Flavia? You want to be this woman on the hill so badly?'

'Yes.'

'No matter how unlikely any of those possibilities happen to be?'

'There's nothing else for me.'

Sirhain put a finger to his forehead, then said, 'This is against my judgement.'

'Please, Sirhain. Anything.'

Sirhain looked up. 'Very well. I won't help you, but I can guide you just a little.' In the darkness, he pursed his lips and looked at the night sky, as if choosing from many options. Then, he looked at Sinistra. 'Ask yourself this question,' he said. 'What's the thing Flavia fears the most?'

Sinistra thought. 'Losing her Hyacinth creature looks.'

'Apart from that.'

'Losing her family's position—all the old families' positions.'

'Yes, but something else. Something more immediate.'

Sinistra's mind darkened. 'Losing Ranant.'

'No, Lieutenant. Try harder. Think of something you saw.'

Sinistra pictured Flavia's raging tantrums, her vanity, and her fears. Then she realized.

'Now you see,' said Sirhain.

'It can't be done, and there isn't time. It can't be done.'

'Well, do as you wish. I've shown you the way, now I must go.'

'But how will I ever get her there?'

'That's up to you.'

'And what if I succeed? What then? How will I win over the crew?'

'It's interesting. You sounded so certain when you were boasting to Owanthan about the phrase "Cometh the hour."'

'I was inspired by the ideas you told me.'

'They were meant to ease your pain, nothing more.'

'Even the part about reigning on Hyacinth?'

'I didn't expect you to act on it.'

'Why don't you just make it happen like you said you would?'

'I can't—not now, not until certain events are determined.'

'Can't or won't?'

'Won't.'

'If I fail, everything else will fail—the crew, the mission, the people on the home planet. Doesn't that bother you?'

'There are other ships. They might launch in time. It's unlikely, but they might.'

'Please, tell me how to do it.'

'No, Sinistra. Your time has run out. So has mine. No, don't say anything more, and don't cry. It won't help.'

And he stepped backward until he became a shadow. Sinistra could no longer see him.

'Sirhain!' Sinistra called. 'Come back!'

But no one answered.

Instead, she heard a terrible groan from the desert, rising above the engine noise. Then she heard the menacing tones of Flavia's voice in her mind.

So, Lieutenant, growled Flavia's voice. It turns out I don't need anybody's help after all. Did you see what I just did to Telepathy? I never knew I possessed such talent and such strength. I never thought I had the stomach. But I did it with my own delicate hands. Oh, yes! Gabinus, if you can hear me, you will be amazed. Totally astonished. But it's nothing, Grenda, compared to what I'll do to you after I catch you.

Sinistra stood overwhelmed in the dark, unable to move. But after a few moments of breathing hard, she calmed down, and said to herself, 'It's better to reign on Hyacinth than to serve the Senate.'

Then she got moving. She hobbled back to the clearing, found the rifle, and slung it over her shoulder. Then, she limped a different route back to the desert, wondering exactly how she was going to do as Sirhain advised.

How was she ever going to lure Flavia to the stern ramp and out into open space—out to the horrible exhaust funnels and their terrible blasts? How was she going to fight her to death?

There were fifty minuta to go until the Acceleration.

84

Sinistra crouched in the shadows by the desert's edge.

In the sky above, the artificial moon watched from a nest of clouds. A soft light shone on the Domun Deck world.

But the deck was anything but calm.

Marines had emerged from the lavender plain. With their rifles at their hips, they crossed into the desert. At least thirty helmet lamps scythed the dunes, sending the shadows scurrying.

Sinistra's heart sank. How would she ever cross the desert? How could she avoid capture or death? Or worse: capture and incarceration? And where was Flavia? How could she lure her across the sand if Flavia wasn't even here?

Sirhain's unlikely idea now seemed ridiculous. All Sinistra had was the image of the woman on the hill on faraway Hyacinth. Would the image be enough? It would have to be. She stood up, slung the rifle, and resettled the iron ring on her boot. Then she stepped onto the sand and crept towards the black ruins of Telepathy's dismembered corpse.

Her plan—if it could be called a plan—was to reach Telepathy's corpse and make herself visible when Flavia tracked her scent back to the forest edge, then she would lead Flavia over dunes to the Domun Deck's stern bulkhead, then blast her way through the bulkhead with the rifle. Then she would climb through the blast hole onto the stern ramp itself. After that, the plan became as vague and empty as the cosmos.

Two minuta later, Sinistra peered over Telepathy's lifeless back, ducking each time a lamp beam flashed.

That's when she heard his voice in her head.

Lieutenant, the sun will soon be up.

Sinistra whispered, 'Telepathy?'

The same. Chief Purser Seta is on the deck. She has ordered the clock to be sped up. Look at the moon. It is sinking. The sun is coming. It will expose you. The marines will shoot you, and in your Hyacinth-creature form, well, you know what will happen when the first blast hits you.

'But you're still alive.'

For now.

'You saved me,' Sinistra said.

Your voice, Lieutenant. How different it sounds since I last heard you speak. You almost sound like Flavia.

'Many things changed on the object.'

Then, I will pretend you are the same Sinistra I knew before. You are the same, aren't you—at least some part of you?

'Yes. Some part of me.'

Where are you going, Lieutenant?

She told him, then ducked beneath a light beam.

You will fail. The dunes are too shallow to hide you. I can hear the marines' thoughts. There are many and they are impatient. They want to be at their stations for the Acceleration. They blame you for keeping them here.

'What about Flavia?'

She can't hear my thoughts, if that's what worries you.

'Can you hear hers?'

Unfortunately, yes. Her mind raves. She pictures catching you, and doing to you what she did to me. Her every second thought is about her ruined looks.

Sinistra looked at the dark lumps of Telepathy's scattered limbs and the sand stained by his black blood.

'But where is she?'

Snuffling for your scent, this way and that.

'So she's in the forest?'

I don't know. What can you see?

Sinistra looked, but no creature disturbed the canopy. Flavia must still be at the clearing.

Telepathy's voice said, The sun, lieutenant. The sun.

'I know. I'm leaving.'

Good luck, wherever you go.

Before she crept away, she said, 'Telepathy, did you hear my thoughts in the forest?'

No. I heard only Flavia's thoughts, delighting in my agony.

'Didn't you hear me talking? Didn't you hear the thoughts of Sirhain?'

Who?

'Sirhain.'

Sirhain? From the Old Book? The demon god? I don't understand you, Lieutenant.

'Didn't you hear me think his name back there in the forest?'

I heard only Flavia. What has Sirhain to do with this?

Sinistra didn't answer. She looked at the moon. It had almost disappeared beneath the false horizon. She crept out from behind Telepathy's wheezing body, out onto the dunes. Then she heard Telepathy's voice distracting the marines.

Marines, said his thought voice. If you don't know, I, Telepathy, originally named Malawg, was murdered here on the sand. That's right. I'm still here, in mind only. But acting Captain Flavia murdered me, against the Navy Code. Corporal Attan! Put down that rifle! There's no need to aim at me like that. What would your poor, sick father, the former navy lieutenant, think? The same with you, Sergeant Krart? Your mother would be ashamed of you. All of your parents would be ashamed of you, hunting Lieutenant Sinistra, who, like me, is wrongfully accused, and horribly abused by the acting Captain.

Then, to Sinistra in private, he said: Go, Lieutenant. Go!

One last thing, said Sinistra in a thought voice. What's in Engineer Gabinus's mind? Is he watching the engines? Are the engines all right?

Gabinus? Nothing is in his mind, or nothing good. He's daydreaming of an engineer's mate named Gallus. No, not daydreaming. He's lusting. You are distracting me, Sinistra. Go away.

Sinistra crept along the shadow between two dunes. It was hard going. The heavy rifle swung on its sling strap and tripped her up. The ring on her left wrist chafed her raw skin, and the ring on her right leg slipped from the boot collar onto her bare ankle. All the while, the engines yowled louder as they strained to increase the revolutions required to fling the Herculaneum across the galaxy.

Now a glow fringed the artificial horizon to the 'east.' Sinistra's limping moon shadow faded. The sand lightened in color to gray-orange. A quarter minuta later, the dawn glowed behind the forest. The dune shadows shortened. The sun climbed up and lit the deck.

Across at the Domum Deck's entrance, Chief Purser Seta stood watching with her chin raised. She had seen Sinistra. Now she waved at the marines on the desert, pointed at Sinistra's location with a jabbing right hand. The marines began jogging.

Sinistra dropped to one knee, pulled the heavy rifle around and aimed at the rear bulkhead, right into the artist's rendition of a desert village.

She fired.

The recoil flung her onto her back in the sand. When she

looked up, she could see a wide blast hole and the white stems of dropships on the stern deck beyond. Behind her, the marines kept on coming, but as yet, no blast knocked her to the sand. No bullet hit her back or her neck. Perhaps Telepathy has persuaded them to hold their fire.

She limped to the bulkhead and climbed through the blast hole. The forest of ships stood before her. Beyond them, out of sight, the stern port waited. If she could get there and somehow hold off the marines until Flavia arrived—*if* Flavia arrived—then maybe, just maybe …

She heard Telepathy's exhausted voice in her mind. Lieutenant, if you ever see the blue oceans on Hyacinth …

Yes? she replied.

But Telepathy's voice said no more. Instead, a male voice shouted from somewhere on the deck. 'Lieutenant Sinistra!' The voice was close enough to hear over the engines.

A tall marine officer stood by the bulkhead's stern side. Sinistra lifted the rifle. The marine raised the face guard on his helmet.

It was Ranant.

85

The engines howled. The bulkheads rattled, and the dropships shivered above their docking pads. The Bactria, the Carpathia, the Anatolia, and the hundreds of other ships seemed nervous, as if they expected the worst was about to happen.

Standing on the vibrating deck, Sinistra calculated how much time remained until the Acceleration: a half hora, perhaps a little more. It wouldn't be enough, unless, perhaps, Ranant had come to help.

At the sight of him, Sinistra's mood softened. Ranant's handsome face displayed the complex expression she found so fascinating: smile and a frown at the same time. Did it mean concern for someone he cared for? Was it the reason he was here?

'I need your help,' Sinistra called.

But Ranant only spoke into the comms device on his helmet. Then, he came closer, and stopped at an arm's length away.

'I've called off the men!' he shouted.

'I have a plan,' Sinistra replied. 'I've just thought of it. We're going to be rid of her—you, me, the crew, the people—all of us. Then I'm going to stop the engines before it's too late. Maybe you could stop them with me. You could order your men to come with us to Engineering.'

Ranant's eyes widened.

'What's the matter?' Sinistra said. 'Why do you look like that?'

'Sin, what do you think you are doing, talking about getting rid of Flavia? You sound upset. Here, give me that, and calm down.' He held out a hand towards the rifle.

'What am I doing? Isn't it obvious? I'm trying to save the mission. I'm saving the people from Flavia and the rest of them. That's what I'm doing.' She didn't mention the vision of the woman on the hill. Instead, she said, 'I've seen how it can be on Hyacinth, Ran. It's like a kind of Elysium.'

'Elysium?' said Ranant. His expression now changed to one Sinistra didn't like. He frowned deeper, but without the smile. He looked down at the deck, then looked up. 'Whose Elysium, Sin?'

Sinistra sensed something was wrong. 'Why are you here, Captain Ranant? If not to help me, why are you here?'

'I have new orders.'

'Orders from Flavia?'

'From Cadmus, on the bridge.'

'And was Cadmus ordered by Flavia?'

'I don't know, Sin. Orders are orders.'

'Orders to do what?'

'Sin, you're not thinking. Flavia is the captain. You were the acting captain till she recovered. Now you're not. That's the way it is. You have to give her a chance.'

'Give her a chance? She's had hundreds of years of chances. Why don't you give *me* a chance? I'm the one who'll save the mission. Flavia will kill me if I don't stop her first.'

'What makes you think so?'

'Necessity makes me think so. Her own words make me think so. The crew and the mission deserve better— especially a better leader.'

'A leader like you?'

'It can only be me. No one else can do what I can.'

'Even if you succeed, Sin, which you won't, do you think the crew will follow you?'

'The crew has been poorly led for too long. They know who is the better captain.'

'How can you be so sure?'

'Are you saying you won't help me?'

'You're not well, Sin. You look fine, but you're unwell. Your mind is not right. You've been through a lot. Give me the weapon and then let's talk about getting you somewhere safe.'

Sinistra considered Ranant with a spurned lover's eye. If he cared so much, why hadn't he come closer? Why hadn't he touched her? Then she realized. She knew. Yet again, she'd been too slow, but now she realized. Her left hand found the rifle forestock.

'I see what's going on,' she said.

'Nothing's going on.'

'Nice try, Captain.'

'That's enough, Sin. Hand me the weapon.'

'No.'

'It's the right thing to do, Sin. Now give it to me.'

'You think you can take it?'

But Ranant didn't answer. Instead, his eyes flicked to something over Sinistra's shoulder. She turned to look. The blast hole in the stern bulkhead quivered. Then, it bulged in and out. A scaled forearm smashed through and Flavia shouldered her way inside, dragging shreds of metal with her. Her great clawed foot followed until she stood on the stern deck, monstrous and angry, as tall and wide as a dropship.

Her thought voice boomed.

So you trapped the little traitor for me. Nice work, Captain Ranant.

Sinistra stepped back toward the forest of dropships. She brought the rifle up to her hip. She swung the muzzle from Ranant to Flavia and back again.

Help me, my love, said Flavia. I'm tired of this creature wasting our time, and ruining our happiness.

Ranant stepped forward, wearing the now hated smile. Sinistra raised the rifle at him. 'Stop,' she said, but Ranant kept coming.

'Stop!' Sinistra shouted one more time. 'Stop!' This time, Ranant came close enough to touch her. He grabbed the rifle's muzzle with his right hand. With his left hand reached for Sinistra's shoulder.

'I said STOP!'

Sinistra pulled the fire button. The blast went down at the deck. It hit the side of Flavia's right claw and ricocheted against the bulkhead near her scaled knee.

Meanwhile, the muzzle flung itself back and up, shrugging off Ranant's hand. It cartwheeled over Sinistra's shoulder and clattered beneath the dropship names Carpathia.

When Sinistra sat up, she saw Ranant was on his back, clutching his jaw. Flavia knelt over him. Black blood swelled into the valleys of her claws.

Sinistra seized her chance. She got up and backed away towards the dropships. She picked up the rifle and swung the muzzle at Ranant, then at Flavia. Then she backed away until she felt the ring on the heel of her right boot knock against the disc of a docking pad.

Only then did she turn and limp deeper into the dropship forest and out of sight.

By now, the Acceleration engines sounded alive and angry, as if they resented being provoked into fury. But to Sinistra's ears, something didn't sound right. One engine sounded ill. There was a mechanical tick, as if something were loose inside Zeus, Apollo, or Mars. Were Gabinus and his boys aware of it? Were they concerned about it?

Sinistra wondered if she'd made the wrong choice. Perhaps she should have gone straight to engineering, barricaded herself inside with the rifle, and forced Gabinus and his hideous crew to shut everything down.

It was too late now.

Sinistra gripped the rifle tighter and limped towards the stern, the great port, open space, and the future.

Several milia forward, on the bridge, acting First Lieutenant Cadmus, turned to Chief Petty Officer Domitian and said, 'I don't think the captain is coming, but let's give her two minuta. Then we'll start.'

He was referring to the final, pre-Acceleration message delivered to the ship and to the Senate and to history. Usually, the captain spoke these words, but since the captain was busy at the stern, Cadmus would make the speech instead. After the speech, his first words would be, 'Chief Engineer Gabinus, please accelerate.'

Back in the dropship forest, Sinistra felt dampness in her right boot. The Goth hide leather squelched with blood from the deep chafe on her shin. The boot was so sodden that every time she swung her leg forward, an arc of black blood splashed over the deck like the spoor of a hunted, wounded animal.

And yet again, she ran through a forest. It was a tall, white forest of metal, machinery and fuel, but a forest all the same. Throughout her two months on the ship, forests were always with her: they were in her dreams; they were on the Domum Deck; and in Sirhain's realm on the object. Now a forest was here again—another forest in which pursuers followed her with violence on their minds.

How much better would be the bare hills on the Hyacinth coast? And how much better would it be to stand tall, beautiful, and strong on one of those very hills? How wonderful to see the valley below and its multitude of adoring Hyacinth creatures chanting her name: Octavia! Octavia! Octavia!

As she limped along and the black blood splattered at the roots of the white ships, she made a pledge: this is the last time I run through a forest in fear. I might live or I might die, but this is the last time.

She limped from the last rank of dropships onto the metallic plain of the stern ramp proper. She could see the great port ahead. It was sealed shut for the Acceleration. Beyond it waited the infinity of open space.

Out there, she thought, on the other side of that hatch—that's what Flavia fears the most. She fears it more than anything.

And so do I.

Back in engineering, Zeus, Apollo, and Mars continued their ascent in pitch and fury. The deck shook, the bulkheads rattled, the dropships shivered.

There were forty minuta to go.

86

Sinistra limped to a stop, turned and surveyed the stern ramp.

No one was there. The hundred crew known as the afterguard were at their Acceleration stations forward of the armory, clipped into their harnesses, praying that this time, the Acceleration would not fail.

Sinistra could read the stenciled names on the last row of dropships: the Scotia, the Dacia, the Alexandria, the Hibernia, the Mesopotamia. The ships appeared still and thoughtful, as if thinking about the terrible duty they must perform on Hyacinth.

But the quiet mood was about to change.

Sinistra scanned the deck beneath the ships. She saw hundreds of black boots running towards her. Then she saw the back row of ships tossed left and right as a large creature forced its way through.

The last moments were drawing near.

She limped to the control panel on the wall to one side. She found the switch that opened and closed the port. Then she turned around, faced the forest, and stood as straight as she could with the rifle on one shoulder and her weight on the shaking right boot.

Come on, she thought. Hurry up!

The first to emerge from the forest were the tall gray marines. They stomped across the ramp, their rifles held by their hips. They halted on the ramp's apron and spun their weapons up into the port arms position, diagonally across their chests.

Behind them, the dropships swung like buoys on a troubled sea as Flavia shoved them aside, and strode across the deck, dragging her right claw and a thick stripe of black blood. The marines parted for her. She stepped forward, planted her feet apart, and smiled wickedly at the lone figure by the control panel.

Sinistra was about to flick the switch to open the port, but then she saw the real reason Flavia waited and did not attack. Out from the forest of ships came the after-guard along with the mechanics, the armourer's mates, and the gunsmiths. They looked at one another, frowning, then they looked at Flavia. It had been six months since they had seen anyone in an expanded state.

Behind them, came crew members from all the various stations: the stewards, the gunner's mates, the able seamen, the astronomers, the wardroom officers, the pilots, the drivers of the terraforming machines, and more. Even Corporal Heva of the master-at-arms came forward, his head bandaged, his neck a dull purple, his face confused like everyone else's.

This cross section of the ship's company, this multitude of Flavia's own design, assembled on the ramp. Their eyes moved from the tall, expanded aristocrat-officer to the beautiful but disheveled Hyacinth creature by the port's edge. Only the two, strange stewards from the Domun Deck never shifted their eyes from Sinistra.

Finally, Chief Petty Officer Seta pushed her way to the front, and then Ranant came forward and stood beside Flavia's ankle. There was blood on his neck. Flavia smiled down at him, revealing long, thick, curving teeth. Then she across up at Sinistra. Over the howl of the engines, her voice spoke in everyone's minds.

Petty Officer Arvina, where are you?

Here, Captain, said an unseen voice.

How much time do we have?

Enough, Captain—just.

Good, said Flavia's voice. Good.

She stood taller and raised her chin.

Shipmates, listen to me. I'm going to explain why I ordered you here so close to the Acceleration, and then I want you to witness something: the punishment of a mutineer and a traitor. It will be the harshest punishment the navy has ever inflicted.

87

Flavia took a step forward, dragging blood. Then she drew herself up to her full height and said in a thought voice, Shipmates, it's time to re-establish the proper order on the Herculaneum—and by order, I mean the traditional order, the way we've always worked. It's the only way for our mission to succeed.

Oh, I know. Many of you don't like it. I understand. I know what people said about Captain Tiberius, that he was past his prime and had lost his judgement. Many have said similar words about myself, about engineer Gabinus, and others. We're not ready nor able to lead during this crisis at home.

And no one has thought this more than Lieutenant Sinistra. She thinks these thoughts so much that she is willing to lead a one-woman mutiny, and put the Herculaneum and its mission at risk, and put our families at home in further peril.

Lieutenant Flavia thinks it's time for the traditional order to go. She thinks it's time for new blood, and for new leaders to take the places of myself, Tiberius, and others. In her mind, these new leaders are not just more competent, they are more deserving.

Is she right? I don't think so. I truly don't believe it.

Without the old order, everyone would fight among themselves for prominence, like animals, like the Goths in spring. You would tear each other apart over the females and the food, and for dominance, just like the Goths do. The North would fight the equatorial regions. The East would fight the West. There would be chaos, destruction and an inevitable end to our civilization.

Now is not the time for change. Not while our people die by the millions in the planet quakes and volcanic eruptions. And the Herculaneum is not the place for change, either. It's a ship whose mission is to pave the way to a new world, not to be the stage for a revolution. The Herculaneum and its crew have more important things to do.

No, shipmates, it's not the time to return to the days of the dictators. That's what poor, foolish Lieutenant Sinistra would like. She is sadly deluded. The natural and proper order, the old order, the order of our ancestors—that's the only way forward. People, like Lieutenant Sinistra, who exploit the tragedies of our families for their own despicable gain, must be punished as severely as the Senate's Navy Code permits.

Then, Flavia's voice said, All right. I've said enough. It's now time to act. Everyone step back. The lieutenant might try to expand and fight me while I punish her, but I don't think she will. She'll go quietly, now that she's trapped, just like the pathetic little upstart she is.

Flavia looked around, checking everyone had understood. There were nods. There was agreement. Flavia smiled. The terrible black hems of her lips slid over the wet, yellow, curved teeth.

But then, the unthinkable happened.

Sinistra's voice rang out in everyone's minds.

Prove it!

Flavia halted. The hems of her lips sank.

It speaks! What did you say, ex-Lieutenant?

I said prove it.

Prove what?

Prove to me and everyone here that you're the natural leader. That you're the right one to captain this ship. Come and prove it.

Prove it how, ex Lieutenant?

By stepping forward and tearing me to pieces.

Flavia smiled. The black hems rose. If you had listened to what I just said, you would know that's what I intend to do.

No, not here, said Sinistra. Not on this ramp where it's safe. I mean out there in space, in the few minuta we have left before the Acceleration.

Sinistra deployed a new Hyacinth creature gesture. She tossed her head back at the great port, indicating the void.

Flavia snorted. Trust me, ex-Lieutenant. You'll soon be going out there yourself—alive and in pieces, swirling in the exhaust blast.

No. You haven't understood me, acting Captain. I mean fight me out there. Demonstrate to everyone how you'll put me in my place. Leave the comfort of this ship like a genuine leader would do. Go on, take me outside. Tear me to pieces out there, in the only place that can kill us, and where true leaders are not afraid to go.

Sinistra reached behind her to the control panel and gripped the lever that would open the towering hatch. She couldn't believe she was actually doing it. Not four Hyacinth days ago, she craved Flavia's approval, as if it were a matter of life and death. Now she challenged Flavia to a duel. It was madness, but she couldn't stop herself.

'Cometh the hour,' she said to herself.

She pulled the switch that opened the port.

A slim stripe of blackness appeared at the port's lower edge. Slowly, the terror of open space appeared like an unwelcome guest who had been waiting just outside. First the black stripe, then a few twinkling stars, then the constellations, and all the yawning expanse of the cosmos.

On the deck, the thin atmosphere rushed out, and the gravity machine switched off. The crew's hair fluttered in the breeze. The engine howls faded to an eery silence. The big marines' rifles floated on their straps and everyone's uniform billowed at the waists and cuffs. The blood pooling between Flavia's claws floated into globules and drifted over the ramp and out into space, like small black ships on missions to their own demise.

Well, acting Captain? Sinistra said.

Flavia slowly shook her head. Her thought voice said, I won't indulge the fantasies of a deranged mind, especially one belonging to a traitor. No, don't look at your weapon, Lieutenant. The marines will hit you before you can lift it. And we both know that if you actually manage to fire at me, one shot won't be enough—not this time. But one shot from any of the marines will be enough to splatter your traitorous self all over the ramp. Is that what you want?

Would you like to find out? Sinistra replied.

I won't have to. I'm going to disarm you. Then, I'm going to dismember you where you stand, right there on the ramp. No, don't think about jumping. I'll snatch you back before you pass the hatch jambs.

Then what? Sinistra said.

Flavia smiled. Captain Ranant, said her voice. Be so good as to disarm this traitor. This time, there won't be any trouble. But don't take long. We don't have all day.

88

Ranant stepped from the crowd.

He came across the deck, his brown eyes level, his smile more endearing, more meaningful than ever.

The smile said, 'I'm sorry about this,' and 'We're old friends,' and 'Both of us see how unnecessary this is,' and 'Let's put what just happened behind us. You know who I am, Sin.'

As always, Sinistra's resolve softened, but she kept the rifle muzzle leveled at Ranant's chest.

Sin, Ranant's voice said. Sin. Listen to me. It's too late now.

Is it?

You know it is. You can't defeat Flavia and the navy, and you can't defeat the Senate. Look around you at the marines and their weapons. Look at the snipers along the bulkheads. You can't defeat fate, Sin. And even if you somehow succeed today, what then? There are ten thousand crew aboard. Imagine how angry they'll be if you disrupt the mission because of a grudge against their captain.

I'm doing this to save the mission, not disrupt it. I'm doing this to save the crew.

Sin, it's not the time to let your exhaustion get the better of you. We're about to accelerate. No one wants to miss the chance and wait six months out here. Just give me the weapon and close the port.

No, it's too late.

Why is it too late?

Because it's better to reign on Hyacinth than to serve the Senate. It's better for the crew, the home planet, and better even for the Hyacinth creatures.

Reign on Hyacinth? What are you talking about? Reign is what kings and queens do. The Senate will govern Hyacinth through Cicero. Just give me the weapon, Sin. Then let me close the port. I think we've all had enough of open space.

Out of nowhere, Sinistra said, Do you love me?

Ranant's let's be reasonable smile returned. Not again, Sin. Please. Not here.

Yes, now and here. Say you love me and I'll think about putting the rifle down.

It's not the time, Sin. Look where you are. Look at the crew.

No. Say it. Choose between me and her and all she represents.

Sin, haven't you had enough of these ideas? They're Hyacinth ideas, not our ideas.

Are you sure? Ask Flavia. You'll find she disagrees.

Let's talk about this later, Ranant said. He looked over his shoulder at the watching crowd, at Flavia, at the marines, at all the sections of the ship's company.

Sinistra said, If you help me, you can join me, on Hyacinth.

Be serious, Sin. How can I help you except by making you see sense?

I've been shown a vision of what's possible, a wonderful vision.

It's madness, Sin. Even if it were true, how could we ever make it happen?

Arvinus's voice spoke. Captain Flavia, it said. Please remember the time.

Quiet, Flavia growled.

Ranant said, Sin, please, listen to me. See reason.

Then say it. Say it! Say it! Don't force me to go out there.

All right! said Flavia's voice. That's enough. It's obvious she's totally mad as well as a traitor. Captain Ranant, tell this creature what you really think of her.

Ranant's voice said, Sorry, Sin. It's too late. His let's-be-reasonable smile had gone.

All right, marines, said Flavia. Do it.

Two of the gray, metallic men shouldered their weapons and came forward. Sinistra pointed the weapon at one, then the other, then at Flavia. Flavia's eyes had narrowed. Her horrible lips retracted once more, sliding over her teeth to reveal the most hideous smile someone in the natural form could make.

Take the weapon, Flavia said. Hold her arms. And for Owanthan's sake, close that port.

Sinistra turned back to Ranant.

And fired the rifle.

Once again, the forestock leaped from Sinistra's hands. The muzzle didn't just climb; it spat. It shot up from her arms so fast that her fingers suddenly held nothing but space.

Then the gun cartwheeled up and back, spinning into the stern port top jamb, denting the metal. Then it spun into the void directly behind the ship and out of sight.

Sinistra followed it.

The thick sling strap had whipped from her shoulder, but not before it yanked her from her feet. In the light gravity, she sailed over the stern ramp and into space, following the wheeling rifle into the gloom.

The two heavy marines snatched at her. Two stern crew mechanics, Sura and Corculum, jumped in from the side to grab at her dripping boots, but without enough gravity to keep their feet on the deck, they flailed as if they were treading water.

As Sinistra sailed away, she saw red blood droplets fanning out and back, splashing onto the acting captain's dark scales. Flavia's grin subsided. A new expression emerged. Her face looked like murder, with yellow eyes filled with astonishment, disbelief, and hate.

89

Sinistra floated backwards into the silent dark.

Over the tips of her boots, the stern ramp receded. So did the crew. She could see the marines, the engineers, the able seaman, the junior petty officers, the astronomers—all of them, receding away, shrinking in a rectangle of light.

She also saw Flavia, on her knees, bent over the remains of Ranant. Soon, even Flavia receded, and to Sinistra's eyes, the terrible scene looked small, distant, and even placid. Space gathered around her and she felt the strangest feeling of relief. How calm it was out there! How peaceful! And how strange, too, especially when she remembered she was traveling at the same astonishing, pre-Acceleration speed as the ship.

Then, the inevitable happened. The terrifying blackness of the Herculaneum's transom announced its presence. From port and starboard, aloft and alow, the transom stretched away like a giant sea creature waking up in the deep ocean. The stern port's bright rectangle became a white ledge in a giant, dark, horrible cliff.

Next, the Herculaneum's exhaust funnels appeared. Active now, not dormant as they were during the crossing to the object, they pressed in with their terrifying black circles, their bottomless caverns tinged with red, from which the silent Acceleration force would send Sinistra so far away she could never be found.

Don't look, Sinistra told herself. Don't think and don't look down. Never look left nor right, and don't look up. Try not to see the ship blocking out the stars. Don't think of being abandoned here. Don't think about the exhaust funnels and what they will do when Cadmus gives the order, and Gabinus sets the engines to work.

And don't think about what you have just done.

Instead, think this.

There is a beautiful woman standing on a hill in the sunlight of Hyacinth. There is a valley beneath her, filled with Hyacinth creatures. The Hyacinth creatures chant the woman's name, 'Octavia! Octavia! Octavia!' Hear their voices. Feel the relief. You are adored. They approve of you. You are good, even if you are bad.

And Sinistra floated on. Maybe, she thought. I can still do it.

But, way back on the Herculaneum, in the receding rectangle of light, the tiny figures and one giant began to move. Flavia stood to her full height. Then she stomped silently towards the yawning mouth of the stern port until she stood on its edge.

All right, boomed Flavia's voice in Sinistra's mind. All right. The monster leaped from the ramp. Sinistra watched it come. She saw Flavia's body blacken as the lanterns fell behind and she became a shape against the immensity of the black cliff.

Sinistra watched in horror but also relief. In a way, she had succeeded. She had drawn Flavia into open space—the thing Flavia feared most. But now the odds of defeating her were overwhelming. The rings still trapped Sinistra's ankle and wrist, and she couldn't expand—not into any useful shape.

Most of all, her only weapon was lost. The rifle had spun away into the dark. There would be no contest now. Instead, Flavia would finish the grisly job she began in the desert, pulling Sinistra apart, limb from limb. If only the rifle strap had stayed on Sinistra's shoulder. If only she could fire one more time. If only she'd thought of a better plan.

And now it was too late.

She closed her eyes in exhaustion and dismay. What have I done? Why couldn't I simply do my duty and nothing more? Why have I brought this on myself? Why?

When Sinistra opened her eyes again, Flavia was shockingly close, almost blocking out the Herculaneum. She stretched out her arms. Her long, yellow claws were unsheathed, and her face was blank. She said nothing. Hatred and fury had silenced her.

Sinistra spoke instead. You don't need to do this, Flavia. Now, it's you who puts the mission at risk, not me. Turn around while there's time to save the ship, the crew, and the people.

But Flavia kept on coming. Soon, her arms glided over the spindly Hyacinth creature's legs. The legs kicked at Flavia's wrists, neck, and face. But all too soon, the terrible claws caught Sinistra's right ankle. Then, Flavia's head and teeth came forward till they were over Sinistra's waist.

On the Herculaneum, a dropship pushed out into space, coming to rescue Flavia after her gruesome task was done.

Further out in space, a leuga away, Flavia began silently dismembering Sinistra alive.

90

Sinistra tried to expand.

She couldn't do much. The rings constricted her ankles and wrists. But if she could make her body into one strong arm and one strong leg, she might beat Flavia's claws away —or at least keep them away long enough to force Flavia to return to the ship.

But she couldn't concentrate. She couldn't picture the shape she wanted. She couldn't focus on anything except the sight of Flavia's terrible, blank face, long teeth, and the excruciating pain.

Flavia was now above her. She stomped one clawed foot down on Sinistra's neck and face, pushing her head down. Her claws seized Sinistra's wrist, piercing the pronator quadratus right through to the other side.

Then, as Flavia's hind claws gouged deep into Sinistra's neck, she pulled and pulled while the tendons in her neck swelled and throbbed.

Then, her voice spoke in Sinistra's mind.

You little murderer. You little upstart. You think you deserve everything, don't you? Everything is yours to take. You are a dangerous little upstart who should never have access to power. I tried to speak up. I tried to keep you out, but Tiberius wouldn't listen. He couldn't see what you were. You fooled him with your cringing and fawning and punctuality. And now look what you've done to the mission and to my Ranant.

Sinistra's joints tore open. Her Hyacinth creature skin stretched, cracked and ripped. Her arm pulled free from her shoulder. Thick, dark blood burst out, spraying into globules. White bone and stringy tendons appeared. The tendon in Sinistra's arm stubbornly held out against Flavia's strength, refusing to snap until Flavia bit through it, and Sinistra's arm came free.

Flavia tossed the arm away. It spun in the gloom till it reached the Herculaneum's starboard exhaust blast, which flung it out of sight. Turning back, Flavia planted one clawed foot between Sinistra's Hyacinth creature's legs. Then she grabbed a flailing ankle and sank her claws deep into the slender calf muscle.

Through her agony, Sinistra replied. You! You are the danger. All of you—Gabinus, Tiberius, and the rest. You are the dangers to the people—not me. I'm the future. I'm the salvation. You are just in my way.

Flavia stomped her foot down. Sinistra's uniform tore as her right leg came free of her pelvis. Flavia held out the limb in front of Sinistra's face, making sure she saw the ragged flesh, the grey femur, the waving tendons, the blood vessels and their final pulses.

Neither of them said a word. Flavia's fury had muted her again, and Sinistra was in too much pain to speak or think. All she could do was hope for the end.

Petty Arvina's voice sounded in their minds.

The dropship, Captain. I'm almost there. Lieutenant Cadmus says he will abort the Acceleration—if you order him.

Not necessary, came Flavia's cold reply.

Would you like to bring the body back with you, Captain?

No. I want Lieutenant Sinistra to say out here until she suffocates or burns.

Sinistra watched, paralyzed. She had finally received the beating she knew she deserved.

Flavia twisted her claws across Sinistra's face, screwing them down into the yielding flesh, until she ruined the beautiful features from Sinistra's mouth to her ears. Then, Flavia kicked outward, flinging Sinistra backward, away from the ship, further into space. Then she turned and swam towards the dropship.

Sinistra was alone, floating among the droplets of her own blood, finally defeated. But then, something caught her attention, out there, to her right, out in space, beyond the Herculaneum's jet stream.

91

It was astonishing.

Out there, against the background of the stars, two great armies faced each other across the void.

The soldiers were giants. Each seemed as large as the Herculaneum, or even larger. Each rode on four-legged creatures with long heads and flowing tails. The riders carried spears, pikes, and cutlasses. They wore quivers of arrows on their backs and carried long bows in their hands.

Some rode in chariots. Others stood atop armored carriages pulled by teams of giant Goths. The soldiers themselves were like Hyacinth creatures, but with three muscled arms sprouting from each of their shoulder joints. Several of the soldiers' heads had more than one face. And their skins were colored vivid green and blue, like the forest and sky in Sirhain's domain.

Sirhain. Was that him riding at the head of one of these armies? Now he was a giant, too—a giant in his gold breastplate and a gleaming gold helmet.

And riding at the head of the army opposing him was Owanthan. Sinistra could see the battered breastplate, the robes, the foolish sandals, and an equally foolish helmet. Behind him swelled an army as vast and fearsome as

Sirhain's. This army was headed by standard bearers, with flags rippling high above them.

Sirhain! Sinistra called. Help me!

Sirhain flinched as he galloped toward Owanthan. He looked over his shoulder in Sinistra's direction. Could he see her, a tiny figure, floating so far away? Would he help? It didn't look like it. He turned back to his army, dug his heels into the creature beneath him, and galloped away to his own battle, the battle to decide who would be adored by the creatures he and Owanthan were supposed to protect.

So that was it.

Sinistra floated, desolate and lost, waiting for her consciousness to fade and vanish. She heard thunder. It rumbled across from where the two armies clashed. Thunder in space defied nature's laws, of course, but after the last few days, thunder in space was just one more challenge to reason and the old understanding of the cosmos.

She looked back at the Herculaneum. There it was, still huge, still dark and terrifying, but less distinct in the gloom. She could see the tiny rectangle of light in the transom's black cliff face, and the dull red fire deep inside each of the exhaust funnels. Between the funnels, the white dropship advanced and Flavia swam towards it.

Soon, the Acceleration engines would fire and the Herculaneum's fate would be revealed at last. If the Acceleration succeeded, the ship would arrive two days later in the Hyacinth solar system. If the Acceleration failed, the ship wouldn't move at all, or worse, it would explode.

Sinistra closed her eyes. Her consciousness faded. At least I will find peace, she thought, just like Sirhain said. I'll find peace and an end to the struggles, a whole life of struggling, a whole life of pain, of never finding relief. And perhaps it won't be the end. Did Sirhain say there was an afterlife? Could there be a second chance?

And for the first time, she wondered if she might meet her

parents, whoever they were.
But that was when she felt the nudge on her shoulder.

92

It wasn't much of a nudge.

It was more like an accidental bump, or a caress, the kind you might feel in the crowded forward-aft shuttle as it trundled beside the Great Passageway.

But her mind presented darker possibilities. The nudge might be her own discarded leg twirling in the gloom. Worse! It might be the touch of Lieutenant Commodus's tentative fingertips—as if Commodus were gently welcoming Sinistra to her bleak, lonely, forever-world. Or perhaps it was one of the crew who failed to make it back to the scuttle after deciding to kill himself.

Probably, it was nothing, but Sinistra's neck tingled all the same.

Then she felt the nudge once more. This time it tugged on the cuff of her one remaining pants leg. It was the slightest pull, like a child tugging at an adult to gain attention.

She looked behind—ready for the worst.

There was nothing to see except droplets of blood and shreds of her uniform. Beyond them, the stars of Gordium twinkled at each other.

But then, there *was* something.

An arm's length away, there was a gleam in the dark. It

was there one moment, and gone the next. She saw it again, then lost it. Then she recognized what it was. No, it wasn't the ghost of Lieutenant Commodus, nor was it her fearful imagination.

It was the blast rifle.

It was still spinning in space, muzzle over stock, stock over muzzle, revolving like a gyroscope. The fire button rolled over the forestock. The muzzle tumbled over the shoulder stock. The strap floated this way and that.

She must have caught it up after Flavia's shove. It was an unlikely piece of luck. The odds of it happening were incredible. Unless Sirhain's guilt at her terrible fate had forced him to intervene.

Was he still out there?

She looked to her right. The warring armies were now far away. They were mere flashes in the darkness—like lightning on a far horizon before the thunder roll. She looked behind her, searching for the rifle. Yes! It was still there, tumbling and rolling in the gloom.

But how? Could Sirhain have sent it?

But it wasn't the time to ask questions. Instead, Sinistra paddled. She scooped with her left hand and kicked with her right foot. She didn't get far. Instead, she twirled in space like the rifle itself, the two of them watching the stars sliding by and reappearing.

She tried something else: scooping and kicking in unison. This time, she remained facing the whirling gun. Twelve paddles and twelve kicks later, she reached out her one remaining hand. She hooked the rifle strap with a cocked wrist. The rifle ceased its spin. Then she pulled the strap over her head, tethering the big floating gun under her armpit.

So far, so good, but now what?

She heard Flavia's voice speak in her mind.

Arvinus.

Yes, Captain Flavia.

Open the hatch.

Aye, Captain.

And Arvinus?

Yes?

Arm the weapons.

The weapons? The cannons?

We might need them.

Beg pardon, Captain Flavia. I don't know how to arm the weapons.

Then who is at the helm?

Lieutenant Cadmus ordered one of the bridge pilots to steer the ship.

Then tell Cadmus to order the pilot to arm the weapons. Then, order him to train them on Lieutenant Sinistra, no matter how far away she is.

Aye, Captain.

Who is the ranking Marine officer on the ramp?

I am, said a different voice. Lieutenant Asina.

All right, Asina, said Flavia. Can you see the traitor, Lieutenant Sinistra?

No, Captain Flavia. I don't see her. She's too far away. To see her, I would need the special rifle sights.

Do you have them?

The snipers have them, Captain.

Good. Have four of them find her and take aim. Then wait for my orders. Petty Officer Arvinus?

Yes, Captain Flavia.

How long until the Acceleration?

Any minuta now, Captain.

Then open the hatch. I'm almost there.

Yes, Captain, but the bridge suggests that, given the shortness of time, you should hold the rail while I tow you to the ramp.

Then hurry up, said Flavia's voice.

93

Sinistra held the rifle and wondered.

What can I do?

The answer was 'not much.'

True, she could fire the rifle at Flavia, who was now a distant speck beside the dropship, but without the strength or the limbs to hold the rifle steady, any shot Sinistra managed would result in only one result: a recoil blast that would knock her backwards, and far, far away.

And what good would that do?

But she could also turn and fire the rifle into space. The blast would send her back towards the Herculaneum—maybe. It might also propel her away from the Herculaneum, or worse, it might send her into the exhaust streams. If that happened, it was all over.

There was also the other question. Supposing she reached the Herculaneum or Flavia's dropship, what then? What could she do with just one arm and one leg, each of which still bore the hated rings?

The answer was nothing.

And what if, against all odds, she reached the stern ramp? Would the crew help her? Almost certainly not. They'd arrest her all over again. It was hopeless. Only one thing was certain: if she remained where she was, nothing would happen at all.

She drifted. The rifle floated in front of her face. Its tiny light still blinked, signaling its readiness. The fire button waited under its guard.

Sinistra made a decision. It was better to do anything rather than nothing. So, she would take action, any action, and let the future take care of itself. Hadn't someone once said that to her?

With her lone hand holding the rifle forestock, she kicked her right leg, twisting her body around, kick by kick, until she faced away from the Herculaneum. Then she kicked the other direction to counter the spin.

Once she was motionless, she looked over her shoulder. Then she paddled with her one arm until her back was square against the Herculaneum's stern. When she was satisfied, she settled the rifle butt on her chest. After a moment's consideration, she lowered the butt to the base of her rib cage. Then she found the fire button, took one last look at the uncaring stars, and pressed.

The blast went out and away into space, traveling to who knew where—to the edge of Gordium perhaps, or to the edge of the galaxy itself, or even into intergalactic space and on to the next galaxy, wherever that might be. There was nothing to slow it down, nothing to block its way, unless it hit a planet or star—or perhaps Sirhain's and Owanthan's armies.

Meanwhile, the stock butt rammed into Sinistra's sternum, turning her about, tearing her uniform, and flattening her ribs against her Hyacinth creature organs until they were forced up under her throat. It also flung her shoulders back so fast that her chin stabbed her collar bone.

She tumbled, head over boot, boot over head—spinning in the gloom. She saw the black ship flash by with its transom and funnels. Then the Gordium constellation came by, followed by more stars, then the black ship again, over and over, with the rifle twisting on its strap above her head.

Kicking her right leg again, she slowed the somersault and added a twist, so that she spun on two axes. More kicking slowed the somersault to a halt. Her paddling left hand slowed the spin until she floated still and upright.

By now, the ship was closer. The stern port rectangle was larger. She could see the crew watching from the ramp, and Flavia watching from the dropship. Flavia had partially transformed back to a Hyacinth creature. She was naked and pale. The goiter floated by her neck. And she held the dropship rail with one claw as it towed her along.

Then Sinistra noticed something else. She wasn't riding towards the stern ramp. Instead, she was sliding to port, toward the terrible black caverns of the exhaust funnels. Already, she could see the exhaust blast's deceptively gentle appearance: a soft distorting of space, like the air on a hot day, rippling over a desert.

She lifted the rifle once more and placed the shoulder stock's heel on her abdomen. She kicked her leg, jerking herself around till she saw nothing but open space, and her back lined up with the rectangle of the stern port.

As she did, she saw the dropship bringing its cannons to bear on her. And she felt something nick her shirt. Was it a bullet fired by the snipers? She didn't wait to find out.

She pulled the fire button.

The rifled bucked. The muzzle struck Sinistra on her left cheek. The shoulder stock punched her Hyacinth-creature solar plexus, shoving her away from the exhaust blast.

But that was as good as it would get.

Her direction was wrong. She shot away from the exhaust, but not toward the stern port. Instead, she crossed the black cliff face diagonally, sliding to starboard, past the rectangle of light and on toward the starboard exhaust stream.

One last try, Sinistra thought. One last try. She raised the rifle butt to her stomach and fired, but without taking care to aim. The blast sent her into a spin. She saw the exhaust, the stars, the exhaust, and the stars again. The blast had only slowed her course across the stern, not altered it.

Soon, the surrounding space wobbled with heat. She braced for the sudden, violent shove. At least it would be quick. At least it would be final.

But three quarters of the way across the stern, something happened.

The galaxy came to a halt.

94

Two and a half minuta before the scheduled Acceleration time, something happened aboard the Herculaneum.

Until this point, First Lieutenant Cadmus, the officer in command, had performed the pre-Acceleration procedures as described in the Acceleration manual.

He had checked with Astronomer Manius regarding the ship's location. The astronomer had confirmed the Herculaneum was on course to reach the Point of Acceleration at the right time, on the right heading. The map showed the way across the galaxy was clear of planets, stars, comets, asteroids, and all detectable obstacles.

Lieutenant Cadmus then contacted Engineering. Chief Engineer Gabinus was unavailable, but one of Gabinus's mates reported the engines were active. They would fire as soon as the Herculaneum crossed the P.O.A. Even Apollo would fire. 'Just say the word, Lieutenant Cadmus,' said the engineer's mate. 'Just say the word.'

So far, so good.

Cadmus called in the reports from the ship's major stations: the gun deck, the hold, the medical deck, the armory, and the stern ramp. All was well, except for the stern ramp, where the port was still open. Captain Flavia and one dropship were still outside.

But Petty Officer Causex explained the stern port would be sealed shut once Captain Flavia was aboard and the Dacia secured on its docking pad. They were coming in now as fast as they could. There was enough time—just.

'What about the crew members who left their stations to watch the disturbance?' asked Cadmus.

'Only the marines are on the stern ramp now,' said Petty Officer Causex. 'When the time comes, they'll have to flatten themselves against the bulkheads.'

Cadmus then called on Petty Officer Eburnus to report the status of the ship's immediate vicinity and the possibility of any objects nearby. Eburnus replied there were no rogue objects fore, aft, to port, to starboard, aloft, or beneath the keel. But one small object drifted near the ship's exhaust funnels. However, this object would soon burn up without disturbing the Acceleration.

At this news, Cadmus felt all eyes on the bridge flick towards him. This small object mentioned by Eburnus caused the bridge crew a degree of anguish. If Cadmus were being honest, the small object caused him a degree of anguish too—perhaps even a high degree of anguish. However, Captain Flavia had ordered him to make the Acceleration his priority—no matter what.

He kept his composure. His young, Hyacinth-creature face remained blank and calm. 'Nothing else out there, Petty Officer Eburnus?'

'No, sir.'

'You are sure? No objects, nothing at all?'

'Well, the sensors detected a rolling boom from starboard, and then something flashed, like lightning, but only for a moment. The boom can only be a glitch in the system. It's happened before. The second, the lightening—well, I don't have an explanation, sir.'

'How long now, Astronomer Manius?'

'A half minuta, Lieutenant Cadmus.'

'Good. Everyone check harnesses.'

The bridge crew pulled at their various straps and buckles, and settled into their chairs. They didn't speak to each other. Everyone was silent. No one dared mention the black thoughts in their minds.

Cadmus spoke into the comms, 'Telepathy,' he said. 'Send the final message to the Senate.' Then, when he saw Manius looking at him, shaking his head. Cadmus cleared his throat, and said, 'Never mind. There will be no message.'

When the countdown clock on the screen said there were only five secunda to go, Cadmus spoke into the comms once more.

'Engineering?' he called. 'Engineering? Are you ready? Engineering?'

He waited for the reply. None came. He tried again. 'Engineering, are you there? Gabinus? Is everything all right? What's that noise? We can hear it from all the way up here. Engineering? You'll have to speak up. I can't ...'

And that's when it happened.

95

Sinistra tumbled through space towards the exhaust blast. She had given up, surrendering to the agony in her shoulder and pelvis, and to her fading senses. Then, just as she spun past the edge of the stern port, something strange occurred.

She wasn't thrown forward. Instead, she carried on her path as before—across the transom. But suddenly, unbelievably, the unimaginable happened. The entire Herculaneum rushed back at her in reverse. The stern port's rectangle of light flung itself at her, snapping her up, swallowing her down into its throat, all in a fraction of a secunda.

Space vanished. The Herculaneum's stern ramp was suddenly all around her in complete chaos. The dropships broke free of their docking pads as if blown down by a hurricane—a hurricane unchaining its fury and letting it loose on the Herculaneum and its crew.

In all the turmoil, Sinistra didn't notice the detritus beside her: globules of blood, fragments of metal, exhaust fuel, chains, boots, rifles, strips of bulkhead, dust, rivets, and the body parts of personnel.

She hit the hull of a ship named Helvetia, and crashed shoulder first into a ship called Polonia, then bounced off the ships Livonia and Iberia, as the entire dropship forest rolled, tumbled, and smashed its way forward.

Then, finally, she floated inside a tangle of upended and dented ships, flailing crew, pieces of the Domun Deck's bulkheads, chunks of soil from the lavender field, and a sand cloud from the desert.

The rifle floated beside her. Together, they drifted in the carnage—the silent, stunned carnage of the Herculaneum's stern ramp and its planet-going fleet.

And then, whether by someone's hand or a remote command from the bridge, the stern port closed, sealing the deck from open space.

The atmosphere pumps hissed into life, as did the gravity simulator. Above the deck, the tangled, dented, ruined dropships sank, settling themselves onto the deck, like slimy sea creatures, sliding hull over hull, pushing their way down, as if each one was suffering a death swoon. The clang and bong of metal grew louder with every pump of air.

Sinistra sank with the ships. Clinging by its strap, the rifle clattered down beside her. As the atmosphere thickened, she heard the swell of bangs and screams coming from forward in the ship, as well as what seemed like every alarm the Herculaneum possessed, ringing out in a hysterical cacophony of bells, sirens, whoops, and spoken warnings for events totally unrelated to the catastrophe: the importance of cleaning your Hyacinth-creature body; the plea to seek help from the medical deck if your Miseria rash is spreading; a news report on the latest volcanic eruptions in the home-planet province of Kanchasta.

Everything was in chaos. Everything was upended, smashed, bent, dented, leaking, twisted, or bearing down on a crushed and screaming marine or a crew member from the after-guard. It was devastation, and it wasn't over. The Herculaneum had slowed but not stopped. Instead, it yawed in space, sliding to starboard, off course, hundreds of thousands of milia from its proper heading, and far away from the Point of Acceleration.

Sinistra guessed she had come to a stop in the Domum Deck itself, in what had been Telepathy's enclosure. Most objects on the stern ramp had come to rest in the artificial forest a milia forward. Some dropships might have gone even further, maybe all the way to the ship's waist, crashing through bulkhead after bulkhead, maiming, crushing, and smashing everything in their paths.

She closed her eyes and listened. There was no engine noise. None. Just the alarms, the screams, the shouts, and metal settling and re-settling itself with the series of bongs, clangs, tears, shrieks, and groans, as if the Herculaneum had suffered a catastrophic and sudden gastronomical illness.

It was awful.

When she looked to her left, she saw a nightmare scene of careened dropships, fallen sections of deckhead, legs and torsos, and purple blood globules turning to mist.

And then, the most terrible sight of all. There, lying not more than three passus away, the length of two Hyacinth creatures, still halfway between giant natural form and Hyacinth creature, lay acting Captain Flavia.

She lay trapped beneath the wreckage of the Dacia. Her great was body crushed. The wounds were devastating. Hyacinth-creature arteries were pierced. Her black blood streamed out, forming a river delta on the white hull beneath her, puddling on the deck, and then smearing to port and starboard as the Herculaneum yawed and the deck slid and spun.

But Flavia still breathed. Her scaled chest rose and fell. And her green eyes were open in her vulnerable, aged, ruined, Hyacinth-creature face. The eyes stared straight back into Sinistra's own blue crystal orbs.

Sinistra reached out her single, now broken arm, and gathered in the rifle. She couldn't lift it, but she could nudge it along the deck until the sights settled on Flavia's ear. The recoil would send the rifle butt into Sinistra's own head, and she would probably miss her mark.

But nothing would stop her from firing.

Flavia watched her, unable to move. She mouthed some words that sounded like 'upstart' in the growls of the native language. Sinistra didn't ask her to repeat them. She turned her head away till she could see some swinging electrical cables disgorging streams of sparks from the deckhead.

Then she closed her eyes.

And fired.

Afterward, she fell unconscious.

The first voice she heard when she woke was Domitian's.

'Forget how she looks,' he said. 'Forget how bad it is. Just keep her alive.'

Doctor Galen's voice answered. 'Are you sure? Shouldn't we be asking ourselves whether she deserves to live?'

'Possibly not,' said Domitian. 'But what will we do if she doesn't? Who else do we have? There's no one.'

'There's Cadmus.'

'You know he can't, Galen. As much as we'd like him to, you know he doesn't have the experience.'

'Well, we'll just have to do what we can?'

'What about the crew? Will they follow her?'

'I don't know.'

'Well, come on. You there! Corporal Heva! Bear a hand.'

And then the world went dark.

Epilogue

96

In the twelfth month of the mission, the great warship Herculaneum decelerated after crossing the galaxy.

The Acceleration engines howled, then groaned, then calmed to an exhausted whine. The harnesses holding the crew in their seats strained as the ship's velocity decreased, and the ship's bulkheads rattled, then quivered, then merely trembled.

Finally, the chief engineer shut the engines down. Then he signaled to the officer of the watch that control of the ship was now returned to the bridge. A short time later, the reverse thrusters fired at the bow, and, over a distance of four million milia, the Herculaneum slowed to cruising speed, after which the cruise engines took over. They pushed the ship forward at a relatively gentle speed towards the destination.

The officer of the watch issued an order to all hands. The crew stood down from their Acceleration stations. Harnesses were unclipped, helmets were lifted from pinched faces, gods were praised, and the timeless rhythm of watches and bells resumed.

Soon, the Herculaneum approached the Hyacinth solar system. It crossed the orbits of the remotest planets and threaded its way through a region thick with tumbling asteroids. Then it pressed on towards the small star.

Four Hyacinth days later, the Herculaneum's forward thrusters fired again, slowing the ship from its cruising speed to a controlled drift. Finally, the officer of the watch, Lieutenant Cadmus, heaved the ship to, and moored it at the location designated by the ship's astronomer: on the dark side of the Hyacinth moon, out of sight of the blue planet's surface.

At the stern, the mechanics inspected the handful of dropships that had survived the devastating incident six months earlier. Though dented and scratched, the ships were deemed useable by the chief mechanic. 'After all,' he remarked. 'What else can we do?'

In the armory, the gunner's mates checked the weapons. The marines received orders to stand by. A descent to the planet's surface might be required at any moment.

After so many upheavals, disease, suffering, and changes to the ship's company, the Herculaneum was on the verge of completing its mission at last. Every crew member waited for what would happen next.

Meanwhile, in the expanse of the great cabin, the captain of the Herculaneum woke from Hyacinth-creature sleep for the two hundred and fiftieth time.

97

As usual, a nightmare had tormented the captain's rest.

The nightmare was always the same: the dark forest, the captain's childhood self running through the gloom, an unseen pursuer calling to her from the trees, and carrying a weapon known as a brak, the word for beak in the native language. The nightmare ended with the captain being caught and thrashed.

The captain's steward, Frumentius, knocked twice and entered the cabin.

'Good morning, Captain Octavia.'

Without looking at him, the captain said, 'You are late, Frumentius.'

'Yes, Captain. I beg your pardon. There was the usual problem with the ship's water heaters.'

Frumentius held out a tray bearing steaming facial towels and a small mirror. The captain selected a towel and pressed it to her eyes. Then she dropped the towel on the tray, took up the mirror, and studied it. Yes, she thought. It's all still there: the oval face; the glowing complexion; the small, inoffensive nose; the glittering cerulean eyes; the tiny cleft in her chin; and, most pleasing of all, the gorgeous waves of her hair.

She dropped the mirror on the tray, pulled back the bedcovers, and climbed from her berth. Then, standing on the soft rug spread across the cabin's deck, she stood naked, and stretched her arms, holding them high above her head, as if reaching for the deckhead above.

Frumentius averted his eyes. He walked to the captain's locker and withdrew the blue and gold uniform from the hanger rail.

'You must look your best today, Captain Octavia.'

When the captain was finally ready, Frumentius helped her dress. With his eyes studying either the bulkhead or the rug, he helped her into the pressed blue trousers, the glistening boots, the icy white shirt, the brushed blue coat, and its brocade of stripes and golden epaulettes.

Then, Frumentius stepped aside, holding the captain's hat under one arm, while Octavia walked across the stateroom to the long mirror.

'Beg pardon, Captain Octavia,' Frumentius said. 'I know I must wait to speak, but I have to say that the uniform will make a great impression on the Hyacinth creatures—a very great impression.'

Someone knocked.

'Veni,' said Octavia.

The door opened. First Lieutenant Cadmus stepped inside and saluted. Like his captain, Cadmus also wore a navy dress uniform of blue, though his first lieutenant's coat was dull compared to the glory of Octavia's.

'Good morning, Captain.'

'Lieutenant Cadmus, why aren't you on the bridge during such a critical watch?'

'Beg pardon, Captain. Third Lieutenant Priscus is in temporary command. I have come to apprise you of certain developments that occurred overnight.'

'What developments, First Lieutenant?'

Cadmus looked at Frumentius, who lowered his eyes,

picked up a cloth, and began dusting the captain's new painting on the forward bulkhead. The new painting's title, like the old painting it replaced, was 'The Fate of The People.'

In this new version of the famous scene, the god Owanthan and the god Sirhain, both stood beside a tall, fair-haired female in Hyacinth-creature form. This new figure wore a scarlet robe. She was neither terrified nor worshipful of the gods, but seemed almost to be a confidante, and a trusted advisor for King Angwor, who stood to the side with Angwere, his wife and queen.

Cadmus brought out a list from his jacket pocket. 'First, our position, Captain. We are . . .' But Octavia interrupted him again.

'What was the jolt I felt during the morning watch? I gave no order to move the ship. What were you doing?'

'Yes, Captain. I adjusted our position.'

'Why?'

'The Hyacinth moon is subject to rapid variations in ... '

'What about the preparations for the descent?'

'Yes, Captain. All is ready, as you ordered. Advisor Cicero is also ready and will join us on the bridge.'

'How is Cicero's mood?'

'Unfortunately, he is still grumbling. He quoted the Admiralty's mission instructions to me again, especially the section stating that the captain must not reveal the ship in case it terrifies the Hyacinth creatures. He said we must be discreet.'

'Tell him if he doesn't want to descend to the surface in the Herculaneum, we can issue him with a dropship and he can wait behind the moon for us to return. Tell him he can travel in the ship he named after himself.'

'Yes, Captain.'

Octavia turned from the mirror and stepped across the stateroom. She sat down in a large chair beneath the painting.

'What else?'

Cadmus continued. 'The Hyacinth location you asked about.'

'Yes.'

'We sent out a scanner. It identified three land masses that match the description.' He looked at his list. 'Rolling brown hills, shallow valleys, a nearby ocean, a temperate climate.'

'And?'

'The first location is on the very continent on which the Roman capital is situated. It matches the description almost exactly. The other location is on the north-west coast of the large continent to the south.'

'And the third?'

'The third is on the west coast of a continent that is mapped but not named in the reports of our previous missions. The Romans have no name for it, either. It seems they haven't discovered it.'

Octavia settled back in her chair. 'Tell me more about about this new continent, First Lieutenant.'

'For the time being, we have named it Ashkanth, after the similarly shaped lands on the home planet. Like them, it has a narrow isthmus connecting two large subcontinents. The location you describe is on the west coast of the northernmost of the two. Its distance from Rome is roughly six thousand Roman milia.'

'Good. We will survey all three locations.'

'Ashkanth looks the most promising, geographically.'

'I look forward to seeing it.'

'Yes, Captain. However, there is one thing more to consider.'

'And what is that?'

'On Ashkanth, we found few Hyacinth creatures. They were not in the numbers you described.'

'That's strange, but not important,' said Octavia.

'Eventually it will populate. What else?'

'Three more items.'

'Quickly, Lieutenant.'

'Yes, Captain. The first is the sea-chest in the hold—the very heavy chest locked in Captain Tiberius's strongroom. We have brought it up to the stern ramp as you ordered. It's now guarded by a detachment of marines. Is it important, Captain—this sea-chest?'

'It's just something mentioned in the mission orders. We'll place it at the designated location when the time comes.'

'May I ask what's inside the chest?'

She told him.

'But why?' said Cadmus. 'It's unthinkable—for all of us, for all our families, let alone the Hyacinth creatures. Did the orders mention the reason it is aboard?'

'Not a thing.'

'But surely they must have warned of the danger.'

She interrupted him. 'Time is short, Cadmus. What is next on your list?'

Cadmus cleared his throat. 'It's about Rome itself, Captain. We have only begun our survey. These are early impressions, but the city of Rome appears to be in ruin. The buildings and temples are not white and red like the ones depicted in the reports. I think it's possible that in our absence, the city was attacked and then abandoned, which implies that Rome might no longer be the dominant civilization. The leaders might no longer control large armies. They might no longer dominate the continent.'

Octavia thought for a moment and then said, 'It might not be important. We shall proceed as if Rome were still the dominant city—at first. If it's not, then we'll soon find out which city defeated it, and then we will pay a visit to the next set of leaders.'

'Yes, Captain. We have identified several centers of power on the Roman continent and one new center of power far to the east on the region the Romans refer to as Cathay.'

'What's the last thing? Tell me on the way to the bridge.'

'It's only brief, Captain. It's about the petty officer who claims he has developed telepathic powers, the one named Egnatius.'

'Not again.'

'Yes, Captain. Unfortunately, Egnatius is still making wild claims. Overnight, he said he had received a message from the Senate. I told him that was impossible. Even Telepathy himself said he couldn't receive messages at this range.

'And what does the supposed Senate message say?'

'It says the Senate demands more information about Captain Agrippa. Petty Officer Egnatius says the Senate received one last message from Agrippa before the Noricum exploded and they lost contact.'

Sinistra raised her chin.

'Please have Petty Officer Egnatius locked in the brig for a month. That might make him rethink his telepathic abilities. Order Doctor Galen to put him to sleep for a few days, too. Egnatius is obviously suffering a disease of the Hyacinth-creature brain.'

'Aye, Captain.'

Octavia stood from the chair, straightened her uniform, and considered the painting of 'The Fate of The People,' as if reassuring herself that, like the tall, fair-haired female in scarlet, she could hear destiny calling her on.

'Frumentius?'

'Yes, Captain?'

'Now.'

98

'Dux in Ponte!' shouted Fourth Lieutenant Basilus. Leader on the bridge!

The bridge crew shot up from their stations and stood to attention. Octavia strode to the raised platform on which the captain's chair waited.

'Second Lieutenant Priscus,' said Octavia. 'Tell your crew they may return to their stations.'

'Sicut eras,' Priscus replied. As you were.

The bridge crew sat down and waited. All was silent except for the hiss of the atmosphere pumps, the bip of the scanners, and the electrical hum of the navigation instruments.

'Lieutenant Priscus,' called Cadmus.

'Sir?'

'Now, if you please.'

'Aye, sir.'

Priscus made his report. Little had altered in the ten minuta since Cadmus had departed. The ship's location had shifted with the Hyacinth moon, of course, but nothing else had altered. Priscus then gave a brief report on the ship's stations.

As Priscus talked, Octavia surveyed the bridge. There

they were—her specialist crew, her favorites. None of them dared smile at her, of course. Not any more. The days of smiling at the captain and receiving a smile in return were over.

The old Herculaneum had been replaced by the new Herculaneum. And the old officers were replaced by Captain Octavia's new officers. These were the most technically competent officers, the most loyal officers, the ones who survived the six months adrift, and more importantly, they were the ones who had endured the captain's purge.

With the change in the leadership, the captain had also changed her Hyacinth name. She was now referred to only as Octavia. This had been the case for several months. Octavia meant 'born eighth' in the Hyacinth language. The captain liked the power implied by the name when spoken aloud. It sounded so much more authoritative than Sinistra, which she never used.

In addition to Octavia, the captain also reserved the name Lavinia. It possessed unquestionably aristocratic credentials. The first woman named Lavinia had been the wife of King Aeneas, the supposed ancestor of the Roman people.

But for the moment, the captain was Octavia—not Sinistra, not Grenda, and never The Lovelorn, a new and disrespectful name originating in the hold. If a crew member was overhead using the word 'lovelorn,' that crew member would find himself or herself incarcerated. If the captain were especially displeased, the crew member would be keelhauled. No one had mouthed the word lovelorn since the great purging five months ago, after the captain's miraculous recovery from her injuries.

The new Herculaneum ran as Captain Octavia had remade it, just as she had remade herself. Once the purge was complete, she ordered a refitting of the engines, a thorough re-armoring, and an eradication of miseria by ordering the crew to spend fifteen minutes each day in sunlight on a new Domum Deck.

She also restructured the hierarchy of command. Some of the older officers now languished in the sickly green lamplight of the brig. Some had been demoted and issued with new Hyacinth creature forms that mirrored their true ages and feeble appearances. Their faces were lined, their hair thin, their bodies bent, their renowned beauty existing only in pre-mission photographs in the purser's files.

All this had been carried out according to the captain's precise instructions, just as her own appearance had been refined to her own tastes. She occupied this new form continuously, never expanding into her natural state. It was said around the ship that the captain now preferred the Hyacinth creature form to the natural one and that she would struggle to expand at all.

With these new measures in place, the ship ran according to proper navy virtues. It ran on discipline, competence, respect for rank, and regard for the strike of the bell. Most of all, it ran on fear. As the new captain discovered, fear was a powerful force. Fear made the ship run smoothly. Fear silenced the sea lawyers and cut short the mutinies, and fear raised the captain's status to infallible.

Captain Octavia explained her new leadership philosophy to Cadmus. 'It is better,' she said, 'far better, to be feared than liked——better for the crew, and better for the mission.' It was certainly better for the captain herself.

It was even better for the home planet, as the Senate reluctantly agreed during the long months in which the Herculaneum refitted itself. In fact, the Senate had no choice but to agree. Their transport ships still waited on the home planet, damaged by the volcanic eruptions. Only the Herculaneum and its new leader could complete their mission. Now, some Senators were actually calling for Captain Octavia to be made an official Senate advisor.

But all that waited in the future, as did the time when she

would become Admiral Octavia and would take her place with the senior senators. And always in her mind, leading her on, was the unwavering vision of the beautiful woman on the hill and the adoring multitude chanting 'Octavia! Octavia! Octavia!'

For now, it was Captain Octavia, not Senator Octavia nor Admiral Octavia, who surveyed the bridge. Cadmus heard the last of Priscus's report, then he turned to address the plinth.

'Your orders, Captain?' he said. Then he stood waiting. 'Captain?' he said again.

But the captain did not reply. She appeared to gaze at nothing as if experiencing a Hyacinth-creature daydream. Then, she smiled. 'What did you say, First Lieutenant?'

'Your orders, Captain.'

'I've had a change of mind. Set course for the areas you researched: the ones with the coasts and the round hills.'

'Not Rome, Captain?'

'Rome can wait. First, let's cruise to the region you mentioned.'

'There are three regions, Captain.'

'Let's go the region named Ashkanth.'

'Ashkanth, Captain?'

'Is your hearing suffering again this morning, First Lieutenant?'

'No, Captain.'

'Well, let us proceed.'

'Yes, Captain, but at Ashkanth, we will arrive as the light is failing. We might not see the land—not for twelve horae. Also, the landing engines can't last that long. They're not designed for it.'

'Then make haste, First Lieutenant.'

'Aye, Captain.'

Lieutenant Basilus stood to attention and called out, 'Senate Advisor on the bridge.' With a stamp of the marines' boots, Advisor Cicero entered. As usual, he wore his robes of white and purple, but he no longer wore the pin bearing his family crest.

'Captain Octavia,' he said. 'If I may…'

'No, Advisor. You may not.'

'Did you read my list of concerns, Captain?'

'Yes, Advisor Cicero. I read them all.'

'I am only concerned for the mission, Captain. The Admiral was definite. We should not alarm the Hyacinth creatures.'

'The Admiral is not here, Advisor.'

'But those are our orders. We must not cause panic by descending to the surface in the Herculaneum.'

'Yes, of course, Advisor. In the meantime, take a seat and enjoy the view of the oceans and the mountains.'

Advisor Cicero sniffed and pulled his robes tighter. Eventually, he sat down in the advisor's seat behind the plinth.

Octavia turned to Cadmus. 'Lieutenant?'

'Yes, Captain.'

'Now. If you please.'

'Aye, Captain,' said Cadmus. He called to the quartermaster. 'Proceed to unmoor the ship.'

'Aye, sir.'

'Engineering,' said Cadmus.

'Aye, First Lieutenant,' said the new chief engineer, Sisenna, who had replaced Gabinus after he was killed by the exploding engine known as Apollo.

'Engage cruise engines,' said Cadmus. 'And prepare to light the landing engines. Gently now. Gently.'

The bulkhead shuddered, and the ship gained way. Several secunda later, the bridge heaved upward as the landing engines fired under the keel. 'This is the first time they've fired since testing,' Octavia said over her shoulder to the frowning Cicero.

Soon, the Herculaneum slid from its hiding place. The gray and crater-pocked Hyacinth moon fell astern, and suddenly the glory of Hyacinth itself filled the viewports. As predicted by previous missions, the planet was beautiful. It astonished every crew member's eye. The seas really were deep blue, the mountains bright white, the plains luminous green, the clouds streaky and clean.

'Just imagine,' said Octavia, 'how the Hyacinth creatures will marvel at us! They'll wonder at the strange object descending from their sky. And they'll be in awe of the amazing creatures aboard it.'

And the great ship Herculaneum descended to the surface.

99

Down on the surface of Hyacinth, it was almost dusk.

Two Hyacinth creatures, a male and female, lay on their backs on a grassy hill, gazing at the sea. Both noticed something creeping across the surface of the pale moon—something like a long, dark centipede, or a like a crab.

When the sun had almost set, people in the villages along the coast witnessed a shadow moving above the clouds—a shadow darker than a thundercloud and swifter than any bird.

Further north, people saw a terrible black island in the sky passing over the sea. It was a terrible sight, with scales like a monstrous snake, and there was a great fire burning beneath it. The heat from its flames drew steam from the waves, like the sea had boiled. On land, a hot wind unsettled the forests. The birds rose from the trees and flew east. The animals fled behind them.

The terrible island moved up the coast, dragging clouds of mist. Further north, more villages witnessed the island's approach. Everyone hid in the forests. Then, the island turned inland, dragging its fire.

100

Cadmus brought the Herculaneum to a halt at an altitude of a leuga over the region resembling the one described by Octavia. It was on the coast of Ashkanth.

At a leuga's altitude, the world was still light. From the bridge, the crew could see all the way to a large mountain range in the east. But down on the planet's surface, it was dark. Cadmus ordered the keel viewports adjusted to make night into day. The land's features lit up. There were round hills, valleys thick with green trees. The sensors reported a warm, dry atmosphere.

'Your orders, Captain? Should we descend?'

'No,' said Octavia. 'We're already too low. If we descended any further, the engines will ignite the land. Look at the stern viewport. See what you've done.' The stern viewport came on. A thick stripe of fire stretched to the coast. Vast areas of forest and grasslands raged in bright orange and a wall of black smoke rose to the clouds.

The Herculaneum ascended to an altitude of a leuga and a half.

Octavia leaned forward in her chair and scanned the hills through the viewport. At first she smiled. Then she frowned. Any number of the hills could be the one. So could any of the valleys. And as Cadmus said, there were no Hyacinth creatures to be seen—not a city, not a village of more than a hundred. Nor were there any signs of land cultivation.

It was hopeless. Of course it was. Octavia had been too eager. What had she expected: that the multitude would waiting for her, chanting her name? Coming to Ashkanth had been a gross indulgence. And yet she needed to see something. After so many months of drifting, silence and struggle, she wanted a sign that everything had really taken place—Sirhain, the vision, everything—even Flavia's demise.

But now, the night had overtaken the Herculaneum. Octavia turned to Cadmus. He was already looking back at her, waiting for orders, anxious about the engines and the fuel.

Advisor Cicero cleared his throat, about to speak. No doubt he would say the ship must withdraw to the moon.

'All right, Advisor,' Octavia said. 'All right. I know what you're going to say.'

'It's the best thing to do,' said Cicero.

'All right,' said Octavia once more. 'Cadmus, to Rome.'

'Rome?' said Cicero. 'Is that wise, Captain? Shouldn't we return to our moorings and make the descent in dropships? Shouldn't we make our approach to the present day power centers, not the fallen ones?'

But Octavia did not reply. She raised an eyebrow at Cadmus, who gave the order. The Herculaneum engaged the cruise engines and proceeded east, ascending to a height of over three leuga. It cleared the large mountain range. Then it crossed the dark plains, a vast lake, and another range of mountains on Ashkanth's eastern coast. Then it increased its velocity and passed over a great storm and an ocean in turmoil. Then, the sun rose to greet it as it approached the region designated as Rome, and Cadmus ordered engineering to slow down.

There were many more people in the Roman region. The Herculaneum's shadow passed over large cities, cultivated land, rivers heavy with traffic, and Hyacinth creatures on the streets, in the fields, in crowds, and fleeing from the shadow —many of them with animals

The Roman coast came closer. The ship tacked northeast until the planetographer's mate, Tullius, pointed out the village of Ostia, and the river to follow inland.

The Herculaneum's shadow soon passed along the river, heading east into the sun, and passing over the towns of Acilia and Vitnia. When the hills and the white buildings came into view, Octavia said, 'Take us up, First Lieutenant Cadmus, up to a leuga and a half, directly over the center.'

The Herculaneum halted. This time, the ship had left no trail of devastation. Instead, the river glittered in the sunlight, and the air was clear except for the exhaust fumes and heat haze.

On the ship's bridge, the viewports magnified the view of the famous city. Everyone was silent as they gazed down at the city and at the buildings they had only ever seen in artist's renderings. There they were: the columned temples, the noble forums, the vast arenas, the roads, the arches, the palaces, the rows of statues of emperors and gods.

But all were in ruins.

All were no longer white and red and proud. The temples had crumbled. The monuments had toppled. The great arena's floor had caved, revealing a skeletal underworld. Elsewhere, the earth had risen, covering the temple podiums. And mournful statues of once-mighty leaders stood on lonely plinths, or atop mossy columns, gazing over the ruins of their city.

Any Hyacinth creatures were hiding or had fled.

'You are right, Cadmus,' said Octavia. 'It is gone.'

'It must have been centuries, Captain' said the now stooped and lined Manius. 'It's hardly worth inspecting.'

'Well,' said Cicero. 'That only leaves us with a decision to make.'

'And what is that, Advisor?' said Octavia.

'We either go west or north to find which new city is the power in this region, or, as much I regret it, we take the other course of action. I think you know the one.'

'It's a pity,' said Manius, 'but I think Cicero might be right. The idea of meeting the leaders was only a fanciful idea. We've always known it might come to this.'

'Manius is right,' Cicero said. 'The Senate will agree, too, once we make some progress. After all, as they say, "Fines iustificant per modum." The ends justify the means. 'The more we achieve before the transports arrive, the better.'

The bridge crew sat at their stations, saying nothing. Around the ship, the ten thousand officers and crew waited and pondered the ranks of terraforming machines and weapons in the hold. No one raised the question of what would happen to the Hyacinth creatures.

'You only have to give the order, Captain,' said Manius. 'We can land the first machines within twenty-four horae.'

'We'll have to forego priceless anthropological research,' said Cicero. 'Galen and Scapula will just have to endure the loss. The mission and the people must come first.'

Octavia listened, saying nothing. She knew Manius and Cicero were right, but how could her own personal vision come about if she ordered so much destruction and so many deaths?

'Captain?' said Cicero. 'Do you agree?'

Octavia ignored him.

'First Lieutenant Cadmus,' she said. 'Send word to the stern ramp.'

'The stern ramp, Captain?'

'Is your hearing failing again, First Lieutenant?'

'No, Captain. Beg pardon.'

'Prepare a dropship for descent to the surface.'

'Why?' said Cicero. 'What purpose can exceed the need to fulfill our mission after six months of delay?'

But Octavia had risen from her chair and was striding from the bridge. The crew stood and saluted.

'And, Cadmus!' said Octavia.

'Yes, Captain.'

'I want the Albus.'

'Yes, Captain. The Albus.'

'And pass the word forward to my steward. Tell him to prepare my white robes.'

101

Crouching behind the columns of a ruined temple, one young Hyacinth male named Asciano, and one female, named Fiorella, watched the white, egg-shaped object push out from the terrible island, high in the sky, and float down towards them.

Fiorella wanted to run away with everyone else, but Asciano held her hand, refusing to move, and said, 'Wait. See what it does.'

'No. They're waiting for us. My mother—she'll ...'

'She'll thank us later. They all will. Think of the story we can tell.'

'I don't want a story. I want to go.'

'Come on. Just for a while. Let's see what it does.'

'It might fall on us.'

'It won't.'

'How do you know?'

'It just won't.'

Apart from the snapping flames above, all was quiet. The whirring cicadas were silent. The thousands of birds that nested in the ruins had fled with the people. So had the grazing flocks. Even the lizards creeping on the chipped and fallen columns were on their way to somewhere else. Only the few remaining statues stood defiantly on the columns, like warriors from a defeated army at the end of a great battle.

The giant, white egg descended all the way down till it met its shadow on the land. It hovered over it, making no sound except for one long hiss. Now that it was closer, the object seemed more like an insect than an egg, a giant, upside-down-teardrop-shaped insect.

Soon, the insect rotated. Four, thin legs pushed out from its underside, just like an insect's legs, and then the object settled on the stony ground. The hissing ceased, and the object was silent except for a series of creaks and cracks, like an old gate. And now that it was still, Asciano and Fiorella could smell it. It smelled like soap.

'Come on!' said Fiorella. 'Please.'

'Too late,' said Asciano.

'But it saw us.'

'No, it didn't.'

'There will be monsters in there.'

'No, there won't. There is a word painted on the other side, so it can't be monsters.'

The object-insect opened and stairs extended till they touched the earth, like a lizard's tongue. Then a giant climbed out, ducking his head. The giant was colored blue with no mouth or nose. He carried a tool across its chest, a kind of bludgeon or cudgel. A second giant emerged. The two giants clomped down the steps to the ground. They stood waiting, not even looking around.

'See. I told you. Monsters. Come on, let's go.'

'Shhhh. There's something more.'

Then, they saw the most extraordinary sight. A tall, fair-haired young woman appeared. She wore bright white robes. Her yellow hair was swept up into a shape like a rolling wave. She looked at the ground, the ruins, the hills. She smiled, as if she were greeting a crowd of people. Then, she stepped down the stairs, her head held high. Asciano and Fiorella could see her legs and sandals.

The woman was followed by a tall man also wearing white robes, with one pale, bare shoulder. Behind him came a second man, wearing a blue tunic and blue leg coverings, like the kind worn by horsemen. He carried a box. The three of them stepped onto the earth beside the two giants.

'What are they saying?' said Fiorella.

'I don't know—something about their breath.'

'No, they weren't.'

'That's how it sounded.'

'They sound strange. Are they from the north?'

'Of course they're not.'

'Then where are they from?'

'Listen.'

The woman and two men walked to one of the old statues, the statue of the man holding a scroll high over his head as if showing it to an imaginary crowd of people. The man in the robes with the bare shoulder pointed at the statue's face, then he swept the ruins with his arm, speaking the strange language. He shook his head. Was he not pleased? The woman listened, saying nothing. The man spoke again. Asciano could hear them. The words sounded almost familiar, like the old language spoken by the priests. But neither Fiorella nor Asciano could understand the priests, either.

'I'm going out there.'

Fiorella grabbed his arm. 'No. Please, no.'

'Maybe there are gifts in that box.'

'Don't be stupid. It could be anything.'

'Like what?'

'I don't know—nothing good. It might be poison.'

'I can find out.'

But he stayed crouching behind the column.

The woman spoke in a clear, round voice. Then, the man

in blue raised a hand to his mouth and shouted something. His voice echoed around the fallen columns, the ruined basilicas, the slabs of marble, the crumbling temples.

'What did he say?'

'He asked if anyone is here?'

'No he didn't.'

'He did.'

'He didn't.'

'I don't care. I'm going out.'

'No, Asciano. Please don't.'

But Asciano stepped out from the column. The giants saw him first. They spun about and raised their bludgeons at him with a flurry of whirs and clicks. Asciano stopped. The woman said something to the giants. They settled the bludgeons back on their chests. Asciano stood up, stood his ground, and squared his shoulders.

The woman took a step forward. The two men came behind her while the giants stayed by the stairs. Then the woman called out. Her soft, round voice was soothing. Most of what she said was gibberish, but Asciano understood one word.

Amicis.

The woman walked to within one arm's length away. Asciano had never seen anyone so—what was the word? Pale? Bright? Healthy? Glowing? Clean? Something like that. She smelled like flowers. Her teeth were so white, small, and even. Her blue eyes sparkled, like the river at dawn. They made him feel uneasy.

Then the woman looked over his shoulder as Fiorella crept out from the column and stood behind Asciano, peering over his shoulder.

After a few moments, the astonishing woman spoke again. As before, the words were familiar, but just out of reach of understanding.

Asciano said, 'Where are you from?'

The woman blinked at him. She turned and looked at the two men. The one wearing the white robes held out his palms, raised his shoulders in a shrug. Then the woman turned back. She smiled and pointed at the island and at the sky. She spoke. It sounded like she said, 'Da Lontano.' From afar.

'What do you want?' replied Asciano. 'Want what?' he added.

The woman pointed with her pale, slender hand at her glittering right eye, then pointed at a temple, the statue of the man and his scroll, and at the hills. Asciano understood the strange words. 'Veni.' To come. 'Videre.' To see.

'Why here?' he said.

'Asciano, let's go,' said Fiorella, tugging at his elbow. 'She frightens me. Look at her.'

'No, I want to ask about the island and what they're doing.'

The woman watched them, her shimmering eyes moving from one to the other.

'Why here?' Asciano repeated.

The man in robes behind the woman said something. He and the other man turned, shaking their heads, and walked back to the egg-insect and the two giants. The woman stayed behind. She raised a hand—a slender, pale, farewell hand.

'Why here?' Asciano repeated before the woman could leave.

The woman spoke a long series of words while Asciano concentrating as hard as he could. But the woman spoke as if she didn't care whether Asciano understood or not. Then, she turned and walked to the stairs.

'What did she say?' said Fiorella. 'Hey! Are you listening?'

'It's strange,' said Asciano.

'What was it? What did she say?'

'I might be wrong.'

'Well, I heard her say a nonsense thing: emperors here,

something like that.'

'No, she didn't,' said Fiorella. 'She said, "My name is Octavia. Here is where emperors are made."'

'She said "live," not "made."'

'No, it was made. I heard her say "fatto."'

'No, you didn't. I would have heard it.'

'She said it.'

'I don't care. I don't like her.'

'I'll ask her.'

But Asciano stayed where he was. The woman and the two men ascended the stairs, followed by the two heavy giants and their bludgeons. Then the stairs pulled back into the white object, which soon began hissing again. Then, it rose up, sending small stones rolling among the billowing grass. Then, without ropes to haul it, the object ascended all the way back to the dark island in the sky. Soon after, the flames from the island turned bright blue and a hot wind forced Asciano and Fiorella to run away until the air was cool again.

When the island breached the clouds above, the rest of the people crept out from their hiding places.

Asciano said, 'Do you think it will come back?'

Fiorella said, 'For all our sakes, I hope we never see it again. I hope it goes up and keeps going, all the way across the sea.'

But the island did not keep going up. Above the clouds, at a height of two leuga from Hyacinth's surface, it turned its bow to the west.

— The End. —

You've reached the series end.
Now it's time to start at the beginning.

Introducing The Burns Series Book 1
The astonishing adventure that started it all.

If you enjoyed 'OCTAVIA,' you'll love the incident that started it all, when an enormous 'sky vessel' descended from the clouds and harassed a British warship in 1803. Here's what it's about.

At the end of the earth, we fought an enemy from beyond the stars.

1803. The Napoleonic War. A Royal Navy warship is ordered to pursue an enemy frigate to the frozen waters far south in the Indian Ocean. There it must capture the enemy ship and retrieve a mysterious sea-chest, contents unknown. Failure not permitted.

For the determined young captain and his crew, this already dangerous mission turns into a battle with a mysterious vessel that appears not in the sea, but, unbelievably, impossibly, in the sky above them.

And it is not friendly.

Embark on an astonishing adventure in 'Fifty Degrees South,' the action-packed, science fiction adventure novel that readers around the world can't put down. Reviewers describe the story as **'Brilliant,'** and **'A unique science fiction novel.'**

Check out the sample first chapter on the following page or go straight to Amazon and search for 'Fifty Degrees South,' and The Alex Burns Series by M.M. Holt. You've never read a science fiction saga like it.

My sincere thanks,

M.M. Holt

Ps: And please, if you liked 'OCTAVIA', don't forget to leave a five-star review on Amazon.

A few words from you could make all the difference.

Thank you for reading 'OCTAVIA.' I hope you enjoyed it.

If you have a few spare moments, would you please do me a huge favor and post a brief review where you purchased it.

Reviews are critical for encouraging more readers to take a chance on the book.

No reviews, no readers.

So if you enjoyed 'OCTAVIA', would you please revisit the page from which you downloaded it, and scroll down to the button that says, 'Write a review.' Then, type, 'This was amazing.'

I'm only kidding. I know you'll put what you think best, but a five-star review would really help.

On the off chance you didn't like the book, could you contact me with your thoughts. I would love to hear them. Email me at mmholt548@gmail.com

My sincere thanks,

M.M. Holt.

Like to be notified when M.M. Holt releases a new book?

It's easy. Visit mmholt.com and find the newsletter signup form on the home page. You'll receive updates on works in progress, access to deleted scenes from the Burns Series, and snaps from my relentless travels. But no spam.

Any problems, email me at mmholt548@gmail.com and I'll put you on the list.

Thank you,

M.M. Holt.

PS: Turn the page to check out the thrilling first chapter from book 1, 'Fifty Degrees South.' You'll find Octavia (under one of her other names) waiting for you in its pages.

'Fifty Degrees South'

Chapter 1

When the first blue beam struck the sea just ahead of HMS Morgause, none of the seventy sailors in the first watch saw it. Instead, they were concentrating on the task known as wearing the ship, changing its heading from southwest to southeast.

At the ship's helm, Jessop, the quartermaster, turned the wheel clockwise, and great ship came into the wind. The Morgause's bow swung to starboard and the compass in the binnacle wobbled around to west-south-west, then west where it paused as Jessop waited for the next command. He was so engrossed in his task of feeling the ship's movement, he missed the sight of the blue beam entirely.

Forward of Jessop, on the main deck, the crew stood ready, the thick ropes in their hands, waiting for the commands to heave the yards of the main mast around to coordinate with Jessop's turn of the helm and with the other crewmen hauling on ropes at the foremast and the mizzen mast.

They too missed the blue beam as it hit the water, thick as a four barrels, and curiously light as it went down into the depths.

High on the mainmast, Trinity Evans was scouring the south for the enemy vessel, the Besançon, which the Morgause had been desperately pursuing for seven long weeks in heavy seas. But when he turned west with the movement of the Morgause's bow, he too missed the blue beam. He didn't see the three-second long blast from the sky, the cylinder-shaped shaft of light, wide and smooth, smacking the dark sea, going through it and straight down and distorting, like a twig in a glass of water. Nor did Trinity Evans hear the hiss of steam that followed.

On the quarterdeck, the view forward was blocked by the mainsail. The officer of the watch, Mr Kyte concentrated on Jessop's shouted compass readings. Mr Kyte didn't see the beam either, nor did he see the smoldering carcass of an enormous white squid surfacing ahead of the Morgause and sliding along its hull to be churned in the ship's wake.

But when the ship hard worn to her new southeast course and was pushing through the dark and swelling water at a good eight knots, the blue beam struck again.

And this time, it was noticed.

Trinity Evans ducked, held up an elbow, and thought it was lightning coming to strike him dead, but this was not like any lightning he'd seen before. For one thing, it was bright blue; for another, it was straight. It also wasn't flashing. It struck sixty yards ahead of the Morgause and blazed for a full five seconds. No lightning ever did that—not in Trinity Evans's experience. Not on your life. Not even after ten too many mugs of grog—the extra strong stuff.

He watched the beam, fascinated. The way it went right down into the water. Only when it finally ceased did he prepare to hail the deck. But still, he hesitated, wondering what he should say. This wasn't a regular sighting. It certainly wasn't the sighting of the Besançon, nor any other ship. This was something else entirely. It wasn't even in his list of hails, which was long. Still, he had better hail something before someone on the deck noticed it first. He slapped a hand to the side of his mouth and peered down at the darkened figures way below.

'On deck there!' he called. 'On deck!'

'Yes, Evans,' came the reply. 'Is it the Besançon?'

'No, sir. Strange light, sir! Strange light.'

'Where away?' came the reply but only after a few moments.

'Straight ahead!' he called.

As he said this, another beam hit the sea. Same place—directly ahead. Same thickness. Same intensity, it was the color of the blue in the plate glass windows back in his church in Penzance—which made Trinity Evans wonder. Was this a sign from the Almighty? Was the Second Coming at hand? Was this something mentioned in the book of Revelations? It certainly didn't look like a friendly light. Tomorrow, he thought. No more grog. No more ale.

'On deck there!' he called again.

'We saw it, Evans,' someone called back.

'Something new!' Trinity Evans countered.

'What?' came the reply.

'The strange light—it came from that big dark cloud.'

On the quarterdeck, Mr Kyte walked to the taffrail and looked up into the gloom at the gray cloud that had settled off the ship's port side, huge and glowering, almost like a ship itself, a ship of the air, with curious bulges. A ship of the air, he thought, then shook his head. His overactive imagination was at work again.

My Kyte made a note of the time. It was three bells in the morning watch, just as dawn was fighting off the night. Possible enemy activity sighted. A strange blue light.

'Did you see it, Poole?' he said to the youth beside him, one of the ship's young midshipman who were training to become officers, just as Mr Kyte himself had trained twenty years ago.

'Yes,' said Poole. 'I saw it, port bow, a quarter cable length away.'

'You mean, "Yes, sir,"' said Mr Kyte. 'You're in His Majesty's Navy, Poole, and we are at war.'

'Yes, sir,' said Poole. 'Beg pardon, sir. The light, sir—it made me forget myself.'

Mr Kyte scanned the darkness again. Nothing but the swelling sea in the soft dawn. Nothing but the shush of the water along the hull, and the creak of ropes as the ship rose and fell. He looked down at the main deck. The seventy men of the morning watch, dressed in their blue jackets and white duck trousers stared into the darkness. Others looked up at Mr Kyte—waiting for a command—and an explanation.

Then, without warning, another blue beam shot from the dark cloud. It was closer this time. He could see it clearly. It was a thick blue shaft of light, straight as a sun ray, coming from the dark cloud, going straight down into the sea, illuminating the underwater world beneath for a good sixty yards or so, and going down into the depths.

Trinity Davies was already hailing him from the upper

deck when a second beam struck the water. Same straight blue shaft of light. Same point of origin in the dark cloud above. Two beams. One to port. One to starboard. They were like a ceremonial gateway of light.

Mt Kyte turned around. Poole was behind him, crouching.

'Stand up straight, Poole,' he said.

'Yes, sir,' said Poole.

'The men must see that you are unafraid, that you are fearless.'

'Yes, sir,' said Poole. 'Beg pardon, sir.'

'Never again, Poole.'

'No, sir. Never again. Fearless.'

'Fearless of even the strangest things produced by war and the heavens.'

'Yes, sir.'

Mr Kyte turned back to the beams.

'Are we going to beat to quarters, sir?' said Poole.

Is was a good question. Beating to quarters meant the bosun's whistle would blow, drums would pound, commands would be shouted, and the crew would scramble for battle, the one hundred and thirty men asleep in the hammocks below would rush to join the men already on the main deck. The gun crews would rush to the cannons ranged along the sides of the Morgause, untying the ropes that held them fast on their wooden carts, readying them for the gunpowder and the cannonballs. The Marines would climb with their muskets into the tops. The powder boys would scramble to the magazine, deep inside the ship, and rush upward with buckets of powder for the gun crews. The wicks would be lit and set in tubs beside each cannon. The boarding crews would assemble for the armourer to hand out the cutlasses, rapiers and pistols. The gun ports on the main deck and below would swing open and the Morgause would be ready to unleash thunderous hell and utterly smash any ship within range.

Beating to quarters.

Mr Kyte made his decision.

'Yes, Poole,' he said. 'Give the order. Beat to quarters.'

Poole almost broke into a run before checking himself. He was eager for something to be done about the beams.

'Mr Pound!' he called to the bosun.

'Sir,' Mr Pound called up from the main deck.

'Per Mr Kyte, we shall beat to quarters.'

'What?' said Mr Pound.

'We shall beat to quarters!' called Mr Kyte.

'Aye,' said Mr Pound.

Instantly, the mood of the ship changed. Mr Pound's whistle piped its shrill two tones, and the ship came alive.

Mr Kyte watched the blue beams and wondered.

The year was 1803 in the Napoleonic war. The location was the Atlantic Ocean in the lonely waters far south the equator, off the west coast of Southern Africa on His Majesty's Ship, Morgause. Seas moderate to heavy. Wind from the northeast. Time at sea: sixty days. Mission: to capture the enemy frigate Besançon and retrieve a certain sea-chest, contents unknown, and return said sea-chest to the Admiralty in London.

Failure not permitted.

'Mr Poole,' said Mr Kyte without taking his eyes off the beams.

'Yes, sir.'

'Pass the word for Captain Burns.'

—/—

To continue reading, search for 'Fifty Degrees South' by M.M. Holt on Amazon. I know you'll enjoy this book.

Acknowledgments

My sincere thanks to the many friends and family who encouraged me to persevere with this novel and the others in the series.

I would also like to acknowledge the mysterious gentlemen known as Awww, Rrrr, and The Hobgoblin. Their encouragement and advice have been invaluable. Yes, the pseudonyms are necessary. All three know the Accord will never forgive them.

Who or what is the Accord? To find out, begin the series from book 1, 'Fifty Degrees South' and treat yourself to an unforgettable adventure. You won't regret it.

M.M. Holt

Author's Notes

The quotations from the Hyacinth poets and the Hyacinth statesman, are correctly attributed as follows.

"Character is destiny" is usually attributed to the Greek philosopher Heraclitus.

"Cometh the hour, cometh the man" is often attributed to Sir Winston Churchill, but its origin predates him. The exact source is unclear.

'What in me is dark illumine' is from 'Paradise Lost,' by John Milton. The line in its full context expresses a plea to the Almighty for divine aid. By restricting the context I intended the line to be a declaration that Sinistra/Octavia wanted to bring her dark side into prominence.

"Our torments also may, in length of time, Become our Elements," is from "Paradise Lost" by John Milton.

"Better to reign in Hell, than serve in Heav'n" is also from 'Paradise Lost,' by John Milton.

"Brevity is the soul of wit" is from "Hamlet," by William Shakespeare.

About M.M. Holt

M.M. Holt is a mysterious figure who lives partly in the real world, but more often in his imagination.

He writes science fiction, horror and adventure novels, often involving a Navy lieutenant named Alex Burns who struggles to keep his sanity in a future world gone mad with political correctness. This same Alex Burns also fights alien invaders. Sometimes Burns's great seafaring ancestors also appear in the books. They are also named Alex Burns, and in their owns times they also battled invaders from beyond the stars. Battling aliens and dystopian regimes is like a family tradition.

M.M. Holt is a relentless traveler. He can usually be found writing in cafes by the sea, or in a bar on the edge of a crowded street, usually in far flung cities. If you see him, he'll be the handsome yet enigmatic stranger pounding the keyboard of his laptop, pausing only to sip black coffee and glance warily over his shoulder. He knows the Accord Of Nations is always one step behind.

Contact M.M. Holt

mmholt548@gmail.com

mmholt.com

Facebook
Search for MM Holt, author

@MMHOLT3

Instagram
Search for mmholt548

Tik Tok
Search for @mm_holt

Printed in Dunstable, United Kingdom

64122187R00285